SO-AYW-616

Praise for Ilf & Petrov

"Ilf & Petrov, two wonderfully gifted writers, decided that if they had a rascal adventurer as protagonist, whatever they wrote about his adventures could not be criticized from a political point of view. . . . Thus Ilf & Petrov . . . managed to publish some absolutely first-rate fiction under that standard of complete independence."

—Vladimir Nabokov

"Ilf & Petrov are the foremost comic novelists of the early Soviet Union."

—*Publishers Weekly*

"*The Golden Calf* is one of the most comic and politically subversive novels written under communism. Smooth operator Ostap Bender—whose sole goal in life was to become a millionaire and move to Rio de Janeiro—is one of the great classic heroes, standing shoulder to shoulder with Cervantes's Don Quixote or Hašek's Švejk."

—Dubravka Ugresic

*Other Books by Ilf & Petrov
in English Translation*

American Road Trip:
The 1935 Travelogue of Two Soviet Writers

Little Golden America

The Twelve Chairs

ILYA ILF AND EVGENY PETROV

THE GOLDEN CALF

A NOVEL

TRANSLATED FROM THE RUSSIAN BY
KONSTANTIN GUREVICH AND HELEN ANDERSON

OPEN LETTER
LITERARY TRANSLATIONS FROM THE UNIVERSITY OF ROCHESTER

Copyright © 2006 by Tekst Publishers Moscow
Copyright © 2003 by Aleksandra Ilf (commentary and arrangement of text)
www.nibbe-wiedling.de

Translation copyright © 2009 by Helen Anderson and Konstantin Gurevich

First edition, 2009
All rights reserved

Library of Congress Control CIP information available.
ISBN-13: 978-1-934824-07-8 / ISBN-10: 1-934824-07-0

Printed on acid-free paper in the United States of America.

Text set in Bembo, an old-style serif typeface based upon face cuts by
Francesco Griffo that were first printed in 1496.

Design by N. J. Furl

Open Letter is the University of Rochester's nonprofit, literary translation press:
Lattimore Hall 411, Box 270082, Rochester, NY 14627

www.openletterbooks.org

CONTENTS

FROM THE TRANSLATORS

The Golden Calf was written in 1929-1931 and first serialized in a popular magazine in 1931. It is generally considered a sequel to the authors' earlier work, *The Twelve Chairs* (1928), although the two novels share only the chief protagonist, Ostap Bender. He was killed at the end of the first novel (see "From the Authors") but resurrected in *The Golden Calf*. The events of the first novel are mentioned in *The Golden Calf* only in passing (in Chapters 12 and 30).

This is the third translation of the novel into English. The first one, by Charles Malamuth, was published under the title *The Little Golden Calf* in 1932; the second, by John H. C. Richardson, in 1962. Some say foreign classics need to be translated anew for every new generation of readers. Either way, both previous translations omitted whole passages from the standard Soviet text, for reasons that we can only speculate about. All these gaps have been restored in this translation; we did not leave out a single paragraph.

In full agreement with our editors, we approached the novel as a work of literature first and foremost, and aimed the translation at a broad English-speaking audience. Thus a few of the more obscure Soviet realia and personalities were simplified or partially deciphered in the text, in order to give the reader at least some frame of reference. There also are a few explanatory notes at the end of the book.

A word about the Ilf-Petrovian character names. Some are simply regular Russian names, others are tongue-in-cheek puns, still others are hilarious word games. Most are untranslatable without rendering them artificial and unwieldy, so we did what we could, leaving most of them alone.

We are grateful to all those who published extensive commentaries to the novel (Alexandra Ilf, A. Wentzel, Ye. Sakharova), but especially to Professor Yuri Shcheglov, whose monumental work (Vienna, 1991 and Moscow, 1995) proved invaluable.

—Konstantin Gurevich & Helen Anderson

FROM THE AUTHORS

Usually our communal literary enterprise inspires perfectly legitimate, though rather unoriginal, questions like: "How do you manage to write together?"

At first, we would give detailed responses and even tell the story of our big fight over whether to kill Ostap Bender, the protagonist of the novel *The Twelve Chairs*, or to let him live. We would painstakingly describe how his fate was decided by drawing lots. We put two pieces of paper in a sugar bowl—one blank, the other with a skull and two chicken bones sketched in a shaky hand. We drew the one with the skull, and in thirty minutes the grand strategist was dead, his throat slashed with a razor.

After a while, our responses grew shorter. First we dropped the story of the skull and chicken bones, then many other details. Finally, our answers lost all vestiges of enthusiasm.

"How do we manage to write together? Well, we just do. Like the Goncourt brothers. Edmond makes the rounds of the publishers, while Jules guards the manuscript, making sure their friends don't steal it."

Suddenly this monotonous line of questioning was interrupted.

"Tell me," asked a stern citizen, one of those who recognized the Soviet government just after England and shortly before Greece, "tell me, why is your writing funny? Why all this giggling during the time of post-revolutionary reconstruction? Have you lost your mind?"

And then he gave us a long and angry lecture, trying to convince us that laughter has no place in these times.

"Laughing is wrong!" he said. "That's right, no laughing! And no smiling either! When I see this new life, these monumental changes, I don't feel like laughing, I feel like praying!"

"But we're not just laughing," we protested. "What we're doing is satirizing exactly those people who do not understand the period of reconstruction."

"Satire should not be funny," said the stern comrade. He then grabbed some Baptist simpleton, whom he mistook for a dyed-in-the-wool proletarian, and led him off to his place. There, he would craft a boring description of the simpleton and write him into a six-volume novel entitled *But Not These Bloody Despots!*

We didn't make this up. If we did, we could have made it funnier.

Cut this sanctimonious toady loose and he would make even men wear the hijab, while he himself would play hymns and psalms on the trumpet from early morning on, convinced that this is the best way to help build socialism.

And so whenever we worked on *The Golden Calf*, we always felt the presence of this stern citizen hovering over us:

"What if this chapter turns out funny? What will the stern citizen say?"

Finally, we resolved as follows:

a) to make the novel as funny as possible;

b) should the stern citizen continue to insist that satire should not be funny, to ask the Prosecutor General, Comr. Krylenko, *to charge the above citizen with the crime of stupidity with malicious intent.*

—I. Ilf & E. Petrov

THE GOLDEN CALF

"Look both ways before crossing the street."
—Traffic regulation

PART 1
THE CREW OF THE ANTELOPE

CHAPTER 1
HOW PANIKOVSKY BROKE THE PACT

You have to be nice to pedestrians.

Pedestrians comprise the greater part of humanity. Moreover, its better part. Pedestrians created the world. They built cities, erected tall buildings, laid out sewers and waterlines, paved the streets and lit them with electricity. They spread civilization throughout the world, invented the printing press and gunpowder, flung bridges across rivers, deciphered Egyptian hieroglyphs, introduced the safety razor, abolished the slave trade, and established that no less than 114 tasty, nutritious dishes can be made from soybeans.

And just when everything was ready, when our native planet had become relatively comfortable, the motorists appeared.

It should be noted that the automobile was also invented by pedestrians. But, somehow, the motorists quickly forgot about this. They started running over the mild-mannered and intelligent pedestrians. The streets—laid out by pedestrians—were taken over by the motorists. The roads became twice as wide, while the sidewalks shrunk to the size of a postage stamp. The frightened pedestrians were pushed up against the walls of the buildings.

In a big city, pedestrians live like martyrs. They've been forced into a kind of traffic ghetto. They are only allowed to cross the streets at the intersections, that is, exactly where the traffic is heaviest—where the thread by which a pedestrian's life hangs is most easily snapped.

In our expansive country, the common automobile—intended by the pedestrians to peacefully transport people and things—has assumed the sinister role of a fratricidal weapon. It puts entire cohorts of union members and their loved ones out of commission. And if on occasion a pedestrian manages to dart out from under a silver grille, he is fined by the police for violating the traffic laws.

In general, the pedestrians' standing is not what it used to be. They, who gave the world such outstanding figures as Horace, Boyle, Mariotte, Lobachevsky, Gutenberg, and Anatole France, have been forced to jump through ridiculous hoops just to remind others of their existence. Lord, oh Lord (who, frankly, doesn't exist), how low you (who don't really exist) have let the pedestrian stoop!

Here he is, walking along a Siberian road from Vladivostok to Moscow, carrying a banner that reads IMPROVE THE LIVING CONDITIONS OF THE TEXTILE WORKERS in one hand, and with an extra pair of Uncle Vanya sandals and a lidless tin kettle dangling from a stick that he's slung over his shoulder. This is a Soviet hiker who left Vladivostok as a young man and who, upon reaching the outskirts of Moscow in his old age, will be run over and killed by a heavy truck. And nobody will even manage to get the license plate number.

Here's another one, the last of the Mohicans of European foot traffic. He is pushing a barrel around the world. He would have been more than happy to walk just like that, without the barrel, but then nobody would notice that he is a long-distance hiker, and the press would ignore him. And so all his life he is forced to push the damn thing, which, to add insult to injury, has a large yellow advertisement extolling the unparalleled qualities of Motorist's Dream engine oil.

This is how far the pedestrian has fallen.

Only in small Russian towns is the pedestrian still loved and respected. In those towns, he still rules, wandering carelessly in the middle of the street and crossing it in the most intricate manner in whatever direction he chooses.

A man wearing a white-topped captain's cap, the kind favored by administrators of summer amusement parks and MCs, undoubtedly belonged to this greater and better part of humanity. He traveled the streets of the town of Arbatov on foot, looking around with somewhat critical curiosity. He carried a small doctor's bag in his hand. Apparently the town made no particular impression on the pedestrian in the artsy cap.

He saw a dozen or so blue, yellow, and pinkish white church towers and noticed the peeling gold of the domes. A flag crackled above a government building.

Near the white gate tower of the provincial citadel, two severe-looking old ladies conversed in French, complaining about the Soviet regime and reminiscing about their beloved daughters. Cold air and a sour wine-like smell wafted from the church basement. Apparently, it was used to store potatoes.

"Church of the Savior on Spilled Potatoes," muttered the pedestrian.

He walked under the plywood arch with the freshly painted banner, WELCOME TO THE 5TH DISTRICT CONFERENCE OF WOMEN AND GIRLS, and found himself at the beginning of a long tree-lined alley named Boulevard of Prodigies.

"No," he said with chagrin, "this is no Rio de Janeiro, this is much worse."

Almost all the benches on the Boulevard of Prodigies were taken up by young women sitting alone with open books in their hands. Dappled shade fell across the pages of the books, the bare elbows, and the cute bangs. When the stranger stepped into the cool alley there was a noticeable stir on the benches. The girls hid their faces behind volumes by Gladkov, Eliza Orzeszkowa, and Seyfullina and eyed the visitor with temerity. He paraded past the excited book lovers and emerged from the alley at his destination, the city hall.

At that moment, a horse cab appeared from around the corner. A man in a long tunic briskly walked next to it, holding on to the dusty, beat-up fender and waving a bulging portfolio embossed with the word *"Musique."* He was heatedly arguing with the passenger. The latter, a middle-aged man with a pendulous banana-shaped nose, held a suitcase between his legs and from time to time shook a finger in his interlocutor's face in vehement disagreement. In the heat of the argument his engineer's cap, sporting a band of plush green upholstery fabric, slid to one side. The adversaries uttered the word "salary" loudly and often.

Soon other words became audible as well.

"You will answer for this, Comrade Talmudovsky!" shouted the Tunic, pushing the engineer's hand away from his face.

"And I am telling you that no decent professional would come to work for you on such terms," replied Talmudovsky, trying to return his finger to its original position.

"Are you talking about the salary again? I'm going to have to launch a complaint about your excessive greed."

"I don't give a damn about the salary! I'd work for free!" yelled the engineer, angrily tracing all kinds of curves in the air with his finger. "I can even retire if I want to. Don't treat people like serfs! You see 'Liberty, equality, brotherhood' everywhere now, and yet I am expected to work in this rat hole."

At this point, Talmudovsky quickly opened his hand and started counting on his fingers:

"The apartment is a pigsty, there's no theater, the salary . . . Driver! To the train station!"

"Whoa!" shrieked the Tunic, rushing ahead and grabbing the horse by the bridle. "As the secretary of the Engineers and Technicians local, I must . . . Kondrat Ivanovich, the plant will be left without engineers . . . Be reasonable . . . We won't let you get away with this, Engineer Talmudovsky . . . I have the minutes here with me . . ."

And then the secretary of the local planted his feet firmly on the ground and started undoing the straps of his "*Musique.*"

This lapse decided the argument. Seeing that the path was clear, Talmudovsky rose to his feet and yelled at the top of his lungs:

"To the station!"

"Wait, wait . . ." meekly protested the secretary, rushing after the carriage. "You are a deserter from the labor front!"

Sheets of thin paper marked "discussed-resolved" flew out of the portfolio.

The stranger, who had been closely watching the incident, lingered for a moment on the empty square, and then said with conviction:

"No, this is definitely not Rio de Janeiro."

A minute later he was knocking on the door of the city council chairman.

"Who do you want to see?" asked the receptionist who was sitting at the desk by the door. "What do you need to see the chairman for? What's your business?"

Apparently the visitor was intimately familiar with the principles of handling receptionists at various governmental, non-governmental, and municipal organizations. He didn't bother to claim that he had urgent official business.

"Private matters," he said dryly and, without looking back at the receptionist, stuck his head in the door. "May I come in?"

Without waiting for an answer, he approached the chairman's desk.

"Good morning, do you recognize me?"

The chairman, a dark-eyed man with a large head, wearing a navy blue jacket and matching pants that were tucked into tall boots with high angled heels, glanced at the visitor rather distractedly and said he did not recognize him.

"You don't? For your information, many people think I look remarkably like my father."

"I look like my father, too," said the chairman impatiently. "What do you want, Comrade?"

"What matters is who the father was," said the visitor sadly. "I am the son of Lieutenant Schmidt."

The chairman felt foolish and started rising from his seat. He instantly recalled the famous image of the pale faced revolutionary lieutenant in his black cape with bronze clasps in the shape of lion's heads. While he was pulling his thoughts together to ask the son of the Black Sea hero an appropriate question, the visitor examined the office furnishings with the eye of a discriminating buyer.

Back in tsarist times, all government offices were furnished in a particular style. A special breed of office furniture was developed: flat storage cabinets rising to the ceiling, wooden benches with polished seats three inches thick, desks on monumental legs, and oak barriers separating the office from the turmoil of the world outside. During the revolution, this type of furniture almost disappeared, and the secret of making it was lost. People forgot how to furnish government offices properly, and official spaces started filling up with objects that until then were thought to belong exclusively in private apartments. Among these were soft lawyer's couches with springs and tiny glass shelves for the seven porcelain elephants that supposedly bring luck, as well as china cabinets, flimsy display shelves, folding leather chairs for invalids, and blue Japanese vases. In addition to a regular desk, the office of the chairman of the Arbatov city council also gave refuge to two small ottomans, which were upholstered with torn pink silk, a striped love seat, a satin screen depicting Mount Fuji with a flowering cherry tree, and a heavy mirrored wardrobe that was slapped together at the local open-air market.

"The wardrobe, I'm afraid, is of the Hey Slavs type," thought the visitor. "The pickings here are slim. Nope, this is no Rio de Janeiro."

"It's very good of you to stop by," said the chairman finally. "You must be from Moscow?"

"Yes, just passing through," replied the visitor, examining the love seat and becoming even more convinced that the city's finances were not in good shape. He much preferred city halls with new, Swedish-style furniture from the Leningrad Woodworks Enterprise.

The chairman was about to ask what brought the Lieutenant's son to Arbatov, but instead, to his own surprise, he smiled meekly and said:

"The churches here are remarkable. We already had some people from Cultural Heritage here, there's talk about restoration. Tell me, do you remember the uprising on the battleship *Ochakov* yourself?"

"Barely," replied the visitor. "In those heroic times, I was very young. I was just a baby."

"Excuse me, what is your name?"

"Nikolay . . . Nikolay Schmidt."

"And your patronymic?"

"Oops, that's not good!" thought the visitor, who did not know his own father's name either.

"Yeah," he said slowly, evading a direct answer, "these days, people don't know the names of our heroes. The frenzy of the New Economic Policy. The enthusiasm of old is gone. As a matter of fact, I'm here entirely by accident. Trouble on the road. Not a penny left."

The chairman was also happy to change the subject. He was genuinely embarrassed that he had forgotten the name of the hero of the *Ochakov*. "That's right," he thought, looking at the hero's exalted features with love, "work deadens your soul. Makes you forget the important things."

"What's that? Not a penny? That's interesting."

"Of course, I could have asked some private citizen. Anybody would be happy to help me out, but, as you understand, that would not be entirely proper from the political standpoint," said the Lieutenant's son, turning mournful. "The son of a revolutionary asking for money from an individual, a businessman . . ."

The chairman noticed the change in the visitor's tone with alarm. "What if he's an epileptic?" he thought. "He could be a lot of trouble."

"And it's a very good thing that you didn't ask a businessman," said the chairman, who was totally confused.

Then, gently, the son of the Black Sea hero got down to business. He asked for fifty rubles. The chairman, constrained by the tight local budget, came up with only eight rubles and three meal vouchers to the Former Friend of the Stomach cooperative diner.

The hero's son put the money and the vouchers in a deep pocket of his worn dappled gray jacket. He was about to get up from the pink ottoman when they heard the sound of stomping and the receptionist's cries of protest coming from behind the door.

The door flew open, and a new visitor appeared.

"Who's in charge here?" he asked, breathing heavily and searching the room with his eyes.

"I am, so?" said the chairman.

"Hiya, Chairman," thundered the newcomer, extending his spade-sized hand. "Nice to meet you! I'm the son of Lieutenant Schmidt."

"Who?" asked the city father, his eyes bulging.

"The son of that great, immortal hero, Lieutenant Schmidt," repeated the intruder.

"But this comrade sitting here, he is the son of Comrade Schmidt. Nikolay Schmidt." In total confusion, the chairman pointed at the first visitor, who suddenly looked sleepy.

This was a very delicate situation for the two con artists. At any moment, the long and nasty sword of retribution could glisten in the hands of the unassuming and gullible chairman of the city council. Fate allowed them just one short second to devise a strategy to save themselves. Terror flashed in the eyes of Lieutenant's Schmidt's second son.

His imposing figure—clad in a Paraguayan summer shirt, sailor's bell bottoms, and light-blue canvas shoes—which was sharp and angular just a moment earlier, started to come apart, lost its formidable edges, and no longer commanded any respect at all. An unpleasant smile appeared on the chairman's face.

But when the Lieutenant's second son had already decided that everything was lost, and that the chairman's terrible wrath was about to fall on his red head, salvation came from the pink ottoman.

"Vasya!" yelled the Lieutenant's firstborn, jumping to his feet. "Buddy boy! Don't you recognize your brother Nick?"

And the first son gave the second son a big hug.

"I do!" exclaimed Vasya, his eyesight miraculously regained. "I do recognize my brother Nick!"

The happy encounter was marked by chaotic expressions of endearment and incredibly powerful hugs—hugs so powerful that the face of the second son of the Black Sea revolutionary was pale with pain. Out of sheer joy, his brother Nick had thrashed him rather badly.

While hugging, both brothers were cautiously glancing at the chairman, whose facial expression remained vinegary throughout the scene. As a result, their strategy had to be elaborated on the spot and enriched with stories of their family life and details of the 1905 sailors' revolt that had somehow eluded official Soviet historians. Holding each other's hands, the brothers sat down on the love seat and began reminiscing, all the while keeping their fawning eyes on the chairman.

"What an incredible coincidence!" exclaimed the first son insincerely, his eyes inviting the chairman to partake in the happy family occasion.

"Yes," said the chairman frostily. "It happens."

Seeing that the chairman was still in the throes of doubt, the first son stroked his brother's red, Irish-setter locks and asked softly:

"So when did you come from Mariupol, where you were staying with our grandmother?"

"Yes, I was staying," mumbled the Lieutenant's second son, "with her."

"So why didn't you write more often? I was very worried."

"I was busy," answered the redhead gloomily.

Afraid that his inquisitive brother might ask him what exactly kept him so busy, which was largely doing time at correctional facilities in various jurisdictions, the second son of Lieutenant Schmidt seized the initiative and asked a question himself:

"And why didn't you write?"

"I did write," replied his sibling unexpectedly. Feeling a great rush of playfulness he added, "I've been sending you registered letters. Here, I've got the receipts."

He produced a pile of frayed slips of paper from his side pocket, which, for some reason, he showed to the chairman of the city council instead of his brother—from a safe distance.

Oddly, the sight of the paper reassured the chairman somewhat, and the brothers' reminiscences grew even more vivid. The redhead became quite comfortable and gave a fairly coherent, albeit monotonous, rendition of the popular brochure "The Revolt on the *Ochakov*." His brother embellished the dry presentation with such picturesque vignettes that the chairman, who had started to calm down, pricked up his ears again.

Nevertheless, he let the brothers go in peace, and they rushed outside with great relief.

They stopped behind the corner of the city hall.

"Talk about childhood," said the first son, "when I was a child, I used to kill clowns like you on the spot. With a slingshot."

"And why is that?" inquired the famous father's second son light-heartedly.

"Such are the tough rules of life. Or, to put it briefly, life imposes its tough rules on us. Why did you barge into the office? Didn't you see the chairman wasn't alone?"

"I thought . . ."

"Ah, you thought? So you do think on occasion? You are a thinker, aren't you? What is your name, Mr. Thinker? Spinoza? Jean-Jacques Rousseau? Marcus Aurelius?"

The redhead kept quiet, feeling guilty as charged.

"All right, I forgive you. You may live. And now let's introduce ourselves. We are brothers, after all, and family ties carry certain obligations. My name is Ostap Bender. May I ask your original name?"

"Balaganov," said the redhead. "Shura Balaganov."

"I'm not asking what you do for a living," said Bender politely, "but I do have some inkling. Probably something intellectual? How many convictions this year?"

"Two," replied Balaganov freely.

"Now that's no good. Why are you selling your immortal soul? A man should not let himself get convicted. It's amateurish. Theft, that is. Beside the fact that stealing is a sin—and I'm sure your mother introduced you to that notion—it is also a pointless waste of time and energy."

Ostap could have gone on and on about his philosophy of life, but Balaganov interrupted him.

"Look," he said, pointing into the green depths of the Boulevard of Prodigies. "See that man in the straw hat?"

"I see him," said Ostap dismissively. "So what? Is that the governor of the island of Borneo?"

"That's Panikovsky," said Shura. "The son of Lieutenant Schmidt."

An aging man, leaning slightly to one side, was making his way through the alley in the shade of regal lindens. A hard straw hat with a ribbed brim sat askew on his head. His pants were so short that the white straps of his long underwear were showing. A golden tooth was glowing beneath his mustache, like the tip of a burning cigarette.

"What, yet another son?" said Ostap. "This is getting funny."

Panikovsky approached the city hall, pensively traced a figure eight in front of the building, grabbed his hat with both hands and set it straight on his head, tidied up his jacket, sighed deeply, and went inside.

"The Lieutenant had three sons," remarked Bender, "two smart ones, one a fool. We have to warn him."

"No, don't," said Balaganov, "next time he'll know better than to break the pact."

"What pact? What are you talking about?"

"Wait, I'll tell you later. Look, he's in, he's in!"

"I am a jealous man," confessed Bender, "but there's nothing to be jealous of here. Have you ever seen a bullfight? Let's go watch."

The children of Lieutenant Schmidt, now fast friends, stepped out from behind the corner and approached the window of the chairman's office.

The chairman was sitting behind the grimy, unwashed glass. He was writing quickly. Like all those engaged in writing, he looked grieved. Suddenly he raised his head. The door swung open, and in came Panikovsky. Holding his hat against his greasy jacket, he stopped in front of the desk and moved his thick lips for a long time. Then the chairman jumped in his chair and opened his mouth wide. The brothers heard a long howl.

Whispering "Fall back, now!" Ostap dragged Balaganov away. They ran to the boulevard and hid behind a tree.

"Take your hats off," said Ostap, "bare your heads. The body is about to be escorted outside."

He was right. The thunderous cadences of the chairman's voice could still be heard when two large men appeared in the doorway of the city hall. They were carrying Panikovsky. One held his arms, the other his legs.

"The remains," narrated Ostap, "were carried out by the friends and family of the deceased."

The men dragged the third, foolish offspring of Lieutenant Schmidt out to the porch and started slowly swinging him back and forth. Panikovsky silently gazed into the blue sky with resignation.

"After a brief funeral service . . ." continued Ostap.

At this very moment the men, having given Panikovsky's body sufficient momentum, threw him out onto the street.

". . . the ashes were interred," concluded Bender.

Panikovsky plopped on the ground like a toad. He quickly got up and, leaning to one side even more than before, ran down the Boulevard of Prodigies with amazing speed.

"All right," said Ostap, "now tell me how the bastard broke the pact and what that pact was all about."

CHAPTER 2
THE THIRTY SONS OF LIEUTENANT SCHMIDT

The eventful morning came to an end. Without discussion, Bender and Balaganov walked briskly away from the city hall. A long, dark-blue steel rail was being carried down the main street in an open peasant cart. The street was ringing and singing, as if the peasant in rough fisherman's clothes was carrying a giant tuning fork rather than a rail. The sun beat down on the display in the window of the visual aids store, where two skeletons stood in a friendly embrace amidst globes, skulls, and the cheerfully painted cardboard liver of an alcoholic. The modest window of the sign shop was largely filled with glazed metal signs that read CLOSED FOR LUNCH, LUNCH BREAK 2–3 P.M., CLOSED FOR LUNCH BREAK, CLOSED, STORE CLOSED, and, finally, a massive black board with CLOSED FOR INVENTORY in gold lettering. Apparently these blunt statements were particularly popular in the town of Arbatov. All other eventualities were covered with a single blue sign, ATTENDANT ON DUTY.

Farther down, three stores—selling wind instruments, mandolins, and bass balalaikas—stood together. Brass trumpets shone immodestly from display stands covered with red fabric. The tuba was particularly impressive. It looked so powerful, and lay coiled in the sun so lazily, that one couldn't help thinking its proper place was not in a window but in a big city zoo, somewhere between the elephant and the boa constrictor. On their days off, parents would bring their kids to see it and would say:

"Look, honey, this is the tuba section. The tuba is now asleep. But when it wakes up, it will definitely start trumpeting." And the kids would stare at the remarkable instrument with their large wondrous eyes.

Under different circumstances, Ostap Bender would have noticed the freshly hewn, log cabin-sized balalaikas, the phonograph records warping in the heat, and the children's marching band drums, whose dashing color schemes suggested that providence is always on the side of the big battalions. This time, however, he was preoccupied with something else. He was hungry.

"I gather you're on the verge of a financial abyss?" he asked Balaganov.

"You mean money?" replied Shura. "I haven't had any for a week now."

"In that case, I'd worry about your future, young man," said Ostap didactically. "The financial abyss is the deepest of them all, and you can be falling into it all your life. Oh well, cheer up. After all, I captured three meal vouchers in my beak. The chairman fell in love with me at first sight."

Alas, the freshly minted brothers did not get to benefit from the kindness of the city father. The doors of the Former Friend of the Stomach diner sported a large hanging lock that was covered with what looked like either rust or cooked buckwheat.

"Of course," said Ostap bitterly, "the diner is closed forever—they're inventorying the schnitzel. We are forced to submit our bodies to the ravages of the private sector."

"The private sector prefers cash," reminded Balaganov gloomily.

"Well, I won't torture you any more. The chairman showered me with gold—eight rubles. But keep in mind, dearest Shura, that I have no intention of nourishing you for free. For every vitamin I feed you, I will demand numerous small favors in return."

But since there was no private sector in town, the brothers ended up eating at a cooperative summer garden, where special posters informed the customers of Arbatov's newest contribution to public dining:

> BEER FOR UNION MEMBERS ONLY

"We'll settle for kvass," said Balaganov.

"Especially considering that the local kvass is produced by a group of private artisans who are friendly with the Soviet regime," added Ostap.

"Now tell me what exactly this devil Panikovsky did wrong. I love stories of petty thievery."

Satiated, Balaganov looked at his rescuer with gratitude and began the story. It took a good two hours to tell and was full of exceptionally interesting details.

In all fields of human endeavor, the supply and demand of labor is regulated by specialized bodies. A theater actor will move to the city of Omsk only if he knows for sure that he need not worry about competition—namely, that there are no other candidates for his recurring role as the indifferent lover or the servant who announces that dinner is ready. Railroad employees are taken care of by their own unions, who helpfully put notices in the papers to the effect that unemployed baggage handlers cannot count on getting work on the Syzran-Vyazma Line or that the Central Asian Line is seeking four crossing guards. A commodities expert places an ad in the paper, and then the entire country learns that there is a commodities expert with ten years' experience who wishes to move from Moscow to the provinces for family reasons.

Everything is regulated, everything flows along clear channels and comes full circle in compliance with the law and under its protection.

And only one particular market was in a state of chaos—that of con artists claiming to be the children of Lieutenant Schmidt. Anarchy ravaged the ranks of the Lieutenant's offspring. Their trade was not producing all the potential gains that should have been virtually assured by brief encounters with government officials, municipal administrators, and community activists—for the most part an extremely gullible bunch.

Fake grandchildren of Karl Marx, non-existent nephews of Friedrich Engels, brothers of the Education Commissar Lunacharsky, cousins of the revolutionary Klara Zetkin, or, in the worst case, the descendants of that famous anarchist, Prince Kropotkin, had been extorting and begging all across the country.

From Minsk to the Bering Strait and from the Turkish border to the Arctic shores, relatives of famous persons enter local councils, get off trains, and anxiously ride in cabs. They are in a hurry. They have a lot to do.

At some point, however, the supply of relatives exceeded the demand, and this peculiar market was hit by a recession. Reform was needed. Little by little, order was established among the grandchildren of Karl Marx, the Kropotkins, the Engelses, and others. The only exception was the unruly guild of Lieutenant Schmidt's children, which, like the Polish parliament, was always torn by anarchy. For some reason, the children were all difficult, rude, greedy, and kept spoiling the fruits of each other's labors.

Shura Balaganov, who considered himself the Lieutenant's firstborn, grew very concerned about market conditions. More and more often he was bumping into fellow guild members who had completely ruined the bountiful fields of Ukraine and the vacation peaks of the Caucasus, places that used to be quite lucrative for him.

"And you couldn't handle the growing difficulties?" asked Ostap teasingly.

But Balaganov didn't notice the irony. Sipping the purple kvass, he went on with his story.

The only solution to this tense situation was to hold a conference. Balaganov spent the whole winter organizing it. He wrote to the competitors he knew personally. Those he didn't know received invitations through the grandsons of Karl Marx whom he bumped into on occasion. And finally, in the early spring of 1928, nearly all the known children of Lieutenant Schmidt assembled in a tavern in Moscow, near the Sukharev Tower. The gathering was impressive. Lieutenant Schmidt, as it turned out, had thirty sons, who ranged in age between eighteen and fifty-two, and four daughters, none of them smart, young, or pretty.

In a brief keynote address, Balaganov expressed hope that the brothers would at last come to an understanding and conclude a pact, the necessity of which was dictated by life itself.

According to Balaganov's plan, the entire Soviet Union was to be divided into thirty-four operational areas, one for everyone present. Each child would be assigned a territory on a long-term basis. All guild members would be prohibited from crossing the boundaries and trespassing into someone else's territory for the purpose of earning a living.

Nobody objected to the new work rules except Panikovsky, who declared early on that he would do perfectly well without any pacts. The division of the country was accompanied by some very ugly scenes, however. All parties to the treaty immediately started fighting and began addressing one another exclusively with rude epithets.

The bone of contention was the assignment of the territories.

Nobody wanted large cities with universities. Nobody cared for Moscow, Leningrad, and Kharkov—these cities had seen it all. To a person, they refused the Republic of the Volga Germans.

"Why, is that such a bad republic?" asked Balaganov innocently. "I think it's a good place. As civilized people, the Germans cannot refuse to help out."

"Oh, come on!" yelled the agitated children. "Try to get anything out of those Germans!"

Apparently, quite a few of them had been thrown into jail by distrustful German colonists.

The distant Central Asian regions, buried in the desert sand, had a very bad reputation as well. They were accused of being unfamiliar with the person of Lieutenant Schmidt.

"You think I'm stupid!" shrieked Panikovsky. "Give me Central Russia, then I'll sign the pact."

"What? The entire Center?" mocked Balaganov. "Would you also like Melitopol on top of that? Or Bobruisk?"

At the word Bobruisk, the children moaned painfully. Everyone was prepared to go to Bobruisk immediately. Bobruisk was considered a wonderful, highly civilized place.

"Fine, not the whole Center," the greedy Panikovsky kept insisting, "give me half. After all, I am a family man, I have two families."

But he didn't get even half.

After much commotion, it was decided to assign the areas by drawing lots. Thirty-four slips of paper were cut up, and each had a geographical name written on it. Lucrative Kursk and questionable Kherson, barely touched Minusinsk and nearly hopeless Ashkhabad, Kiev, Petrozavodsk, Chita—all the republics and regions lay in somebody's rabbit-fur hat waiting for their masters.

The drawing was accompanied by cheers, suppressed moans, and swearing.

Panikovsky's unlucky star played a role in the outcome. He ended up with the barren republic of the vindictive Volga Germans. He joined the pact, but he was mad as hell.

"I'll go," he yelled, "but I'm warning you: if they don't treat me well, I'll violate the pact, I'll trespass!"

Balaganov, who drew the golden Arbatov territory, became alarmed. He declared then and there that he would not tolerate any violations of the operational guidelines.

Either way, order was established, and the thirty sons and four daughters of Lieutenant Schmidt headed for their areas of operation.

"And now, Bender, you just saw for yourself how that bastard broke the pact," said Shura Balaganov, concluding the story. "He's been creeping around my territory for a while, I just couldn't catch him."

Against Shura's expectations, Ostap did not condemn Panikovsky's infraction. Bender was leaning back in his chair and staring absentmindedly into the distance.

The back wall of the restaurant garden was high and painted with pictures of trees, symmetrical and full of leaves, like in a school reader. There were no real trees in the garden, but the shade of the wall provided a refreshing coolness which satisfied the customers. Apparently, they were all union members, since they were drinking nothing but beer—without any snacks.

A bright green car drove up to the gate of the garden, gasping and backfiring incessantly. There was a white semi-circular sign on its door which read LET'S RIDE! Below the sign were the rates for trips in this cheerful vehicle. Three rubles per hour. One-way fares by arrangement. There were no passengers in the car.

The customers started nervously whispering to each other. For about five minutes, the driver stared pleadingly through the latticed fence of the garden. Apparently losing hope of getting any passengers, he dared them:

"The taxi is free! Please get in!"

But nobody showed any desire to get into the LET'S RIDE! car. Even the invitation itself had the most peculiar effect on people. They hung their heads and tried not to look towards the car. The driver shook his head and slowly drove off. The citizens of Arbatov followed him glumly with their eyes. Five minutes later, the green vehicle whizzed by in the opposite direction at top speed. The driver was bouncing up and down in his seat and shouting something unintelligible. There were still no passengers. Ostap followed it with his eyes and said:

"Well, let me tell you, Balaganov, you are a loser. Don't be offended. I'm just trying to point out your exact position in the grand scheme of things."

"Go to hell!" said Balaganov rudely.

"So you took offense anyway? Do you really think that being the Lieutenant's son doesn't make you a loser?"

"But you are a son of Lieutenant Schmidt yourself!" exclaimed Balaganov.

"You are a loser," repeated Ostap. "Son of a loser. Your children will be losers, too. Look, kiddo. What happened this morning was not even a phase, it was nothing, a pure accident, an artist's whim. A gentleman in search of pocket money. It's not in my nature to fish for such a miserable rate of return. And what kind of a trade is that, for God's sake! Son of Lieutenant Schmidt! Well, maybe another year, maybe two. And then what? Your red locks will grow familiar, and they'll simply start beating you up."

"So what am I supposed to do?" asked Balaganov, alarmed. "How am I supposed to win my daily bread?"

"You have to think," said Ostap sternly. "I, for one, live off ideas. I don't beg for a lousy ruble from the city hall. My horizons are broader. I see that you love money selflessly. Tell me, what amount appeals to you?"

"Five thousand," answered Balaganov quickly.

"Per month?"

"Per year."

"In that case, we have nothing to talk about. I need five hundred thousand. A lump sum preferably, not in installments."

"Would you accept installments, if you had to?" asked Balaganov vindictively.

Ostap looked back at him closely and replied with complete seriousness: "I would. But I need a lump sum."

Balaganov was about to crack a joke about this as well, but then raised his eyes to look at Ostap and thought better of it. In front of him was an athlete with a profile that could be minted on a coin. A thin white scar ran across his dark-skinned throat. His playful eyes sparkled with determination.

Balaganov suddenly felt an irresistible urge to stand at attention. He even wanted to clear his throat, which is what happens to people in positions of moderate responsibility when they talk to a person of much higher standing. He did indeed clear his throat and asked meekly:

"What do you need so much money for . . . and all at once?"

"Actually, I need more than that," said Ostap, "Five hundred thousand is an absolute minimum. Five hundred thousand fully convertible rubles. I want to go away, Comrade Shura, far, far away. To Rio de Janeiro."

"Do you have relatives down there?" asked Balaganov.

"Do you think I look like a man who could possibly have relatives?"

"No, but I thought . . ."

"I don't have any relatives, Comrade Shura, I'm alone in this world. I had a father, a Turkish subject, but he died a long time ago in terrible convulsions. That's not the point. I've wanted to go to Rio de Janeiro since I was a child. I'm sure you've never heard of that city."

Balaganov shook his head apologetically. The only centers of world culture he knew other than Moscow were Kiev, Melitopol, and Zhmerinka. Anyway, he was convinced that the earth was flat.

Ostap threw a page torn from a book onto the table.

"This is from *The Concise Soviet Encyclopedia*. Here's what it says about Rio de Janeiro: 'Population 1,360,000 . . .' all right . . . '. . . substantial Mulatto population . . . on a large bay of the Atlantic Ocean . . .' Ah, there! 'Lined with lavish stores and stunning buildings, the city's main streets rival those of the most important cities in the world.' Can you imagine that, Shura? Rival! The mulattos, the bay, coffee export, coffee dumping, if you will, the charleston called 'My Little Girl Got a Little Thing,' and . . . Oh well, what can I say? You understand what's going on here. A million and a half people, all of them wearing white pants, without exception. I want to get out of here. During the past year, I have developed very serious differences with the Soviet regime. The regime wants to build socialism, and I don't. I find it boring. Do you understand now why I need so much money?"

"Where are you going to get five hundred thousand?" asked Balaganov in a low voice.

"Anywhere," answered Ostap. "Just show me a rich person, and I'll take his money from him."

"What? Murder?" asked Balaganov in an even lower voice, quickly glancing at the nearby tables, where the citizens of Arbatov were raising their glasses to each other's health.

"You know what," said Ostap, "you shouldn't have signed the so-called Sukharev Pact. This intellectual effort apparently left you mentally exhausted. You're getting dumber by the minute. Remember, Ostap Bender has never killed anybody. Others tried to kill him, that's true. But he is clean before the law. I'm no angel, of course. I don't have wings, but I do revere the criminal code. That's my weakness, if you will."

"Then how are you going to take somebody else's money?"

"How am I going to take it? The method of swiping money varies, depending on the circumstances. I personally know four hundred relatively honest methods of taking money. That's not a problem. The problem is that there are no rich people these days. That's what's really frustrating. Of course, somebody else might simply go after a defenseless state institution, but that's against my rules. You already know how I feel about the criminal code. It's not a good idea to rob a collective. Just show me a wealthy individual instead. But that individual doesn't exist."

"Oh, come on!" exclaimed Balaganov. "There are some very rich people out there."

"Do you know people like that?" asked Ostap quickly. "Can you give me the name and exact address of at least one Soviet millionaire? Yet they do exist, they gotta exist. As long as monetary instruments are circulating within the country, there must be people who have a lot of them. But how do you find such a fox?"

Ostap sighed heavily. He must have been dreaming of finding a wealthy individual for quite some time.

"It is so nice," he said pensively, "to work with a legal millionaire in a properly functioning capitalist country with long established bourgeois traditions. In such places, a millionaire is a well-known figure. His address is common knowledge. He lives in a mansion somewhere in Rio de Janeiro. You go to see him in his office and you take his money without even having to go past the front hall, right after greeting him. And on top of that, you do it nicely and politely: "Hello, Sir, please don't worry. I'm going to have to bother you a bit. All right. Done." That's it. That's civilization for you! What could be simpler? A gentleman in the company of gentlemen takes care of a bit of business. Just don't shoot up the chandelier, there's no need for that. And here . . . my God! This is such a cold country. Everything is hidden, everything is underground. Even the Commissariat of Finance, with its mighty fiscal apparatus, cannot find a Soviet millionaire. A millionaire may very well be sitting at the next table in this so-called summer garden, drinking forty-kopeck Tip-Top beer. That's what really upsets me!"

"Does that mean," Balaganov asked after a pause, "that if you could find such a secret millionaire, then . . .?"

"Hold it right there. I know what you're going to say. No, it's not what you think, not at all. I won't try to choke him with a pillow or pistol-whip him. None of that silliness. Oh, if only I could find a millionaire! I'll make sure he'll bring me the money himself, on a platter with a blue rim."

"That sounds really good," chuckled Balaganov simple-heartedly. "Five hundred thousand on a platter with a blue rim."

Balaganov got up and started circling the table. He smacked his lips plaintively, stopped, opened his mouth as if he was going to say something, sat down without uttering a word, and then got up again. Ostap watched his routine nonchalantly.

"So he'd bring it himself?" asked Balaganov suddenly in a raspy voice. "On a platter? And if he doesn't? Where is that Rio de Janeiro? Far away?

I don't believe that every single man there wears white pants. Forget it, Bender. With five hundred thousand one can live a good life even here."

"Absolutely," said Ostap smiling, "one certainly can. But don't get worked up for no reason. You don't have the five hundred thousand, do you?"

A deep wrinkle appeared on Balaganov's smooth, virginal forehead. He looked at Ostap uncertainly and said slowly:

"I know a millionaire."

Bender lost his lively expression immediately; his face turned harsh and began to resemble the profile on a coin again.

"Go away," he said, "I give to charity only on Saturdays. Don't pull my leg."

"I give you my word, Monsieur Bender . . ."

"Listen, Shura, if you insist on switching to French, please call me *citoyen*, not *monsieur*. It means citizen. And what, incidentally, is this millionaire's address?"

"He lives in Chernomorsk."

"Of course, I knew that. Chernomorsk! Down there, even before the war, a man with ten thousand rubles was called a millionaire. And now . . . I can imagine! No, I'm sure this is pure nonsense!"

"Wait, just let me finish. He's a real millionaire. You see, Bender, I was in their detention center recently . . ."

Ten minutes later, the half-brothers left the cooperative beer garden. The grand strategist felt like a surgeon who is about to perform a rather serious operation. Everything is ready. Gauze and bandages are steaming in the electric sterilizers, a nurse in a white toga moves silently across the tiled floor, the medical glass and nickel shine brightly. The patient lies languorously on a glass table, staring at the ceiling. The heated air smells like German chewing gum. The surgeon, his arms spread wide, approaches the operating table, accepts a sharp sterilized dagger from an assistant, and says to the patient dryly: "Allrighty, take off your nightie."

"It's always like this with me," said Bender, his eyes shining, "I have to start a project worth a million while I'm noticeably short of monetary instruments. My entire capital—fixed, working, and reserve—amounts to five rubles . . . What did you say the name of that underground millionaire was?"

"Koreiko," said Balaganov.

"Oh yes, Koreiko. A very good name. Are you sure nobody knows about his millions?"

"Nobody except me and Pruzhansky. But I already told you that Pruzhansky will be in prison for about three more years. If you could only see how he moaned and groaned when I was about to be released. He probably had a hunch that he shouldn't have told me about Koreiko."

"The fact that he disclosed his secret to you was no big deal. That's not why he moaned and groaned. He must have had a premonition that you would tell the whole story to me. That is indeed a big loss for poor Pruzhansky. By the time he gets out of prison, Koreiko's only consolation will be the cliché that there's no shame in poverty."

Ostap took off his summer cap, waved it in the air, and asked:

"Do I have any gray hair?"

Balaganov sucked in his stomach, spread his feet to the width of a rifle butt, and boomed like a soldier:

"No, Sir!"

"I will. Great battles await us. Your hair, Balaganov, will turn gray too."

Balaganov suddenly giggled childishly:

"How did you put it? He'll bring the money himself on a platter with a blue rim?"

"A platter for me," said Ostap, "and a small plate for you."

"But what about Rio de Janeiro? I want white pants too."

"Rio de Janeiro is the cherished dream of my youth," said the grand strategist seriously, "keep your paws off it. Now back to business. Send the forward guards to my command. Troops are to report to the city of Chernomorsk ASAP. Full dress uniform. Start the music! I am commanding the parade!"

CHAPTER 3
GAS IS YOURS, IDEAS OURS

A year before Panikovsky violated the pact by trespassing on someone else's territory, the first automobile appeared in the town of Arbatov. The town's trailblazing automotive pioneer was a motorist by the name of Kozlevich.

It was his decision to start a new life that brought him to the steering wheel. The old life of Adam Kozlevich was sinful. He repeatedly violated the Criminal Code of the Russian Socialist Republic, specifically Article 162, which deals with the misappropriation of another person's property (theft).

This article has many sections, but sinful Adam had no interest in Section A (theft committed without the use of technical devices). That was too primitive for him. Section E, which carried the penalty of incarceration for up to five years, did not suit him either. He didn't want to spend too much time in prison. Having been interested in all things technical since he was a child, Kozlevich devoted his energies to Article C (felonious misappropriation of another person's property committed with the use of technical devices, or repeatedly, or in collusion with other individuals, at train stations, in ports, on boats, on trains, or in hotels).

But Kozlevich had very bad luck. He was caught whether he utilized his beloved technical devices or made do without them. He was caught at train stations, in ports, on boats, and in hotels. He was also caught on trains. He was caught even when, in total despair, he resorted to grabbing property in collusion with other individuals.

After a total of about three years in jail, Adam Kozlevich decided that it was much better to accumulate your own property honestly and overtly than to take it from others covertly. This decision brought peace to his restless soul. He became a model inmate, published denunciatory poems in the prison newsletter, *Day In and Day Out*, and worked hard in the machine shop. The penitentiary system had a salutary effect on him. Adam Kazimirovich Kozlevich, 46, single, of peasant origin, of the former Czestochowa District, multiple repeat offender, came out of prison an honest man.

After two years of working in a Moscow garage, he bought a used car; it was so ancient that its appearance on the market could only be explained by the closing of an automotive museum. Kozlevich paid 190 rubles for this curiosity. For some reason, the car came with a fake palm tree in a green pot. He had to buy the palm tree as well. The tree was passable, but the car needed plenty of work. He searched flea markets for missing parts, patched up the seats, replaced the entire electric system, and, as a final touch, painted the car bright lizard green. The car's breed was impossible to determine, but Adam claimed it was a Lorraine-Dietrich. As proof of that, he attached a brass plate with the Lorraine-Dietrich logo to the radiator. He was ready to start a private taxi business, which had been Adam's dream for quite some time.

The day when Adam introduced his creation to the public at a taxi stand was a sad day for private taxi drivers. One hundred and twenty small, black Renault taxicabs, that looked like Browning pistols, were introduced to the streets of Moscow by the authorities. Kozlevich didn't even attempt to compete with them. He put the palm tree in the Versailles cabdrivers' tearoom, for safekeeping, and went to work in the provinces.

Arbatov, which totally lacked automotive transport, was much to his liking, so he decided to stay there for good.

Kozlevich imagined how hard, cheerfully, and, above all, honestly he would toil in the field of cabs for hire. He pictured himself on early arctic-cold mornings, waiting at the station for the train from Moscow. Wrapped in a thick ruddy-colored fur coat, his aviator goggles raised to his forehead, he jovially offers cigarettes to the porters. Somewhere behind him, the freezing coachmen are huddling. They cry from the cold and shiver in their thick dark-blue capes. And then the station bell begins to ring. It's a sign that the train has arrived. Passengers walk out onto the station square and stop in front of the car, pleasantly surprised. They didn't think that the idea of the taxi had reached the boondocks of Arbatov. Sounding the horn, Kozlevich whisks his passengers to the Peasants' Hostel.

There's enough work for the whole day, and everyone is happy to take advantage of his services. Kozlevich and his faithful Lorraine-Dietrich invariably participate in all of the town's weddings, sightseeing trips, and other special occasions. Summers are particularly busy. On Sundays, whole families go to the country in Adam's car. Children laugh foolishly, scarves and ribbons flutter in the wind, women chatter merrily, fathers look at the driver's leather-clad back with respect and ask him about automotive developments in the United States of North America. For example, is it true that Ford buys himself a new car every day?

That's how Kozlevich pictured his blissful new life in Arbatov. The reality, however, quickly destroyed Adam's castle in the air, with all its turrets, drawbridges, weathervanes, and standards.

The first blow was inflicted by the train schedule. Fast trains passed through Arbatov without making a stop, picking up single line tokens and dropping express mail on the move. Slow trains arrived only twice a week. For the most part, they only brought insignificant people: peasants and shoemakers with knapsacks, boot trees, and petitions to the local authorities. As a rule, these people did not use taxis. There were no sightseeing trips or special occasions, and nobody hired Kozlevich for weddings. People in Arbatov were accustomed to using horse-drawn carriages for weddings. On such occasions, the coachmen would braid paper roses and chrysanthemums into the horses' manes. The older men, who were in charge of the festivities, loved it.

On the other hand, there were plenty of outings, but those were very different from the ones Adam had pictured. No children, no fluttering scarves, no merry chatter.

On the very first evening, when the dim kerosene street lamps were already lit, Adam was approached by four men. He had spent the whole day pointlessly waiting on Holy Cooperative Square. The men stared at the car for a long time without saying a word. Then one of them, a hunchback, asked uncertainly:

"Can anybody take a ride?"

"Yes, anybody," replied Kozlevich, surprised by the timidity of the citizens of Arbatov. "Five rubles an hour."

The men whispered among themselves. The chauffeur heard some strange sighs and a few words: "Why don't we do it after the meeting,

Comrades . . .? Would that be appropriate . . .? One twenty-five per person is not too much . . . Why would it be inappropriate . . .?"

And so for the first time, the spacious car took a few locals into its upholstered lap. For a few minutes, the passengers were silent, overwhelmed by the speed, the smell of gasoline, and the whistling wind. Then, as if having a vague premonition, they started quietly singing: "The time of our lives, it's fast as waves . . ." Kozlevich shifted into third gear. The sombre silhouette of a boarded-up roadside stand flew by, and the car tore out into the fields on the moonlit highway.

"Every day brings the grave ever closer to us," crooned the passengers plaintively. They felt sorry for themselves, sorry that they had never gone to university and had never sung student songs. They belted out the chorus rather loudly:

"Let's have a glass, a little one, tra-la-la-la, tra-la-la-la."

"Stop!" shouted the hunchback suddenly. "Turn around! I can't take it any more!"

Back in town, the riders picked up a large number of bottles that were filled with clear liquid, as well as a broad-shouldered woman from somewhere. Out in the fields, they set up a picnic, ate dinner with vodka, and danced the polka without music.

Exhausted from the night's adventures, Kozlevich spent the next day dozing off behind the wheel at his stand. Towards evening, the same gang showed up, already tipsy. They climbed into the car and drove like mad through the fields surrounding the city all night long. The third night saw a repeat of the whole thing. The nighttime feasts of the fun-loving gang, headed by the hunchback, went on for two weeks in a row. The joys of automotive recreation affected Adam's clients in a most peculiar way: in the dark, their pale and swollen faces resembled pillows. The hunchback, with a piece of sausage hanging from his mouth, looked like a vampire.

They grew anxious and, at the height of the fun, occasionally wept. One night, the adventurous hunchback arrived at the taxi stand in a horse-drawn carriage with a big sack of rice. At sunrise, they took the rice to a village, swapped it for moonshine, and didn't bother going back to the city. They sat on haystacks and drank with the peasants, hugging them and swearing eternal friendship. At night, they set up bonfires and wept more pitifully than ever.

The following morning was gray and dull, and the railroad-affiliated Lineman Co-op closed for inventory. The hunchback was its director, his fun-loving friends members of the board and the control commission. The auditors were bitterly disappointed to discover that the store had no flour, no pepper, no coarse soap, no water troughs, no textiles, and no rice. The shelves, the counters, the boxes, and the barrels had all been completely emptied. A pair of enormous hip boots, size fifteen with yellow glued-leather soles, towered in the middle of the store. A National cash register, its lady-like nickel-plated bosom covered with numerous keys, sat in a glass booth. That was all that was left. Kozlevich, for his part, received a subpoena from a police detective; the driver was wanted as a witness in the case of the Lineman Co-op.

The hunchback and his friends never showed up again, and the green car stood idle for three days.

All subsequent passengers, like the first bunch, would appear under the cover of darkness. They would also start with an innocent drive to the country, but their thoughts would turn to vodka after the first half-mile. Apparently, the people of Arbatov could not imagine staying sober in an automobile. They clearly regarded Adam's vehicle as a refuge for sinful pleasures, where one ought to behave recklessly, make loud obscene noises, and generally live one's life to the fullest. Kozlevich finally understood why the men who walked past his stand during the day winked at one another and smiled wryly.

Things were very different from what Adam had envisioned. At night, he was whizzing past the woods with his headlights on, listening to the passengers' drunken fussing and hollering behind him. During the day, in a stupor from lack of sleep, he sat in detectives' offices giving statements. For some reason, the citizens of Arbatov paid for their high living with money that belonged to the state, society, or the co-ops. Against his will, Kozlevich was once again deeply entangled with the Criminal code, this time its Part III, the part that informatively discusses white-collar crimes.

The trials soon commenced. In all of them, the main witness for the prosecution was Adam Kozlevich. His truthful accounts knocked the defendants off their feet, and they confessed everything, choking on tears and snot. He ruined countless organizations. His last victim was a branch of the regional film studio, which was shooting a historical movie, *Stenka Razin and the Princess*, in Arbatov. The entire staff of the branch was locked up for six years, while the film, which was of legal interest only, joined the pirate boots from the Lineman Co-op at the material evidence exhibit.

After that, Adam's business crashed. People avoided the green vehicle like the plague. They made wide circles around Holy Cooperative Square, where Kozlevich had erected a tall sign: AUTOMOBILE FOR HIRE. He earned nothing at all for several months and lived off the savings from earlier nocturnal rides.

Then he had to make a few sacrifices. He painted a white sign on the car's door that said LET'S RIDE!, and lowered the fare from five to three rubles an hour. The sign looked rather enticing to him, but people resisted anyway. He would drive slowly around town, approaching office buildings and yelling into open windows:

"The air is so fresh! Why not go for a ride?"

Officials would stick their heads out and yell back over the clatter of the Underwood typewriters:

"Go take a ride yourself, you hangman!"

"Hangman?" Kozlevich asked, on the verge of tears.

"Of course you are," answered the officials, "you'd put us all in the slammer."

"Then why don't you pay with your own money?" asked the driver. "For the rides?"

At this point the officials would exchange funny looks and shut the windows. They thought it was ridiculous to use their own money to pay for car rides.

The owner of LET'S RIDE! was at loggerheads with the entire city. He no longer exchanged greetings with anybody. He became edgy and mean-spirited. Seeing an office worker in a long Caucasus-style shirt with puffy sleeves, he would drive up and yell, laughing bitterly:

"Thieves! Just wait, I'm going to set all of you up! Article 109!"

The office worker shuddered, pulled up his silver-studded belt (that looked like it belonged on a draft horse), pretended that the shouting had nothing to do with him, and started walking faster. But vindictive Kozlevich would continue to follow him and goad the enemy by monotonously reading from a pocket edition of the Criminal code, as if from a prayer book:

"Misappropriation of funds, valuables, or other property by a person in a position of authority who oversees such property as part of his daily duties shall be punished . . ."

The worker would flee in panic, his derriere, flattened by long hours in an office chair, bouncing as he ran.

". . . by imprisonment for up to three years!" yelled Kozlevich after him.

But this brought him only moral satisfaction. Financially, he was in deep trouble; the savings were all but gone. He had to do something fast. He could not continue like this.

One day, Adam was sitting in his car in his usual state of anxiety, staring at the silly AUTOMOBILE FOR HIRE sign with disgust. He had an inkling that living honestly hadn't worked out for him, that the automotive messiah had come too early, when citizens were not yet ready to accept him. Kozlevich was so deeply immersed in these depressing thoughts that at first he didn't even notice the two young men who had been admiring his car for some time.

"A unique design," one of them finally said, "the dawn of the automotive industry. Do you see, Balaganov, what can be made out of a simple Singer sewing machine? A few small adjustments—and you get a lovely harvester for the collective farm."

"Get lost," said Kozlevich grimly.

"What do you mean, 'get lost'? Then why did you decorate your thresher with this inviting LET'S RIDE! sign? What if my friend and I wish to take a business trip? What if a ride is exactly what we're looking for?"

The automotive martyr's face was lit by a smile—the first of the entire Arbatov period of his life. He jumped out of the car and promptly started the engine, which knocked heavily.

"Get in, please" he said. "Where to?"

"This time, nowhere," answered Balaganov, "we've got no money. What can you do, Comrade driver, poverty . . ."

"Get in anyway!" cried Kozlevich excitedly. "I'll drive you for free! You're not going to drink? You're not going to dance naked in the moonlight? Let's ride!"

"All right, we'll accept your kind invitation," said Ostap, settling himself in next to the driver. "I see you're a nice man. But what makes you think that we have any interest in dancing naked?"

"They all do it here," replied the driver, turning onto the main street, "those dangerous felons."

He was dying to share his sorrows with somebody. It would have been best, of course, to tell his misfortunes to his kindly, wrinkle-faced mother. She would have felt for him. But Madame Kozlevich had passed away a long time ago—from grief, when she found out that her son Adam was gaining notoriety as a thief. And so the driver told his new passengers the whole story of the downfall of the city of Arbatov, in whose ruins his helpless green automobile was buried.

"Where can I go now?" concluded Kozlevich forlornly. "What am I supposed to do?"

Ostap paused, gave his red-headed companion a significant look, and said:

"All your troubles are due to the fact that you are a truth-seeker. You're just a lamb, a failed Baptist. I am saddened to encounter such pessimism among drivers. You have a car, but you don't know where to go. We're in a worse bind: we don't have a car, but we know where we want to go. Want to come with us?"

"Where?" asked the driver.

"To Chernomorsk," answered Ostap. "We have a small private matter to settle down there. There'd be work for you, too. People in Chernomorsk appreciate antiques and enjoy riding in them. Come."

At first Adam was just smiling, like a widow with nothing to look forward to in this life. But Bender gave it his eloquent best. He drew striking perspectives for the perplexed driver and quickly colored them in blue and pink.

"And here in Arbatov, you've got nothing to lose but your spare chains. You won't be starving on the road, I will take care of that. Gas is yours, ideas ours."

Kozlevich stopped the car and, still resisting, said glumly:

"I don't have much gas."

"Enough for thirty miles?"

"Enough for fifty."

"In that case, there's nothing to worry about. I have already informed you that I have no shortage of ideas and plans. Exactly forty miles from here, a large barrel of aviation fuel will be waiting for you right on the road. Do you fancy aviation fuel?"

"I do," answered Kozlevich, blushing.

Life suddenly seemed easy and fun. He was prepared to go to Chernomorsk immediately.

"And this fuel," continued Ostap, "will cost you absolutely nothing. Moreover, they'll be begging you to take it."

"What fuel?" whispered Balaganov. "What the hell are you talking about?"

Ostap disdainfully studied the orange freckles spread across his half-brother's face and answered in an equally low voice:

"People who don't read newspapers have no right to live. I'm sparing you only because I still hope to re-educate you."

He did not explain the connection between reading newspapers and the large barrel of fuel allegedly sitting on the road.

"I now declare the grand Arbatov-Chernomorsk high-speed rally open," said Ostap solemnly. "I appoint myself the captain of the rally. The driver of the vehicle will be . . . what's your last name? Adam Kozlevich. Citizen Balaganov is confirmed as the rally mechanic, with additional duties as Girl Friday. One more thing, Kozlevich: you have to paint over this LET'S RIDE! sign right away. We don't need to attract any attention."

Two hours later the car, with a freshly painted dark green spot on the side, slowly climbed out of the garage and drove through the streets of Arbatov for the last time. Adam's eyes sparkled hopefully. Next to him sat Balaganov, who was diligently carrying out his role as the rally's mechanic by thoroughly polishing the car's brass with a piece of cloth. The captain of the rally sat behind them, leaning into the ruddy-colored seat and eyeing his staff with satisfaction.

"Adam!" he shouted over the engine's rumble, "what's your buggy's name?"

"Lorraine-Dietrich," answered Kozlevich.

"What kind of a name is that? A car, like a naval ship, ought to have a proper name. Your Lorraine-Dietrich is remarkably fast and incredibly graceful. I therefore propose to name it the Gnu Antelope. Any objections? Unanimous."

The green Antelope, all of its parts creaking, sped down the outer lane of the Boulevard of Prodigies and flew out onto the market square.

An odd scene greeted the crew of the Antelope on the square. A man with a white goose under his arm was running from the square, in the direction of the highway. He held a hard straw hat on his head with his left hand, and he was being chased by a large howling crowd. The man glanced back frequently, and there was an expression of terror on his decent-looking actor's face.

"That's Panikovsky!" cried Balaganov.

"The second phase of stealing a goose," remarked Ostap coldly. "The third phase comes after the culprit is apprehended. It is accompanied by painful blows."

Panikovsky apparently knew that the third phase was coming. He was running as fast as he could. He was so frightened that he kept holding on to the goose, which irritated his pursuers to no end.

"Article 116," recited Kozlevich from memory. "Covert or overt theft of large domestic animals from persons engaged in agriculture or animal husbandry."

Balaganov burst out laughing. He loved the thought that the violator of the pact would finally receive his due punishment.

The car cut through the noisy crowd and drove onto the highway.

"Help me!" yelled out Panikovsky as the car caught up with him.

"Not today," said Balaganov, hanging over the side.

The car shrouded Panikovsky with clouds of crimson dust.

"Take me with you!" screamed Panikovsky, desperately trying to keep up with the car. "I am good!"

The voices of the individual pursuers blended into a roar of disapproval.

"Shall we take the bastard?" enquired Ostap.

"No, don't," said Balaganov harshly, "that'll teach him to break pacts."

But Ostap had already made the decision.

"Drop the bird!" he yelled to Panikovsky; then he turned to the driver and added quietly, "Dead slow."

Panikovsky immediately obeyed. The goose got up from the ground looking displeased, scratched itself, and started walking back to town as if nothing had happened.

"Get in," invited Ostap. "What the hell. But don't sin any more, or I'll rip your arms out of their sockets."

Panikovsky grabbed the edge of the car, then leaned into it and, beating the air with his legs, rolled himself inside, like a swimmer into a boat. He fell to the floor, his stiff cuffs knocking loudly.

"Full speed ahead," ordered Ostap. "Our deliberations continue."

Balaganov squeezed the rubber bulb, and the brass horn produced the cheerful strains of an old-fashioned Brazilian tango that cut off abruptly:

> The Maxixe is fun to dance. Ta-ra-ta . . .
> The Maxixe is fun to dance. Ta-ra-ta . . .

And the Antelope tore out into the wilderness, towards the barrel of aviation fuel.

CHAPTER 4
A PLAIN-LOOKING SUITCASE

A man without a hat walked out of the small gate of building number sixteen, his head bowed. He wore gray canvas pants, leather sandals without socks, like a monk, and a white collarless shirt. Stepping onto the flat, bluish stones of the sidewalk, he stopped and said quietly to himself:

"Today is Friday. That means I have to go to the train station again."

Having uttered these words, the man in sandals quickly looked over his shoulder. He had a hunch that a man, wearing the impenetrable expression of a spy, was standing behind him. But Lesser Tangential Street was completely empty.

The June morning was just beginning to take shape. Acacia trees were gently trembling and dropping cold metallic dew on the flat stones. Little birds were chirping some cheerful nonsense. The heavy molten sea blazed at the end of the street below, beyond the roofs. Young dogs, looking around sadly and making tapping sounds with their nails, were climbing onto trash cans. The hour of the street sweepers had ended, and the hour of the milk delivery women hadn't started yet.

It was that time, between five and six in the morning, when the street sweepers, having swung their bristly brooms enough, returned to their shacks, and the city is light, clean, and quiet, like a state bank. At moments like this, one feels like crying and wants to believe that yogurt is indeed tastier and healthier than vodka. But one can already hear the distant rumble of the milk delivery women, who are getting off commuter trains with their cans. They will rush into the city and bicker with housewives at back doors. Factory workers with lunch bags will appear for a brief moment and then immediately disappear behind factory gates. Smoke will start billowing from the stacks. And then, jumping angrily on their night stands, myriad alarm clocks will start ringing their hearts out (those of the Paul Buhre brand a bit quieter, those from the Precision Mechanics State Trust a bit louder), and half-awake office workers will start bleating and falling off their high single beds. The hour of the milk delivery women will be over, and the hour of the office dwellers will begin.

But it was still early, and the clerks were still asleep under their ficus. The man in sandals walked through the entire city, seeing almost no one on the way. He walked under the acacias, which performed certain useful functions in Chernomorsk: some had dark blue mailboxes that were emblazoned with the postal logo (an envelope with a lightning bolt) hanging on them, others had metal water bowls, for dogs, attached to them with chains.

The man in sandals arrived at the Seaside Station just when the milk delivery women were leaving the building. After a few painful encounters with their iron shoulders, the man approached the luggage room and handed over a receipt. The attendant glanced at the receipt—with the unnatural seriousness that is unique to railroad personnel—and promptly tossed a suitcase to him. For his part, the man opened a small leather wallet, sighed, took out a ten-kopeck coin, and put it on the counter, which was made of six old rails that had been polished by innumerable elbows.

Back on the square in front of the station, the man in sandals put the suitcase down on the pavement, looked it over carefully, and even touched the small metal lock. It was a plain-looking suitcase that had been slapped together from a few wooden planks and covered with man-made fabric.

If this kind of suitcase belongs to a younger passenger, it usually contains cotton Sketch socks, two spare shirts, a hairnet, some underwear, a brochure entitled *The Goals of the Young Communist League in the Countryside,* and three squished boiled eggs. Plus, there's always a roll of dirty laundry wrapped in the newspaper *Economic Life* and tucked in the corner. Older passengers use this kind of suitcase to carry a full suit and a separate pair of pants (made of "Odessa Centennial" checkered fabric), a pair of suspenders, a pair of closed-back slippers, a bottle of eau-de-cologne, and a white Marseilles blanket. It should be noted that in these cases there's also something wrapped in *Economic Life* and tucked in the corner, except that instead of dirty laundry it's a pale boiled chicken.

Satisfied with this perfunctory inspection, the man in sandals picked up the suitcase and boarded a tropical-white streetcar that took him to the Eastern Station at the other end of the city. Here, he reversed the process he had just completed at the Seaside Station—he checked his suitcase in at the luggage room and obtained a receipt from the imposing attendant.

Having completed this unusual ritual, the owner of the suitcase left the station just as the streets were beginning to fill up with the most exemplary of the clerks. He quickly joined their disorderly ranks, and his outfit immediately lost all its strangeness. The man in sandals was an office worker, and almost every office worker in Chernomorsk followed an unwritten dress code: a night shirt with sleeves rolled up above the elbows, light, orphanage-style pants, and those same sandals, or canvas shoes. Nobody wore a hat. One could occasionally spot a cap, but a mane of wild black hair standing on end was much more common, and a bald, sun-tanned pate, glimmering like a melon lying in the field and tempting you to write something on it with an indelible pencil, was more common still.

The organization where the man in sandals worked was called The Hercules, and it occupied a former hotel. Revolving glass doors with brass steamboat handles propelled him into a large, pink marble hallway. The elevator was permanently moored on the first floor, and it served as an information booth—one could already see a woman's laughing face inside. Having run a few steps, thanks to the momentum given to him by the door, the newcomer stopped in front of an old doorman, who was wearing a cap with a golden zigzag, and asked cheerily:

"So, old man, are you ready for the crematorium?"

"Ready, my friend," answered the doorman with a broad smile, "ready for our Soviet columbarium."

He even waived his hands in excitement. His kindly face showed a willingness to submit himself to the fiery ritual at any moment.

The Chernomorsk authorities were planning to build a crematorium—along with a space called a columbarium, for funeral urns—and for some reason this novelty, courtesy of the municipal cemetery department, delighted the citizens to no end. Maybe they thought the new words—crematorium and columbarium—were funny, or maybe they were particularly amused by the thought that a human body can be burned like a log. Either way, they pestered elderly people in the streets and on streetcars with comments like: "Where are you charging off to, old woman? To the crematorium?" Or: "Let the old man pass, he's off to the crematorium."

Surprisingly, the old folks liked the idea of cremation very much, and they responded good-naturedly to all jokes on the subject. In general, all that talk about dying, which was previously considered inappropriate and impolite, had come to enjoy universal popularity in Chernomorsk and was considered as entertaining as Jewish and Armenian jokes.

The man skirted a naked marble woman that stood at the bottom of the stairs, an electric torch in her raised hand, and threw a quick annoyed look at the poster that said, THE PURGE OF THE HERCULES BEGINS. DOWN WITH THE CONSPIRACY OF SILENCE AND CRONYISM. Then he climbed the stairs to the second floor. He worked in the Department of Finance and Accounting. It was still fifteen minutes before the official start of the workday, but the others—Sakharkov, Dreyfus, Tezoimenitsky, Musicant, Chevazhevskaya, Kukushkind, Borisokhlebsky, and Lapidus Jr.—were already at their desks. They weren't worried about the purge at all, and repeatedly reassured one another that they weren't, but lately, for some reason, they had started coming to work earlier and earlier. Taking advantage of the few minutes of free time, they were chatting loudly among themselves. Their voices boomed across the huge hall, which was once the hotel's restaurant. Its oak-paneled ceiling, which was covered with carvings, and the murals of frolicking dryads and other nymphs, with dreadful smiles on their faces, were evidence of its past.

"Have you heard the news, Koreiko?" Lapidus Jr. asked the new arrival. "You really haven't? Then you won't believe it."

"What news? Good morning, Comrades," said Koreiko. "Good morning, Anna Vasilevna."

"You can't even imagine!" said Lapidus Jr. gleefully. "Accountant Berlaga is in the nuthouse."

"Are you serious? Berlaga? He's the most normal person in the world!"

"Was the most normal until yesterday, but now he's the least normal," chimed in Borisokhlebsky. "It's true. His brother-in-law called me. Berlaga has a very serious mental illness, the heel nerve disorder."

"The only surprising thing is that the rest of us don't have this nerve disorder yet," remarked old Kukushkind darkly, looking at his co-workers through his round, wire-rimmed glasses.

"Bite your tongue," said Chevazhevskaya. "He's always so depressing."

"It's really too bad about Berlaga," said Dreyfus, turning his swivel chair towards the others.

The others silently agreed with Dreyfus. Only Lapidus Jr. smirked mysteriously. The conversation moved on to the behavior of the mentally ill. They mentioned a few maniacs, and told a few stories about notorious madmen.

"I had a crazy uncle," reported Sakharkov, "who thought he was simultaneously Abraham, Isaac, and Jacob. You can imagine the ruckus he raised!"

"The only surprising thing," said old Kukushkind in a scratchy voice, methodically wiping off his glasses with the flap of his jacket, "the only surprising thing is that the rest of us don't yet think that we are Abraham . . ." The old man started puffing, ". . . Isaac . . ."

"And Jacob?" asked Sakharkov teasingly.

"That's right! And Jacob!" shrieked Kukushkind suddenly. "And Jacob! Yes, Jacob. We live in such unnerving times . . . When I worked at the banking firm of Sycamorsky and Cesarewitch they didn't have any purges."

Hearing the word "purge," Lapidus Jr. perked up, took Koreiko by the elbow, and pulled him toward the enormous stained-glass window, which depicted two gothic knights.

"You haven't heard the most interesting bit about Berlaga yet," he whispered. "Berlaga is healthy as a horse."

"What? So he's not in the nuthouse?"

"Oh yes, he is."

Lapidus smiled knowingly.

"That's the trick. He was simply afraid of the purge and decided to sit this dangerous period out. Faked mental illness. Right now, he's probably growling and guffawing. What an operator! Frankly, I'm envious."

"Is there a problem with his parents? Were they merchants? Undesirable elements?"

"Yes, his parents were problematic, and he himself, between you and me, used to own a pharmacy. Who knew the revolution was coming? People took care of themselves the best they could: some owned pharmacies, others even factories. Personally, I don't see anything wrong with that. Who knew?"

"They should have known," said Koreiko icily.

"That's exactly what I'm saying," agreed Lapidus quickly, "people like this do not belong in a Soviet organization."

He gave Koreiko a wide-eyed look and returned to his desk.

The hall was filled with employees. Flexible metal rulers, shining and silvery like fish scales, abacuses with palm beads, heavy ledgers with pink and yellow stripes on their pages, and a multitude of other pieces of stationery great and small were pulled out of desk drawers. Tezoimenitsky tore yesterday's page off the wall calendar, and the new day began. Somebody had already sunk his young teeth into a large chopped mutton sandwich.

Koreiko settled down at his desk as well. He firmly planted his suntanned elbows on the desk and started making entries in a current accounts ledger.

Alexander Ivanovich Koreiko, one of the lowest-ranking employees of the Hercules, was approaching the very end of his youth. He was thirty-eight. His brick-red face sported white eyes and blonde eyebrows that looked like ears of wheat. His thin English mustache was the color of ripe cereal, too. His face would have looked quite young had it not been for the rough drill-sergeant's jowls that cut across his cheeks and neck. At work, Alexander Ivanovich carried himself like an army volunteer: he didn't talk too much, he followed instructions, and he was diligent, deferential, and a bit slow.

"He's too timid," the head of Finance and Accounting said, "too servile, if you will, too dedicated. The moment a new bond campaign is announced, he's right there, with his one-month salary pledge. The first to sign up. And his salary is a measly forty-six rubles a month. I would love to know how he manages to live on that . . ."

Alexander Ivanovich had one peculiar talent: he could instantly divide and multiply three- and four-digit numbers in his head. Despite this talent, they still thought Koreiko was somewhat slow.

"Listen, Alexander Ivanovich," an office mate would ask, "how much is 836 times 423?"

"Three hundred and fifty-three thousand six hundred and twenty-eight," Koreiko would answer after a moment's hesitation.

The co-worker wouldn't even bother to check the result because he knew that the slow Koreiko never made a mistake.

"Someone else would have made a career out of this," Sakharkov, Dreyfus, Tezoimenitsky, Musicant, Chevazhevskaya, Borisokhlebsky, Lapidus Jr., the old fool Kukushkind, and even Berlaga, the one who escaped to the nuthouse, often repeated. "But this one is a loser. He'll spend his whole life making forty-six rubles a month."

Of course, his co-workers, or the head of Finance and Accounting, Comrade Arnikov himself, or even Impala Mikhailovna, the personal secretary to the director of the entire Hercules, Comrade Polykhaev—all of them would have been shocked had they found out what exactly Alexander Ivanovich Koreiko, the quietest of the clerks, had been up to just one hour earlier. For whatever reason, he dragged a particular suitcase from one train station to another. The suitcase contained not Odessa Centennial pants, nor a boiled chicken, and certainly not *The Goals of the Young Communist League in the Countryside*, but ten million rubles in Soviet and foreign currency.

In 1915, Alex Koreiko, twenty-three, the ne'er-do-well son of middle class parents, was one of those who are deservedly known as "retired high-schoolers." He didn't finish school, didn't take up any trade, he just hung out on the boulevards and lived off his parents. His uncle, the manager of the regional military office, had shielded him from the draft, so he could listen to the cries of the half-witted paperboy without worrying:

"The latest cables! Our troops are advancing! Thank God! Multiple casualties! Thank God!"

Back then, Alex Koreiko pictured his future in the following way: he's walking down the street and suddenly, near a downspout covered with zinc stars, right next to the wall, he sees a burgundy leather wallet that's squeaky like a new saddle. There's a lot of money in the wallet, 2,500 rubles . . . After that, everything would be swell.

He pictured finding the money so often that he knew exactly where it was going to happen—on Poltava Victory Street, in an asphalt corner formed by the jutting wall of a building, near the star-studded downspout. There it lies, his leather savior, dusted with dry acacia flowers, next to a flattened cigarette butt. Alex walked to Poltava Victory Street every day, but to his great surprise, the wallet was never there. He'd poke the garbage with a student's walking stick and mindlessly stare at the glazed metal sign that hung by the front door: YU. M. SOLOVEISKY, TAX ASSESSOR. Then he would wander home in a daze, throw himself on the red velvet couch and dream of riches, deafened by the ticking of his heart and pulse. His pulse was shallow, angry, and impatient.

The revolution of 1917 chased Koreiko off his velvet couch. He realized that he could become the lucky heir to some wealthy strangers. He felt in his guts that the country was awash in unclaimed gold, jewelry, expensive furniture, paintings and carpets, fur coats and dining sets. One just had to move fast and grab the riches, the sooner the better.

At the time, however, he was still young and foolish. He took over a large apartment—whose owner was smart enough to escape to Constantinople on a French ship—and started living there openly. Over the course of a week, he grew accustomed to the lavish lifestyle of the fugitive businessman: he drank the muscat wine he found in the cupboard with pickled herring from his food ration and sold knickknacks at the flea market. He was quite surprised when he was arrested.

He got out of prison five months later. He hadn't given up the idea of becoming rich, but he came to realize that such an undertaking has to be secret, hidden, and gradual. First, he had to acquire some camouflage. In the case of Alexander Ivanovich, the camouflage came in the form of tall orange boots, huge dark-blue breeches, and the long military-style jacket of a food-supply official.

In those distressing times, everything that had been made by human hands wasn't working as well as it had before: houses no longer gave any protection from the cold, food wasn't filling, the electricity was only turned on to round up deserters and bandits, running water didn't reach beyond the first floor, and streetcars did not run at all. At the same time, the elements became more ferocious and dangerous: the winters were colder than before, the winds were stronger, and the common cold, which used to put a person in bed for three days, killed him within the same three days. Groups of young men without any discernible occupation wandered the streets, singing a devil-may-care ditty about money that had lost its value:

> I am standing at the till,
> Not a single smaller bill.
> Can you break a hundred million fo-o-o-r me?

Alexander Ivanovich watched in consternation as the money that he had gone to incredible lengths to acquire was turning into dust.

Typhoid was killing people by the thousands. Alex was selling medications that had been stolen from a warehouse. He made five hundred million on the typhoid, but inflation turned it into five million within a month. Then he made a billion on sugar; inflation turned it into dust.

During that period, one of his most successful operations was the heist of a scheduled food train that was headed for the famished Volga region. Koreiko was in charge of the train. The train left Poltava for Samara but never reached Samara and did not return to Poltava either. It disappeared en route without a trace. Alexander Ivanovich disappeared with it.

CHAPTER 5
THE UNDERGROUND KINGDOM

The orange boots surfaced in Moscow toward the end of 1922. Above the boots, a thick greenish leather coat lined with golden fox fur reigned supreme. A raised sheepskin collar with a quilted lining protected a cocky-looking mug, with short Sebastopol-style sideburns, from the elements. A lovely Caucasian hat made of curly fleece adorned the head of Alexander Ivanovich.

Meanwhile, Moscow was already beginning to fill with brand new automobiles that sported crystal headlights, and the nouveau riche, in tony sealskin skull caps and coats lined with patterned Lyre fur, paraded in the streets. Pointy gothic shoes and briefcases with luggage-style belts and handles were coming into vogue. The word "citizen" started to replace the familiar "comrade," and some young people, who were quick to appreciate the real joys of life, were already dancing the Dixie One-step and even the Sunflower Foxtrot in the restaurants. The city echoed with the shouts of smart coachmen in expensive carriages, while inside the grand building of the Foreign Ministry the tailor Zhurkevich sewed tailcoats, day and night, for Soviet diplomats who were preparing to go abroad.

To his surprise, Alexander Ivanovich realized that his outfit, which projected valor and wealth in the provinces, was seen as a curious anachronism in Moscow and cast an unfavorable light on its owner.

Two months later, a new company called Revenge, the Industrial Chemicals Cooperative, opened on Sretensky Boulevard. The Cooperative occupied two rooms. The first room was decorated with a portrait of Friedrich Engels, one of the founders of socialism. Beneath it sat Alexander Ivanovich himself, with an innocent smile on his face. He wore a gray English suit with red silk stripes. The orange pirate boots and the crude sideburns were gone. Koreiko's cheeks were clean shaven. The manufacturing plant was located in the back room. It consisted of two oak barrels with pressure gauges and water-level indicators, one on the floor, the other in the loft. The barrels were connected by a thin enema hose through which some liquid babbled busily. When all the liquid ran from the upper barrel into the lower one, a boy in felt boots would appear on the shop floor. Sighing like an adult, the boy scooped the liquid from the lower barrel with a bucket, dragged the bucket to the loft, and emptied it into the upper barrel. After completing this complex manufacturing process, the boy would go to the office to warm up, while the enema hose would start sobbing again. The liquid continued on its usual path from the upper reservoir to the lower.

Alexander Ivanovich himself wasn't quite sure which chemicals were being produced by the Revenge Cooperative. He had more important things to do. Even without the chemicals his days were already full. He moved from bank to bank, applying for loans to expand the operation. He signed agreements with state trusts to supply the chemicals and obtained raw materials at wholesale prices. Loans were also coming in. Reselling the raw materials to state factories at ten times wholesale was very time-consuming, and the black-market currency operations he conducted at the foot of the monument to the heroes of the battle of Plevna were also extremely labor-intensive.

After a year, the banks and the trusts developed a desire to find out how much the Revenge Industrial Cooperative benefited from all the financial and material aid it received, and they wanted to know whether the healthy private establishment needed any further assistance. The commission, decked out in scholarly beards, arrived at the Revenge in three coaches. The chairman stared into Engels's dispassionate face for a long time and kept banging on the fir counter with a cane, in an attempt to summon the administrators and members of the cooperative. Finally the door of the manufacturing plant opened, and a teary-eyed boy with a bucket in his hand appeared in front of the commission.

An interview with the young representative of the Revenge revealed that the manufacturing process was going full-throttle, and that the owner had been gone for a week. The commission didn't spend much time at the production plant. In its taste, color, and chemical composition, the liquid that babbled so busily in the enema hose resembled ordinary water, and that's exactly what it was. Having established this incredible fact, the chairman said "Hmm" and looked at the other members, who also said "Hmm." Then the chairman looked at the boy with a terrible smile and asked:

"And how old are you?"

"Twelve," answered the boy.

And then he burst out crying so inconsolably that the members ran outside, pushing each other on the way, climbed into their coaches, and left in total confusion. As for the Revenge Cooperative, all of its operations were duly recorded in the profit and loss balance sheets of bank and trust ledgers, specifically in the sections that say nothing about profits and deal exclusively with losses.

On the same day that the commission had such a meaningful exchange with the boy at the Revenge, Alexander Ivanovich Koreiko got off the sleeper car of an express train two thousand miles from Moscow, in a small grape-growing republic.

He opened his hotel room window and saw a small oasis town, complete with bamboo water lines and a shoddy mud-brick fortress. The town was separated from the sands by poplars and was filled with Asiatic hubbub.

The next day he learned that the republic had started building a new electric power plant. He also learned that money was short, and that the construction, which was crucial to the future of the republic, might have to be halted.

And so the successful entrepreneur decided to help out. He got into a pair of orange boots again, put on an embroidered Central Asian cap, and headed to the construction office with a fat briefcase in his hand.

They didn't receive him very warmly, but he carried himself with dignity, didn't ask anything for himself, and insisted that the idea of bringing electricity to backward hinterlands was especially dear to his heart.

"Your project is short of money," he said. "I'll get it for you."

He proposed to create a profitable subsidiary within the construction enterprise.

"What could be easier! We will sell postcards with views of the construction site, and that will bring the funds that the project needs so badly. Remember, you won't be giving anything, you will only be collecting."

Alexander Ivanovich cut the air with his hand for emphasis. He sounded convincing, and the project seemed sure-fire and lucrative. Koreiko secured the agreement—giving him a quarter of all profits from the postcard enterprise—and got down to work.

First, he needed working capital. It had to come from the money allocated for construction. That was the only money the republic had.

"Don't worry," he reassured the builders, "and remember that starting right now, you will only be collecting."

Alexander Ivanovich inspected the gorge on horseback. The concrete blocks of the future power plant were already in place, and Koreiko sized up the beauty of the granite cliffs with a glance. Photographers followed him in a coach. They surrounded the site with tripods on long jointed legs, hid under black shawls, and clicked their shutters for a while. When all of the shots were taken, one of the photographers lowered his shawl and said thoughtfully:

"Of course, it would've been better if the plant was farther to the left, in front of the monastery ruins. It's a lot more scenic over there."

It was decided that they would build their own print shop to produce the postcards as soon as possible. The money, as before, came from the construction funds. As a result, certain operations at the power plant had to be curtailed. But everybody took solace in the thought that the profits from the new enterprise would allow them to make up for lost time.

The print shop was built in the same gorge, across from the power plant. Soon the concrete blocks of the print shop appeared right beside those of the plant. Little by little, the drums with concrete mix, the iron bars, the bricks, and the gravel all migrated from one side of the gorge to the other. The workers soon followed—the pay at the new site was better.

Six months later, train stations across the country were inundated with salesmen in striped pants. They were selling postcards that showed the cliffs of the grape-growing republic, where construction proceeded on a grand scale. Curly-haired girls spun the glass drums of the charitable lottery in amusement parks, theaters, cinemas, on ships, and at resorts, and everyone won a prize—a postcard of the electric gorge.

Koreiko's promise came true: revenues were pouring in from all sides. But Alexander Ivanovich was not letting the money slip through his hands. One quarter was already his under the agreement. He apprehended another quarter by claiming that some of the sales squads hadn't submitted their reports yet. He used the rest to expand the charitable enterprise.

"One has to be a good manager," he would say quietly, "first we'll set up the business properly, then the real profits will start pouring in."

By then the Marion excavator taken from the power plant site was already digging a large pit for a new printing press building. The work at the power plant had come to a complete halt. The site was abandoned. The only ones still working there were the photographers with their black shawls.

Business was booming, and Alexander Ivanovich, always with an honest Soviet smile on his face, began printing postcards with portraits of movie stars.

As was to be expected, a high-level commission arrived one evening in a jolting car. Alexander Ivanovich didn't linger. He threw a farewell glance at the cracked foundation of the power plant, at the imposing, brightly lit building of the subsidiary, and skipped town in a jiffy.

"Hmm," said the chairman, picking at the cracks in the foundation with a cane. "Where's the power plant?"

He looked at the commission members, who in turn said "Hmm." The power plant was nowhere to be found.

In the print shop, however, the commission saw the work going full-speed ahead. Purple lights shone; flat printing presses busily flapped their wings. Three of them produced the gorge in black-and-white, while the fourth, a multi-color machine, spewed out postcards: portraits of Douglas Fairbanks with a black half-mask on his fat teapot face, the charming Lya de Putti, and a nice bulgy-eyed guy named Monty Banks. Portraits flew out of the machine like cards from a sharper's sleeve.

That memorable evening was followed by a long series of public trials that were held in the open air of the gorge, while Alexander Ivanovich added a half-million rubles to his assets.

His shallow, angry pulse was as impatient as ever. He felt that at that moment, when the old economic system had vanished and the new system was just beginning to take hold, one could amass great wealth. But he already knew that striving openly to get rich was unthinkable in the land of the Soviets. And so he looked with a condescending smile at the lonely entrepreneurs rotting away under signs like: GOODS FROM THE WORSTED TRUST B. A. LEYBEDEV, BROCADE AND SUPPLIES FOR CHURCHES AND CLUBS, or GROCERIES, X. ROBINSON AND M. FRYDAY.

The pressure from the state is crushing the financial base under Leybedev, under Fryday, and under the owners of the musical pseudo co-op "The Bell's A-Jingling."

Koreiko realized that in these times, the only option was to conduct underground commerce in total secrecy. Every crisis that shook the young economy worked in his favor; every loss of the state was his gain. He would break into every gap in the supply chain and extract his one hundred thousand from it. He traded in baked goods, fabrics, sugar, textiles—everything. And he was alone, completely alone, with his millions. Both big- and small-time crooks toiled for him all across the country, but they had no idea who they were working for. Koreiko operated strictly through frontmen. He alone knew the entire length of the channels that ultimately brought money to him.

At twelve o'clock sharp, Alexander Ivanovich set the ledger aside and prepared for lunch. He took an already peeled raw turnip out of the drawer and ate it, looking straight ahead with dignity. Then he swallowed a cold soft-boiled egg. Cold soft-boiled eggs are quite revolting; a nice, good-natured man would never eat them. But Alexander Ivanovich wasn't really eating, he was nourishing himself. He wasn't having lunch; he was performing the physiological process of delivering the right amounts of protein, carbohydrates, and vitamins to his body.

Herculeans usually capped their lunch with tea, but Alexander Ivanovich drank a cup of boiled water with sugar cubes on the side. Tea makes the heart beat harder, and Koreiko took good care of his health.

The owner of ten million was like a boxer who is painstakingly preparing for his triumph. The fighter follows a strict regimen: he doesn't drink or smoke, he tries to avoid any worries, he practices and goes to bed early—all with the aim of one day jumping into the glittering ring and leaving a jubilant winner. Alexander Ivanovich wanted to be young and fresh on the day when everything came back to normal, when he could emerge from the underground and open his plain-looking suitcase without fear. Koreiko never doubted that the old days would return. He was saving himself for capitalism.

And in order to keep his second, true life hidden from the world, he lived like a pauper, trying not to exceed the forty-six rubles a month he was paid for the miserable and tedious work he did beside the nymph- and dryad-covered walls of the Finance and Accounting Department.

CHAPTER 6
THE GNU ANTELOPE

The green box with the four con artists went flying in leaps and bounds along the dusty road.

The car was subjected to the same natural forces that a swimmer experiences during a storm. It would be suddenly thrown off track by an unexpected bump, sucked into a deep pothole, rocked from side to side, and showered with sunset-red dust.

"Listen, young man," said Ostap to the new passenger, who had already recovered from his recent misadventure and was sitting next to the captain as if nothing had happened. "How dare you violate the Sukharev Pact? It's a respectable treaty which was approved by the League of Nations Tribunal."

Panikovsky pretended he didn't hear and even looked the other way.

"And in general, you play dirty," continued Ostap. "We have just witnessed a most unpleasant scene. The people of Arbatov were chasing you because you took off with their goose."

"Miserable, wretched people!" mumbled Panikovsky angrily.

"Really?" said Ostap. "And you are, apparently, a public health physician? A gentleman? Keep in mind, though, that if you decide to make notes on your cuffs like a true gentleman, you're going to have to use chalk."

"Why is that?" asked the new passenger grumpily.

"Because your cuffs are pitch black. That wouldn't be dirt, by any chance?"

"You're a miserable, wretched man!" retorted Panikovsky quickly.

"You're saying this to me, your savior?" asked Ostap gently. "Adam Kazimirovich, could you stop the car for a moment? Thank you kindly. Shura, my friend, would you please restore the status quo?"

Balaganov had no idea what "status quo" meant, but he took his cue from the tone with which these words were uttered. With a nasty smile on his face, he put his hands under Panikovsky's arms, pulled him out of the car, and lowered him onto the road.

"Go back to Arbatov, young man," said Ostap dryly. "The owners of the goose can't wait to see you there. We don't need boors here. We are boors ourselves. Let's go."

"It won't happen again!" pleaded Panikovsky. "My nerves are bad!"

"Get on your knees," said Ostap.

Panikovsky instantly dropped on his knees, as if his legs had been cut out from under him.

"Good!" said Ostap. "I find your posture satisfactory. You are accepted conditionally, until the first violation, as the new Girl Friday."

The Antelope re-admitted the chastened boor and went rolling on again, swaying like a hearse.

Half an hour later, the car turned onto the big Novozaitsev highway and, without slowing down, entered a village. People were gathered near a log house with a crooked and knotty radio mast growing from its roof. A clean-shaven man stepped out of the crowd resolutely, a sheet of paper in his hand.

"Comrades!" he shouted sternly, "I now declare our meeting of celebration open! Allow me, comrades, to consider your applause . . ."

He had evidently prepared a speech and was already looking at his paper, but then he realized that the car wasn't stopping and cut it short.

"Join the Road Club!" he said hastily, looking at Ostap, who was just then riding past him. "Let's mass-produce Soviet motorcars! The iron steed is coming to replace the peasant horse."

And then, as the car was already speeding away, he blurted out the last slogan over the congratulatory rumble of the crowd:

"The car is not a luxury but a means of transportation!"

With the exception of Ostap, all the Antelopeans were somewhat unnerved by this elaborate reception. Not knowing what to make of it, they fidgeted in the car like little sparrows in their nest. Panikovsky, who generally disliked large gatherings of honest people, crouched on the floor just in case, so that the villagers could see only the dirty top of his straw hat. Ostap, on the other hand, was totally unfazed. He took off his white-topped cap and acknowledged the greetings by nodding left and right with dignity.

"Improve the roads!" he shouted as a farewell. "*Merci* for the reception!"

The car was back on the white road cutting though a large, quiet field.

"They're not going to chase us?" asked Panikovsky anxiously. "Why the crowd? What happened here?"

"These people have never seen an automobile before, that's all," said Balaganov.

"Continuing our discussion," commented Ostap. "Let's hear from the driver. What's your assessment, Adam Kazimirovich?"

The driver thought for a moment, sounded the maxixe to shoo off a silly dog that had run into the road, and allowed that the crowd had gathered to celebrate a local church holiday.

"Holidays of this nature are common among country people," explained the driver of the Antelope.

"Right," said Ostap. "Now I know for sure that I'm in the company of unenlightened people. In other words, bums without university education. Children, dear children of Lieutenant Schmidt, why don't you read newspapers? One must read newspapers. They quite often sow the seeds of reason, good, and the everlasting."

Ostap pulled a copy of *Izvestiya* out of his pocket and loudly read to the crew a short article about the Moscow—Kharkov—Moscow auto rally.

"We are now on the route of the rally," he said smugly, "roughly one hundred miles ahead of its lead car. I suppose now you understand what I'm talking about?"

The low-ranking Antelopeans were quiet. Panikovsky unbuttoned his jacket and scratched his bare chest under his dirty silk tie.

"So you still don't get it? Apparently, even reading newspapers doesn't help in some cases. Fine, I'll give you more details, even though it goes against my principles. First: the peasants thought the Antelope was the lead car of the rally. Second: we don't deny it. Moreover, we will appeal to all organizations and persons for proper assistance, underscoring the fact that we are the lead car. Third . . . Oh well, the first two points should be enough for you. It's abundantly clear that we will keep ahead of the rally for a while and will milk, skim off, and otherwise tap this highly civilized undertaking."

The grand strategist's speech made a huge impression. Kozlevich looked at the captain with admiration. Balaganov rubbed his wild red locks with his palms and laughed uncontrollably. Panikovsky shouted "Hooray!" in anticipation of worry-free looting.

"All right, enough emotion," said Ostap. "On account of the falling darkness, I now declare the evening open. Stop!"

The car stopped, and the tired Antelopeans climbed out. Grasshoppers hopped around in the ripening crops. The passengers were already seated in a circle near the road, but the old Antelope was still huffing and puffing, its body creaking here and there and its engine rattling occasionally.

The novice Panikovsky made such a large fire that it seemed like a whole village was ablaze. The wheezing flames blew in all directions. While the travelers fought the pillar of fire, Panikovsky bent down and ran into the fields, returning with a warm, crooked cucumber in his hand. Ostap promptly snatched the cucumber from him, saying: "Don't make a cult out of eating."

Then he ate the cucumber himself. They dined on the sausage that the practical Kozlevich brought from home and went to sleep under the stars.

"And now," said Ostap to Kozlevich at sunrise, "get ready. Your mechanical tub has never seen a day like this before, and it will never see one like this again."

Balaganov grabbed a small bucket, that was inscribed "Arbatov Maternity Hospital," and ran to the river to fetch some water.

Adam raised the hood of the car, squeezed his hands into the engine, and, whistling along, started fiddling with its little copper intestines.

Panikovsky leaned against the spare wheel and stared pensively and unblinkingly at the cranberry-colored sliver of sun that had appeared above the horizon. The light revealed a multitude of small age-related details on his wrinkled face: bags, pulsating veins, and strawberry-colored splotches. This was the face of a man who had lived a long, honorable life, has adult children, drinks healthy acorn coffee in the morning, and writes for his organization's newsletter under the pen name "The Antichrist."

"Panikovsky," asked Ostap suddenly, "do you want to hear how you're going to die?"

The old man flinched and turned toward him.

"It'll be like this. One day, when you return to a cold, empty room at the Hotel Marseilles—which will be in some small town where your line of work takes you—you'll start feeling sick. One of your legs will be paralyzed. Hungry and unshaven, you will lie on a wooden bench, and nobody will come to see you, Panikovsky, nobody will feel sorry for you. You didn't have kids because you were too cheap, and you dumped your wives. You will suffer for an entire week. Your agony will be horrible. Your death will be slow, and everyone will be sick and tired of it. You will not be quite dead yet when the bureaucrat in charge of the hotel will already be requesting a free coffin from the municipal authorities . . . What is your full name?"

"Mikhail Samuelevich," replied the stunned Panikovsky.

". . . requesting a free coffin for Citizen M. S. Panikovsky. But don't cry, you'll still last for a couple of years. Now back to business. We need to take care of the promotional and educational aspects of our campaign."

Ostap pulled his doctor's bag out of the car and put it down on the grass.

"My right hand," said the grand strategist, patting the bag on its fat sausage-like side. "Everything that an elegant man of my age and ambition might possibly need is right here."

Bender squatted over the bag like an itinerant Chinese magician and started pulling various objects out of it. First he took out a red armband with the word "Administrator" embroidered on it in gold. It was joined on the grass by a policeman's cap with the crest of the city of Kiev, four decks of playing cards with identically patterned backs, and a pack of official documents with round purple stamps on them.

The entire crew of the Antelope looked at the bag with respect. Meanwhile, new objects kept coming out of it.

"You are amateurs," said Ostap, "I'm sure you'd never understand why an honest Soviet pilgrim like me can't get by without a doctor's coat."

The bag contained not only the coat but a stethoscope as well.

"I'm not a surgeon," remarked Ostap. "I am a neuropathologist, a psychiatrist. I study the souls of my patients. For some reason, I always get very silly souls."

An ABC for the deaf-and-dumb came out of the bag next, followed by charity postcards, enamel badges, and a poster, which featured Bender himself in traditional Indian pants and a turban. The poster read:

THE HIGH PRIEST IS HERE
(The Famous Brahmin-Yogi from Bombay)
- Son of Brawny -
The Favorite of Rabindranath Tagore

IOCANAAN MARUSIDZE
(Distinguished Artist of Many Republics)

Magic, Sherlock-Holmes Style—Indian Fakir—Invisible Hen
Candles from Atlantis—Tent from Hell
Samuel the Prophet Answers Questions from the Audience
Materialization of Spirits and Distribution of Elephants

TICKETS FROM 50 KOP. TO 2 RUB.

The poster was followed by a dirty, greasy turban.

"I resort to this kind of amusement very rarely," said Ostap. "Believe it or not, it's the progressive-minded people, like the directors of railway workers' clubs, who are the most likely to buy into the high priest story. The job is easy but irksome. Personally, I find being the favorite of Rabindranath Tagore distasteful. And Samuel the Prophet invariably gets the same old questions: 'Why is there no butter in the stores?' or 'Are you Jewish?'"

Ostap finally found what he was looking for—a lacquered tin with honey-based paints in porcelain cups and two paintbrushes.

"The car that leads the rally has to be decorated with at least one slogan," said Ostap.

He then proceeded to paint brown block letters on a long band of yellowish linen:

MAY THE RALLY FIGHT ROADLESSNESS AND IRRESPONSIBILITY!

They hung the banner above the car on two long tree branches. The moment the car started moving, the banner arched in the wind and looked so dashing that it left no doubt about the need to use the rally as a weapon against roadlessness, irresponsibility, and maybe even red tape as well. The passengers of the Antelope started puffing and preening.

Balaganov covered his red hair with the cap that he always carried in his pocket. Panikovsky turned his cuffs inside out and made them show exactly three-quarters of an inch below the sleeves. Kozlevich was more concerned about the car than about himself. He washed it thoroughly before starting out, and the sun was glimmering on the Antelope's dented sides. The captain squinted playfully and teased his companions.

"Village on the port side!" yelled Balaganov, making a visor with his hand. "Are we stopping?"

"We are followed by five top-notch vehicles," said Ostap. "A rendezvous with them is not in our interest. We must skim off what we can, and fast. Therefore, we'll stop in the town of Udoev. Incidentally, that's where the drum of fuel should be waiting for us. Step on it, Adam."

"Do we respond to the crowds?" asked Balaganov anxiously.

"You can respond with bows and smiles. Kindly keep your mouth shut; God knows what might come out of it."

The village greeted the lead car warmly, but the usual hospitality had a rather peculiar flavor here. The citizens must have been informed that someone would be passing through, but they didn't know who or why. So, just in case, they dug up all the slogans and mottoes from previous years. The street was lined with schoolchildren who were holding a hodgepodge of obsolete banners: "Greetings to the Time League and its founder, dear Comrade Kerzhentsev!," "The bourgeois threats will come to naught, we all reject the Curzon note!," "For our little ones' welfare please organize a good daycare."

Besides that, there were many banners of various sizes, written primarily in Old Church Slavonic script, all saying the same thing: "Welcome!"

All this flew swiftly by. This time, the crew waved their hats with confidence. Panikovsky couldn't resist and, despite his orders, jumped up and shouted a confused, politically inappropriate greeting. But nobody could make it out over the noise of the engine and the roar of the crowd.

"Hip, hip, hooray!" cried Ostap.

Kozlevich opened the choke, and the car emitted a trail of blue smoke— the dogs that were running after them started sneezing.

"How are we doing on gas?" asked Ostap. "Will we make it to Udoev? We only have twenty miles to go. Once we're there, we'll take everything."

"Should be enough," Kozlevich replied uncertainly.

"Keep in mind," said Ostap, looking at his troops with a stern eye, "that I will not tolerate any looting. No violation of the law whatsoever.

I am commanding the parade."

Panikovsky and Balaganov looked embarrassed.

"The people of Udoev will give us everything we need anyway. You'll see. Make room for bread and salt."

The Antelope covered twenty miles in an hour and a half. During the last mile, Kozlevich fussed a lot, pressed on the accelerator, and shook his head in despair. But all his efforts, as well as Balaganov's shouting and encouraging, were in vain. The spectacular finale planned by Adam Kazimirovich did not materialize, due to the lack of fuel. The car disgracefully stopped in the middle of the street, a hundred yards short of a reviewing stand that had been decorated with conifer garlands in honor of the intrepid motorists.

With loud cries, people rushed to the Lorraine-Dietrich, which had arrived from the dark ages. The thorns of glory promptly pierced the noble foreheads of the travelers. They were unceremoniously dragged out of the car and wildly thrown into the air, as if they drowned and had to be brought back to life at any cost.

Kozlevich stayed with the car while the rest of the crew were led to the stand—a short three-hour event had been planned. A young man who was dressed like a motorist made his way to Ostap and asked:

"How are the other cars?"

"Fell behind," replied Ostap indifferently. "Flat tires, breakdowns, exuberant crowds. All this slows you down."

"Are you in the captain's car?" The automotive enthusiast wouldn't let go. "Is Kleptunov with you?"

"I took him out of the rally," said Ostap dismissively.

"And Professor Pesochnikov? Is he in the Packard?"

"Yes, in the Packard."

"And how about the writer Vera Cruz?" the quasi-motorist continued to grill him. "I would love to take a peek at her. Her and Comrade Nezhinsky. Is he with you too?"

"You know," said Ostap, "I am exhausted by the rally."

"Are you in a Studebaker?"

"You can think of our car as a Studebaker," answered Ostap angrily, "but up until now it's been a Lorraine-Dietrich. Are you satisfied now?"

But the enthusiast was not satisfied.

"Wait a minute!" he exclaimed with youthful persistence. "There aren't any Lorraine-Dietrichs in the rally! The paper said that there are two Packards, two Fiats, and a Studebaker."

"Go to hell with your Studebaker!" exploded Ostap. "Who is this Studebaker? Is he a relative of yours? Is your Daddy a Studebaker? What do you want from me? I'm telling you in plain Russian that the Studebaker was replaced with a Lorraine-Dietrich at the last moment, and you keep bugging me! Studebaker my foot!"

The young man had long been eased away by officials yet Ostap kept waving his arms and muttering:

"Experts! Such experts should go to hell! Just give him his Studebaker, or else!"

The chairman of the welcoming committee embellished his opening speech with such a long chain of subordinate clauses that it took him a good half hour to finish them all. Meanwhile, the captain of the rally was worried. He followed the suspicious activities of Balaganov and Panikovsky, who were a little too busy weaving through the crowd, from his perch on the stand. Bender kept making stern faces at them and finally his signals stopped the children of Lieutenant Schmidt in their tracks.

"I am happy, comrades," declared Ostap in his response, "to break the age-old silence in the town of Udoev with the horn of an automobile. An automobile, comrades, is not a luxury but a means of transportation. The iron steed is coming to replace the peasant horse. Let's mass-produce Soviet motorcars! May the rally fight roadlessness and irresponsibility! This concludes my remarks, comrades. After a snack, we will continue our long journey."

While the crowd stood still around the podium and absorbed the captain's words, Kozlevich wasted no time. He filled the tank with gas which, just as Ostap promised, was of the highest quality, and shamelessly took three large cans of extra fuel as a reserve. He replaced the tires and the tubes on all four wheels, even picked up a pump and a jack. This completely decimated both the long-term and the current inventories of the Udoev branch of the Road Club.

The trip to Chernomorsk was now well-supplied with materials. The only thing missing was money, but that didn't really bother the captain. The travelers had a very nice dinner in Udoev.

"Don't worry about pocket money," said Ostap. "It's lying on the road. We'll pick it up as needed."

Between ancient Udoev, founded in A.D. 794, and Chernomorsk, founded in A.D. 1794, lay a thousand years and a thousand miles of both paved and unpaved roads.

A variety of characters appeared along the Udoev—Black Sea highway over those thousand years.

Traveling salesmen with merchandize from Byzantine trading firms moved along this road. They were greeted by Nightingale the Robber, a boorish man in an Astrakhan hat who would step out of the howling forest to meet them. He'd seize the merchandise and do away with the salesmen. Conquerors followed this road with their soldiers, as did peasants and singing pilgrims.

Life in this land changed with every new century. Clothing changed, weapons became more sophisticated, potato riots were put down. People learned to shave off their beards. The first hot air balloon went up. The iron twins, the steamboat and the steam engine, were invented. Cars started honking.

But the road remained the same as it was during the time of Nightingale the Robber. Humped, buried in volcanic mud, or covered with a dust as toxic as pesticide, our Russian road stretched past villages, towns, factories, and collective farms like a thousand-mile-long trap. The yellowing, poisoned grasses along the route are littered with the skeletal remains of carriages and the bodies of exhausted, expiring automobiles.

An émigré, going mad from selling newspapers amid the asphalt fields of Paris, may remember the Russian country road as a charming feature of his native landscape: the young moon sitting in a small puddle, crickets praying loudly, an empty pail clattering gently against a peasant's cart.

But the moonlight has already received a new assignment. The moon will shine perfectly well on paved highways. Automobile sirens and horns will replace the symphonic clatter of the peasant's pail, and one will be able to hear crickets in special nature preserves. They'll build bleachers, and visitors, warmed up by the introductory remarks of a white-haired cricketologist, will be able to enjoy the singing of their favorite insects to their heart's content.

CHAPTER 7
THE SWEET BURDEN OF FAME

The captain of the rally, the driver, the rally mechanic, and the Girl Friday all felt great.

The morning was chilly. The pale sun floated in a pearly sky. A collection of small birdies screeched in the grass.

Little roadside birds, known as water rails, slowly walked across the road, right in front of the car. The grassland horizons produced such a cheerful smell that if instead of Ostap, there was a mediocre peasant writer from a literary group called the Iron Udder or something, he wouldn't have been able to control himself. He would have leapt out of the car, installed himself in the grass, and immediately started writing a new story in his notebook. Something like this:

"Them winter crops got mighty toasty. The sun got awful strong and went a-pushing its rays 'crost the whole wide world. Old-timer Romualdych sniffed his sock real good and went, I'll be darned . . ."

But Ostap and his companions had no time for poetry. It was their second day running ahead of the rally. They were greeted with music and speeches. Children beat drums in their honor. Adults fed them lunches and dinners, provided them with the automobile parts they had prepared in advance. In one tiny town they were even given bread and salt on a carved oak platter with a cross-stitched towel. The bread and salt sat on the floor between Panikovsky's feet. He kept picking at the round loaf until finally he made a mouse hole in it. The squeamish Ostap threw the bread and salt out on the road. The Antelopeans spent the night in a village, in the caring arms of the local activists. They left with a big jug of baked milk and sweet memories of the fragrant scent of the hay in which they slept.

"Milk and hay, what could possibly be better?" said Ostap as the Antelope was leaving the village at sunrise. "One always thinks, 'I'll do this some other time. There will still be plenty of milk and hay in my life.' But in fact, there won't be anything like this ever again. Make note of it, my poor friends: this was the best night of our lives. And you didn't even notice."

Bender's companions looked at him with respect. They absolutely loved the easy life that was suddenly theirs.

"Life is beautiful!" said Balaganov. "Here we are, driving along, our stomachs full. Maybe happiness awaits us . . ."

"Are you sure?" asked Ostap. "Happiness awaits us on the road? Maybe it even flaps its wings in anticipation? 'Where, it wonders, is Admiral Balaganov? Why is he taking so long?' You're crazy, Balaganov! Happiness isn't waiting for anybody. It wanders around the country in long white robes, singing children's songs: 'Ah, America, there's the land, people there drink straight from the bottle.' But this naïve babe must be caught, you have to make her like you, you have to court her. Sadly, Balaganov, she won't take up with you. You're a bum. Just look at yourself! A man dressed like you will never achieve happiness. Come to think of it, the entire crew of the Antelope is dressed atrociously. I'm surprised people still believe we're part of the rally!"

Ostap looked his companions over with disappointment and continued:

"Panikovsky's hat really bothers me. He's dressed far too ostentatiously. The gold tooth, the underwear straps, the hairy chest poking out from under the tie . . . You should dress more modestly, Panikovsky! You're a respectable old man. You need a long black jacket and a felt hat. Balaganov would look good in a checkered cowboy shirt and leather leggings. He could easily pass as a student-athlete, but now he looks like a merchant sailor fired for drunkenness. Not to mention our esteemed driver. Hard luck has prevented him from dressing in a way that befits his position. Can't you see how well leather overalls and a black calfskin cap would go with his inspired, oil-smudged face? Whatever you say, boys, you have to update your wardrobe."

"There's no money," said Kozlevich, turning around.

"The driver is correct," replied Ostap courteously. "Indeed, there is no money. None of those little metal discs that I love so dearly."

The Gnu Antelope glided down a small hill. The fields continued to slowly rotate on both sides of the car. A large brown owl was sitting by the side of the road, its head bent to one side, its unseeing yellow eyes bulging foolishly. Disturbed by the Antelope's creaking, the bird spread its wings, soared above the car and quickly flew away to take care of its boring owlish business. Other than that, nothing interesting was happening on the road.

"Look!" cried Balaganov suddenly. "A car!"

Just in case, Ostap ordered them to take down the banner that called on the citizens to fight against irresponsibility. While Panikovsky was carrying out this task, the Antelope approached the other car.

A gray hard-top Cadillac was parked on the shoulder, listing slightly. The landscape of central Russia was reflected in its thick shiny windows, looking neater and more scenic than it actually was. The driver was on his knees, taking the tire off a front wheel. Three figures in sand-colored travel coats hovered behind him, waiting.

"Your ship's in distress?" asked Ostap, tipping his cap politely.

The driver raised his tense face, said nothing, and went back to work.

The Antelopeans climbed out of their green jalopy. Kozlevich walked around the magnificent vehicle several times, sighing with envy. He squatted down next to the driver and struck up a technical conversation. Panikovsky and Balaganov stared at the passengers with childlike curiosity. Two of the passengers had a rather standoffish, foreign look to them. The third one was a fellow Russian, judging by the overpowering smell of galoshes coming from his State Rubber Trust raincoat.

"Your ship's in distress?" repeated Ostap, politely touching the rubber-clad shoulder of his fellow countryman, while at the same time eyeing the foreigners pensively.

The Russian started complaining about the blown tire, but his grumbling went in one of Ostap's ears and out the other. Two plump foreign chicklets were strolling around the car—on a highway some eighty miles from the nearest town of any significance, right in the middle of European Russia. That got the grand strategist excited.

"Tell me," he interrupted, "these two wouldn't be from Rio de Janeiro, by any chance?"

"No," said the Russian. "They're from Chicago. And I am their interpreter, from Intourist."

"What on earth are they doing here in this ancient wilderness in the middle of nowhere? So far from Moscow, from the Red Poppy ballet, from the antique stores and Repin's famous painting *Ivan the Terrible Kills his Son*? I don't get it! Why did you drag them out here?"

"They can go to hell!" said the interpreter bitterly. "We've been racing from village to village like mad for three days now. I can't take it any more. I've dealt with foreigners quite a bit, but I've never seen anything like this." He waved in the direction of his ruddy-faced companions. "Normal tourists run around Moscow, buying handmade wooden bowls in gift shops. But these two broke away and went driving around the back-roads."

"That's commendable," said Ostap. "America's billionaires are learning about life in the new Soviet countryside."

The two citizens of Chicago looked on sedately as their car was being repaired. They wore silvery hats, frozen starched collars, and red matte shoes.

The interpreter looked at Ostap indignantly and blurted out, "Yeah, right! Like they need your new countryside! They need the country moonshine, not the countryside!"

Hearing the word "moonshine," which the interpreter had stressed, the two gentlemen looked around nervously and edged closer.

"See!" said the interpreter. "Just hearing the word gets them all excited."

"Interesting. There's a mystery here," said Ostap. "I don't understand why one would want moonshine when our native land offers such a large selection of superb hard liquors."

"This is much simpler than you think," said the interpreter. "They're just searching for a decent moonshine recipe."

"Of course!" exclaimed Ostap. "Prohibition! I get it now . . . So have you found a recipe? Of course not. You might as well have shown up in a three-car motorcade! Obviously, people think you're officials. I can assure you that you'll never find a recipe this way."

The interpreter began to complain about the foreigners again.

"You won't believe it, but they've even started pestering me: 'Just tell us the secret of the moonshine!' For God's sake, I'm not a moonshiner. I'm a member of the education workers' union. I have an elderly mother in Moscow."

"And how badly do you want to go back to Moscow? To be with your mother?"

The interpreter sighed dejectedly.

"In that case, our deliberations continue," declared Ostap. "How much will your bosses pay for a recipe? 150, perhaps?"

"They'll pay two hundred," whispered the interpreter. "Do you really have a recipe?"

"I can give it to you this very moment—I mean, the moment I get the money. Made from anything you want: potatoes, wheat, apricots, barley, mulberry, buckwheat. One can even brew moonshine from an ordinary chair. Some people enjoy the chair brew. Or you can have a simple raisin or plum brew. In other words, any of the 150 kinds of moonshine known to me."

Ostap was introduced to the Americans. Their politely raised hats floated in the air for a long time. Then they got down to business.

The Americans chose the wheat moonshine—the simplicity of the brewing process appealed to them. They painstakingly recorded the recipe in their notebooks. As a bonus, Ostap sketched out a design for a compact still that could be hidden in an office desk. The seekers assured Ostap that, given American technology, making such a still would be a breeze. For his part, Ostap assured the Americans that the device he described would produce two gallons of beautiful, fragrant *pervach* per day.

"Oh!" cried the Americans.

They had already heard this word in a very respectable home in Chicago, where *pervach* was highly recommended. The man of the house had been in Archangel, with the American expeditionary force. He drank *pervach* there and never forgot the alluring sensation that it gave him.

On the lips of the enchanted tourists, the crude word *pervach* sounded both tender and enticing.

The Americans easily parted with two hundred rubles and endlessly shook Bender's hand. Panikovsky and Balaganov also got to shake hands with the citizens of the transatlantic republic, who had been suffering under Prohibition for so long. The interpreter was thrilled; he pecked Ostap on his cheek and invited him to stop by, adding that his elderly mother would be delighted. For some reason, however, he neglected to give his address.

The new friends climbed into their respective cars. Kozlevich played a farewell maxixe, and to the accompaniment of these cheerful sounds, the cars flew off in opposite directions.

"See," said Ostap when the American car disappeared in a cloud of dust, "everything happened just like I told you. We were driving. Money was lying on the road. I picked it up. Look, it didn't even get dusty."

And he crackled the stack of bills in his hand.

"Actually, this isn't much to brag about, a trivial job. But it was clean and honest, that's what counts. Two hundred rubles in five minutes. And not only did I not break the law, I even did some good. I provided the crew of the Antelope with financial backing. The elderly mother is getting her son the interpreter back. And finally, I quenched the spiritual thirst of the citizens of a country that does, after all, maintain trade relations with us."

It was almost time for lunch. Ostap immersed himself in the rally map that he had torn out of an automotive magazine and announced the upcoming town of Luchansk.

"The town is very small," said Bender, "that's not good. The smaller the town, the longer the welcoming speeches. So let's ask our amiable hosts to give us lunch for starters and speeches for the second course. In the intermission, I will equip you with more appropriate gear. Panikovsky! You are beginning to neglect your duties. Return the banner to its original position."

Kozlevich, who had become an expert in spectacular finales, brought the car to a dramatic halt right in front of the reviewing stand. Bender kept his remarks very short. They arranged to postpone the ceremonies for two hours. Fortified by a free lunch, the motorists were in high spirits, and they headed for a clothing store. They were surrounded by the curious. The Antelopeans carried the sweet burden of their new-found fame with dignity. They walked in the middle of the street, holding hands and swaying like sailors in a foreign port. The red-headed Balaganov, looking every inch the young boatswain, broke into a seaman's song.

The store that sold clothing "For men, ladies, and children" was located under an enormous sign that covered the entire façade of the two-story building. The sign showed dozens of figures: yellow-faced men with pencil mustaches wearing winter coats whose open flaps revealed fitch-fur lining, women with muffs in their hands, short-legged children in little sailors' suits, Young Communist League girls in red kerchiefs, and gloomy industrial managers sinking up to their hips in large felt boots.

All this splendor was ruined by a small hand-made sign on the front door:

OUT OF PANTS

"Ugh, how vulgar," said Ostap, entering the store. "I can see that I'm in the provinces. Why don't they say, 'Out of trousers,' like they do in Moscow? That would be proper and decent. The customers would go home satisfied."

They didn't spend much time in the store. For Balaganov, they found a canary yellow cowboy shirt with large checks and a Stetson hat with vent holes. Kozlevich got his calfskin cap, as promised, but had to settle for a black calfskin jacket, which shined like pressed caviar. Outfitting Panikovsky took much longer. They had to forget about the long pastor's coat and the fedora, which Bender thought would give the violator of the pact a more refined look. The store's only alternative was a fireman's dress uniform: a jacket with golden pumps on its collar patches, fuzzy wool-blend pants, and a cap with a blue strap. Panikovsky jumped around in front of the wavy mirror for a long time.

"I don't understand why you don't like the fireman's uniform," said Ostap. "It's certainly better than the exiled king outfit that you're wearing now. Come now, turn around, my boy! Excellent! Let me tell you, this suits you much better than the coat and hat that I had in mind for you."

They went outside in their new outfits.

"Me, I need a tuxedo," said Ostap, "but they didn't have any. Oh well, some other time."

Ostap opened the ceremonies in a great mood, unaware of the storm that was gathering over the Antelopeans' heads. He was witty; he told funny driving stories and Jewish jokes. The public loved him. The final portion of his speech was devoted to the analysis of pressing automobile-related issues.

"The car," he boomed, "is not a luxury but . . ."

At that point he noticed a boy run up to the chairman of the welcoming committee and hand him a telegram.

While still uttering the words "not a luxury but a means of transportation," Ostap leaned to the left and glanced at the telegram over the chairman's shoulder. What he read startled him. He had thought they had one more day. The long list of towns and villages where the Antelope had misappropriated materials and funds flashed through his mind.

The chairman was still wiggling his mustache, trying to digest the message, when Ostap jumped off the stand in mid-sentence and started making his way through the crowd. The green Antelope was waiting at the intersection. Fortunately, the other passengers were already in their seats. Bored, they were waiting for the moment when Ostap would order them to haul the town's offerings into the car. This usually happened after the ceremonies.

When the chairman finally grasped what the telegram was saying, he raised his eyes only to see the captain of the rally running away.

"They're con artists!" he shouted in agony.

He had spent the whole night preparing his welcoming speech, and now his writer's ego was wounded.

"Hold them, guys!"

The chairman's shrieking reached the ears of the Antelopeans. They began fussing nervously. Kozlevich started the engine and leapt into his seat. The car jumped forward without waiting for Ostap. In their great hurry, the Antelopeans didn't even realize they were abandoning their captain to grave danger.

"Stop!" yelled Ostap, making giant leaps. "I'll get you! You're all fired!"

"Stop!" yelled the chairman.

"Stop, you bonehead!" Balaganov yelled at Kozlevich. "Can't you see we've lost the chief?"

Adam hit the brakes, and the Antelope screeched to a halt. The captain lunged into the car and screamed, "Full speed ahead!" Despite his open-minded and cool-headed nature, he hated the idea of physical reprisal. In a panic, Kozlevich jumped into third gear and the car jerked forward, forcing a door open and throwing Balaganov to the ground. All this happened in a flash. While Kozlevich was braking again, the shadow of the approaching crowd was already falling on Balaganov. Huge hands were already stretching out to grab him, but then the Antelope crept back in reverse, and the captain's steely hand seized him by his cowboy shirt.

"Full speed!" screamed Ostap.

And that's when the citizens of Luchansk understood the advantages of automotive transport for the first time. The car rattled away, delivering the four lawbreakers from their well-deserved punishment.

For the first mile, they just breathed heavily. Balaganov, who valued his good looks, examined the red scratches left by the fall with the help of a pocket mirror. Panikovsky was shaking in his fireman's uniform. He feared the captain's retribution, and it came promptly.

"Did you tell the driver to take off before I could get in?" asked the captain harshly.

"I swear . . ." began Panikovsky.

"Don't deny it! It's all your doing. So you're a coward on top of everything else? I'm in the company of a thief and a coward? Fine! I am demoting you. You were a fire chief in my eyes, but from now on, you're just a simple fireman."

And Ostap solemnly tore the golden pumps off of Panikovsky's red collar patches.

After this procedure, Ostap apprised his companions of the contents of the telegram.

"We're in trouble. The telegram says to seize the green car that's running ahead of the rally. We need to get off to the side somewhere right away. Enough of the triumphs, palm branches, and free dinners cooked with cheap oil. This idea has outlived itself. Our only option is to turn off onto the Griazhsk Road. But that's still three hours away. And I'm sure that a very warm welcome will be awaiting us in every town between here and there. This blasted telegraph has planted its stupid wired posts all over the place."

The captain was right.

The Antelopeans never learned the name of the next small town they encountered, but they wished they had, so that they could curse it from time to time. At the town line, the road was blocked with a heavy log. The Antelope turned and, like a blind puppy, started poking around with its nose, looking for a detour. But there wasn't any.

"Let's turn back!" said Ostap, becoming very serious.

And suddenly the impostors heard a very distant, mosquito-like buzz. This must have been the cars of the real rally. There was no way back, so the Antelopeans rushed forward again.

Kozlevich frowned and raced the Antelope toward the log. The people standing around it rushed aside, fearing a wreck. But Kozlevich decelerated abruptly and slowly climbed over the obstacle. The passers-by grumbled and cursed the passengers as the Antelope drove through town, but Ostap kept quiet.

The Antelope was approaching the Griazhsk Road, and the rumble of the still invisible cars grew stronger and stronger. The moment they turned off the damned highway, hiding the car behind a small hill in the falling darkness, they heard the bursts and the firing of the engines. The lead car appeared in the beams of light. The con artists hid in the grass on the side of the road and, suddenly losing their usual arrogance, quietly watched the passing motorcade.

Banners of blinding light flapped over the road. The cars creaked softly as they passed the crushed Antelopeans. Dust flew from under the wheels. Electric horns howled. The wind blew in all directions. It was over in a minute, and only the ruby taillights of the last car danced and jumped in the dark for a long time.

Real life flew by, trumpeting joyously and flashing its glossy fenders. All that was left for the adventurers was a tail of exhaust fumes. They sat in the grass for a long while, sneezing and dusting themselves off.

"Yes," said Ostap, "now even I see that the car is not a luxury but a means of transportation. Aren't you jealous, Balaganov? I am."

CHAPTER 8
AN ARTISTIC CRISIS

Some time after 3 A.M., the hounded Antelope stopped at the edge of a bluff. An unfamiliar city lay below, neatly sliced, like a cake on a platter. Multicolored morning mists swirled above it. The dismounted Antelopeans thought they heard a distant crackling and an ever so slight whistling. This must have been the citizens snoring. A jagged forest bordered the city. The road looped down from the bluff.

"A valley from heaven," said Ostap. "It's nice to plunder cities like this early in the morning, before the sun starts blazing. It's less tiring."

"It is early morning right now," observed Panikovsky, looking fawningly into the captain's eyes.

"Quiet, Goldilocks!" exploded Ostap. "You're such a restless old man! No sense of humor whatsoever."

"What are we going to do with the Antelope?" asked Kozlevich.

"A good point," replied Ostap, "we can't drive this green washtub into the city under the circumstances. They'd put us in jail. We're going to have to follow the lead of the most advanced nations. In Rio de Janeiro, for example, stolen cars are repainted a different color. This is done for purely humanitarian reasons, so that the previous owner doesn't get upset when he sees a stranger driving his car. The Antelope has acquired a dicey reputation; it needs to be repainted."

They decided to enter the city on foot and find some paint, leaving the car in a safe place outside the city limits.

Ostap walked briskly down the road along the edge of the bluff and soon saw a lopsided log house, its tiny windows gleaming river-blue. A shed behind the house looked like the perfect hiding place for the Antelope.

The grand strategist was thinking up a good excuse to enter the little house and make friends with its residents when the door flew open and a respectable-looking man, in soldier's underwear with black metal buttons, ran out onto the porch. His paraffin-pale cheeks sported neatly styled gray sideburns. At the end of the nineteenth century, a face like this would have been common. In those times, most men cultivated such government-issue, conformist hair devices on their faces. But when the sideburns were not sitting above a dark-blue uniform, or some civilian medal on a silk ribbon, or the golden stars of a high-ranking imperial official, this kind of face seemed unnatural.

"Oh my Lord," mumbled the toothless log house dweller, his arms outstretched toward the rising sun. "Lord, oh Lord! The same dreams! Those very same dreams!"

After this lament, the old man started crying and ran, shuffling his feet, along the footpath around the house. An ordinary rooster, who was about to sing for the third time, and who had already positioned itself in the middle of the yard for that purpose, darted away. In the heat of the moment it took several hurried steps and even dropped a feather, but soon composed itself, climbed on top of the wattle fence, and from this safe position finally notified the world that morning had come. Its voice, however, betrayed the anxiety that the untoward behavior of the owner of the little house had caused.

"Those goddamn dreams," the old man's voice reached Ostap.

Bender was staring in surprise at the strange man and his sideburns—nowadays, the only place to see sideburns like that is on the imperious face of a doorman at the symphony hall, if anywhere.

Meanwhile, the extraordinary gentleman completed a full circle and once again appeared near the porch. Here he lingered for a moment and then went inside, saying, "I'll go try again."

"I love old people," whispered Ostap to himself, "they're always entertaining. I have to wait and see how this mysterious test will turn out."

He didn't have to wait long. Shortly thereafter, howling could be heard from the house, and the old man crawled out onto the porch, moving backwards, like Boris Godunov in the final act of Mussorgsky's opera.

"Begone! Begone!" he cried out, sounding like Shalyapin. "That same dream! Aaaa!"

He turned around and started walking straight towards Ostap, stumbling over his own feet. Deciding that it was the time to act, the grand strategist stepped out from behind the tree and took the Sideburner into his powerful embrace.

"What? Who's that? What's that?" cried the restless old man. "What?"

Ostap carefully opened his embrace, grabbed the old man's hand, and shook it warmly.

"I feel for you!" he declared.

"Really?" asked the owner of the little house, leaning against Bender's shoulder.

"Of course I do," replied Ostap. "I myself have dreams quite often."

"And what do you dream about?"

"This and that."

"No, seriously?" insisted the old man.

"Well, all kinds of things. A mishmash really. What the newspapers call 'All things from all places' or 'World panorama.' The other day, for example, I dreamed of the Mikado's funeral, and yesterday it was the anniversary celebration at the Sushchevsky Fire Brigade headquarters."

"My God!" said the old man. "My God, what a lucky man you are! A lucky man! Tell me, have you ever dreamt of a Governor General or . . . maybe even an imperial minister?"

Bender wasn't going to be difficult.

"I have," he said playfully. "I sure have. The Governor General. Last Friday. All night. And right next to him, I recall, was the chief of police in patterned breeches."

"Oh, how nice!" said the old man. "And have you, by any chance, dreamt of His Majesty's visit to the city of Kostroma?"

"Kostroma? Yes, I had that dream. Wait, wait, when was that? Ah yes, February third of this year. His Majesty was there, and next to him, I recall, was Count Frederiks, you know . . . the Minister of the Imperial Court."

"Oh my!" the old man became excited. "Why are we standing here? Please, please come in. Forgive me, you're not a Socialist, by any chance? Not a party man?"

"Of course not," said Ostap good-naturedly. "Me, a party man? I'm an independent monarchist. A faithful servant to his sovereign, a caring father to his men. In other words, soar, falcons, like an eagle, ponder not unhappy thoughts . . ."

"Tea, would you like some tea?" mumbled the old man, steering

Bender towards the door.

The little house consisted of one room and a hallway. Portraits of gentlemen in civilian uniforms covered the walls. Judging by the patches on their collars, these gentlemen had all served in the Ministry of Education in their time. The bed looked messy, suggesting that the owner spent the most restless hours of his life in it.

"Have you lived like such a recluse for a long time?" asked Ostap.

"Since the spring," replied the old man. "My name is Khvorobyov. I thought I'd start a new life here. And you know what happened? You must understand . . ."

Fyodor Nikitich Khvorobyov was a monarchist, and he detested the Soviet regime. He found it repugnant. He, who had once served as a school district superintendent, was forced to run the Educational Methodology Sector of the local Proletkult. That disgusted him.

Until the end of his career, he never knew what Proletkult stood for, and that made him detest it even more. He cringed with disgust at the mere sight of the members of the local union committee, his colleagues, and the visitors to the Educational Methodology Sector. He hated the word "sector." Oh, that sector! Fyodor Nikitich had always appreciated elegant things, including geometry. Never in his worst nightmares would he imagine that this beautiful mathematical term, used to describe a portion of a circle, could be so brutally trivialized.

At work, many things enraged Khvorobyov: meetings, newsletters, bond campaigns. But his proud soul couldn't find peace at home either. There were newsletters, bond campaigns, and meetings at home as well. And Khvorobyov's acquaintances talked exclusively about vulgar things: remuneration (what they called their salaries), Aid to Children Month, and the social significance of the play *The Armored Train*.

He was unable to escape the Soviet system anywhere. Even when Khvorobyov walked the city streets in frustration he would overhear detestable phrases, like:

". . . So we determined to remove him from the board . . ."

". . . And that's exactly what I told them: if you insist on the PCC, we'll appeal to the arbitration chamber!"

Khvorobyov was distressed to see posters calling upon citizens to implement the Five-Year Plan in four years, and he repeated to himself indignantly:

"Remove! From the board! The PCC! In four years! What a crass regime!"

When the Educational Methodology Sector switched to the continuous work-week, and Khvorobyov's days off became some kind of mysterious purple fifth days instead of Sundays, he retired in disgust and went to live far beyond the city limits. He did it in order to escape the new regime—it had taken over his entire life and deprived him of his peace.

The lone monarchist would sit above the bluff all day long, look at the city, and think about pleasant things: church services celebrating the birthday of a member of the royal family, school exams, or his relatives who had served in the Ministry of Education. But, to his surprise, his thoughts almost immediately returned to Soviet, and therefore unpleasant, things.

"What's new at the blasted Proletkult?" he would think.

After the Proletkult, his mind would wander to downright outrageous things: May Day and Revolution Day rallies, family evenings at the workers' club with lectures and beer, the projected semiannual budget of the Methodology Sector.

"The Soviet regime took everything from me," thought the former school district superintendent, "rank, medals, respect, bank account. It even took over my thoughts. But there's one area that's beyond the Bolsheviks' reach: the dreams given to man by God. Night will bring me peace. In my dreams, I will see something that I'd like to see."

The very next night, God gave Fyodor Nikitich a terrible dream. He dreamt that he was sitting in an office corridor that was lit by a small kerosene lamp. He sat there with the knowledge that, at any moment, he was to be removed from the board. Suddenly a steel door opened, and his fellow office workers ran out shouting: "Khvorobyov needs to carry more weight!" He wanted to run but couldn't.

Fyodor Nikitich woke up in the middle of the night. He said a prayer to God, pointing out to Him that an unfortunate error had been made, and that the dream intended for an important person, maybe even a party member, had arrived at the wrong address. He, Khvorobyov, would like to see the Tsar's ceremonial exit from the Cathedral of the Assumption, for starters.

Soothed by this, he fell asleep again, only to see Comrade Surzhikov, the chairman of the local union committee, instead of his beloved monarch.

And so night after night, Fyodor Nikitich would have the same, strictly Soviet, dreams with unbelievable regularity. He dreamt of union dues, newsletters, the Goliath state farm, the grand opening of the first mass-dining establishment, the chairman of the Friends of the Cremation Society, and the pioneering Soviet flights.

The monarchist growled in his sleep. He didn't want to see the Friends of the Cremation. He wanted to see Purishkevich, the far-right deputy of the State Duma; Patriarch Tikhon; the Yalta Governor, Dumbadze; or even just a simple public school inspector. But there wasn't anything like that. The Soviet regime had invaded even his dreams.

"Those same dreams!" concluded Khvorobyov tearfully. "Those cursed dreams!"

"You are in serious trouble," said Ostap compassionately. "Being, they say, determines consciousness. Since you live under the Soviets, your dreams will be Soviet too."

"Not one break," complained Khvorobyov. "Anything, anything at all. I'll take anything. Forget Purishkevich. I'll take Milyukov the Constitutional Democrat. At least he was a university-educated man and a monarchist at heart. But no! Just these Soviet anti-Christs."

"I'll help you," said Ostap. "I've treated several friends and acquaintances using Freud's methods. Dreams are not the issue. The main thing is to remove the cause of the dream. The principal cause of your dreams is the very existence of the Soviet regime. But I can't remove it right now. I'm in a hurry. I'm on a sports tour, you see, and my car needs a few small repairs. Would you mind if I put it in your shed? As for the cause of your dreams, don't worry, I'll take care of it on the way back. Just let me finish the rally."

The monarchist, dazed by his troublesome dreams, readily allowed the sympathetic, kind-hearted young man to use his shed. He threw on a coat over his shirt, stuck his bare feet into galoshes, and went outside with Bender.

"So you think there's hope for me?" he asked, mincing behind his early morning guest.

"Don't give it another thought," replied the captain dismissively. "The moment the Soviet regime is gone, you'll feel better at once. You'll see!"

Within half an hour the Antelope was stowed away in Khvorobyov's shed and left under the watchful eyes of Kozlevich and Panikovsky. Bender, accompanied by Balaganov, went to the city to get paint.

The half-brothers walked towards the sun, making their way into the town center. Gray pigeons promenaded on the roof edges. Sprayed with water, the wooden sidewalks were clean and cool.

For a man with a clear conscience, it was a good morning to step outside, linger at the gate for a moment, take out a box of matches (emblazoned with an airplane that had a fist in place of a propeller and a slogan, "Our answer to Curzon"), admire the fresh pack of cigarettes, and then light up, puffing out a small cloud of smoke that chases away a bumble bee with golden stripes on its belly.

Bender and Balaganov fell under the spell of the morning, the clean streets, and the carefree pigeons. For a brief moment they felt as if their consciences were as clear as a whistle, that everybody loved them, and that they were off to a date with their fiancées.

Suddenly a man with a portable easel and a shiny paintbox in his hands blocked their path. He had the wild-eyed look of a man who had just escaped from a burning building, and the easel and the box were all he had managed to salvage.

"Excuse me," he said loudly. "Comrade Platonikov-Pervertov was supposed to pass by here a moment ago. You haven't seen him, by any chance? Was he here?"

"We never see people like that," answered Balaganov rudely.

The artist bumped into Bender's chest, mumbled "*Pardon!*," and rushed on.

"Platonikov-Pervertov?" grumbled the grand strategist, who hadn't had his breakfast yet. "I personally knew a midwife whose name was Medusa-Gorgoner, and I didn't make a big fuss over it. I didn't run down the street shouting: 'Have you by any chance seen Comrade Medusa-Gorgoner? She's been out for a walk here.' Big deal! Platonikov-Pervertov!"

The moment Bender finished his tirade, he was confronted by two more men with black easels and shiny paintboxes. The two couldn't have looked more different. One of them evidently believed that an artist had to be hairy: his facial hair qualified him for the role of deputy of Henri de Navarre in the Soviet Union. The mustache, his hair, and his beard made his flat features very lively. The other man was simply bald, his head shiny and smooth like a glass lampshade.

"Comrade Platonikov . . . ," said the deputy of Henri de Navarre, panting.

"Pervertov," added the Lampshade.

"Have you seen him?" cried de Navarre.

"He was supposed to be taking a stroll here," explained the Lampshade.

Balaganov had already opened his mouth to utter a curse, but Bender pushed him aside and said with stinging courtesy:

"We haven't seen Comrade Platonikov, but if you are really interested in seeing him, you'd better hurry. He's already being sought by some character who looks like an artist. A con artist, that is."

Bumping against each other and getting their easels stuck together, the artists ran off. Then a horse cab careened from around the corner. Its passenger was a fat man whose sweaty gut was barely concealed by the folds of his long tunic. The passenger's general appearance brought to mind an ancient advertisement for a patented ointment that began with the words: "The sight of a naked body covered with hair makes a revolting impression." The fat man's profession wasn't hard to guess. His hand held down a large easel. Under the coachman's feet lay a big shiny box which undoubtedly contained paint.

"Hello!" Ostap called out. "Are you searching for Pervertov?"

"Yessir," confirmed the fat artist, looking plaintively at Ostap.

"Hurry! Hurry! Hurry!" cried Ostap. "Three artists are already ahead of you. What's going on here? What happened?"

But the horse, banging its shoes on the cobblestones, had already carried away the fourth practitioner of fine arts.

"What a center of culture!" said Ostap. "You must have noticed, Balaganov, that of the four citizens we encountered thus far, all four were artists. How curious."

When the half-brothers stopped in front of a small hardware store, Balaganov whispered to Ostap:

"Aren't you ashamed?"

"Of what?" asked Ostap.

"That you're actually going to pay money for the paint."

"Oh, I see," said Ostap. "Frankly, I am a little bit. It's silly, you're right. But what can you do? We're not going to run to the city council and ask them to supply the paint for Skylark Day. They would, of course, but that could take us all day."

The brilliant colors of the dry paint in jars, glass cylinders, sacks, caskets, and torn paper bags gave the hardware store a festive look.

The captain and the rally mechanic started the painstaking process of picking a color.

"Black is too mournful," said Ostap. "Green won't do: it's the color of lost hope. Purple, no. Let the chief of police ride around in a purple car. Pink is trashy, blue is banal, red is too conformist. We're going to have to paint the Antelope yellow. A bit too bright, but pretty."

"And what would you be? Artists?" asked the salesman, whose chin was lightly powdered with cinnabar.

"Yes, artists," answered Bender, "scenic and graphic."

"Then you're in the wrong place," said the salesman, removing the jars and the bags from the counter.

"What do you mean, the wrong place?" exclaimed Ostap. "What's the right place?"

"Across the street."

The clerk led the two friends to the door and pointed at the sky-blue sign across the street. It had a brown horse head and the words OATS AND HAY written in black letters.

"Right," said Ostap, "soft and hard feed for livestock. But what does it have to do with us artists? I don't see the connection."

It turned out there was a connection, and a very meaningful one at that. Ostap grasped it shortly after the clerk began his explanation.

The city had always loved fine paintings, and the four resident artists formed a group called the Dialectical Easelists. They painted portraits of officials and sold them to the local fine arts museum. With time, the pool of yet-unpainted officials grew smaller and smaller, and the income of the Dialectical Easelists had decreased accordingly, but they still managed to get by. The truly lean years began when a new artist, Feofan Smarmeladov, came to the city.

His first painting made quite a stir. It was a portrait of the director of the local hotel authority. Feofan Smarmeladov left the Easelists in his dust. The director of the hotel authority was not depicted in oil, watercolors, coal, crayons, gouache, or lead pencil; he was done in oats. While Smarmeladov was taking the portrait to the museum in a horse cart, the horse looked back nervously and whinnied.

Later, Smarmeladov began to use other grains as well.

He made portraits in barley, wheat, and poppy seeds, bold sketches in corn and buckwheat, landscapes in rice, and still-lifes in millet—every one a smashing success.

At the moment, he was working on a group portrait. A large canvas depicted a meeting of the regional planning board. Feofan was working in dry beans and peas. Deep in his heart, however, he remained true to the oats that had launched his career and undermined the Dialectical Easelists.

"You bet it's better with oats!" exclaimed Ostap. "And to think those fools Rubens and Raphael kept messing with oils. Like Leonardo da Vinci, we're fools, too. Give us some yellow enamel."

While paying the talkative clerk, Ostap asked:

"Oh yes, by the way, who's this Platonikov-Pervertov? We're not from around here, you know, so we aren't up to date."

"Comrade Pervertov is a prominent figure in Moscow, although he's from here originally. He's here on vacation."

"I see," said Ostap. "Thanks for the information. Goodbye!"

Outside, the half-brothers spotted the Dialectical Easelists again. All four of them stood at the intersection, looking sad and melodramatic, like Gypsy performers. Next to them were their easels, placed together like a stack of rifles.

"Bad news, fellows?" asked Ostap. "Did you lose Platonikov-Pervertov?"

"We did," groaned the artists. "And we almost had him."

"Feofan snatched him, didn't he?" asked Ostap, casually revealing his familiarity with the scene.

"He's already painting him, that charlatan," said the deputy of Henri de Navarre. "In oats. Says he's going back to his old method. The hack is complaining that he's having an artistic crisis."

"And where's this operator's studio?" inquired Ostap. "I'd like to take a look."

The artists, who had plenty of time on their hands, were happy to take Ostap and Balaganov to Feofan Smarmeladov's place. Feofan was working outside in his yard. Comrade Platonikov, apparently a timid man, sat in front of him on a stool. He held his breath and looked at the artist who, like the sower on a thirty-ruble bill, was grabbing oats from a basket by the handful and throwing them across the canvas. Smarmeladov frowned. The sparrows were bothering him. They brazenly flew onto the painting and pecked at the smaller details.

"How much are you going to get for this painting?" asked Platonikov shyly.

Feofan stopped sowing, examined his creation with a critical eye, and tentatively replied:

"Well, I think the museum will pay something like 250 for it."

"That's kind of pricey."

"But who can afford oats these days?" said Smarmeladov melodically. "They're not cheap, those oats."

"So how are the crops doing?" asked Ostap, sticking his head through the garden fence. "I see the sowing season is well under way. A hundred percent success! But this is nothing compared to what I saw in Moscow. One artist there made a painting out of hair. A large painting with multiple figures, mind you, and ideologically flawless, too, although, admittedly, he used the hair of non-party members. But ideologically, I repeat, the painting was absolutely impeccable. It was called "Grandpa Pakhom and His Tractor on the Night Shift." It was such a mischievous painting they really didn't know what to do with it. Sometimes, the hair on it would literally stand on end. And one day it turned completely gray, so Grandpa Pakhom and his tractor disappeared without a trace. But the author was fast enough to collect some fifteen hundred for his bright idea. So don't get too confident, Comrade Smarmeladov! The oats might germinate, your painting will start sprouting, and then you'll never harvest again."

The Dialectical Easelists laughed supportively, but Feofan was unfazed.

"This sounds like a paradox," he remarked, returning to his sowing.

"All right," said Ostap, "keep sowing the seeds of reason, good, and the everlasting, and then we'll see. And you, fellows, goodbye to you, too. Forget your oils. Switch to mosaics made of screws, nuts, and spikes. A portrait in nuts! What a splendid idea!"

The Antelopeans spent the whole day painting their car. By evening, it was unrecognizable and glistened with all the different colors of an egg-yolk.

At sunrise the next morning, the transformed Antelope left the cozy shed and set a course toward the south.

"Too bad we didn't have a chance to say goodbye to our host. But he was sleeping so peacefully that I didn't have the heart to wake him. Perhaps at this very moment, he's finally dreaming of Archbishop Inclement, blessing the Ministry of Education officials on the 300th anniversary of the House of Romanov."

And then they heard the howling cries that were already familiar to Ostap. They came from the little log house.

"The same dream!" cried old Khvorobyov. "Lord, oh Lord!"

"I was wrong," observed Ostap. "Instead of Archbishop Inclement, he must have seen a plenary session of The Forge and the Farm literary group. To hell with him, though. Business calls us to Chernomorsk."

CHAPTER 9
ANOTHER ARTISTIC CRISIS

It's amazing what some people do for a living.

Parallel to the big world inhabited by big people and big things, there's a small world with small people and small things. In the big world, they invented the diesel engine, wrote the novel *Dead Souls*, built the Dnieper Hydroelectric Station, and flew around the globe. In the small world, they invented the blowout noisemaker, wrote the song *Little Bricks*, and built Soviet Ambassador-style pants. People in the big world aspire to improve the lives of all humanity. The small world is far from such high-mindedness. Its inhabitants have only one desire—to get by without going hungry.

The small people try to keep up with the big people. They understand that they must be in tune with the times, since only then will their small offerings find a market. In Soviet times, when ideological monoliths have been created in the big world, the small world is in a state of commotion. All the small inventions from the world of ants are given rock-solid foundations of Communist ideology. The noisemaker is adorned with the likeness of Chamberlain, very similar to the one that appears in *Izvestiya* cartoons. In a popular song, a savvy metalworker wins the love of a Young Communist League girl by meeting, and even exceeding, his quotas in three stanzas. And while the big world is torn by vehement arguments about what the new life should look like, the small world has already figured everything out: there's the Shockworker's Dream necktie; the Fyodor Gladkov tunic; the plaster statuette, called A Collective Farm

Woman Bathing; and the Love of the Worker Bees brand ladies' absorbent armpit pads.

Fresh winds are blowing in the field of riddles, puzzles, anagrams, and other brainteasers. The old ways are out. The newspaper and magazine sections like *At Your Leisure* or *Use Your Brain* flatly refuse to accept non-ideological material. And while the great country was moving and shaking, building assembly lines for tractors and creating giant state farms, old man Sinitsky, a puzzle-maker by trade, sat in his room, his glazed eyes on the ceiling, and worked on a riddle based on the fashionable word *industrialisation*.

Sinitsky looked like a garden gnome. Such gnomes often appeared on the signs of umbrella stores. They wear pointy red hats and wink amicably at the passers-by, as if inviting them to hurry up and buy a silk parasol or a walking stick with a silver dog-head knob. Sinitsky's long yellowish beard descended below the desk right into the waste basket.

"Industrialisation," he whispered in despair, wiggling his old-man's lips, which were as pale as uncooked ground meat.

And then he divided the word into parts for the puzzle, like he always did:

"In. Dust. Rial. Is. Ation."

Everything was wonderful. Sinitsky was already picturing an elaborate word puzzle—rich in meaning, easy to read, yet hard to solve. The only problem was the last part, *ation*.

"What in the world is *ation*?" struggled the old man. "If only it was *action* instead! Then it would have been perfect: *industrialisaction*."

Sinitsky agonized over the capricious ending for half an hour, but he couldn't find a good solution. He then decided that it would come to him later on and got down to work. He started his poem on a sheet of paper which had been torn from a ledger that had *Debit* printed at the top.

Through the white glass door of his balcony, he could see the acacias in bloom, patched-up roofs, and the sharp blue line of the horizon in the sea. The Chernomorsk noon filled the city with a thick gooey heat.

The old man thought for a while and wrote down the opening lines:

My first one is a little word,

It is a preposition, truly . . .

"It is a preposition, truly," repeated the old man, satisfied.

He liked what he had so far, but he was struggling to find rhymes for *word* and *truly*. The puzzle-maker walked around the room and fiddled with his beard. And suddenly it came to him:

The second is the finest dirt
That every maid expunges duly.

The *rial* and *is* weren't too difficult either:

My third one lines the pockets of
A Persian, if his God is kindly.
The fourth one is a simple verb,
You see it everywhere, mind you.

Tired from this last effort, Sinitsky leaned back in his chair and closed his eyes. He was seventy years old. For fifty of those years he had been composing puzzles, riddles, and other brainteasers. But the good old puzzle-maker had never had such a hard time professionally. He wasn't up to date, he was politically ignorant, and his younger rivals were beating him hands down. The puzzles they brought to their editors had such impeccable ideological underpinnings that the old man cried with envy just reading them. How could he possibly compete with something like this:

A NUMBERS PUZZLE

Three train stations—Larkovo, Storkovo, and Chickadeevo—had an equal number of clerks. Chickadeevo had one sixth of the combined number of Young Communist League members at the other two, while Larkovo had 12 more Communist Party members than Storkovo. However, the latter station had 6 more non-party members than the first two. How many clerks did each station have, and how strong was the presence of the Party and Young Communist League at each of the three?

The old man shook off his depressing thoughts, and was about to go back to his "debit" sheet, when a young woman, with wet bobbed hair and a black swimsuit hanging over her shoulder, entered the room.

Without saying a word, she stepped out onto the balcony, hung her soggy swimsuit on the chipped railing, and looked down. She saw the same meager courtyard that she had been looking at for years—actually, it was a destitute-looking courtyard, with broken crates lying around, wandering cats covered with coal dust, and a tinsmith noisily fixing a bucket. Housewives on the ground floor were talking about their hard lives.

It wasn't the first time the young woman had heard these complaints. She also knew the cats by name, while the tinsmith had been fixing the same bucket for years—or so it seemed. Zosya Sinitsky went back into the room.

"This ideology is killing me," she heard her grandfather mumble. "What does puzzle-making have to do with ideology? Puzzle-making . . ."

Zosya looked at the old man's scribbles and exclaimed:

"What have you written here? What is this? 'A Persian, if his God is kindly.' What God? Weren't you telling me that the editors no longer accept puzzles with religious expressions?"

Sinitsky gasped. Crying, "Where's God? There's no God there!" he pulled his white-rimmed glasses onto his nose with shaking hands and picked up the sheet.

"There is a God," he admitted brokenheartedly. "Snuck in . . . I messed up again. What a shame! Such a good line wasted."

"Why don't you replace *God* with *fate*?" suggested Zosya.

But the frightened Sinitsky rejected *fate*.

"That's mysticism too. I know. Oh, I messed up again! What's going to happen, Zosya sweetheart?"

Zosya gave her grandfather a cold look and advised him to start a new puzzle from scratch.

"Either way," she said, "you always struggle with words that end in -tion. Remember how you struggled with *levitation*?"

"Of course," replied the old man. "I used 'levit' as the first part and wrote: 'The first one will not challenge you, it is the last name of a Jew.' They rejected that riddle: 'Not up to snuff, won't do.' I messed up!"

Then the old man settled down at his desk and went to work on a large, ideologically correct picture puzzle. First he sketched a goose holding a letter L in his beak. The letter was large and heavy, like an upside down gallows. The work proceeded smoothly.

Zosya began setting the table for dinner. She moved between a china cabinet with mirrored portholes and the table, unloading the dishes. She brought a glazed soup bowl with broken handles; plates, some decorated with little flowers and some not; forks, yellowed with age; and even a punch bowl, although punch wasn't on the menu.

On the whole, the Sinitskys were in dire straits. The riddles and puzzles brought home more worries than money. The homemade dinners that the old puzzle-maker had been offering to his acquaintances were their chief source of income. But that was in trouble, too. Subvysotsky and Bomze were away on vacation. Stoolian married a Greek woman and started eating at home. Pobirukhin was purged from his organization under Category Two. He was so upset that he lost his appetite and stopped coming to dinner. He just wandered around the city, accosting his acquaintances and repeating the same sarcasm-laden question: "Have you heard the news? I got purged under Category Two." Some of his acquaintances commiserated with him: "Look what they did, those bandits Marx and Engels!" Others wouldn't say anything; they'd fix a fiery eye on Pobirukhin and race past him, rattling their briefcases. In the end, there was only one diner left, and even he hadn't paid for the whole week, blaming it on delayed wages.

Zosya shrugged her shoulders unhappily and went to the kitchen. When she came back, the only remaining diner was already sitting at the table. It was Alexander Ivanovich Koreiko.

Outside the office, Alexander Ivanovich did not act timid or servile. Nevertheless, a vigilant expression never left his face even for a minute. At the moment he was carefully studying Sinitsky's new puzzle. Its mysterious drawings included a sack spilling letter Ts, a fir tree with the sun rising behind it, and a sparrow sitting on a line from a musical score. It all ended in an upside-down comma.

"This one won't be easy to solve," said Sinitsky, pacing slowly behind the diner's back. "You're going to have to sweat over it!"

"Right, right," replied Koreiko with a smirk. "I'm just not sure about this goose. What's with the goose? Ah! Got it! 'Through struggle you will attain your rights'?"

"That's correct," drawled the old man, disappointed. "How did you solve it so quickly? You must be gifted. No wonder you're Bookkeeper First Class."

"Second Class," corrected Koreiko. "And what's this puzzle for? For publication?"

"Yes, for publication."

"That's too bad," said Koreiko, glancing with curiosity at the borscht with gold medals of fat floating in it. There was something meritorious about this borscht, something of a decorated veteran. "'Through struggle you will attain your rights' is the motto of the Socialist Revolutionaries, not the Bolsheviks. It's no good for publication."

"Oh my God!" moaned the old man. "Merciful Mother of God! I messed up again! You hear, Zosya sweetheart? I messed up. What am I going to do now?"

They tried to calm the old man down. After eating dinner half-heartedly, he rose quickly, collected the week's puzzles, put on a huge straw hat, and said:

"Well, Zosya dear, I'm off to *The Youth Courier*. I'm a bit concerned about the algebraic puzzle, but I'm sure they'll give me some money."

The editors at the Young Communist League magazine *The Youth Courier* often rejected the old man's material, and admonished him for his backwardness, but they treated him kindly—the magazine was the only source of the tiny stream of money that came his way. Sinitsky was bringing in the puzzle that began with "My first one is a little word," two collective-farm anagrams, and an algebraic puzzle which, through some very complex division and multiplication, proved the superiority of the Soviet system over all other systems.

After the puzzle-maker left, Alexander Ivanovich began to examine Zosya gloomily. He had started eating at the Sinitskys' because their dinners were good and inexpensive. Besides, his first and foremost rule was to always remember that he was just a lowly clerk. He liked to talk about how hard it was to live in a big city on a meager salary. After a while, however, the price and the taste of the food lost its abstract, camouflaging value for him. If he had to—and if he could do it openly—he would gladly pay not 60 kopecks for dinner, but three or even five thousand rubles.

Alexander Ivanovich—this hermit who deliberately tormented himself with financial chains, who forbade himself to touch anything that cost more than fifty kopecks, and who at the same time was irked that he couldn't openly spend a hundred rubles for fear of losing his millions—fell in love with the abandon of a strong, austere man who had been embittered by an endless wait.

Today he finally decided to open his heart to Zosya and to offer her his hand, with its small, mean, ferret-like pulse, and his heart, which was bound by enchanted hoops.

"Yes," he said, "that's the way things are, Zosya Victorovna."

Having made this pronouncement, Citizen Koreiko grabbed an ashtray—it had the pre-revolutionary motto "Husband, don't vex your wife" printed on the side—and began studying it very carefully.

One needs to point out here that there isn't a young woman in the whole world who doesn't sense an upcoming declaration of love at least a week in advance. That's why Zosya Victorovna sighed uneasily as she lingered in front of the mirror. She had that sporty look that every pretty young woman had acquired in recent years, and after reaffirming her beauty in the mirror, she sat down in front of Alexander Ivanovich and prepared to hear him out. But Alexander Ivanovich said nothing. He knew only two roles: clerk and secret millionaire. He hadn't known anything else.

"Have you heard the news?" asked Zosya. "Pobirukhin was purged."

"It started at our place, too," said Koreiko, "heads will roll. Lapidus Jr., for example. Come to think of it, Lapidus Sr. isn't squeaky clean either . . ."

At this point, Koreiko realized that he was playing the role of a poor clerk, and he fell back into his leaden thoughtfulness.

"Yes," he said, "one lives like this, alone, without any bliss."

"Without any what?" Zosya perked up.

"Without a woman's affection," said Koreiko tensely.

Seeing that Zosya wasn't offering any help, he elaborated.

He's quite old. Well, not exactly old, but not young. Well, not exactly not young, but time passes, you know, the years go by. Time flies, in other words. And this passage of time makes him think of various things. Of marriage, for example. Let nobody think that he is something like, you know . . . He's actually not bad. A totally harmless man. One should feel for him. He even thinks that one might be able to love him. He's not a show-off, like some, and he means what he says. So why shouldn't a certain young lady marry him?

Having expressed his feelings in such a timid way, Alexander Ivanovich gave Zosya an angry look.

"So they really might purge Lapidus Jr.?" asked the puzzle-maker's granddaughter.

And without waiting for an answer, she delved into the subject at hand.

She understands everything perfectly well. Time really does fly. She was nineteen just recently, and now she's already twenty. And in a year, she'll be twenty-one. She never thought that Alexander Ivanovich was something like, you know . . . On the contrary, she's always been convinced that he is a good man. Better than many. And, of course, he deserves a lot. But right now she is seeking something, she doesn't yet know what. In other words, she can't get married at the moment. Plus, what kind of life would they have? She is seeking. And he, in all honesty, only makes forty-six rubles a month. And besides, she doesn't love him yet, which, frankly speaking, is rather important.

"Forget the forty-six rubles!" exploded Alexander Ivanovich, rising to his feet. "I . . . me . . ."

But that was all he said. He chickened out. The role of the millionaire would only lead to disaster. He was so scared he even mumbled something to the effect that money can't buy happiness. At this very moment, a puffing sound came from behind the door. Zosya rushed out into the hallway.

Her grandfather stood there in his huge hat, its straw crystals sparkling. He couldn't bring himself to come in. His grief had caused his beard to open up like a broom.

"Why so fast?" cried Zosya. "What happened?"

The old man slowly raised his eyes to her. They were filled with tears.

Worried, Zosya grabbed her grandfather's prickly shoulders and pulled him into the room. For half an hour Sinitsky just lay on the couch and shivered.

After a good amount of cajoling, the old man finally told his story.

At first, everything was wonderful. He made it to the office of *The Youth Courier* without incident. The head of the *Exercise Your Brain* section was exceptionally nice to him.

"He shook my hand, Zosya dear," sighed the old man. "Comrade Sinitsky, he said, have a seat. And that's when he hit me with it. Our section, he said, is closing. The new editor-in-chief has arrived, and he announced that our readers don't need brain teasers anymore. What they need, Zosya dear, is a special section on the game of checkers. So what's going to happen? I asked. Nothing, he said, it's just that we can't accept your material, that's all. He praised my riddle, though. Sounds like Pushkin's verse, he said, especially this: "The second is the finest dirt that every maid expunges duly."

The old puzzle-maker kept trembling on the couch and complaining about the omnipresent Soviet ideology.

"All that drama again!" exclaimed Zosya.

She put her hat on and headed for the door. Alexander Ivanovich followed her, even though he knew it wasn't a good idea.

Outside, Zosya took Koreiko by the arm.

"We'll still be friends, right?"

"I'd much rather you married me," grumbled Koreiko candidly.

Bare-headed young men in white shirts, their sleeves rolled up above their elbows, were crowding the wide open soda bars. Dark-blue siphons with metal faucets stood on the shelves. Tall glass cylinders on rotating stands, filled with syrup, cast out glimmering drugstore light. Sad-looking Persians roasted chestnuts on open grills, enticing the strollers with pungent fumes.

"I want to go to the movies," said Zosya capriciously. "I want some nuts, I want some soda."

For Zosya, Koreiko was prepared to do anything. He was even prepared to lift his disguise a bit and splurge to the tune of five rubles or so. He happened to have a flat metal Caucasus cigarette box in his pocket. The box contained ten thousand rubles in 250-ruble bills. But even if he had lost his mind and was bold enough to produce a single bill, no movie theater would have been able to break it anyway.

"Wages are delayed again," he said in complete despair, "they pay very irregularly."

Then, a young man wearing very nice sandals on his bare feet stepped out from the crowd. He raised his hand to greet Zosya.

"Hi there," he said, "I've got two free passes to the movies. Wanna come? But it has to be right now."

And then the young man in fabulous sandals led Zosya under the dim sign of the Whither Goest movie theater, formerly the Quo Vadis.

The millionaire bookkeeper didn't spend the night asleep in his bed. He wandered aimlessly through the city, stared blankly at the photos of naked babies in photographers' display windows, kicked up the gravel on the boulevard with his feet, and gazed into the dark hollow of the port. There, invisible steamers exchanged greetings, policemen whistled, and the lighthouse flashed its red flare.

"What a wretched country!" grumbled Koreiko. "A country where a millionaire can't even take his fiancée to the movies."

Somehow he already thought of Zosya as his fiancée.

By dawn, Alexander Ivanovich, pale from lack of sleep, found himself on the outskirts of the city. As he was walking down Bessarabian Street, he heard the sound of the maxixe. Surprised, he stopped.

A yellow car was coming down the hill towards him. The driver, in a leather jacket, crouched over the wheel, looking tired. Next to him dozed a broad-shouldered fellow in a Stetson hat with vent holes, his head hanging to one side. Two more passengers slouched in the back seat:

a fireman in full dress uniform and an athletic-looking man wearing a white-topped seaman's cap.

"Greetings to our first Chernomorskian!" hollered Ostap as the car drove past Koreiko, rumbling like a tractor. "Are the warm seawater baths still open? Is the theater functioning? Has Chernomorsk been declared a free city?"

Ostap didn't get any answers. Kozlevich opened the choke, and the Antelope drowned the first Chernomorskian in a cloud of blue smoke.

"Well," said Ostap to the awakened Balaganov, "our deliberations continue. Just bring me your underground Rockefeller. I'm going to peel his skins off. Those princes and paupers, let me tell you!"

PART 2
THE TWO STRATEGISTS

CHAPTER 10
A TELEGRAM FROM THE BROTHERS KARAMAZOV

At some point, the underground millionaire began to feel that he was the subject of someone's unflagging attention. At first, it wasn't anything in particular. It was just that his familiar and comfortable feeling of privacy had somehow disappeared. Then came far more sinister signs.

One day, when Koreiko was walking to work with his usual measured gait, a pushy street bum with a golden tooth accosted him right in front of the Hercules. Stepping on the underwear straps he was dragging behind him, the bum grabbed Alexander Ivanovich by the hand and muttered:

"Gimme a million, gimme a million, gimme a million!"

Then the bum stuck out his fat dirty tongue and began blurting out complete nonsense. It was just a half-crazy bum, a common sight in southern cities. Nevertheless, Koreiko went up to his desk in Finance and Accounting with a heavy heart.

After that encounter, all hell broke loose.

Alexander Ivanovich was awakened at three o'clock in the morning. A telegram arrived. His teeth chattering from the morning chill, the millionaire tore the seal and read:

"COUNTESS WITH STRICKEN FACE RUNS TO POND."

"What countess?" whispered the baffled Koreiko, standing barefoot in the hallway.

There was no answer. The postman was gone. Pigeons cooed passionately in the courtyard. The neighbors were all asleep. Alexander Ivanovich looked at the gray sheet of paper again. The address was correct. His name was, too.

"LESSER TANGENTIAL 16 ALEXANDER KOREIKO COUNTESS WITH STRICKEN FACE RUNS TO POND."

Alexander Ivanovich didn't understand a thing, but he was so distressed that he burned the telegram with a candle.

At 5:35 P.M. on the same day, another telegram arrived:

"DELIBERATIONS CONTINUE COMMA MILLION KISSES."

Alexander Ivanovich went pale with fury and tore the telegram into small pieces. But the very next night, two more urgent cables arrived.

The first read:

"LOAD ORANGES BARRELS BROTHERS KARAMAZOV."

The second read:

"ICE HAS BROKEN STOP I AM COMMANDING PARADE."

After that, Alexander Ivanovich had an unsettling accident at work. While multiplying 985 by thirteen, at Chevazhevskaya's request, he made a mistake and gave her the wrong answer. This had never happened before. But he was incapable of focusing on mathematical problems. He just couldn't get the crazy telegrams out of his mind.

"Barrels," he whispered, staring at the old Kukushkind. "Brothers Karamazov. That's shameless, plain and simple."

He tried to calm himself down with the thought that these telegrams were a cutesy joke being played by some friends of his, but this theory had to be rejected on the spot: he had no friends. As for his co-workers, they were serious people and joked only once a year, on April Fools' Day. And even on this day of cheerful merriment and joyful pranks, they invariably played the same depressing trick: they used the typewriter to concoct a fake pink slip for Kukushkind and put it on his desk. And each time, seven years in a row, the old man would gasp in horror, which entertained everybody to no end. Besides, they weren't wealthy enough to waste money on telegrams.

After the telegram in which a mysterious person announced that he, rather than anybody else, was commanding the parade, things quieted down. No one bothered Alexander Ivanovich for three days. He had already started getting used to the idea that these strange occurrences had nothing to do with him when a thick registered letter arrived. It contained a book *The Capitalist Sharks: Biographies of American Millionaires.*

Under different circumstances, Koreiko would have bought such a curious little book himself, but he literally squirmed in horror. The first sentence, underlined in blue pencil, read: "All large modern-day fortunes were amassed through the most dishonest means." Just in case, Alexander Ivanovich decided to stop checking on his treasured suitcase at the train station for the time being. He was very alarmed.

"The main thing is to create panic in the enemy camp," said Ostap, leisurely pacing around the spacious room in the Carlsbad Hotel. "The opponent must lose his peace of mind. It's not that difficult to pull off. After all, what scares people the most is the unknown. I myself was once a lone mystic and got to the point where I could be scared with a simple sharp knife. That's right. More of the unknown. I am convinced that my latest telegram, 'You're in our thoughts,' had a crushing effect on our counterpart. All this is just the superphosphate, the fertilizer. Let him agonize. The client must get used to the idea that he'll have to part with his money. He must be disarmed psychologically, his reactionary, proprietary instincts must be suppressed."

After finishing the speech, Bender gave his subordinates a stern look. Balaganov, Panikovsky, and Kozlevich sat stiffly in their plush, fringed, and tasseled red armchairs. They felt awkward. They were troubled by the captain's lavish lifestyle, by the golden draperies, by the bright, chemically-colored carpets, and by the print of *The Appearance of Christ to the People*. They were staying in a hostel, along with the Antelope, and came to the hotel only to receive instructions.

"Panikovsky," said Ostap, "your assignment for today was to encounter our defendant and again ask him for a million, accompanying your request with idiotic laughter."

"The moment he saw me he crossed to the other side of the street," replied Panikovsky smugly.

"Good. Everything is going according to plan. The client is getting nervous. Right now he is progressing from stupefied confusion to unprovoked fear. I have no doubt that he wakes up in the middle of the night and babbles meekly: 'Mama, Mama . . .' Another small push, the slightest thing, the last stroke of the brush, and he'll be ripe for the picking. Wailing, he'll open his cupboard and take out a blue-rimmed platter . . ."

Ostap winked at Balaganov, Balaganov winked at Panikovsky, Panikovsky winked at Kozlevich. And even though the honest Kozlevich didn't understand a thing, he too began winking with both of his eyes.

For a while after that, the room in the Carlsbad Hotel was filled with friendly winking, giggling, tongue clicking, and even some jumping up from the red plush armchairs.

"Enough of that," said Ostap. "For now, the money platter is still in Koreiko's hands—that is, if this magic platter does exist."

And then Bender sent Panikovsky and Kozlevich back to the hostel, with instructions to have the Antelope ready at a moment's notice.

"Well, Shura," he said, once he was alone with Balaganov, "no more telegrams. Our preparatory work can be considered complete. The active struggle begins. We're going to go and observe our precious calf at his place of employment."

Staying in the transparent shade of the acacias, the half-brothers walked through the public garden, where a thick water jet from the fountain was melting like a candle, passed by a few mirrored beer joints, and stopped at the corner of Mehring Street. Flower ladies with red sailor's faces bathed their delicate wares in glazed bowls. The asphalt, heated by the sun, sizzled under their feet. People were coming out of the blue-tiled milk bar, wiping kefir from their lips.

A welcoming glow came from the fat, noodle-shaped, gilded-wood letters that formed the word *Hercules*. The sun frolicked in the huge glass panels of the revolving door. Ostap and Balaganov entered the hallway and joined the crowd of people who were there on business.

CHAPTER 11
THE HERCULEANS

A long procession of the Hercules' directors tried to banish the ghosts of the hotel from the building, but no matter how hard each of them tried, they all ultimately failed. No matter how many times Maintenance painted over the old signs, they still showed through everywhere. One day, the words *Private Dining Rooms* popped up in the Sales Department, then a watermark, *Maid on Duty,* suddenly became visible on the frosted-glass door of the typing pool; another time, painted golden fingers, with the word *Ladies'* in French, appeared on the walls. The hotel just wouldn't quit.

Lower-level employees sat in one-ruble rooms on the fourth floor—the kind that used to be frequented by country priests who were attending diocesan conferences, or minor salesmen with Warsaw-style mustaches. These rooms had pink metal sinks and still smelled of armpits. Department heads, their assistants, and the head of Maintenance occupied the nicer rooms, where pool sharks and provincial actors used to stay. These rooms were a bit better: they had mirrored wardrobes and floors covered with reddish-brown linoleum. The top administrators nested in deluxe rooms with bathtubs and alcoves. The white bathtubs were filled with files, while the walls of the dim alcoves were covered with diagrams and charts that depicted the organizational structure of the Hercules and its network of local affiliates. Rooms like this still contained silly gold-painted love seats, carpets, and night stands with marble tops. Some alcoves even had heavy nickel-plated beds with ball knobs. The beds were also covered with files and all kinds of correspondence. It was very convenient, since the papers were always at hand.

Back in 1911, the famous writer Leonid Andreev stayed in one of these rooms—No. 5. All the Herculeans knew about it, and for some reason, No. 5 had a bad reputation in the building.

Every administrator who had set up their offices in this room had gotten into some kind of trouble. The moment a No. 5 would become more or less comfortable with his new responsibilities, he'd be demoted and transferred to another position. If he was lucky, there would be no formal reprimand. But at times there was a reprimand; at other times there would be an article in the paper; and sometimes it was much worse—it's unpleasant even to think about it.

"That room is cursed," complained the victims afterwards. "But who knew?"

And so the author of the scary story, *The Seven Who Were Hanged*, was held responsible for terrible things: Comr. Lapshin giving jobs to his own six mighty brothers; Comr. Spravchenko, hoping that the tree-bark collection campaign would somehow take care of itself, thus making said campaign a total failure; or Comr. Indochinov losing 7,384.03 rubles of state funds in a game of cards. And no matter how Indochinov wiggled, no matter how he tried to convince the authorities that the 0.03 rubles were spent on state business, and that he could produce documentation in support of this claim, nothing helped. The ghost of the late writer was implacable, and one fall evening, Indochinov was escorted to the slammer. Room No. 5 was definitely no good.

The director of the entire Hercules, Comr. Polykhaev, had his office in what used to be the winter garden, and his secretary, Impala Mikhailovna, would pop up here and there amid the surviving palms and ficus. This same area also contained a long table, like a train station platform, that was covered with thick crimson fabric; this was the site of frequent and lengthy board meetings. In addition, Room 262, which used to be the snack bar, was recently taken over by the Purge Committee, eight unremarkable men with dull gray eyes. They came in punctually every day and were always reading some kind of official-looking papers.

As Ostap and Balaganov were climbing the stairs, an alarm bell went off, and the staff immediately started pouring out of every room. Everyone moved quickly, it felt like an emergency on a ship. The bell didn't signal an emergency, however; it called for the morning break. Some of the employees rushed to the cafeteria, in order to secure a red caviar sandwich for themselves. Others walked up and down the hallways, eating on the go.

A remarkably noble-looking man came out of the Planning Department. A young, rounded beard hung from his pale, kind face. He was holding a cold meat patty, which he kept bringing to his mouth, examining it carefully each time.

His routine was almost interrupted by Balaganov, who wished to know where they could find Finance and Accounting.

"Can't you see, Comrade, that I'm having a bite to eat?" said the man, turning away from Balaganov indignantly.

And then, ignoring the half-brothers, he immersed himself in studying the last remaining morsel of the meat patty. He examined it carefully from all sides, even sniffed it goodbye, and finally placed it in his mouth. Then he puffed out his chest, cleaned the crumbs off his jacket, and slowly approached another employee, who was standing near the door to his department.

"So, how are you feeling?" he asked after looking around.

"Don't even ask, Comrade Bomze," the other one answered. Then he looked around and added: "What kind of life is that? No room for individuality. Same stuff over and over again: the Five-Year Plan in four years, in three years . . ."

"I know," whispered Bomze, "it's just terrible! I couldn't agree more. Like you said, no room for individuality, no incentives, no personal growth. My wife stays at home, of course, and even she says there are no incentives, no personal growth."

Sighing, Bomze moved on to another co-worker.

"So, how are you feeling?" he asked, a sad smile already on his face.

"You know," said the other, "I just came back from a business trip. Got to see a state farm. Incredible. A grain factory! You can't imagine, my friend, what the Five-Year Plan means, what the will of the collective really means!"

"But that's exactly what I was just saying!" Bomze exclaimed enthusiastically. "That's right, the will of the collective! The Five-Year Plan in four years, even in three—that's the incentive that . . . Take my own wife. She stays at home—yet even she appreciates industrialisation. The new life is emerging in front of our eyes, damn it!"

He stepped aside and shook his head cheerfully. A minute later he was already holding the quiet Borisokhlebsky by the sleeve and saying:

"You're right, I agree with you. Why build all those Magnitogorsks, state farms, and combine harvesters when there's no private life, when individuality is suppressed?"

The next minute, his somewhat weak voice was already murmuring in the stairwell:

"And that's exactly what I was saying to Comrade Borisokhlebsky just now. Why mourn individuality and private life when grain factories are rising in front of our eyes? Magnitogorsks, combine harvesters, concrete mixers; when the collective . . ."

During the break, Bomze, who greatly enjoyed these meaningful exchanges, managed to shoot the breeze with about a dozen of his co-workers. The mood of each exchange could be determined from his facial expression, which quickly moved from sadness about the suppression of individuality to a bright enthusiastic smile. But whatever emotions he experienced at any given moment, an expression of innate nobility never left his face. And everybody, from the ideologically up-to-snuff members of the local union committee to the politically backward Kukushkind, considered Bomze an honest man and even a man of principle. Then again, his own opinion of himself was no different.

The new bell announced an end to the emergency and returned the employees to their hotel rooms. Work resumed.

As a matter of fact, the words "work resumed" did not exactly describe the activities at the Hercules, which, according to its charter, was supposed to be engaged in the lumber and timber trade. During the last year, however, the Herculeans had abandoned all thoughts of such mundane things as logs, plywood, export-quality cedar, and the like. Instead, they immersed themselves in a more exhilarating pursuit: the fight for their building, their dearly beloved hotel.

It all started with a small sheet of paper that a slow-moving messenger from the city's Municipal Affairs Department brought in his canvas delivery bag.

"Upon receiving this," read the paper, "you are *requested* to vacate the premises of the former Hotel Cairo within a period of one week and to transfer the building, along with all the equipment of the former hotel, to the jurisdiction of the Hotel Department. You are assigned the premises of the former Tin and Bacon Co. *See*: City Council resolution of June 12, 1929."

In the evening, the paper was placed in front of Comrade Polykhaev, who sat in the electric shade of the palms and the ficus.

"What!" exploded the director of the Hercules indignantly. "They tell me I'm 'requested!' Me, who reports directly to the Center! What is wrong with them? Are they out of their minds?"

"They might as well have said 'instructed,'" Impala Mikhailovna said, adding fuel to the fire. "Such arrogance!"

"They can't be serious," said Polykhaev, smiling ominously. A most forthright response was composed immediately. The director of the Hercules flatly refused to vacate the premises.

"Next time they'll know I'm not their night watchman, and they'd better not write 'requested' to me," mumbled Comrade Polykhaev, taking a rubber stamp with his signature out of his pocket and applying it upside down in agitation.

Once again a slow-moving messenger, this time the one from the Hercules, trudged down the sun-drenched streets, stopping at refreshment stands, getting involved in all the street squabbles on the way, and waving his delivery bag with abandon.

For the entire week after that, the Herculeans discussed the new situation. The employees basically agreed that Polykhaev was not about to swallow such a challenge to his authority.

"You don't know our Polykhaev," said the eagles from Finance and Accounting. "He's seen it all. He won't budge because of some lousy resolution."

Shortly thereafter, Comrade Bomze emerged from the principal's office with a list of select employees in his hand. He went from department to department, leaning over each person named on the list and whispering secretively:

"A small get-together. Three rubles each. To say goodbye to Polykhaev."

"What?" the chosen people would react with alarm. "Is Polykhaev leaving? Is he being reassigned?"

"No, no. He's going to the Center to see about the building. So don't be late. Eight o'clock sharp, at my place."

The good-bye party was a lot of fun. Polykhaev sat holding a goblet, while the employees looked at him admiringly and clapped their hands in unison, singing:

> Drink it up, drink it up, drinkitup.
> Drink it up, drink it up, drinkitup.

They sang until their beloved director had emptied a substantial number of goblets and a few tall thin glasses as well. He then took his turn and started singing in an unsteady voice: "On that old Kaluga Highway, near milepost forty-nine . . ." But nobody ever found out what exactly happened near that milepost, because Polykhaev, without warning, switched to a different song:

> On the streetcar number four
> Someone dropped dead by the door.
> Now they drag the stiff away,
> Whooptie-doo! Hop, hey-hey . . .

After Polykhaev left, productivity at the Hercules dropped a little. It would have been silly to work hard without knowing whether you're staying put or will be forced to traipse to the Tin and Bacon Co. with all your stationery. But it would have been even sillier to work hard after Polykhaev came back. He returned a conquering hero, as Bomze put it: the Hercules got to keep its building, and so the employees spent their office hours making fun of Municipal Affairs.

The crushed opponent asked to at least be given the sinks and the armored beds, but Polykhaev, riding the crest of his success, didn't even respond. Then the hostilities resumed. The Center was inundated with complaints. Polykhaev went there in person to refute them. The triumphant "drinkitup" was heard at Bomze's place with ever-increasing frequency, and an ever-increasing number of Herculeans were sucked into the fight for the building. Lumber and timber were gradually forgotten. When Polykhaev occasionally found something relating to export-quality cedar or plywood on his desk, he was so flabbergasted that, at first, he didn't even understand what they wanted from him. At the moment, he was immersed in a crucial task—luring two particularly dangerous employees from Municipal Affairs with an offer of higher salaries.

"You're in luck," said Ostap to his companion. "You're witnessing an amusing exercise—Ostap Bender in hot pursuit. Watch and learn! A petty criminal like Panikovsky would have written Koreiko a note: 'Put six hundred rubles under the trash can outside or else'—and added a cross, a skull, and a candle at the bottom. Sonka the Golden Hand, whose skills I am by no means trying to denigrate, in the end would have resorted to a simple honeytrap, which would have brought her perhaps fifteen hundred. A woman, what can you expect? Or take Cornet Savin, if you will. An outstanding swindler. As the saying goes, a swindler through and through. And what would he have done? He would have gone to Koreiko's home, claiming to be the Tsar of Bulgaria, made a scene at the building manager's office, and messed the whole thing up. Me, I'm not in a hurry, you can see that. We've been in Chernomorsk for a full week, and I'm only now headed to our first date . . . Ah, here's Finance and Accounting. Well, rally mechanic, show me the patient. You are an expert on Koreiko, after all."

The deafening hall was full of visitors. Balaganov led Bender to the corner where Chevazhevskaya, Koreiko, Kukushkind, and Dreyfus sat behind a yellow divider. Balaganov raised his hand to point out the millionaire, when Ostap angrily whispered:

"Why don't you yell at the top of your lungs: 'There he is, the rich guy! Hold him!' Quiet now. Let me guess. Which one of the four?"

Ostap settled down on the cool marble window sill and, dangling his feet like a child, began thinking aloud:

"The young lady doesn't count. That leaves three choices: the red-faced toady with white eyes, the little old man in steel glasses, and the fat pooch with the dead-serious expression on his face. I indignantly reject the little old man. He's got no valuables, unless you count the cotton stuck in his furry ears. That leaves two: the pooch-face and the white-eyed toady. Which one of them is Koreiko? Let me think."

Ostap stuck his neck out and began comparing the two candidates. He turned his head quickly, as if he was watching a game of tennis and following every volley with his eyes.

"You know, mechanic," he said finally, "the fat pooch-face fits the image of an underground millionaire better than the white-eyed toady. Note the twinkle of alarm in the pooch's eyes. He's restless, he can't wait, he wants to run home and sink his paws into his bags of gold. No doubt he's the one collecting carats and dollars. Can't you see his fat mug is nothing but an egalitarian blend of the faces of Shylock, the Miserly Knight, and Harpagon? And White Eyes—he's nothing, a zero, a Soviet mouseling. He does have a fortune, of course—twelve rubles in the savings bank. His dreams don't stretch beyond the purchase of a fuzzy coat with a calfskin collar. This is not Koreiko. This is a mouse that . . ."

At this point the grand strategist's brilliant speech was interrupted by a lion-hearted shout that came from the depths of Finance and Accounting, and it clearly belonged to somebody who had the right to shout:

"Comrade Koreiko! Where are the stats on what Municipal Affairs owes us? Comrade Polykhaev needs them right now."

Ostap kicked Balaganov with his foot. But Pooch-Face continued to scratch with his pen, unperturbed. His face—the one that combined the characteristics of Shylock, Harpagon, and the Miserly Knight—showed no emotion. The red-faced blond with white eyes, on the other hand, this zero, this Soviet mouseling who dreamed of nothing but a coat with a calfskin collar, became very agitated. He started banging his desk drawers hurriedly, grabbed a sheet of paper, and rushed off to answer the call.

The grand strategist grunted and gave Balaganov a piercing look. Shura laughed.

"Yes," said Ostap after a long silence. "This one is not going to bring us the money on a platter. Only if I really beg him. This client deserves our respect. Let's go outside. My brain has just produced an amusing plan. Tonight, God willing, we'll give Mr. Koreiko's udder the first squeeze. You, Shura, will do the squeezing."

CHAPTER 12
HOMER, MILTON, AND PANIKOVSKY

The orders were very simple:
1. Run into Citizen Koreiko on the street as if by chance.
2. Do not beat him up under any circumstances, and in general avoid violence.
3. Take everything found in the pockets of the above-mentioned citizen.
4. Report upon completion of the task.

Even though the grand strategist's instructions were perfectly simple and clear, Balaganov and Panikovsky still had a heated argument. The Lieutenant's sons were sitting on a green bench in the public garden, glancing pointedly at the doors of the Hercules. Arguing, they didn't even notice that the wind was bending the fire-hose jet from the fountain and spraying them with mist. They just jerked their heads, stared blankly into the clear sky, and continued to bicker.

Panikovsky, who had changed from the thick fireman's jacket into an open-collared cotton shirt, due to the heat, was acting snooty. He was very proud of the assignment.

"Gotta be a theft," he insisted.

"Gotta be a mugging," argued Balaganov, who was also proud of the captain's trust in him.

"You're a miserable, wretched person," declared Panikovsky, looking at his counterpart with disgust.

"And you are an invalid," retorted Balaganov. "I'm in charge here."

"Who's in charge?"

"I'm in charge. It's my assignment."

"Yours?"

"Mine."

"Really?"

"Who else's? You think it's yours?"

The conversation entered a realm that had nothing to do with the task at hand. The crooks got so agitated they even started pushing each other, ever so slightly, and hissing; "And who are you?" Such actions usually serve as a prelude to an all-out fight, in which the opponents throw their hats on the ground, ask passers-by to be their witnesses, and rub childlike tears all over their scrubby faces.

But it didn't come to a fight. Just when the moment was right for the first slap on the face, Panikovsky suddenly pulled his hands away and recognized Balaganov as his direct superior.

Panikovsky must have remembered the thrashings he had received from individuals and entire collectives, and how painful those thrashings were. Having seized power, Balaganov immediately became more amenable.

"Why not mug him?" he said less vehemently. "Is it that difficult? Koreiko walks down the street at night. It's dark. I approach him from the left. You approach him from the right. I bump him from the left, you bump him from the right. This fool stops and says to me: 'You punk!' 'Who's the punk?' I ask. You ask who the punk is too and push from the right. Then I throw him a good . . . No, beating is forbidden!"

"That's the thing, beating is forbidden," Panikovsky sighed hypocritically. "Bender wouldn't allow it."

"I know, I know . . . Well, fine, then I grab his hands and you check if there's anything interesting in his pockets. He, naturally, cries 'Police!' and then I . . . Oh, damn, no beating. Right, then we go home. So how's the plan?"

Panikovsky avoided giving a straight answer. He took a carved souvenir cane from Balaganov's hands—it had a V rather than a knob—drew a straight line in the sand, and said:

"Look here. First, we have to wait until dark. Second . . ."

Panikovsky drew a shaky perpendicular from the right side of the first line.

"Second, he may not even go out tonight. And if he does, then . . ."

Now Panikovsky connected the two lines with a third, making something like a triangle in the sand, and concluded:

"Who knows? He might be out with a whole bunch of people. Then what?"

Balaganov looked at the triangle with respect. He didn't find Panikovsky's arguments particularly convincing, but the triangle projected such compelling hopelessness that Balaganov hesitated. Panikovsky noticed it and pounced.

"Go to Kiev!" he said suddenly. "Then you'll see that I'm right. Yes, you have to go to Kiev!"

"What are you talking about!" mumbled Shura. "Why Kiev?"

"Go to Kiev and ask what Panikovsky did there before the revolution. Do it!"

"Leave me alone," said Balaganov gloomily.

"No, you should ask!" demanded Panikovsky. "Go and ask! And they'll tell you that before the revolution, Panikovsky was a blind man. Do you think I would have become a son of Lieutenant Schmidt if it hadn't been for the revolution? I used to be a wealthy man. I had a family and a nickel-plated samovar on my table. And how did I make my living? With dark glasses and a cane."

He took a black cardboard case with dull silver stars out of his pocket and showed Balaganov his dark-blue glasses.

"These glasses fed me for many years," he said with a sigh. "I would put them on, take a cane, go out to Kreshchatik Street, and ask some nice-looking gentleman to help the poor blind man across the street. The gentleman would take me by the arm and walk with me. When we reached the opposite sidewalk, he would already be missing his watch, if he had a watch, or his wallet. Some people used to carry wallets, you know."

"So why did you quit?" asked Balaganov, perking up.

"The revolution!" answered the former blind man. "I used to pay a cop standing on the corner of Kreshchatik and Proreznaya five rubles a month, and nobody bothered me. The cop even made sure I was safe. He was a good man! His name was Semen Vasilyevich Nebaba. I ran into him recently—he's a music critic nowadays. And now? Can you really mess with the police these days? I've never seen nastier guys. They're so principled, such idealists. And so, Balaganov, in my old age I had to become a swindler. But for such an important task, I can make use of my old glasses again. It's much better than a mugging."

Five minutes later, a blind man in dark-blue glasses stepped out of a public restroom that was surrounded by tobacco and mint plants. His chin raised to the sky, he headed for the park exit, constantly tapping in front of him with a souvenir cane. Balaganov followed him. Panikovsky was unrecognizable. Holding his shoulders back and carefully placing his feet on the sidewalk, he almost walked into buildings, tapped on display window railings with his cane, bumped into people, and moved on, looking right through them. He was so diligent he even dispersed a small lineup that had formed at a bus stop. Balaganov watched this agile blind man with amazement.

Panikovsky continued wreaking havoc until Koreiko showed up in the doorway of the Hercules. Balaganov lost his cool. First he positioned himself too close to the action, then he ran too far away. Finally, he found a spot near a fruit stand that was good for surveying the scene. For some reason, he developed an unpleasant taste in his mouth, as if he had been sucking on a brass doorknob for half an hour. But when he saw Panikovsky's maneuvers, he calmed down.

Balaganov saw the blind man turn towards the millionaire, brush his leg with the cane, and then bump him with his shoulder. They apparently exchanged a few words. Then Koreiko smiled, took the blind man by the arm, and helped him off the curb onto the street. To stay in character, Panikovsky was banging the paving stones with the cane as hard as he could, and he held his head so far back that it looked as though he were bridled. He proceeded with such skill and precision that Balaganov even felt pangs of envy. Panikovsky put his arm around Koreiko's waist. His hand slid down Koreiko's left side and lingered over the canvas pocket of the millionaire bookkeeper for just a fraction of a second.

"Good, good," whispered Balaganov. "Go, gramps, go!"

But at that moment, glass suddenly sparkled, a horn honked nervously, the earth shook, and a large white bus ground to a halt in the middle of the street, barely managing to stay on its wheels. Simultaneously, two cries were heard:

"Idiot! Can't you see a bus!" shrieked Panikovsky, jumping out from under the wheels and shaking the glasses that had fallen off of his nose in the direction of his helper.

"He's not blind!" exclaimed Koreiko. "Thief!"

The scene disappeared in a cloud of blue smoke, the bus moved on, and when the fumes parted, Balaganov saw Panikovsky surrounded by a small crowd. There was some kind of commotion around the phony blind man. Balaganov ran closer. Panikovsky had an ugly smile on his face. He was oddly indifferent to what was happening, even though one of his ears was so ruby-red that it would probably glow in the dark—one could have developed photographic plates in its light.

Pushing aside the people who came pouring in from all directions, Balaganov rushed to the Carlsbad Hotel.

The grand strategist sat at a bamboo table, writing.

"They're beating Panikovsky!" cried Balaganov, picturesquely appearing in the doorway.

"Already?" asked Bender calmly. "That's a bit too soon."

"They're beating Panikovsky!" repeated the red-headed Shura in desperation. "Right by the Hercules."

"Stop bawling like a polar bear on a warm day," said Ostap sternly. "Has it been long?"

"Maybe five minutes."

"Then why didn't you say so right away? What a cranky old man! Well, let's go enjoy the view. You can tell me everything on the way."

Koreiko had already left by the time the grand strategist arrived, but a huge crowd still heaved around Panikovsky, blocking the street. Cars yelped impatiently, their noses stuck against the mass of people. Nurses in white uniforms looked out of the windows of the clinic. Dogs were running around, their tails curved like sabers. The fountain in the public garden ceased playing. Bender sighed decisively and elbowed his way into the crowd.

"*Pardon*," he was saying, "*pardon* once again. Excuse me, *madame*, did you drop a ration coupon for jam on the corner? Run, it's still there. Come on, guys, let the experts through. Let me through, you delinquent, can't you hear me!"

Applying the policy of carrots and sticks, Bender finally reached the hounded Panikovsky. By this time, his other ear was also red enough to be used for various photographic operations. Panikovsky caught sight of the captain and hung his head in shame.

"Is that him?" asked Ostap dryly, giving Panikovsky a shove in the back.

"Yes, that's him," confirmed the numerous truth-tellers eagerly. "We saw it with our own eyes."

Ostap appealed for calm, took a notebook out of his pocket, glanced at Panikovsky, and said in a commanding voice:

"Witnesses, your names and addresses, please. Step forward, please!"

One would have thought that the citizens, who had shown such eagerness in catching Panikovsky, would readily offer their damning evidence against the lawbreaker. In reality, however, when the truth-tellers heard the word "witnesses," they lost their spunk, started fussing around, and backed off. Breaks and openings began to form in the crowd. It was falling apart right in front of Bender's eyes.

"So where are the witnesses?" repeated Ostap.

Panic ensued. Working their elbows, the witnesses cut through the crowd, and within a minute, the street was back to normal. Cars sprung forward, the clinic's windows shut, dogs began carefully examining the sidewalk posts, and the water jet rose again from the fountain in the public garden, hissing like a siphon.

After the street cleared and Panikovsky was safely out of danger, the grand strategist grumbled:

"You're a useless old man! A failed madman! Meet yet another blind great—Panikovsky! Homer, Milton, and Panikovsky! What a bunch! And you, Balaganov? A sailor from a shipwreck. 'They're beating Panikovsky, they're beating Panikovsky!' And where were you? All right, let's go to the public garden. I'll make you a scene by the fountain."

At the fountain, Balaganov promptly blamed everything on Panikovsky. The disgraced blind man cited his nerves, frayed by years of hardship, and, while he was at it, blamed everything on Balaganov, a miserable and wretched person, as everyone knows. Here, the brothers started pushing each other again. Already the familiar shouts "And who are you?" were heard, already Panikovsky's orbs released a large tear—a precursor to an all-out fight—when the grand strategist called "Break!" and separated the opponents like a referee in a ring.

"You can box on your days off," he said. "What a match: Balaganov as a bantamweight, Panikovsky as a chickenweight! However, my dear champions, you're about as competent at your jobs as a sieve made of dog tails. It can't continue like this. I'm going to dismiss you, especially considering that your social value is nil."

Forgetting their argument, Panikovsky and Balaganov began to swear up and down that they would go through Koreiko's pockets that night, no matter what. Bender only smirked.

"You'll see," boasted Balaganov. "A street mugging. Under the cover of darkness. Right, Mikhail Samuelevich?"

"I give you my word," echoed Panikovsky. "Shura and I . . . Don't you worry! You're dealing with Panikovsky."

"That's exactly what bothers me," said Bender. "But what the heck. How did you put it? Under the cover of darkness? Fine, under the cover it is. The idea is rather flimsy, of course. The implementation will probably be pitiful, too."

After several hours of surveillance, all the necessary pieces fell into place—namely, the cover of darkness and the patient himself, who left the old puzzle-maker's home in the company of a young woman. The woman was not part of the plan, though. All they could do was follow the couple, who were heading towards the sea.

The burning hunk of the moon hung low above the cooling shore. Black basalt couples sat on the cliffs in eternal embrace. The sea whispered about love until death, unrequited passion, broken hearts, and other trifles like that. A star talked to a star in Morse code, twinkling on and off. The tunnel of light from a searchlight connected the two sides of the bay. When it disappeared, it left a lingering black beam in its place.

"I'm tired," whined Panikovsky, trudging from bluff to bluff behind Koreiko and his lady friend. "I'm old. It's hard for me."

He kept stumbling over gopher holes and falling down, grabbing dried-up cow-pies with his hands. He wanted to go back to the hostel, to homey Kozlevich, with whom it was so nice to have some tea and shoot the breeze.

But the moment Panikovsky firmly decided to go home and suggest that Balaganov finish the task by himself, they heard voices ahead of them:

"It's so warm! You don't swim at night, Alexander Ivanovich? Then wait for me here. I'll just take a dip and will be right back."

Then they heard small stones roll down the cliff, and the white dress disappeared. Koreiko remained alone.

"Hurry up!" whispered Balaganov, pulling Panikovsky's sleeve. "So, I approach from the left, you approach from the right. Move it!"

"I approach from the left," said the cowardly violator of the pact.

"All right, fine, you approach from the left. I bump him from the left, no, from the right, and you bump him from the left."

"Why from the left?"

"Oh, come on! Fine, from the right. He says: 'You punk!' And you respond: 'Who's the punk?'"

"No, you respond first."

"Fine. I'll tell Bender everything. Go, go! So, you're on the left."

And the Lieutenant's valiant sons, shaking with fear, approached Alexander Ivanovich.

The plan fell apart from the very beginning. Instead of approaching the millionaire from the right and pushing him, as called for in the plan, Balaganov hesitated and suddenly blurted out:

"Got a light?"

"I don't smoke," answered Koreiko coldly.

"I see," said Balaganov foolishly, looking back at Panikovsky. "And do you know what time it is?"

"Around twelve."

"Twelve," repeated Balaganov. "Hmm . . . I had no idea."

"A warm evening," said Panikovsky deferentially.

In the ensuing pause, only the raging crickets could be heard. The moon turned pale; its light accentuated the powerful shoulders of Alexander Ivanovich. Panikovsky couldn't bear the tension anymore; he stepped behind Koreiko and screeched:

"Hands up!"

"What?" asked Koreiko, surprised.

"Hands up," repeated Panikovsky meekly.

The next moment he received a sharp and very painful blow to the shoulder and fell on the ground. When he got up, Koreiko was already grappling with Balaganov. They both breathed heavily, as if they were moving a grand piano. Mermaid-like laughter and splashing came from below.

"Why are you hitting me?" bellowed Balaganov. "I just asked you for the time! . . ."

"I'll show you the time!" hissed Koreiko, putting the age-old hatred of a rich man for a thief into his blows.

Panikovsky got closer on all fours and slipped his hands into the Herculean's pockets. Koreiko kicked him, but it was too late. A metal Caucasus cigarette box had already relocated itself from Koreiko's left pocket to Panikovsky's hands. Pieces of paper and various membership cards fell from the other pocket and were strewn about on the ground.

"Run!" cried Panikovsky from the dark.

The last blow landed on Balaganov's back. A few minutes later, the thrashed and agitated Alexander Ivanovich saw two blue, moonlit silhouettes high above his head. They were running up the crest of the hill toward the city.

Zosya, fresh and smelling of sea-salt, found Alexander Ivanovich engaged in an odd pursuit. He was crawling on his knees, lighting matches with trembling fingers, and picking up pieces of paper from the grass. But before Zosya was able to ask what happened, he had already found the receipt for a suitcase that was quietly sitting in the luggage room between a woven basket full of cherries and a baize holdall.

"I dropped it accidentally," he said, smiling anxiously and carefully putting the receipt away.

And only as they were entering the city did he remember the Caucasus cigarette box with the ten thousand that he hadn't transfered to the suitcase.

While the titans struggled on the seashore, Ostap Bender decided that staying in the hotel brought unwanted visibility to the venture they had embarked upon. Having read in the evening paper an ad saying: "FR: exl. rm. all am. s.v. r. bac."—and quickly deciphering it as: "For rent: an excellent room with all the amenities and a sea view, a respectable bachelor only"—Ostap thought to himself: "Looks like I'm a bachelor now. Just recently, the Stargorod city court informed me that my marriage to Citizen Gritsatsueva was dissolved at her request, and that I was to assume my premarital name, O. Bender. Well, I'm going to have to lead a premarital life. I'm a bachelor and I'm respectable, so the room is definitely mine."

And so the grand strategist pulled on his cool white pants and headed to the address listed in the paper.

CHAPTER 13
BASILIUS LOKHANKIN AND HIS ROLE IN THE RUSSIAN REVOLUTION

At precisely 4:40 P.M., Basilius Lokhankin went on a hunger strike.

He was lying on an oilcloth-covered couch, his back to the world, his face to the curved back of the couch. He wore suspenders and green socks—known as *karpetki* in Chernomorsk.

Having spent about twenty minutes of his hunger strike in this position, Lokhankin moaned, rolled over, and looked at his wife. The green *karpetki* traced a small arc in the air. Meanwhile, his wife was throwing her stuff into a colorful travel bag: decorative perfume bottles, a rubber massage bolster, two dresses with tails and an old one without, a tall felt hat decorated with a glass crescent, copper cartridges of lipstick, and a pair of stretch pants.

"Barbara!" called out Lokhankin in a nasal voice.

She remained silent, breathing heavily.

"Barbara!" he repeated. "Are you really leaving me for Ptiburdukov?"

"Yes," she answered. "I'm leaving. That's how it should be."

"But why, why?" asked Lokhankin with bovine passion.

His nostrils, already large, flared in despair. His pharaonic beard quivered.

"Because I love him."

"But what about me?"

"Basilius! I already made it known to you yesterday that I don't love you anymore."

"But I do! I love you, Barbara!"

"That's your problem, Basilius. I'm leaving you for Ptiburdukov. That's how it should be."

"No!" exclaimed Lokhankin. "That's not how it should be! A person cannot leave if the other person loves her!"

"Yes, she can," said Barbara testily, looking at herself in a pocket mirror. "Stop acting silly, Basilius."

"In that case, I'm still on a hunger strike!" cried the heartbroken husband. "I will starve until you come back to me. A day. A week. I'll starve for a year!"

Lokhankin rolled over again and stuck his beefy nose into the cold slippery oilcloth.

"I'll lie like this, in my suspenders, until I die," came from the couch. "And it'll be your fault, yours and that engineer Ptiburdukov's."

His wife thought for a moment, pulled a fallen strap back onto her dough-white shoulder, and suddenly burst out:

"You can't talk about Ptiburdukov like that! He's better than you!"

This was too much for Lokhankin. He jerked as if an electric charge went through his entire body, from his suspenders to the green *karpetki*.

"You're a floozy, Barbara," he whined. "You're a tramp!"

"Basilius, you're a fool!" his wife retorted calmly.

"You she-wolf you," continued the whiny Lokhankin. "I truly do despise you. You leave me for your lover, do you not? You leave me for Ptiburdukov. You, ghastly you, you leave me now, forever, for that contemptible Ptiburdukov. So that's for whom you're leaving me forever! You want to give yourself to him in lust. An old she-wolf you are, yes, old and ghastly too!"

Wallowing in his grief, Lokhankin didn't even notice that he was speaking in iambic pentameter, even though he never wrote any poetry and didn't like to read it.

"Basilius! Stop being such a clown," said the she-wolf, closing her bag. "Just look at yourself. You should wash. I'm leaving. Goodbye, Basilius! I put your ration card for bread on the table."

With that, Barbara picked up her bag and headed for the door. Seeing that his incantations didn't work, Lokhankin quickly jumped off the couch, ran to the table, cried "Help!" and tore the card to pieces. Barbara was frightened. She pictured her husband emaciated from starvation, with a barely discernible pulse and cold extremities.

"What have you done?" she said. "Don't you dare starve yourself!"

"I will!" declared Lokhankin stubbornly.

"It's stupid, Basilius. It's the revolt of individuality."

"And that's what makes me proud," retorted Lokhankin somewhat iambically. "You're underestimating the importance of individuality and of the intelligentsia as a whole."

"But society will condemn you."

"So be it," replied Basilius resolutely, falling back on the couch.

Barbara said nothing, threw her bag on the floor, hastily tore a straw bonnet from her head and, muttering "crazed pig," "tyrant," "slave-master," quickly made a chopped eggplant sandwich.

"Eat!" she said, bringing the food to her husband's scarlet lips. "You hear me, Lokhankin? Eat up! Now!"

"Leave me alone," he said, pushing his wife's hand away.

Taking advantage of the fact that the hunger striker's mouth was open for a moment, Barbara deftly tucked the sandwich into the gap that appeared between the pharaonic beard and the trim Moscow-style mustache. But the striker forced the food out with a strong push from his tongue.

"Eat, you bastard!" Barbara yelled in desperation, trying to reinsert the sandwich. "Intellectual!"

But Lokhankin turned his face away and bellowed in protest. After a few minutes, Barbara, flushed and covered in green eggplant paste, gave up. She sat down on her bag and burst into icy tears.

Lokhankin brushed the crumbs off his beard, threw his wife a cautious, evasive glance, and quieted down on his couch. He really didn't want to part with Barbara. Despite numerous shortcomings, Barbara had two very important merits: a large white bosom and a steady job. Basilius had never had a job. A job would have interfered with his reflections on the role of the Russian intelligentsia, the social group of which he considered himself a member. As a result, Lokhankin's prolonged ruminations boiled down to pleasant and familiar themes: "Basilius Lokhankin and His Significance," "Lokhankin and the Tragedy of Russian Liberalism," "Lokhankin and His Role in the Russian Revolution." It was easy and comforting to think about all of that while walking around the room in little felt boots (bought with Barbara's money) and glancing at his favorite bookcase, where the spines of the *Brockhaus Encyclopedia* glimmered with ecclesiastical gold. Basilius spent hours standing in front of the bookcase and moving his eyes from spine to spine. Splendid examples of the art of bookbinding were neatly arranged on the shelves: *The Great Medical*

Encyclopedia, The Animals of the World, the massive *Man and Woman,* and *The Earth and Its Inhabitants* by Elisée Reclus.

"Proximity to these treasures of human reflection is purifying, somehow makes you grow spiritually," thought Basilius unhurriedly. Arriving at this conclusion, he would sigh happily, pull out an 1899 copy of *Motherland,* an illustrated magazine, its binding the color of frothy, foamy sea water, that sat under the bookcase, and look at the pictures from the Boer War, an ad by an unknown lady entitled "How I Enlarged My Bust By Six Inches," and other curious miscellany.

If Barbara were to leave, she'd take with her the financial foundation on which the well-being of this most deserving member of the intellectual class has been resting.

In the evening, Ptiburdukov arrived. For a long time, he couldn't bring himself to enter the Lokhankins' rooms, and he loitered in the kitchen, amid the blazing Primus stoves and the crisscrossing lines for laundry, which was hard as plaster and stained by bluing. The apartment came to life. Doors were banging, shadows were darting, the tenants' eyes were shining, and somebody sighed passionately: a man had arrived.

Ptiburdukov took off his cap, tugged on his engineer's mustache, and finally steeled himself.

"Barb," he said pleadingly, entering the room, "didn't we agree . . ."

"Look at this, Sasha!" cried Barbara, grabbing his hand and pushing him towards the couch. "There he is! On the couch! The pig! The dirty slave-master! See, this tyrant went on a hunger strike because I want to leave him."

Catching sight of Ptiburdukov, the striker promptly unleashed his iambic pentameter.

"Ptiburdukov, I truly do despise you," he whined. "And don't you dare touch my dear wife. You are a lout, Ptiburdukov, a bastard! Whither are you now taking her?"

"Comrade Lokhankin," said the dumbfounded Ptiburdukov, grabbing his mustache again.

"Go, go away, I truly do abhor you," continued Basilius, rocking like an old Jew at prayer, "you are a lout, sad and ghastly too. An engineer you're not—you are a scoundrel, a lowly creep, a pimp, and bastard too!"

"You should be ashamed of yourself, Basilius Andreevich," said Ptiburdukov, who was getting tired of all this. "It's foolish, plain and simple. Look what you're doing! In the second year of the Five-Year Plan . . ."

"He dares tell me that I'm acting foolish! He, he, the one who stole my wife away! Go now, Ptiburdukov, or else a thrashing, that is, a beating, I will give to thee!"

"A sick man," said Ptiburdukov, trying to stay within the confines of decency.

For Barbara, however, these confines were too tight. She grabbed the dried-up green sandwich from the table and approached the hunger striker again. Lokhankin defended himself desperately, as if he was about to be castrated. Ptiburdukov turned away and looked through the window at the horse chestnut that was blooming with white candles. Behind him he heard Lokhankin's disgusting bellowing and Barbara's cries: "Eat, you nasty man! Eat, you slave-master!"

The next day, Barbara didn't go to work because she was too upset about this unexpected obstacle. The hunger striker turned for the worse.

"I already have stomach cramps," he reported with satisfaction, "then comes scurvy due to malnutrition, the hair and teeth start falling out."

Ptiburdukov brought in his brother, an army doctor. Ptiburdukov the second held his ear to Lokhankin's torso for a long time and listened to the functioning of his organs with the concentration of a cat listening to a mouse that had snuck into a sugar bowl. During the examination, Basilius stared at his naked chest, shaggy like a woolen overcoat, his eyes full of tears. He felt very sorry for himself. Ptiburdukov the second looked at Ptiburdukov the first and reported that the patient had no need to follow a diet. He could eat everything: for example, soup, meat patties, fruit drinks. Bread, vegetables, and fresh fruit were also allowed. Fish was permitted. Smoking was fine—within reason, of course. Drinking was not recommended, but in order to boost the appetite, it might be a good idea to introduce a small glass of nice port into his system. In other words, the doctor hadn't quite grasped the Lokhankins' drama. Puffing self-importantly and stomping with his boots, he departed, his final piece of advice being that the patient could also swim in the sea and ride a bicycle.

But the patient had no intention of introducing any fruit, fish, meat, or other delicacies into his system. He didn't want to go to the beach for a swim. Instead, he continued to lie on the couch and shower those around him with spiteful pentameters. Barbara started feeling sorry for him. "He's starving because of me," she thought proudly, "what remarkable passion. Is Sasha capable of such powerful feelings?" And she kept glancing anxiously at the well-fed Sasha, who looked like no romantic drama would stop him from introducing lunches and dinners into his system on a regular basis. Once, when Ptiburdukov stepped out, she even called Basilius "poor dear." With that, a sandwich once again appeared at the hunger striker's lips, and was once again rejected. "A little more endurance," he thought to himself, "and Ptiburdukov can kiss my Barbara goodbye."

He listened to the voices from the other room with satisfaction.

"He'll die without me," Barbara was saying. "We're going to have to wait. Don't you see that I can't leave him right now?"

That night, Barbara had a bad dream. Basilius, emaciated by his powerful feelings, gnawed on the silver-colored spurs that the army doctor wore on his boots. It was terrifying. The doctor's face expressed the same resignation as a cow who was being milked by the village thief. The spurs banged, the teeth chattered. Barbara woke up in horror.

A yellow Japanese sun was shining directly into the room, wasting all its power on illuminating such trifles as the cut-glass stopper from a Turandot toilet water bottle. The oilcloth-covered couch was empty. Barbara moved her eyes and saw Basilius. He was standing in front of the open cupboard with his back to the bed and making loud chomping noises. Greedy and impatient, he was leaning forward, tapping his foot clad in a green sock and making whistling and squelching sounds with his nose. He emptied a tall tin can, carefully took the lid off a pot, dipped his fingers into the cold borscht, and extracted a chunk of meat. Basilius would have been in deep trouble even if Barbara had caught him doing this during the best times of their marriage. His fate was sealed.

"Lokhankin!" she called out in a terrifying voice.

The startled hunger striker let go of the meat, which fell back into the pot, producing a small fountain of shredded cabbage and carrot medallions. Basilius leaped back onto the couch with a wounded howl. Barbara was dressing quickly and quietly.

"Barbara!" he whined. "Are you really leaving me for Ptiburdukov?"

There was no answer.

"You she-wolf you," declared Lokhankin uncertainly, "I truly do despise you. You're leaving me for that Ptiburdukov . . ."

But it was too late. Lokhankin whined about love and about dying of hunger all in vain. Barbara left him for good, dragging her travel bag with the colorful stretch pants, felt hat, decorative perfume bottles, and other objects of female necessity.

And so a period of agonizing reflection and moral suffering began for Basilius Andreevich. There are people who don't know how to suffer, it just doesn't work for them somehow. And if they do suffer, they try to get through it as fast as they can, without calling attention to themselves. Lokhankin, on the other hand, suffered openly and grandly. He gulped his misery in large draughts, he wallowed in it. His cosmic grief offered him yet another chance to reflect on the role of the Russian intelligentsia, as well as on the tragedy of Russian liberalism.

"Maybe this had to be," he thought, "maybe this is the redemption, and I will emerge from it purified. Isn't this the fate of every refined person who dared to stand above the crowd? Galileo, Milyukov, A. F. Koni. Yes, Barbara was right, this had to be!"

His depression, however, didn't stop him from placing an ad in the paper offering his second room for rent.

"That will give me some material support for the time being," decided Basilius. And then he again immersed himself in vague theorizing about the suffering of the flesh and the significance of the soul as the source of goodness.

Nothing could distract him from these thoughts, not even his neighbors' persistent requests that he turn the lights off after he used the bathroom. In his discombobulated state, Lokhankin kept forgetting, which irritated the frugal tenants to no end.

It should be noted that the tenants of communal apartment No. 3, where Lokhankin resided, had a reputation for being ornery, and were famous throughout the building for their frequent squabbles and fierce feuds. The apartment was even dubbed the Rookery. Long communal coexistence had hardened these people, and they knew no fear. Equilibrium was maintained by competing coalitions of tenants. At times, all the residents of the Rookery banded together against one of their number, which spelled big trouble for that person. The centripetal force of litigiousness would pick him up, suck him into legal offices, carry him through smoked-filled courthouse hallways, and push him into countless courtrooms. The defiant tenant would be adrift for years, searching for truth all the way to the office of the country's president, Comrade Kalinin himself. For the rest of his life, the tenant would speak the legalese that he had picked up in various government offices, saying "penalize" instead of "punish" and "perpetrated" instead of "did." He would refer to himself not as Comrade Zhukov, which had been his name since birth, but as "the injured party." But most often and with particular glee, he'd utter the phrase "to launch legal action." His life, which hadn't been all milk and honey to begin with, would become downright miserable.

Long before the Lokhankin family drama erupted, the pilot Sevry-ugov, who had the misfortune of residing in apartment No. 3, had been urgently dispatched by the Society for Defense and Aviation to fly beyond the Arctic Circle. The whole world was anxiously following Sevryugov's progress. A foreign expedition that had been headed for the North Pole had disappeared, and Sevryugov was supposed to find it. The world's hopes rested upon the success of his mission. Radio stations from every continent talked to each other, meteorologists warned the brave Sevry-ugov about geomagnetic storms, ham radio operators filled the airwaves with noise, and all the while the newspaper *Kurier Poranny*, which was close to the Polish Foreign Ministry, was already demanding the restoration of Poland's 1772 borders. Sevryugov had been flying over the icy desert for a month, and the roar of his engines was heard around the world.

Finally, Sevryugov did something that totally confused the newspaper which was close to the Polish foreign ministry. He found the expedition lost in the ice ridges, radioed their exact location, and then disappeared himself. The world exploded in a frenzy. Sevryugov's name was uttered in 320 different languages and dialects, including the language of the Black-foot. Pictures of Sevryugov, clad in animal skins, were printed on every available sheet of paper. Meeting with the press, Gabriele d'Annunzio announced that he had just finished his new novel and was immedi-ately embarking on a search for the brave Russian. A charleston named *I'm Warm at the Pole with My Baby* was released. The old Moscow hacks Usyshkin-Werther, Leonid Trepetovsky, and Boris Ammiakov, who had been engaged in literary dumping for years, and periodically flooded the market with their production at throwaway prices, were already working on an article entitled "Aren't You Cold?" In other words, the planet was living out a great sensation.

All this caused an even greater sensation in apartment No. 3 at 8 Lemon Lane, better known as the Rookery.

"Our tenant is missing," cheerfully reported the retired janitor Nikita Pryakhin, who was drying a felt boot over a Primus stove. "He's missing, that boy. Well, who forced him to fly? A man should walk, not fly. Yes, walk, that's right."

And he repositioned the boot over the whooshing fire.

"That's what you get for flying, goggle-face," muttered an old grand-ma whose name nobody knew. She lived in the loft over the kitchen, and although the entire apartment had electricity, the grandma used a kerosene lamp with a reflector in her loft. She didn't believe in electricity. "Now we've got a spare room, some spare footage!"

The grandma was the first to name what had long been burdening the hearts of everyone in the Rookery. Everybody started talking about the missing pilot's room, among them: a former Prince from the Caucasus mountains, lately a proletarian from the East, Citizen Hygienishvili; Dunya, a woman who was renting a bed in Auntie Pasha's room; Auntie Pasha herself, a street vendor and a hopeless boozer; Alexander Dmitrievich Sukhoveiko, once Chamberlain at His Imperial Majesty's Court, known to his neighbors simply as Mitrich; and other minor apartment characters, all headed by the chief leaseholder, Lucia Franzevna Pferd.

"Well," said Mitrich, straightening his gold-rimmed glasses as the kitchen filled up with tenants, "since the comrade is missing, we have to divvy it up. I, for example, have long been entitled to some extra footage."

"Why should a man get the footage?" countered Dunya the bed renter. "Shouldn't it be a woman? This might be the only time in my life that a man suddenly goes missing."

She continued lingering in the crowd for a long time, offering various arguments in her own favor and frequently repeating the word "man."

The one thing all the tenants agreed upon was that the room had to be taken immediately.

That same day, the world was shaken by yet another sensation. The brave Sevryugov was no longer missing. Nizhny Novgorod, Quebec City, and Reykjavik had heard his radio signals. He was stranded at the eighty-fourth parallel with damaged landing gear. The airwaves teemed with reports: "The brave Russian is in excellent condition," "Sevryugov sends a message to the Society for Defense and Aviation," "Charles Lindbergh calls Sevryugov the world's top pilot," "Seven icebreakers are on their way to rescue Sevryugov and the expedition he found." Apart from these reports, the newspapers printed nothing but photos of some icy shores and banks. The following words were constantly repeated: "Sevryugov," "North Cape," "parallel," "Sevryugov," "Franz Joseph Land," "Spitsbergen," "King's Bay," "sealskin boots," "fuel," "Sevryugov."

The gloom that this news brought to the Rookery was soon replaced by quiet confidence. The icebreakers were moving slowly, the ice fields were hard to crack.

"Let's take the room—and that's that," said Nikita Pryakhin. "He's sitting pretty on that ice over there, while Dunya here, for example, has all the rights. Especially since, by law, a tenant cannot be absent for more than two months."

"You should be ashamed of yourself, Citizen Pryakhin!" argued Barbara—still Mrs. Lokhankin at the time—waving a copy of *Izvestiya*. "He's a hero! He's on the eighty-fourth parallel now!"

"Whatever that parallel is," Mitrich responded vaguely. "Maybe it doesn't even exist, that parallel. We don't know that. We didn't attend classical gymnasiums."

Mitrich was telling the truth. He hadn't attended a gymnasium. He had graduated from His Majesty's Corps of Pages.

"Look here," argued Barbara, putting the newspaper right in front of the Chamberlain's nose. "Here's the article. See? *Amid ice ridges and icebergs.*"

"Icebergs!" sneered Mitrich. "Yes, we can understand that. Ten long years of nothing but tears. Icebergs, Weisbergs, Eisenbergs, all those Rabinovitzes. Pryakhin is right. Let's just take it, end of story. Especially since Lucia Franzevna here agrees about the law."

"And his stuff can go into the stairwell, to hell with it!" exclaimed the former Prince, lately a proletarian from the East, Citizen Hygienishvili, in his throaty voice.

Barbara got a good pecking and ran to her husband to complain.

"But maybe that's how it should be," replied the husband, raising his pharaonic beard, "maybe the Great Russian Homespun Truth speaks through the simple peasant Mitrich. Just think of the role of the Russian intelligentsia and its significance."

On that extraordinary day when the icebreakers finally reached Sevryugov's tent, Citizen Hygienishvili broke the lock on Sevryugov's door and threw all of the hero's belongings out into the hallway, including a red propeller that was hanging on the wall. The room was taken by Dunya, who immediately brought in six paying bed renters. The conquered territory was the site of a night-long feast. Nikita Pryakhin played the concertina, and Chamberlain Mitrich did Russian folk dances with a drunken Auntie Pasha.

If Sevryugov had been slightly less famous, if his incredible flights over the Arctic hadn't given him international celebrity, he would never have seen his room again. He would have been sucked in by the centripetal force of litigiousness, and for the rest of his life he would have referred to himself not as "the brave Sevryugov," not as "the hero of the ice," but as "the injured party." But this time the Rookery was hit back hard. The room was returned (although Sevryugov soon moved to a new build-ing), while the daring Hygienishvili spent four months in jail for acting without proper authority; he came back mad as hell.

He was the one who first pointed out the need to turn off the bath-room lights regularly to the orphaned Lokhankin. As he spoke, his eyes looked decidedly devilish. The absentminded Lokhankin failed to appre-ciate the importance of this démarche by Citizen Hygienishvili and thus completely missed the beginnings of the conflict that was soon to lead to a horrifying event, unheard of even in the history of communal living.

Here's how it all happened. Basilius Andreevich continued to leave the lights on in the shared facilities. How could he possibly remember such a trivial thing when his wife had left him, when he found himself penni-less, when the multifaceted significance of the Russian intelligentsia was not yet entirely understood? Could he even imagine that the lousy, dim light from an eight-watt bulb would inspire such powerful feelings in his neighbors? At first they warned him several times each day. Then they sent him a letter, which had been composed by Mitrich and signed by all the other tenants. In the end, they stopped issuing warnings and sending letters. Lokhankin still didn't appreciate the gravity of the situation, but he had developed a vague premonition that some kind of circle was about to close around him.

On Tuesday evening, one of Auntie Pasha's girls came running in and reported in a single breath:

"They're telling you one last time to turn it off."

But it somehow happened that Basilius Andreevich got distracted again, and the bulb continued to shine nefariously through the cobwebs and dirt. The apartment gave a sigh. A minute later, Citizen Hygienishvili appeared at Lokhankin's door. He was wearing light-blue canvas boots and a flat brown sheepskin hat.

"Come," he said, beckoning Basilius with his finger.

Holding his hand tightly, Citizen Hygienishvili led Lokhankin down the dark hallway, where Basilius got antsy and even started kicking a bit. The former Prince pushed him into the middle of the kitchen with a blow to his back. Grabbing onto the laundry lines, Lokhankin managed to stay on his feet and looked around fearfully. The whole apartment was present. Lucia Franzevna Pferd stood there in silence. Creases of purple ink ran across the imperious face of the leaseholder-in-chief. Next to her, a boozed-up Auntie Pasha slumped forlornly on the stove. Barefoot Nikita Pryakhin was looking at the frightened Lokhankin with a smirk.

The head of nobody's grandma dangled from the loft. Dunya was gesturing at Mitrich. The former Chamberlain of the Imperial Court was smiling and hiding something behind his back.

"What? Are we having a meeting?" asked Basilius Andreevich in a high-pitched voice.

"Just wait," said Nikita Pryakhin, moving closer to Lokhankin, "you'll have everything. Champagne, caviar, everything . . . Lie down!" he yelled suddenly, breathing either vodka or turpentine on Basilius.

"What do you mean, lie down?" asked Basilius Andreevich, beginning to tremble.

"There's no point in talking to this bad man!" said Citizen Hygienishvili. He squatted and started feeling around Lokhankin's waist to unbutton his suspenders.

"Help me!" whispered Basilius, fixing a crazed stare on Lucia Franzevna.

"You should have been turning the lights off!" replied Citizen Pferd sternly.

"We're no moneybags here, we can't afford to waste electricity like that," added Chamberlain Mitrich, dipping something into a bucket of water.

"Its not my fault!" squeaked Lokhankin, trying to free himself from the former Prince, lately a proletarian from the East.

"It's nobody's fault," muttered Nikita Pryakhin, restraining the quivering tenant.

"I didn't do anything!"

"Nobody did anything."

"I'm depressed."

"Everybody's depressed."

"You can't touch me. I'm anemic."

"Everybody's anemic."

"My wife left me!" cried Basilius.

"Everybody's wife left," replied Nikita Pryakhin.

"Get going, Nikita!" interrupted Chamberlain Mitrich, bringing some shining wet birches into the light. "Talking won't get us anywhere."

Basilius Andreevich was placed face down on the floor. His legs glowed like milk in the light. Hygienishvili swung his arm as far back as he could, and the birch made a high-pitched sound as it cut through the air.

"Mama!" screamed Basilius.

"Everybody has a mama!" said Nikita didactically, holding Lokhankin down with his knee.

And suddenly Basilius fell silent.

"Maybe that's how it should be," he thought, flinching from the blows and looking at Nikita's dark, armored toenails. "Maybe this is all about atonement, cleansing, a great sacrifice . . ."

And so while he was being flogged—while Dunya giggled sheepishly and the grandma cheered from her loft: "Give it to him, just give it to him!"—Basilius Andreevich thought hard about the significance of the Russian intelligentsia, and that Galileo had also suffered in the name of truth.

Mitrich was the last to take up the switch.

"Well, let me try now," he said, raising an arm. "A few good switches to his rear end."

But Lokhankin never got the chance to taste the Chamberlain's switches. There was a knock on the back door. Dunya rushed to open it. (The front door of the Rookery had been nailed shut a long time ago because the tenants couldn't decide who would wash the stairs first. The room with the bathtub was also permanently locked for the same reason.)

"Basilius Andreevich, some strange man is asking for you," said Dunya, as if nothing had happened.

And indeed, everyone saw a strange man in white gentleman's pants standing in the doorway. Basilius Andreevich jumped up from the floor, adjusted his wardrobe, and, with an unnecessary smile on his face, turned toward Bender, who had just come in.

"I'm not interrupting anything?" inquired the grand strategist courteously, squinting.

"Well," murmured Lokhankin, bowing slightly, "you see, I was, how should I put it, somewhat busy . . . But . . . it looks like I'm free now?"

And he looked around inquiringly. But there was nobody left in the kitchen except for Auntie Pasha, who had fallen asleep on the stove while the punishment was being meted out. Only a few twigs and a white canvas button with two holes were left on the wooden floor.

"Why don't you come in," invited Basilius.

"But maybe I interrupted something after all?" asked Ostap, entering Lokhankin's first room. "No? All right, fine. So tell me, is that your ad: "FR: exl. rm. all am. s.v. r.bac.?" Is it really "exl." with "all am.?"

"Absolutely," said Lokhankin, brightening up. "An excellent room, all amenities. And I'm not asking much. Fifty rubles a month."

"I'm not going to haggle," said Ostap politely, "but the neighbors . . . what about them?"

"Wonderful people," replied Basilius, "not to mention all amenities. And it's inexpensive."

"But it looks like they resort to corporal punishment here?"

"Oh," said Lokhankin with affectation, "after all, who knows? Maybe that's how it should be. Maybe that's what the Great Russian Homespun Truth is all about."

"Homespun?" repeated Ostap pensively. "Also known as homegrown, homebred, and home-brewed? I see. So tell me, which grade of the gymnasium did you flunk out of? Sixth?"

"Fifth," replied Lokhankin.

"Ah, that golden grade. So you never made it as far as physics? And you've been leading a strictly intellectual life ever since, haven't you? Then again, what do I care. It's your life. I'm moving in tomorrow."

"What about the deposit?" asked the ex-student.

"You're not in church, nobody's going to fleece you," said the grand strategist weightily. "You'll get your deposit. In due course."

CHAPTER 14
THE FIRST DATE

Returning to the Carlsbad Hotel, Ostap walked past countless reflections of himself in the mirrors that lined the entryway, stairwell, and hallway (that are so popular in establishments of this sort), and went to his room. He was surprised to find everything upside down. The plush red chair was lying on its back, exposing its short legs and unattractive jute underbelly. The braided velvet tablecloth had slid off the table. Even *The Appearance of Christ to the People* was tilted to one side and lost most of the didacticism intended by the artist. Fresh sea breezes blew from the balcony, rustling the bills that were scattered across the bed. Amid the bills lay the metal Caucasus cigarette box. Panikovsky and Balaganov, were silently grappling on the carpet, kicking the air with their legs.

Disgusted, the grand strategist stepped over the combatants and went out to the balcony. On the boulevard below, people chatted, gravel crunched under their feet, and the harmonious breath of a symphony orchestra soared above the black maples. In the dark depths of the port, a refrigerator ship that was under construction flaunted its lights and banged its steel parts. Beyond the breakwater, an invisible steamer bellowed insistently, probably asking to be let into the harbor.

Stepping back into the room, Ostap found the half-brothers already sitting on the floor face to face, pushing each other wearily with their hands, and mumbling: "And who are you?"

"Couldn't you share?" asked Bender, closing the curtain.

Panikovsky and Balaganov quickly jumped to their feet and launched into their story. Each claimed the success of the entire mission for himself and denigrated the role of the other. Each skipped the facts that were not particularly flattering to himself, invoking instead the many details that shed a positive light on his own mettle and skill.

"That's enough!" said Ostap. "Don't bang your skull on the hardwood. I get the picture. So you're saying he had a girl with him? That's good. Well, let's see: a lowly clerk happens to have in his pocket . . . looks like you've already counted? How much? Wow! Ten thousand! Mr. Koreiko's wages for twenty years of dedicated service. A sight for the gods, as the most astute of the editorialists would have it. But it looks like I interrupted something? Weren't you doing something on the floor here? You were dividing up the money? Please, please continue, I'll watch."

"I wanted it to be honest and fair," said Balaganov, collecting the money from the bed. "Everybody gets an equal share—twenty-five hundred."

He put the money into four piles and modestly stepped aside, saying: "You, me, him, and Kozlevich."

"Very good," said Ostap. "Now let Panikovsky do it. Looks like he has a dissenting opinion on the subject."

The author of the dissenting opinion dove into the task with gusto. Leaning over the bed, Panikovsky moved his fat lips, wetted his fingers, and endlessly shuffled the bills, as if he was playing a game of solitaire. All these complex maneuvers produced three piles on the blanket: a large one, composed of clean new bills, another large one, but with less pristine bills, and a third one, with small and dirty bills.

"You and I get four thousand each," said Panikovsky to Bender, "and Balaganov gets two. Even that's too much for what he did."

"And what about Kozlevich?" asked Balaganov, angrily closing his eyes.

"Why should Kozlevich get anything?" shrieked Panikovsky. "That's highway robbery! Who's this Kozlevich and why should we share with him? I don't know any Kozlevich!"

"Are you finished?" asked the grand strategist.

"Yes, finished," answered Panikovsky, his eyes fixed on the pile of clean bills. "How can you talk about Kozlevich at a moment like this?"

"And now it's my turn," said Ostap firmly.

He slowly put all the piles back together, placed the money in the metal box, and stuck the box in the pocket of his white pants.

"All this money," he announced, "will immediately be returned to the victim, Citizen Koreiko. How do you like that?"

"I don't," blurted out Panikovsky.

"Don't joke around, Bender," said Balaganov testily. "We have to split it fair and square."

"Not going to happen," said Ostap coldly. "I wouldn't joke around at this late hour."

Panikovsky clasped his purplish old-man's hands. He glanced at the grand strategist with horror in his eyes, stepped back into a corner, and said nothing. Only his gold tooth gleamed occasionally in the dark.

Balaganov's face turned shiny, as if it had been burned by the sun.

"So all this work was for nothing?" he asked, puffing. "That's not right. That's . . . please explain."

"To you, the Lieutenant's favorite son," said Ostap politely, "I can only repeat what I already told you in Arbatov. I revere the Criminal Code. I'm not a bandit, I'm a highly principled pursuer of monetary instruments. Mugging is not on my list of four hundred honest methods of taking money, it just doesn't fit. On top of that, we didn't come here for a mere ten thousand. I myself need at least five hundred of those thousands."

"Then why did you send us?" asked Balaganov, cooling off. "We tried really hard . . ."

"In other words, you mean to ask if the esteemed captain knows why he undertook this latest action? The answer is: Yes, I do. You see . . ."

At this moment, the gold tooth stopped gleaming in the corner. Panikovsky turned, lowered his head, and, screaming "And who are you?" rushed Ostap in a rage. Without changing his position, or even turning his head, the grand strategist hit the deranged violator of the pact with his rubber fist, sending him back to his original position. He then continued:

"You see, Shura, this was a test. A clerk who makes forty rubles a month has ten thousand in his pocket, which is a bit unusual. It improves our chances, or, as racing fans would say, it gives us good odds for scoring big. Five hundred thousand is definitely a big score. And here's how we're going to get it. I will return the ten thousand to Koreiko, and he'll take it. I have yet to see a man who wouldn't take his money back. And that'll be the end of him. His greed will be his undoing. The moment he confesses to his riches, I'll get him with my bare hands. As a smart man, he'll understand that a portion is less than the whole, and he'll give me that portion for fear of losing everything. And then, Shura, a certain platter with a rim will appear on the scene . . ."

"That's right!" exclaimed Balaganov.

Panikovsky was weeping in the corner.

"Give me back my money," he moaned, "I have nothing! I haven't had a bath in a year. I'm old. Girls don't love me."

"Contact the World League for Sexual Reform," said Ostap. "Maybe they'll be able to help you."

"Nobody loves me," continued Panikovsky, shuddering.

"And why should anybody love you? Girls don't love people like you. They love the young, the long-legged, the politically up-to-date. And you will soon die. And nobody will write about you in the paper: "Yet another one worked himself to death." There will be no beautiful widow with Persian eyes sitting at your grave. And teary-eyed kids won't be asking: "Papa, papa, can you hear us?"

"Don't say that!" cried out the frightened Panikovsky. "I'll outlive you all. You don't know Panikovsky yet. Panikovsky will buy and sell you all, you'll see. Give me back my money."

"Just tell me, will you continue to serve or not? I'm asking you for the last time."

"I will," answered Panikovsky, wiping away his sluggish, old-man's tears.

Night, dark, deep night, shrouded the whole country.

In the port of Chernomorsk, cranes swung back and forth rapidly, lowering their steel cables into the deep holds of foreign ships, and then they swung back again, carefully lowering, with cat-like caution, pine-wood crates filled with equipment for the tractor factory onto the dock. Pink comet-like flames burst out of the tall smokestacks of cement plants. The star clusters of the Dnieper hydroelectric site, Magnitogorsk, and Stalingrad were ablaze. The star of the Red Putilov rose over the north, followed by a multitude of the brightest stars. These were factories and plants, power stations and construction sites. The entire Five-Year Plan was aglow, eclipsing the old sky that even the ancient Egyptians knew all too well.

A young man who stayed at the workers' club late into the night with his girl would hastily turn on the electric map of the Five-Year Plan and whisper:

"Look at this little red light. That's where the Siberian Combine Factory is going to be. We can go there together. Do you want to?"

And the girl would quietly laugh and pull her hands away.

Night, dark, deep night, as mentioned before, shrouded the whole country. The monarchist Khvorobyov groaned in his sleep because he saw a giant union card in his dream. Engineer Talmudovsky snored on the upper bunk on the train headed from Kharkov to Rostov, lured by a higher salary. The two American gentlemen rolled on the broad Atlantic waves, carrying the recipe for a delicious wheat moonshine home. Basilius Lokhankin was tossing on his couch and stroking his injured parts. The old puzzle-maker Sinitsky was wasting electricity, working on a picture puzzle entitled "Find the chairman of the pumping station general staff meeting, convened to elect local union officials," which he intended for *The Plumbing Journal.* He was trying to be quiet, so as not to wake Zosya. Polykhaev lay in bed with Impala Mikhailovna. Other Herculeans slept nervously in various parts of the city. Alexander Ivanovich Koreiko, worried about his riches, couldn't sleep. If he had nothing, he'd be sleeping well. We already know what Bender, Balaganov, and Panikovsky were doing. Only Kozlevich, the owner-driver of the Antelope, will not be mentioned here, even though he had already got himself into trouble of a very sensitive nature.

Early in the morning, Bender opened his doctor's bag, took out the policeman's cap with the crest of the city of Kiev, stuck it in his pocket, and went to see Alexander Ivanovich Koreiko. On his way, he pestered the milk delivery women—as the hour of these resourceful ladies had already begun, while the hour of the office dwellers hadn't yet—and murmured the lyrics of the love song: "But now the joys of our first date no longer move me like before." The grand strategist wasn't being entirely honest; his first date with the millionaire clerk excited him. Entering No. 16 Lesser Tangential Street, he stuck his official cap on his head, frowned, and knocked on the door.

Alexander Ivanovich stood in the middle of the room. He was wearing a sleeveless fishnet undershirt and had already slipped into his lowly clerk pants. The room was furnished with exemplary austerity, which in tsarist times was typical of orphanages and other such institutions that were under the patronage of Empress Maria Fyodorovna. There were just three pieces: a small metal field-hospital bed, a kitchen cabinet with doors that were held shut by wooden latches that one normally sees on country outhouses, and a beat-up Vienna chair. There were a few dumbbells in the corner, along with two large kettle-bell weights, the joy of a weightlifter.

Seeing a policeman, Alexander Ivanovich took a heavy step forward.

"Citizen Koreiko?" asked Ostap, smiling radiantly.

"That's me," answered Alexander Ivanovich, also expressing his joy at seeing a representative of law and order.

"Alexander Ivanovich?" inquired Ostap, smiling even more radiantly.

"Precisely," confirmed Koreiko, turning up the heat of his joy as high as he could.

After that, the only thing left to the grand strategist was to sit down on the Vienna chair and generate a supernatural smile. Having accomplished this, he looked at Alexander Ivanovich. But the millionaire clerk made a huge effort and projected God knows what on his face: adoration, delight, happiness, and quiet admiration all at once. All on account of his happy encounter with a representative of law and order.

This escalation of smiles and emotions was reminiscent of a manuscript by the composer Franz Liszt, where a note on the first page said to play "fast"; on the second page—"very fast"; on the third—"much faster"; on the fourth—"as fast as possible"; and on the fifth—"still faster."

Seeing that Koreiko was already on page five, and that any further competition was simply impossible, Ostap got down to business.

"Actually, I have something for you," he said, turning serious.

"Please, be my guest," replied Alexander Ivanovich, also clouding over.

"We've got good news for you."

"I'd love to hear it."

Sad beyond measure, Ostap delved into his pocket. Koreiko watched him with an altogether funereal expression. A metal Caucasus cigarette box emerged. However, there was no exclamation of surprise, as Ostap had expected. The underground millionaire stared at the box blankly. Ostap took out the money, carefully counted it, pushed the pile towards Alexander Ivanovich, and said:

"Ten thousand, even. Kindly make out a receipt for me."

"This is a mistake, Comrade," said Koreiko very quietly. "What ten thousand? What receipt?"

"What do you mean? Weren't you robbed yesterday?"

"No."

"What do you mean—no?" Ostap grew animated. "Yesterday, by the sea. And they took the ten thousand. The robbers were apprehended. Just make out the receipt."

"I swear, nobody robbed me," said Koreiko, and something flickered momentarily on his face. "This is clearly a mistake."

Not yet realizing the full extent of his defeat, the grand strategist stooped to an unseemly state of discomposure, which later made him squirm whenever he thought about it. He persisted, he became angry, he tried to push the money into Koreiko's hands, and in general lost face, as the Chinese saying goes. Alexander Ivanovich shrugged his shoulders, and smiled politely, but he wouldn't take the money.

"So, nobody robbed you?"

"That's right, nobody robbed me."

"And nobody took ten thousand from you?"

"Of course not. How could I possibly have that much money?"

"That's true," said Ostap, cooling off. "How could a simple clerk have such a pile of money? So, everything's fine with you?"

"Everything!" replied the millionaire with a charming smile.

"And your stomach is fine, too?" asked Ostap, smiling even more seductively.

"It's perfect. I'm a very healthy man, you know."

"And no bad dreams either?"

"No, none."

After that, the smiles closely followed Liszt's instructions: fast, very fast, much faster, as fast as possible, and still faster. The way the new friends were saying goodbye, one might have thought they really adored each other.

"Don't forget your police cap," said Alexander Ivanovich. "You left it on the table."

"Don't eat raw tomatoes before bedtime," advised Ostap, "it might hurt your stomach."

"All the best to you," said Koreiko, bowing cheerfully and clicking his heels.

"See you later," replied Ostap. "You're such an interesting man. Everything's fine with you. All that luck—and you're still at large. Amazing!"

Finally, the grand strategist bolted outside; he was still smiling, even though it was no longer necessary. He walked briskly for a few blocks, forgetting that he was still wearing the policeman's cap with the crest of the city of Kiev, which was completely out of place in the city of Chernomorsk. And only when he walked into a crowd of respectable-looking old men, who were babbling away in front of the covered porch of City Diner No. 68, did he come back to his senses and start assessing the situation rationally.

While he strolled back and forth absentmindedly, immersed in his thoughts, the old men continued to do what they did here every day. These were odd people, preposterous in this day and age. Nearly all of them wore white piqué vests and straw boater hats. Some even sported panamas that had darkened with age. And, of course, they all had yellowed starched collars around their hairy chicken necks. This spot near Diner No. 68, formerly the fabled Florida Café, was the gathering place for the remnants of long-gone commercial Chernomorsk. They were brokers left without their brokerage firms, commissioned salesmen who had faded in the absence of commissions, grain traders, accountants who had gone off the deep end, and other such riffraff. In the old days, they used to gather here to cut deals. But it was long-time habit, combined with a need to exercise their old tongues, that kept bringing them to this sunny street corner. Every day, they read Moscow's *Pravda* —they had no respect for the local press—and interpreted anything that was going on anywhere in the world as a prelude to Chernomorsk becoming a free city. About a hundred years earlier, Chernomorsk was indeed a free city, which brought so much fun and so much profit that the legend of *porto franco* still shone its golden light on the sunny street corner near the Florida Café.

"Have you read about the disarmament conference?" one Piqué Vest would inquire of another. "Count Bernstorff's speech?"

"Bernstorff is a real brain!" replied the other Vest, as if he had known the Count personally for many years. "And have you read the speech that Snowden gave at the electoral meeting in Birmingham, that Conservative stronghold?"

"Goes without saying . . . Snowden is a real brain! Listen, Valiadis," said the first, turning to yet another old fogey in a panama. "What's your take on Snowden?"

"I have to be honest with you," replied the Panama, "Snowden is a tough cookie. Personally, I wouldn't try to pull the wool over his eyes."

And showing no concern for the fact that Snowden would never let Valiadis pull anything over his eyes, the old man continued:

"But whatever you say, I have to be honest with you: Chamberlain is a real brain, too."

The Piqué Vests would shrug their shoulders. They didn't deny that Chamberlain was a real brain, too. But their absolute favorite was Briand.

"Briand!" they would say enthusiastically. "Now there's a brain! With his pan-Europe proposal . . ."

"I'll tell you honestly, *Monsieur* Funt," whispered Valiadis, "everything's going to be fine. Beneš has already agreed to pan-Europe, but you know on what condition?"

The Piqué Vests gathered around and stuck their chicken necks out.

"On the condition that Chernomorsk is declared a free city. Beneš is a real brain. They need to sell their agricultural machinery to somebody, right? Well, we'll be the ones buying it."

Upon hearing this, the eyes of the old men began to sparkle. For many years, they'd been dying to buy and sell, sell and buy.

"Briand is a real brain," they sighed. "Beneš is a real brain, too."

When Ostap finally managed to shake off his heavy thoughts, he realized that an old man in a beat-up straw hat with a greasy black ribbon was clutching his jacket. His clip-on tie was off kilter, and a brass clasp glared right into Ostap's face.

"I'm telling you," shouted the old man into the grand strategist's ear, "MacDonald is not going to take this bait! He will not take this bait! You hear me?"

Ostap moved the agitated geezer aside and made his way out of the crowd.

"Hoover is a real brain!" came from behind. "And Hindenburg is a brain, too."

By then, Ostap had already decided what to do next. He went through all the four hundred honest methods of taking money, and although they included such gems as starting a company to salvage gold that had sunk with a ship during the Crimean War, organizing a big carnival to benefit the prisoners of capital, or obtaining a concession to remove the ever-changing storefront signs—none of them quite suited the project at hand. So Ostap invented method number 401.

"Our surprise attack on the fortress failed," he thought, "so now we're forced to set up a regular siege. We've established the main thing: the defendant has money. And judging by how easily he declined the ten thousand—without as much as a blink—we're talking big money. Well, since the two sides failed to reach an agreement, our deliberations continue."

On his way home, he bought a yellow cardboard folder with shoelace straps.

"So?" asked Balaganov and Panikovsky in unison, barely able to contain themselves.

Ostap walked silently to the bamboo table, put the folder in front of him, and wrote on it in large letters:

"The Case of Alexander Ivanovich Koreiko. Opened June 25, 1930. Closed . . . , 193 . . ."

The half-brothers stared at it over Bender's shoulder.

"What's inside?" asked the curious Panikovsky.

"Ah!" said Ostap. "Inside, there's everything: palms, girls, the Blue Express, the azure ocean, a white ship, a barely used tuxedo, a Japanese butler, your own pool table, platinum teeth, socks with no holes, dinners cooked with real butter, but most importantly, my little friends, the power and fame that come with money."

With that, he opened the empty folder and showed it to the dumbfounded Antelopeans.

CHAPTER 15
HORNS AND HOOFS

Once there was a poor merchant. He was a fairly rich man, the owner of the haberdashery near the Capital Hill movie theater. He peacefully sold underwear, lace, neckties, buttons, and other small, but profitable, wares. One day he came home looking shaken. Without saying a word, he opened the cupboard, took out a cold chicken, and ate it all while pacing around the room. Then he opened the cupboard again, took out a loop of Polish sausage that weighed exactly one pound, sat down, and slowly consumed the whole thing, staring straight ahead with glazed-over eyes. When he reached for the boiled eggs that were sitting on the table, his wife became alarmed and asked:

"What happened, Boris?"

"Disaster!" he replied, stuffing a hard rubbery egg into his mouth. "They're taxing me to death. You can't even imagine."

"But why are you eating so much?"

"I need a distraction," answered the merchant. "I'm scared."

All that night, he stumbled around his rooms, which contained no less than eight chests of drawers, and kept on eating. He ate all the food in the house. He was scared.

The next day, he sublet half of the store to a stationer. So one window displayed neckties and suspenders, while the other was taken up by a huge yellow pencil hanging from two strings.

Then things got even tougher. A third co-owner set up shop inside the store. He was a watchmaker. He pushed the pencil to the side and filled half of the window with a magnificent brass clock in the shape of the goddess Psyche yet missing its minute hand. And so the poor haberdasher, whose ironic smile had become permanent, had to face not just the tiresome pencil man but also the watchmaker with a black magnifying glass stuck in his eye.

Disaster struck two more times, and two more tenants moved in: a plumber, who immediately fired up some kind of a soldering furnace, and a downright bizarre merchant, who had decided that A.D. 1930 was just the right year for the people of Chernomorsk to pounce on his wares—starched collars.

The once-proud and respectable storefront started to look ghastly:

HABERDASHERY

Habertrade

B. KULTURTRIGGER

CLOCK AND WATCH

Repairs

Frm. Paul Buhre

GLASSIUS-SCHENKER

OFFISUPPL

Everything for Artists and Offices

LEO SOKOLOVSKY

PIPE, SINK & TOILET

Repairs

M. N. FANATIUK

SPECIALTY

Starched Collars From Leningrad

KARL BABOONIAN

Clients and customers entered the formerly sweet-smelling store with trepidation. The watchmaker Glassius-Schenker, surrounded by tiny wheels, watch glasses, and springs, sat under a collection of clocks, one of them big enough for the city tower. Alarm clocks were constantly going off. Schoolchildren crowded in the back of the store, inquiring about notebooks that were always in short supply. Karl Baboonian killed time while waiting for his clients by trimming his collars with scissors. And the moment the courteous B. Kulturtrigger asked a customer: "What would you like?," Fanatiuk the plumber would hit a rusty pipe with a hammer, producing a loud bang. Soot from the soldering furnace settled on the delicate haberdashery items.

In the end, the oddball commune of private merchants fell apart. Karl Baboonian rode a horse cab into oblivion, taking his anachronistic merchandise with him. Then Habertrade and Offisuppl disappeared too, with tax inspectors on horseback in hot pursuit. Fanatiuk became an alcoholic. Glassius-Schenker joined the New Times Co-op. The corrugated iron shutters fell down with a bang. The peculiar storefront signage disappeared as well.

Soon, however, the shutters in front of the merchants' ark went back up and a small but neat sign appeared:

> ARBATOV BUREAU
> FOR THE COLLECTION OF HORNS AND HOOFS
> CHERNOMORSK BRANCH

If an idle Chernomorskian were to peek inside, he would have noticed that the shelves and counters were gone, and the floor was sparkling clean. There were egg yolk-colored desks, and the walls displayed the usual posters regarding office hours and the harmful effects of handshaking. The brand new little office was already equipped with a barrier to protect it from visitors, even though there weren't any yet. A messenger with a gold tooth sat at a small table, where a yellow samovar was already puffing away, emitting high-pitched complaints about its samovarian fate. Drying teacups with a towel, the messenger hummed irritably:

> That's the oddest time we live in,
> That's the oddest time we live in.
> Everybody stopped believing,
> Everybody stopped believing.

A strapping red-headed fellow loitered behind the barrier. He would occasionally approach the typewriter, hit a key with his fat, unbending finger, and burst out laughing. The grand strategist, illuminated by a desk lamp, sat in the back of the office, under the sign BRANCH PRESIDENT.

The Carlsbad Hotel had long been abandoned. All the Antelopeans, except Kozlevich, had moved into the Rookery to stay with Basilius Lokhankin, which scandalized him to no end. He even tried to protest, pointing out that he had offered the room to one person, not three, and to a respectable bachelor at that. "*Mon dieu*, Basilius Andreevich," said Ostap nonchalantly, "stop torturing yourself. Of the three of us, I'm the only one who's respectable, so your conditions have been met." As the landlord continued to lament, Bender added weightily: "*Mein Gott*, dear Basilius! Maybe that's exactly what the Great Homespun Truth is all about." Lokhankin promptly gave in and hit Bender up for twenty rubles. Panikovsky and Balaganov fit in very well at the Rookery, and their self-assured voices soon joined the apartment's chorus. Panikovsky was even accused of stealing kerosene from other people's Primus stoves at night. Mitrich, never one to miss an opportunity, made some nitpicking remark to Ostap. In response, the grand strategist silently shoved him in the chest.

The Bureau for the Collection of Horns and Hoofs had been established for numerous reasons.

"Investigating Koreiko's case might take a long time," said Ostap. "God only knows how long. And since there is no God, nobody knows. We are in a terrible bind. It might be a month, it might be a year. Either way, we need some legal standing. We need to blend in with the cheery masses of office workers. That's what the bureau is all about. I have long been interested in administration. I am a bureaucrat and a mis-manager at heart. We will be collecting something very funny, for example, teaspoons, dog tags, or bells and whistles. Or horns and hoofs. That's perfect! Horns and hoofs to supply the manufacturers of combs and cigarette holders. How about that? Besides, I already have some excellent blank forms that are suitable for any occasion and a round rubber stamp in my bag."

The money that Koreiko had declined, and that the scrupulous Ostap decided could be put to use, was deposited in the bank account of the new organization. Panikovsky rebelled again, demanding his share. As a punishment, he was assigned the low-paying position of messenger, which offended his freedom-loving nature. Balaganov was appointed to the important post of Vice President for Hoofs, which paid ninety-two rubles a month. An old Adler typewriter was purchased at the flea market. It was missing the letter "s," so "z" had to be used instead. As a result, the very first official missive that Ostap sent to a stationery store read like this:

Pleaze izzue the bearer, mezzenger Comr. Panikovzky, office zuppliez in the amount of 150 (one hundred and fifty) rublez for the Chernomorzk branch, to be charged to the Head Office in the zity of Arbatov.

Enclozure: None

"God sent me an idiot for a Vice President for Hoofs!" grumbled Ostap. "I can't rely on him for anything. He bought a typewriter with a German accent! So I'm the Branch Prezident? You're a zwine, Shura, plain and simple."

But even the typewriter and its curious accent could not dampen the grand strategist's enthusiasm. He loved this new field of endeavor. He'd return to the office with a new toy almost every hour. He bought such complex office machines and equipment that the messenger and the Vice President couldn't believe their eyes. There were hole punches, duplicating machines, a swivel stool, and an expensive bronze inkwell set that was shaped like several little log cabins—each contained a different color of ink. This concoction was called "Face the Country" and cost 150 rubles. The crowning achievement was a cast-iron railway ticket punch that Ostap obtained from the train station. Finally, Bender brought in a large rack of deer antlers. Groaning and complaining about his pay, Panikovsky hung it above the boss's desk. Everything went well, splendidly even. The only thing that hampered the smooth functioning of the bureau was the inexplicable absence of the automobile and its glorious driver, Adam Kozlevich.

The first visitor appeared on the third day of the bureau's existence. To everyone's surprise, it was the postman. He delivered eight envelopes, had a chat with Panikovsky about this and that, and left. The envelopes contained three official letters that urgently summoned a representative of the bureau to attend various meetings and conferences. All three emphasized that attendance was mandatory. The other correspondence contained requests from unfamiliar, but apparently industrious, organizations that demanded all kinds of information, reports, and records in multiple copies—all of this was urgent and mandatory as well.

"What the hell is that?" thundered Ostap. "Just three days ago, I was as free as a mountain eagle, I flapped my wings wherever I pleased, and now look at this—attendance is mandatory! Turns out there's plenty of people in this city who can't do without Ostap Bender. Plus, who's going to take care of all this amicable correspondence? We'll have to incur additional expenses and revise our staffing structure. We need an experienced sec-retary. Let her deal with all this."

Two hours later, a new disaster struck. A peasant showed up carrying a heavy sack.

"Who's taking horns here?" he asked, dumping his load on the floor. The grand strategist looked at the visitor and his offerings without any enthusiasm. The horns were small, crooked, and dirty. Ostap was disgusted.

"But are these any good?" asked the branch president cautiously.

"Just look at them horns!" The man grew agitated and held up a yel-low horn to the grand strategist's nose. "Beauties, first class! Meets the standards."

They had no choice but to accept such high-quality merchandise. After that, the man endlessly drank tea with Panikovsky and talked about life in the country. Bender was understandably irked, like anybody who had just wasted fifteen rubles.

"If Panikovsky lets in one more of those horn blowers," said Ostap the moment the visitor finally left, "he's out of here. I'll fire him without severance pay. Either way, enough of these official pursuits. Time to get down to business."

The branch president put the LUNCH BREAK sign on the glass door and took out the folder that ostensibly contained the azure ocean and a white ship, gave it a slap and announced:

"This is what our bureau will be working on. Right now, there's nothing here, but we'll dig up the leads even if we have to dispatch Pan-ikovsky and Balaganov to collect evidence in the Karakum Desert, or Kremenchug, or some such place."

At this point, the door handle started rattling. Behind the glass stood an old man wearing a panama hat that had been mended with white thread and a large woven silk jacket with a piqué vest showing under-neath. The old man stretched out his chicken neck and held his large ear to the glass.

"We're closed!" shouted Ostap hastily. "The collection of hoofs is temporarily suspended."

But the old man continued to gesture.

Had Ostap not let the old White Vest in, the novel could have gone in a totally different direction. Many of the amazing events featuring the grand strategist, his irritable messenger, his carefree Vice President for Hoofs, and lots of other people, including a certain sage from the East, the granddaughter of the old puzzle-maker, a prominent activist, the boss of the Hercules, as well as numerous Soviet and foreign citizens, could never have taken place.

But Ostap opened the door. Smiling mournfully, the old man walked past the barrier and lowered himself into a chair. Then he closed his eyes and said nothing for about five minutes. One could only hear a faint whistling that his pale nose emitted from time to time. When the staff finally concluded that the visitor wouldn't utter another word ever again, and started whispering about the best ways to dispose of the body, the old man raised his brown eyelids and said in a low-pitched voice:

"My name is Funt. Funt."

"And you think this is reason enough to barge into offices that are closed for lunch?" asked Ostap light-heartedly.

"I see you're laughing," replied the old man, "but my name is Funt. I'm ninety years old."

"So what can I do for you?" asked Ostap, starting to lose his patience.

But then Citizen Funt fell silent again, and he remained silent for quite a while.

"You have a bureau," he said finally.

"That's right, a bureau," encouraged Ostap. "Go on."

But the old man just patted his knee.

"You see these pants I'm wearing?" he said after a long silence. "These are my Easter pants. I used to wear them only for Easter, but now I wear them every day."

And even though Panikovsky slapped him on the back, in an effort to help the old man's words flow without interruption, Funt fell silent again. He spoke quickly, but his sentences were separated by pauses that occasionally lasted as long as three minutes. For those who were not accustomed to Funt's manner of speaking, talking to him was torture. Ostap was about to grab Funt by his starched dog collar and show him the door, when the old man opened his mouth again. Then the exchange took such a fascinating turn that Ostap had to reconcile himself to the Funtian method of conversation.

"Do you need a chairman, by any chance?" inquired Funt.

"A chairman?" exclaimed Bender in surprise.

"The official chairman. The head of the organization, in other words."

"I'm the head myself."

"So you're planning to do the time yourself? You should have said so right away. Why did you waste two hours of my time?"

The old man in Easter pants became angry, but that didn't make the pauses between his sentences any shorter.

"I am Funt," he repeated proudly. "I am ninety years old. All my life, I've done time for others. That's my line of work—to suffer for others."

"Oh, so you're a frontman?"

"Yes," said the old man, nodding with dignity. "I'm the dummy chairman Funt. I've been doing time forever. I did time under Alexander II the Liberator, under Alexander III the Peacemaker, under Nicholas II the Bloody."

The old man kept counting the tsars on his fingers.

"Under Kerensky's Provisional Government, I did time as well. True, I didn't do any time under Military Communism: there was no commerce to speak of, and hence no work. But how I did time under the NEP! Oh, how I did time under the NEP! Those were the best days of my life. In four years, I barely spent three months out of prison. I married off my granddaughter, Golconda Yevseevna, and gave her a grand piano, a silver bird, and eighty rubles in gold coins as a dowry. But now I walk around and I don't recognize our Chernomorsk. Where did it all go? Where's the private capital? Where's the First Society for Mutual Credit? Where's the Second Society for Mutual Credit, I'm asking you? Where are the trust companies? Where are the mixed-capital partnerships? Where did it all go? It's an outrage!"

This short speech didn't take long—just half an hour. Panikovsky was very moved. He took Balaganov aside and whispered with respect:

"You can tell he's a man from the old days. People like this aren't around anymore, and pretty soon they'll be gone for good."

He graciously handed the old man a cup of sweet tea. Ostap dragged the dummy chairman to his executive desk, ordered the office closed, and began to patiently interview the eternal prisoner who had laid down his life for his brethren. The dummy chairman clearly enjoyed the chat. If it hadn't been for the lengthy gaps between sentences, one could have said that he just wouldn't shut up.

"Do you happen to know a certain Alexander Ivanovich Koreiko?" asked Ostap, glancing at the folder with shoelace straps.

"No," replied the old man. "I don't know that one."

"And have you had any dealings with the Hercules?"

Hearing the word Hercules, the dummy chairman stirred ever so slightly. Ostap didn't even notice this tiny motion, but any of the Piqué

Vests from the Florida Café who had known Funt for ages—Valiadis for instance—would have thought: "Funt is very excited, he's beside himself."

How could Funt not know the Hercules? His last four prison stints were directly linked to that organization! Several private partnerships fed off the Hercules. The firm named Intensivnik, for example. Funt was offered the chairman's post. The Intensivnik received a large advance from the Hercules to supply something related to timber—a dummy chairman doesn't have to know exactly what. The firm promptly went under. Somebody bagged the money, while Funt got six months in jail. After the Intensivnik, the Toiling Cedar Trust Partnership came about—with the respectable-looking Funt as chairman, naturally. Then, naturally, came an advance from the Hercules to supply seasoned cedar, followed by sudden bankruptcy, naturally. Somebody got rich, while Funt had to earn his chairman's keep in jail. Then the Sawing Aid—the Hercules—advance—bankruptcy—someone scored—jail. And again: advance—the Hercules—the Southern Lumberjack—Funt goes to jail—somebody gets a bundle.

"But who?" probed Ostap, pacing around the old man. "Who was behind all this?"

The old man silently sucked the tea from his cup, barely raising his heavy eyelids.

"Who knows?" he said forlornly. "Nobody told Funt anything. All I have to do is time, that's my job. I did time under Alexander II, and Alexander III, and Nicholas Romanov, and Alexander Kerensky. And during the NEP: before the frenzy, during the frenzy, and after the frenzy. And now I'm out of work, and I have to wear my Easter pants every day."

Ostap dragged the words out of the old man one by one. He was like a gold prospector, tirelessly washing through tons and tons of mud and sand in order to find a few specks of gold on the bottom. He nudged Funt with his shoulder, woke him up, and even tickled him under his arms. After all this effort, he finally learned that in Funt's opinion, the same person was definitely behind all those failed companies and partnerships. As for the Hercules, it had been milked to the tune of hundreds of thousands.

"In any case," added the frail dummy chairman, "this mystery man is a real brain. Do you know Valiadis? Valiadis wouldn't try to pull the wool over this man's eyes."

"How about Briand?" asked Ostap with a smile, remembering the crowd of Piqué Vests near the old Florida Café. "Would Valiadis try to pull the wool over Briand's eyes? What do you think?"

"Never!" answered Funt. "Briand is a real brain."

He flapped his lips in silence for three minutes and then added: "Hoover is a brain. Hindenburg is also a brain. Hoover and Hindenburg, that's two brains."

Ostap grew very concerned. The oldest of the Piqué Vests was preparing to plumb the depths of world politics. At any moment, he might have launched into a discussion of the Kellogg-Briand Pact or the Spanish dictator Primo de Rivera, and then nothing, absolutely nothing would stop him from this commendable pursuit. A gleam of madness appeared in his eyes, his Adam's apple began trembling above the yellowed starched collar, heralding the advent of a new sentence—when Bender unscrewed a light bulb and threw it on the floor. The bulb broke with the cold cracking noise of a rifle shot. It distracted the dummy chairman from international affairs. Ostap quickly took advantage of the opportunity.

"But have you met anybody from the Hercules, ever?" he asked. "To discuss the advances?"

"I only dealt with Berlaga, an accountant from the Hercules. He was on their staff. But me, I knew nothing. They never told me anything. People only need me to do time. I did time under the tsars, under Socialism, under the Ukrainian Hetman, and under the French occupation. Briand is a brain."

Nothing else could be squeezed out of the old man. But what he had already said was enough to start the hunt.

"Feels like Koreiko's hand," thought Ostap.

The president of the Chernomorsk Branch of the Arbatov Bureau for the Collection of Horns and Hoofs sat down at his desk and recorded the dummy chairman's speech on paper. He did, however, leave out Funt's thoughts on the complex relationship between Valiadis and Briand.

The first page of the underground investigation of the underground millionaire was numbered, punched through properly, and filed away.

"So, are you going to hire a chairman or not?" asked the old man, putting his mended panama back on. "I can tell that your bureau needs a chairman. I'm not asking much: 120 rubles a month while I'm outside, and 240 while I'm in prison. There's a one hundred percent surcharge for hazardous duty."

"Well, I guess we are," said Ostap. "Submit your application to the Vice President for Hoofs."

CHAPTER 16
JAHRBUCH FÜR PSYCHOANALYTIK

The workday in the Finance and Accounting Department at the Hercules started at 9 A.M. sharp, as usual.

Kukushkind had already raised the flap of his jacket to wipe his glasses, preparing to inform his colleagues that working at the banking firm of Sycamorsky and Cesarewitch was far less unnerving than working at this Sodom, the Hercules; Tezoimenitsky had already turned in his swivel chair towards the wall and reached out to tear a page off the calendar; and Lapidus Jr. had already opened his mouth wide to welcome a piece of bread slathered with chopped herring when the door opened—and in came the accountant Berlaga.

His unexpected appearance caused much commotion in Finance and Accounting. Tezoimenitsky slipped on his rotating saucer, and the calendar page remained in place for the first time in perhaps three years. Lapidus Jr. forgot to bite into his sandwich and just moved his jaws idly. Dreyfus, Chevazhevskaya, and Sakharkov were flabbergasted. Koreiko raised his head and lowered it again. Old Kukushkind quickly put his glasses back on, forgetting to wipe them for the first time in his thirty years of service. Berlaga sat down at his desk, as if nothing had happened, and opened his ledgers, ignoring Lapidus Jr.'s expressive smirk.

"How are you feeling?" asked Lapidus anyway. "How's your heel nerve?"

"It's fine now," said Berlaga without raising his head. "It's as if it doesn't even exist."

Up until the lunch break, everybody in Finance and Accounting fidgeted on their stools and cushions, dying of curiosity. When the alarm bell finally went off, all the bright lights of bookkeeping gathered around Berlaga. But the fugitive hardly answered any questions. He took four of his most trusted friends aside, made sure that no one else was listening, and told them about his incredible adventures at the insane asylum. The fugitive accountant's story was interwoven with numerous interjections and intricate expressions that are omitted here for the sake of coherence.

THE STORY OF THE ACCOUNTANT BERLAGA,
detailing what happened to him at the insane asylum,
as told by himself in the strictest confidence to Borisokhlebsky,
Dreyfus, Sakharkov, and Lapidus Jr.

As we already know, Berlaga fled to the insane asylum to escape the purge. He was hoping to wait out the dangerous period at this medical institution and return to the Hercules after the storm was over and the eight men with gray eyes had moved on to the next organization.

His brother-in-law slapped the whole thing together. He got hold of a book about the manners and customs of the mentally ill, and after much discussion, they selected delusions of grandeur from the available manias.

"You won't have to do anything," explained the brother-in-law, "you just have to yell in everybody's face: 'I'm Napoleon!' or 'I'm Émile Zola!' or 'Prophet Mohammed!' if that's what you want."

"How about the Viceroy of India?" asked Berlaga naïvely.

"Why not? Crackpots can be anything they want. So, the Viceroy of India, yes?"

The brother-in-law spoke with authority, as if he were at the very least a junior intern at a mental hospital. In reality, however, he was just a salesman who pushed subscriptions to lavishly printed book sets from the State Publishing House. The silk-lined bowler hat that he kept in his storage chest was the only reminder of his past commercial greatness.

The brother-in-law rushed to the phone to call an ambulance, while the new Viceroy of India took off his tunic, tore up his cotton undershirt, and just in case, poured a bottle of the best, premium-quality iron gall copying ink onto his head. Then he lay on the floor face down and, when the orderlies arrived, started bellowing:

"I'm none other than the Viceroy of India! Where are my trusted nawabs and maharajas, my abreks and kunaks, my elephants?"

Listening to his megalomaniacal ravings, the brother-in-law shook his head in doubt. He wasn't convinced that the abreks and the kunaks fell under the purview of the King of India. But the orderlies just wiped the premium-quality ink from the accountant's face with a wet cloth, picked him up, and stuffed him into the ambulance. The shiny doors slammed shut, the siren went off, and the vehicle whisked Viceroy Berlaga to his new domain.

On the way to the hospital, the patient flailed his arms and babbled incoherently, all the while worrying about his first encounter with real madmen. He was afraid that they would be nasty to him, and maybe even kill him.

The hospital was very different from what Berlaga had pictured. People in light-blue robes sat on couches, lay in beds, or strolled around a large, well-lit ward. The accountant noticed that the madmen hardly ever spoke to one another. They didn't have time to talk. They were busy thinking. They were thinking all the time. They had many thoughts, they had to recall something, something very important that their happiness depended upon. But their thoughts were falling apart, and, worst of all, they were simply disappearing, wiggling their tails. And so one had to start anew, think everything over again, finally understand what had happened and why everything was so bad when everything had been so good before.

The same disheveled and miserable madman had already walked past Berlaga several times. Holding his chin in his hand, he walked along the same line—from the window to the door, from the door to the window, back to the door, back to the window. So many thoughts roared in his poor head that he had to put his other hand on his forehead and accelerate his pace.

"I'm the Viceroy of India!" cried Berlaga, giving the orderly a quick glance.

The madman didn't even look at the accountant. Wincing, he went back to gathering the thoughts that Berlaga's wild cries had scattered. Then the Viceroy was approached by a short idiot, who put his arm around Berlaga's waist and chirped something in his ear.

"What?" asked the frightened Berlaga cautiously.

"Ene, bene, raba, quinter, finter, baba," his new friend enunciated clearly.

Berlaga said "Oh my God" and moved away from the idiot. He then found himself near a man with a bald, lemon-like pate. The man quickly turned away to the wall, giving the accountant an anxious look.

"Where are my maharajas?" Berlaga asked him, feeling he had to maintain his reputation.

But then a patient who was sitting on a bed deep inside the large ward stood up on his legs, which were thin and yellow like church candles, and yelled out with pain:

"Freedom! Freedom! To the pampas!"

Later, the accountant learned that the man who longed for the pampas was an old geography teacher, the author of the textbook from which the young Berlaga had learned about volcanoes, capes, and isthmuses many years ago. The geographer went mad quite unexpectedly: one day he looked at the map of the two hemispheres and couldn't find the Bering Strait. The old teacher spent the whole day studying the map. Everything was where it was supposed to be: Newfoundland; the Suez Canal; Madagascar; the Sandwich Islands with their capital city, Honolulu; even the Popocatépetl volcano. But the Bering Strait was missing. The old man lost his mind right then and there, in front of the map.[1] He was a harmless madman who never hurt anybody, but he scared Berlaga to death. The shouting broke his heart.

"Freedom!" the geographer yelled out again. "To the pampas!"

He knew more about freedom than anyone else in the world. He was a geographer: he knew of the wide open spaces that regular people, busy doing their mundane things, can't even imagine. He wanted to be free, he wanted to ride a sweating mustang through the brush . . .

A young woman doctor with doleful blue eyes entered the room and went straight to Berlaga.

"How are you feeling, dear?" she asked, touching the accountant's forearm with her warm hand. "You're better now, aren't you?"

"I'm the Viceroy of India!" he reported, blushing. "Give me back my favorite elephant!"

"You're having a delusion," said the doctor gently. "You're in a hospital, we'll help you recover."

"Oooh! My elephant!" cried Berlaga defiantly.

---

1. The authors have discovered that the map which drove the poor geographer mad was indeed missing the Bering Strait. This was due to negligence at The Book and the Pole Publishers. The culprits were duly punished. The director was demoted, while the rest got away with reprimands and warnings.—Authors' note.

"But you must understand," said the doctor even more gently, "you're not the Viceroy. This is a delusion, you understand? A delusion."

"No, it's not!" objected Berlaga, who knew that he was supposed to be difficult.

"Yes, a delusion!"

"No, it's not!"

"Delusion!"

"Is not!"

Seeing that the iron was hot, the accountant struck. He gave the gentle doctor a shove and emitted a lengthy howl that startled the other patients, especially the little idiot, who sat down on the floor and said, drooling:

"Un, dun, trois, quatre, Mademoiselle Jourauvatre."

Then, to his delight, Berlaga overheard the woman doctor telling an orderly:

"We need to put him in with those other three, or else he'll scare the whole ward silly."

Two even-tempered orderlies took the cantankerous Viceroy to a smaller ward, for disruptive patients, where three men lay quietly. And it was there that the accountant finally learned what true madmen were like. Seeing the visitors, the patients grew extremely agitated. A fat man rolled out of bed, quickly got down on all fours, stuck out his rear end—it looked like a mandolin in his tight clothes—and started barking in bursts, digging the hardwood floor with his slipper-clad hind legs. The other one wrapped himself in a blanket and started shouting: "Et tu, Brute, sold out to the Bolsheviks!" This man clearly thought he was Gaius Julius Caesar. At times, however, something would snap in his deeply disturbed head, and he'd get confused and yell: "I'm Heinrich Julius Zimmermann!"

"Go away! I'm naked!" shouted the third man. "Don't look! I'm ashamed! I'm a naked woman."

As a matter of fact, he was a fully dressed man with a mustache.

The orderlies left. The Viceroy of India was so petrified that he lost any interest in demanding the return of his favorite elephant, the maharajas, the faithful nawabs, never mind the mysterious abreks or kunaks.

"These guys will kill me just like that," he thought, breaking into a cold sweat.

He kicked himself for making such a scene in the quiet ward. It would have been so nice to sit near the kindly geographer and listen to the comforting babble of the little idiot: "Ene, bene, raba, quinter, finter, baba." But nothing terrible happened. The dog man yelped a few more times, growled, and went back to bed. Julius Caesar kicked off his blanket, yawned deeply, and had a good stretch. The mustachioed woman lit up his pipe, and the sweet smell of Our Capstan tobacco calmed Berlaga's tormented soul.

"I'm the Viceroy of India," he declared, recovering his bravery.

"Shut up, bastard!" replied Julius Caesar dismissively, and he added with the directness of a Roman: "Or you're dead meat."

This remark by the bravest of the warriors and emperors brought the fugitive accountant to his senses. He hid under the blanket, sadly reflected on his grueling life, and drifted off to sleep.

In the morning, still half-asleep, he overheard a strange conversation:

"They stuck a real lunatic in here, goddamit. It was so nice with just the three of us, and now look . . . He's trouble! This damn Viceroy could very well bite us all."

Berlaga recognized the voice: it was Gaius Julius Caesar. A few minutes later, he opened his eyes and saw that the dog man was staring at him with keen interest.

"That's it," thought the Viceroy, "now he'll bite me!"

But the dog man suddenly clasped his hands and asked in a perfectly human voice:

"Excuse me, aren't you the son of Foma Berlaga?"

"I am," answered the accountant, but then he came to his senses and started hollering: "Give the poor Viceroy his faithful elephant back!"

"Please look at me," invited the mongrel man. "Don't you recognize me?"

"Mikhail Alexandrovich!" exclaimed the accountant, regaining his sight. "I'm so happy to see you!"

The Viceroy and the dog man gave each other a friendly hug and a kiss. Their foreheads collided, clapping like billiard balls. Mikhail Alexandrovich had tears in his eyes.

"So you're not crazy?" asked Berlaga. "Then why are you playing the fool?"

"And you, why are you playing the fool? Look at him! Just give him his elephants or else! Besides, my dear Berlaga, I have to tell you that if you want to make a good madman, the Viceroy is not a very convincing role, not at all."

"My brother-in-law told me it was fine," said Berlaga dejectedly.

"Take me, for example," said Mikhail Alexandrovich, "a subtle act. A dog man. Schizophrenia complicated by bipolar disorder and on top of that,

Berlaga, de–personalization. Do you think it was easy to pull off? I studied the literature. Did you read *Autistic Thinking* by Professor Bleuler?"

"I'm afraid not," answered Berlaga, sounding like a Viceroy who had just been stripped of the Order of the Garter and demoted to officer's orderly.

"Gentlemen!" called out Mikhail Alexandrovich. "He hasn't read Bleuler! Don't be scared, come over here. He's no more a Viceroy than you are Caesar."

The two remaining denizens of the small ward for disruptive patients came closer.

"You haven't read Bleuler?" asked Julius Caesar with surprise. "But then what did you use to prepare?"

"He probably subscribed to the German magazine *Jahrbuch für Psychoanalytik und Psychopathologie*," suggested the mustachioed psychopath.

Berlaga felt like a complete fool. Meanwhile, the experts continued spouting abstruse terminology relating to the theory and practice of psychoanalysis. Everybody agreed that Berlaga was in deep trouble, and that the head physician, Titanushkin, who was expected back from a business trip at any moment, would see through him in five minutes. They failed to mention that they themselves were not looking forward to Titanushkin's return.

"Maybe I should switch delusions?" asked Berlaga meekly. "What if I become Émile Zola, or the Prophet Mohammed?"

"Too late, " said Caesar. "Your case history already says that you're the Viceroy. A madman cannot change his manias like socks. For the rest of your life, you'll be the stupid Viceroy. We've been here for a week, and we know how it works."

Within the next hour, Berlaga had learned the real case histories of his companions in great detail.

Mikhail Alexandrovich had entered the insane asylum for very simple, mundane reasons. He was an important businessman who had inadvertently underpaid his income tax by forty-three thousand rubles. This could mean an involuntary trip way up north, whereas business urgently required his presence in Chernomorsk. Duvanov, the man who pretended he was a woman, was apparently a petty criminal with good reasons to fear arrest. But Gaius Julius Caesar, or, according to his papers, I. N. Starokhamsky, a former attorney-at-law, was a different matter entirely.

Gaius Julius Starokhamsky had entered the madhouse for lofty, ideological reasons.

"In Soviet Russia, the only place where a normal person can live is an insane asylum," he said, draping himself in a blanket. "Everything else is super-bedlam. I cannot live with the Bolsheviks, no sir! I'd rather live here, among common lunatics. At least they aren't building socialism. Plus, here they feed you, while out there, in bedlam, you need to work. And I have no intention of working for their socialism. Finally, I have my personal freedom here. Freedom of conscience, freedom of speech . . ."

Seeing an orderly who was passing by, Gaius Julius Starokhamsky started screaming:

"Long live the Constitutional Assembly! Everyone to the Forum! Et tu, Brute, sold out to the party apparatchiks!" He turned to Berlaga and added: "See? I yell whatever I please. Try that outside."

For most of the day and a good part of the night, the four disruptive patients played sixty-six with twenty and forty removed, a tricky card game that requires self-control, sharp wits, purity of spirit, and clarity of mind.

In the morning, Professor Titanushkin returned from his business trip. He examined all four of them briefly and promptly had them thrown out of the hospital. Neither Bleuler's book, nor de-personalization complicated by bipolar disorder, nor *Jahrbuch für Psychoanalytik und Psychopathologie* were of any help. Professor Titanushkin had no patience for malingerers.

And so they ran down the street, pushing people aside with their elbows. Julius Caesar led the pack, followed by the man-woman and the dog man. Behind them trudged the deposed Viceroy, cursing his brother-in-law and contemplating his future with horror.

After finishing his highly instructive story, Berlaga wistfully looked first at Borisokhlebsky, then at Dreyfus, then at Sakharkov, and finally at Lapidus Jr. In the semi-darkness of the hallway, it seemed to him that they were nodding their heads sympathetically.

"Now look where all your fantasies got you," said the cold-hearted Lapidus Jr. "You wanted to escape one purge and got yourself into another. Now you're in trouble. Since you were already purged from the madhouse, surely you'll be purged from the Hercules as well."

Borisokhlebsky, Dreyfus, and Sakharkov didn't say anything. Without a word, they started to fade slowly into the darkness.

"Friends!" cried the accountant meekly. "Where are you all going?"

But his friends had already broken into a gallop; their orphanage-style pants flashed in the stairwell for the last time and disappeared.

"Shame on you, Berlaga," said Lapidus coldly. "You should know better than to drag me into your dirty anti-Soviet schemes. Adieu!"

And the Viceroy of India was left alone.

So what have you done, Berlaga? Where were your eyes? What would your father Foma have said if he had found out that his son became a Viceroy in his declining years? That's where you ended up, dear accountant, thanks to your shady dealings with the chairman of many partnerships with mixed and tainted capital, Mr. Funt. It's hard even to think of what old Foma would have said about his favorite son's risky antics. But Foma had long been lying in the 2nd Christian Cemetery, under a stone seraph with a broken wing, and only the boys who went there to steal lilacs would occasionally throw an incurious glance at the epitaph that read: "Your path has ended. Rest right here, Beloved F. Berlaga dear." But maybe the old man wouldn't have said anything. Come to think of it, he certainly wouldn't have said anything, as he himself hadn't exactly lived the life of a holy man. He would simply have advised his son to be more careful and not to rely on his brother-in-law in serious matters. Yes, Berlaga, you've gotten yourself into quite a mess!

The heavy thoughts that consumed the ex-regent of George V in India were interrupted by shouting from the stairwell:

"Berlaga! Where is he? Someone's looking for him. Ah, there he is! Please, go right in."

The Vice President for Hoofs appeared in the hallway. Swinging his huge arms like an Imperial Guardsman, Balaganov marched up to Berlaga and handed him a summons:

To Comr. Berlaga. Upon receipt of thiz zummonz, you are to inztantly report for the purpoze of clarifying certain circumztancez.

The summons bore the letterhead of the Chernomorsk Branch of the Arbatov Bureau for the Collection of Horns and Hoofs, as well as an official-looking round stamp whose details would have been difficult to decipher, even if it had occurred to Berlaga to try. But the fugitive accountant was so overwhelmed by his troubles that he only asked:

"May I call home?"

"Why bother?" said the Vice President for Hoofs, frowning.

Two hours later, the crowd that stood in front of the Capital Hill movie theater, waiting for the first show and gawking at the passersby, for lack of anything better to do, spotted a man leaving the horn collection bureau. Holding his hand over his heart, he slowly stumbled away. It was Berlaga. At first, he moved his legs limply, then started to accelerate. Turning the corner, the accountant crossed himself surreptitiously, and bolted. Soon, he was sitting at his desk back in Finance and Accounting, his crazed stare fixed on the master ledger. The numbers leaped and somersaulted before his eyes.

The grand strategist snapped Koreiko's case folder shut, looked at Funt, who was sitting under a new sign, CHAIRMAN OF THE BOARD, and said:

"When I was very young and very poor, I earned my living by showing a fat monk with breasts at the fair in Kherson, claiming he was an inexplicable natural wonder—a bearded woman. But even then I hadn't stooped as low as this lout Berlaga."

"A miserable, wretched man," agreed Panikovsky as he was bringing tea to the others. He relished the thought that there were people out there who were even lowlier than him.

"Berlaga is not much of a brain," offered the dummy chairman in his typically unhurried fashion. "MacDonald is a real brain. His idea of industrial peace . . ."

"All right, all right," said Bender. "One day we'll have a special meeting just to discuss your views on MacDonald and other bourgeois statesmen. But right now I'm busy. Berlaga is no brain, that's true, but he did tell us a few things about the life and works of those self-destructing partnerships."

The grand strategist felt great. Things were going well. Nobody was bringing any more foul-smelling horns. The work of the Chernomorsk Branch could be deemed satisfactory, even though the latest mail delivery brought a new pile of circulars, memos, and requests, and Panikovsky had been to the employment office twice already to look for a secretary.

"Oh yes!" Ostap exclaimed suddenly. "Where's Kozlevich? Where's the Antelope? How can you have an organization without a car? I need to go to a meeting. They all want me, they can't live without me. Where's Kozlevich?"

Panikovsky looked away and sighed:

"There's a problem with Kozlevich."

"What do you mean—a problem? Is he drunk or something?"

"Worse," replied Panikovsky, "we were even afraid to tell you. Those Catholic priests put a spell on him."

The messenger looked at the Vice President for Hoofs, and the two of them shook their heads sadly.

CHAPTER 17
THE RETURN OF THE PRODIGAL SON

The grand strategist didn't care for Catholic priests. He held an equally negative opinion of rabbis, Dalai Lamas, Orthodox clergy, muezzins, shamans, and other purveyors of religion.

"I'm into deception and blackmail myself," he said. "Right now, for example, I'm trying to extract a large amount of money from a certain intransigent individual. But I don't accompany my questionable activities with choral singing, or the roar of the pipe organ, or silly incantations in Latin or Old Church Slavonic. I generally prefer to operate without incense or astral bells."

And while Panikovsky and Balaganov, interrupting each other, were telling him about the terrible fate that had befallen the driver of the Antelope, Ostap's brave heart was filling with frustration and anger.

The priests apprehended the soul of Adam Kozlevich at the hostel, where the Antelope was sitting in mud thick with manure, alongside Moldovan fruit carts and two-horse wagons that belonged to some German colonists. Father Kuszakowski frequented the hostel, where he conducted spiritual conversations with the Catholic colonists. The cleric noticed the Antelope, walked around it, and poked a tire with his finger. Then he had a chat with Kozlevich and found out that Adam Kazimirovich was indeed a Roman Catholic, but hadn't been to confession for some twenty years. Saying: "Shame on you, *Pan Kozlewicz*," Father Kuszakowski left, holding up his black skirt with both hands and jumping over the frothy beer-colored puddles.

Early next morning, as the wagon drivers were preparing to take some agitated vendors to the small market town of Koshary, stuffing fifteen of them into each wagon, Father Kuszakowski appeared once again. This time, he was accompanied by another priest, Aloisius Moroszek. While Kuszakowski was greeting Adam, Father Moroszek carefully inspected the automobile, not only poking a tire with his finger but even squeezing the horn, which played the maxixe. The two priests exchanged glances, approached Kozlevich from both sides, and started to cast their spells on him. They kept at it the whole day. The moment Kuszakowski stopped talking, Moroszek chimed in. And the moment he paused to wipe the sweat off his brow, Kuszakowski took over again. At times Kuszakowski would raise his yellow index finger towards the heavens, while Moroszek worked his rosary beads. At other times, it was Kuszakowski who fingered his beads, while Moroszek pointed toward the heavens. Several times, the priests sang quietly in Latin, and toward the end of the day, Kozlevich started to join in. At this point, both Fathers glanced at the car with interest.

After a while, Panikovsky noticed a change in the Antelope's owner. Adam Kazimirovich took to uttering vague words about the kingdom of heaven. Balaganov saw the change, too. Then Kozlevich started disappearing for long periods of time, and he finally moved out of the hostel altogether.

"So why didn't you inform me?" asked the grand strategist angrily.

They wanted to, but they were afraid of the captain's wrath. They were hoping that Kozlevich would come to his senses and return on his own. But they had given up hope. The priests had put a spell on him. Just the day before, the messenger and the Vice President for Hoofs had run into Kozlevich by accident. He was sitting in his car in front of the cathedral. They didn't even have a chance to talk to him. Father Aloisius Moroszek came out, accompanied by a boy decked out in lace.

"Can you believe it, Bender," said Shura, "the whole gang got into our Antelope, Kozlevich—the poor sucker—took off his hat, the boy rang a bell, and they took off. I felt really sorry for our Adam. The Antelope is as good as gone."

Without saying a word, the grand strategist put on his captain's cap, with its glossy black visor, and headed for the door.

"Funt," he said, "you're staying here. Do not accept any horns or hoofs no matter what. If there's any new mail, dump it in the basket. The secretary will figure it out later. Do you understand?"

By the time the dummy chairman opened his mouth to reply—which happened exactly five minutes later—the orphaned Antelopeans were long gone. The captain ran at the head of the pack, taking huge strides. He looked back occasionally and muttered: "You lost our sweet Kozlevich, you daydreamers! Consider yourself repudiated! Those bishops and archbishops, let me tell you!" The rally mechanic marched quietly, pretending that the reprimands had nothing to do with him. Panikovsky limped forward like a monkey, working up his anger against Kozlevich's abductors, even though he had a large cold toad sitting on his heart. He was afraid of the black priests, believing they possessed many magic powers.

Maintaining formation, the entire branch of the Horns and Hoofs Bureau reached the foot of the cathedral. The empty Antelope was parked in front of the wrought-iron fence made of interwoven spirals and crosses. The cathedral was enormous. Thorny and sharp, it ripped into the sky like a fish bone. It stuck in your throat. Polished red bricks, tiled roofs, tin flags, massive buttresses, graceful stone idols hiding from the rain in niches—all these Gothicisms, frozen at attention like soldiers, overwhelmed the Antelopeans from the start. They felt tiny. Ostap climbed into the car, sniffed the air, and said with disgust:

"Ugh! Sickening! Our Antelope already reeks of candles, collection baskets, and heavy priests' boots. Of course it's much nicer to carry the rites around in a car than in a horse cab. Plus, it's free! Well, sorry, dear Fathers, but our rites are more important!"

With that, Bender entered the gate and, walking through a group of kids who were playing hopscotch, climbed the imposing granite steps to the cathedral entrance. The thick door panels were enforced with iron hoops and decorated with reliefs of saints, each one in his own little square. The saints were blowing kisses at each other, or waved their hands in various directions, or amused themselves by reading thick little books in which the meticulous woodcarver had even cut tiny Roman letters. The grand strategist pulled the door, but it didn't move. The gentle sounds of a harmonium wafted through the door.

"The spells are being cast!" reported Ostap loudly, coming down the steps. "They're hard at it as we speak! To the sweet sound of the mandolin."

"Maybe we'd better leave?" asked Panikovsky, fiddling with the hat in his hands. "This is God's temple, you know. It's not right."

Ignoring him, Ostap walked up to the Antelope and started squeezing the horn impatiently. He played the maxixe until they heard keys jingling behind the thick doors. The Antelopeans raised their heads. The door panels opened, and the jolly saints slowly rode back in their little oak squares. Adam Kazimirovich stepped out of the dark portal onto the tall, bright porch. He was pale. His long train conductor's mustache had grown damp and drooped dejectedly from his nostrils. He had a prayer book in his hands. The priests were propping him up on both sides. On his left was Father Kuszakowski, on his right—Father Aloisius Moroszek. Their eyes were awash in saccharine piety.

"Hey, Kozlevich!" shouted Ostap from below. "Haven't you had enough of that already?"

"Good afternoon, Adam Kazimirovich," said Panikovsky brashly, ducking behind the captain's back, just in case.

Balaganov raised his hand in a greeting and made a face, which must have meant: "Stop fooling around, Adam!"

The body of the Antelope's driver took a step forward, but his soul lurched back under the piercing stares of both Kuszakowski and Moroszek. Kozlevich looked at his friends with anguish and lowered his eyes.

And then the great battle for the driver's soul began.

"Hey, you, cherubim and seraphim!" said Ostap, challenging his opponents to a debate. "There is no God!"

"Yes, there is," countered Father Aloisius Moroszek, shielding Kozlevich with his body.

"This is outrageous," mumbled Father Kuszakowski.

"No, there isn't," continued the grand strategist, "and there never has been. It's a medical fact."

"I think this conversation is highly inappropriate," declared Kuszakowski angrily.

"And taking the car away—is that appropriate?" shouted the tactless Balaganov. "Adam! They just want to take the Antelope."

Hearing this, the driver raised his head and looked at the holy fathers inquiringly. The priests began to get nervous and tried to take Kozlevich back inside, their silk robes rustling about. But he wouldn't budge.

"So, on the subject of God?" persisted the grand strategist.

The priests were forced into a debate. The children stopped hopping and came closer.

"How can you say there is no God," started Aloisius Moroszek earnestly, "when He created all living things!"

"Yeah, yeah," said Ostap, "I am an old Catholic and Latinist myself. *Puer, socer, vesper, gener, liber, miser, asper, tener.*"

These Latin exceptions, which Ostap had to learn by heart in the third grade of Iliadi's private gymnasium, and which his brain still retained for no reason, made a powerful impression on Kozlevich. His soul rejoined his body, and as a consequence of this reunion, the driver inched tentatively forward.

"My son," said Kuszakowski, looking at Bender furiously, "you are confused, my son. God's miracles demonstrate . . ."

"Quit yapping, Father!" said the grand strategist sternly. "I have performed miracles myself. Just four years ago in some God-forsaken town, I was Jesus Christ for a few days. And it went very smoothly. I even fed several thousand of the faithful with five loaves of bread. I did that all right, but imagine the mayhem!"

The debate continued in the same oddball vein. Ostap's arguments, unconvincing yet funny, had the most invigorating effect on Kozlevich. Color appeared on the driver's cheeks, and the tips of his mustache gradually started to look up.

"You tell them!" Cries of encouragement came from behind the spirals and the crosses of the fence, where a sizable crowd of onlookers had already gathered. "Tell them about the Pope, tell them about the Crusade!"

Ostap told them about the Pope. He condemned Alexander Borgia for bad behavior, mentioned St. Seraphim of Sarov for no apparent reason, and laid particularly hard into the Inquisition that persecuted Galileo. He got so carried away that he ended up laying the blame for the great scientist's misfortunes directly on the shoulders of Kuszakowski and Moroszek. That was the last straw. When he heard about Galileo's terrible fate, Adam quickly put the prayer book down on the steps and fell into Balaganov's bear-like embrace. Panikovsky was right there, stroking the prodigal son's scratchy cheeks. The air was filled with happy kissing.

"*Pan Kozlewicz!*" groaned the priests. "Where are you going? Come to your senses, *Pan!*"

But the heroes of the auto rally were already getting into their car.

"See!" shouted Ostap to the disconsolate priests while settling into the captain's seat, "I told you there's no God! It's a scientific fact. Farewell, Fathers! See you later!"

Hailed by the crowd, the Antelope took off, and soon the tin flags and the tiled roofs of the cathedral disappeared from view. To celebrate, the Antelopeans stopped at a beer joint.

"Thank you so much, guys!" said Kozlevich, holding a heavy beer mug in his hand. "I was as good as gone. Those priests really put a spell on me, especially Kuszakowski. He's one sneaky devil! He forced me to fast, can you believe it? Or else, he said, I wouldn't make it to heaven."

"Heaven!" said Ostap. "There's nothing going on in heaven these days. Wrong times, wrong historic period. The angels want to come down to earth now. It's nice down here: we have municipal services, the planetarium. You can watch the stars and listen to an anti-religious lecture all at once."

After the eighth mug Kozlevich ordered a ninth, raised it high above his head, sucked on his conductor's mustache, and asked excitedly:

"So there's no God?"

"No," answered Ostap.

"No? Well, to our health then."

And that's how he continued drinking, preceding each new mug with:

"Is there God? No? To our health then."

Panikovsky drank along with everybody else but kept mum on the subject of God. He didn't want to get involved in a controversy.

The return of the prodigal son, and the Antelope, gave the Chernomorsk Branch of the Arbatov Bureau for the Collection of Horns and Hoofs the glamor it had been lacking. The car was always waiting by the door of what used to be the five-merchant commune. It wasn't quite the same as a blue Buick or a stretch Lincoln, of course, or even a little Ford coupe, but it was still a car, an automobile, a vehicle which, in Ostap's words, despite all its flaws, could occasionally move around without the aid of horses.

Ostap immersed himself in his work. Had he devoted all his energies to the collection of horns or hoofs, the manufacturers of cigarette holders and combs would likely have had enough supplies to last them through the end of the current fiscal century. But the Branch President was involved in something totally different.

Having finished with both Funt and Berlaga, whose stories were very informative but hadn't lead directly to Koreiko, Ostap determined that, in the interests of business, he would make friends with Zosya Sinitsky and clear up a few things about Alexander Ivanovich—well, not as much about him as about his finances—in between polite kisses under a dark acacia tree. But a lengthy surveillance conducted by the Vice President for Hoofs revealed that there was no love between Zosya and Koreiko, and that the latter, as Shura put it, was just wasting his moves.

"Where there's no love," Ostap commented with a sigh, "there's no talk of money. Let's forget about the girl for now."

And while Koreiko recalled the charlatan in a police cap and his pathetic attempt at third-rate blackmail with a smile, the Branch President was racing all over town in a yellow car, looking for people great and small that the millionaire clerk had long forgotten about. But they remembered him very well. A few times, Ostap called Moscow and spoke to a businessman he knew, who was an expert on commercial secrets. The branch had begun receiving letters and telegrams that Ostap quickly separated from the bulk of the mail, which still largely consisted of urgent invitations, requests for horns, and admonishments over the slow rate of hoof collection. Some of those letters and telegrams went straight into the folder with shoelace straps.

In late July, Ostap set out on a trip to the Caucasus. Business required that the grand strategist make a personal visit to a small grape-growing republic.

On the day of the President's departure, the branch was rocked by a scandal. Panikovsky was issued thirty rubles to purchase a ticket at the port and came back within thirty minutes, drunk, with no ticket and no money left. He didn't offer any excuses; he just pulled out his pockets, which made them look as if they belonged on a pool table, and laughed incessantly. Everything made him laugh, whether it was the captain's wrath, or Balaganov's reproachful expression, or the samovar that was entrusted to him, or Funt, who was dozing off at his desk with the panama hat covering his nose. But when Panikovsky's eyes fell on the deer antlers—the pride and joy of the office, he cracked up so hard that he fell on the floor and soon fell asleep with a happy smile on his purple lips.

"Now we have all the attributes of a real organization," said Ostap, "even our own embezzler, who also doubles as the boozer doorman. The presence of these two characters gives all our undertakings a solid footing."

While Ostap was away, Fathers Moroszek and Kuszakowski appeared at the bureau several times. At the sight of the priests, Kozlevich would hide in the farthest corner of the office. The priests would open the door, peek inside, and quietly call out:

"*Pan Kozlewicz! Pan Kozlewicz!* Do you hear the voice of our Heavenly Father? Come to your senses, *Pan!*"

And Father Kuszakowski would point his finger toward the heavens, while Father Moroszek would work his rosary beads. Then Balaganov would confront the clerics and silently show them his flame-colored fist. The priests would retreat, casting a few wistful looks at the Antelope.

Ostap returned two weeks later. The entire staff came to greet him at the port. From his perch atop the tall black wall of the docking ship, the grand strategist looked at his subordinates with warmth and kindness. He had a whiff of roasted young lamb and excellent Georgian wine about him.

In addition to the secretary, who had been hired even before Ostap went away, two young men in heavy boots were also waiting at the Chernomorsk branch. They were agriculture students who had been sent to do internships.

"Oh, great!" said Ostap unenthusiastically. "The new generation is stepping in. But here, my dear comrades, you'll have to work very hard. I'm sure you know that horns, or pointed projections covered with either fur or hard fibers, represent outgrowths of the skull, and are found primarily in mammals?"

"We know that," said the students firmly, "we just need to do the internship."

The way he got rid of the students was complex and rather expensive. The grand strategist sent them to the steppes of Kalmykia to organize collection outposts. It cost the Bureau 600 rubles, but there was no other choice: the students would have been in the way of finishing the project, which was moving forward so nicely.

When Panikovsky found out how much was spent on the students, he took Balaganov aside and whispered angrily:

"And me, I don't get to go on business trips. I don't get vacation either. I need to go to the Yessentuki resort, to take care of my health. I get no days off and no work clothes. No, Shura, I don't like it here. Actually, I heard the pay at the Hercules is better. I'm going to go and be a messenger over there. As God is my witness, I am!"

In the evening, Ostap summoned Berlaga once again.

"On your knees!" shouted Ostap the moment he saw the accountant, sounding like Tsar Nicholas I.

The conversation itself, however, was quite amicable and went on for two hours. After it was over, Ostap ordered the Antelope to wait outside the Hercules the next morning.

CHAPTER 18
ON LAND AND AT SEA

Comrade Sardinevich arrived at the beach with a personalized briefcase. A silver business card, with a folded corner and a lengthy engraving in italics, was attached to it, and this card attested to the fact that Yegor Sardinevich had already celebrated five years of service at the Hercules.

He had a clean, open, gallant face, like that of the shaving Englishman from the ads. Sardinevich paused in front of the board where the water temperature was marked in chalk and then moved on to look for a good spot, his feet getting stuck in the hot sand.

The beachgoers' camp was crowded. Its makeshift structures rose in the morning, only to disappear at sunset, leaving behind the usual urban litter in the sand: shriveled melon peels, eggshells, and scraps of newspaper, which then proceed to lead a secret nocturnal life on the beach, whispering about this and that and flying around under the cliffs.

Sardinevich struggled past little huts made of waffle weave towels, past umbrellas and sheets stretched between tall stakes. Young women in skimpy swim skirts were hiding underneath. Most of the men were also wearing swimsuits, but not all. Some wore nothing but fig leaves, and even those covered not the private parts of the gentlemen of Chernomorsk but rather their noses—to prevent them from peeling. Having clad themselves in this way, the men were lying in the most uninhibited positions. Occasionally, they would cover their private parts with a hand, go into the water for a quick dip, and hurry back to the comfortable hollows made in the sand by their bodies, so as not to miss a single cubic inch of the curative sun bath.

The dearth of clothing on these people was more than compensated for by a gentleman of a totally different type. He wore leather boots with buttons, formal trousers, and a fully buttoned-up jacket, along with a stiff collar, a necktie, a pocket watch chain, and a fedora. A thick mustache, and the cotton that was stuck into his ears, completed this man's appearance. Next to him was a cane with a glass knob that was protruding vertically from the sand.

He suffered greatly from the heat. His collar was soaked with sweat. His armpits were as hot as a blast furnace, hot enough to smelt ore. Nevertheless, he continued to lie there, motionless. There's a man like this on every beach in the world. Nobody knows who he is, why he's here, or why he's lying in the sand in full dress uniform. But these people are out there, one for every beach. Maybe they are members of some clandestine League of Fools, or the remnants of the once powerful Rosicrucian Order, or half-crazed bachelors—who knows . . .

Yegor Sardinevich settled next to the member of the League of Fools and quickly took off his clothes. Sardinevich naked looked nothing like Sardinevich dressed. His gaunt English head sat on a white, feminine body with sloping shoulders and very broad hips. Yegor approached the water, tested it with his foot, and squealed. Then he put his other foot into the water and squealed again. Then he took several steps forward, plugged his ears with his thumbs, covered his eyes with his index fingers, closed his nostrils with his middle fingers, emitted a heart-wrenching shriek, and dunked himself four times in a row. Only after this elaborate procedure did he start swimming, paddling with his arms and turning his head up with every stroke. The rippling waters embraced Yegor Sardinevich, a model Herculean and an outstanding activist. Five minutes later, when the tired activist turned onto his back and his globular gut started rocking on the waves, the sound of the Antelope's maxixe came from the bluff above the beach.

Out stepped Ostap Bender, Balaganov, and the accountant Berlaga, whose face expressed full acceptance of his fate. All three of them climbed down to the beach and began searching for someone, peering unceremoniously into people's faces.

"These are his pants," said Berlaga finally, stopping in front of the pile of clothing that belonged to the unsuspecting Sardinevich. "He's probably far out in the sea."

"I've had it!" exclaimed the grand strategist. "I'm not waiting any longer. We're forced to take action both on land and at sea."

He slipped out of his suit and shirt, revealing his swim trunks, and marched into the water, waving his arms. On his chest, the grand strategist had a gunpowder-blue tattoo of short-armed Napoleon in a tricorne, holding a beer mug in his hand.

"Balaganov!" called Ostap from the water. "Undress Berlaga and get him ready. I might need him."

With that, the grand strategist swam away on his side, splitting the waters with his bronze shoulder and charting a north-northeasterly course, toward the pearly belly of Yegor Sardinevich.

Before submerging himself in the ocean's depths, Ostap had worked hard on dry land. The trail had led the grand strategist to the golden letters of the Hercules, and that was where he had been spending most of his time. He was no longer amused by rooms with alcoves and sinks, or by the statues, or the doorman in a cap with a golden zigzag who liked to gab about the fiery ritual of cremation.

Berlaga's desperate and muddled testimony brought to light the semi-executive figure of Comrade Sardinevich. At the Hercules, he occupied a large room with two windows, the kind of room once favored by foreign boat captains, lion tamers, and rich students from Kiev.

Two telephones rang in the room often and irritably, sometimes separately, sometimes together. But nobody answered the calls. Even more often, the door would crack open, a closely cropped bureaucratic head would pop in, glance around perplexed, and disappear, only to make way for the next head, this one not closely cropped but with a mane of wild stiff hair, or simply bald and purple, like an onion. But the onion skull wouldn't linger in the doorway either. The room was empty.

When the door opened for perhaps the fiftieth time that day, it was Bender who peeked into the room. Like everybody else, he turned his head from left to right and from right to left and, like everybody else, realized that Comrade Sardinevich was not in. Expressing his displeasure brazenly, the grand strategist started making the rounds of the departments, units, sections, and offices, inquiring about Comrade Sardinevich everywhere. And, everywhere, the answer was always the same: "He was here just a moment ago," or, "He just left."

The semi-executive Yegor was one of those office dwellers who either "were here just a moment ago" or "have just left." Some of them never even make it to their office during the entire workday. At 9 A.M. sharp, a person like this enters the building and, with the best of intentions, lifts his foot in order to put it on the first step. Great deeds await him. His schedule includes eight important appointments and two big meetings and a small one, all in his office. On his desk, there's a stack of papers, all requiring urgent action. There's so much to do and so little time. So this executive, or semi-executive, purposefully lifts his foot toward the first marble step. But setting it down is not that simple. "Comrade Parusinov, just one second," someone coos, "I just wanted to go over one small issue with you." Parusinov is gently taken by the arm and led into a corner. From this moment on, the executive—or the semi-executive—is a complete loss to the country. He's been taken over. The moment he clears up the small issue and runs three steps up, he's picked up again, taken to the window, or into a dark hallway, or to a secluded nook where the messy head of maintenance left some empty boxes lying around. People explain things to him, request things, urge him to do something, and plead with him to resolve certain matters urgently. By 3 P.M., and against all the odds, he finally makes it up the first flight of stairs. By 5 P.M., he even manages to break through to the second floor. But as his own office is on the third floor, and the workday is already over, he promptly runs downstairs and leaves the building, in order to make it to an urgent regional meeting. Meanwhile, the phones in his office are ringing off the hook, the scheduled appointments fall through, and his correspondence remains unanswered, while the attendees of the two big and one small meetings drink tea peacefully and chat about problems with public transportation.

The case of Yegor Sardinevich was particularly acute because of the extracurricular activities to which he dedicated himself with far too much zeal. He was especially adept at exploiting the universal mutual fraud that had somehow become the norm at the Hercules, which was for some reason referred to as extracurricular duties.

Sometimes the Herculeans would spend three straight hours in these meetings, listening to Sardinevich's demeaning blather.

They were all dying to grab Yegor by his plump thighs and throw him out a window from a considerable height. Sometimes they even felt that all extracurricular activities everywhere have always been a fiction, even though they were aware of some real activities of this kind taking place outside the Hercules. "What an asshole," they thought dejectedly, fiddling with pencils and teaspoons, "a goddamn phony!" But catching Sardinevich, and exposing him, was beyond their reach. Yegor gave all the right speeches about Soviet society, cultural pursuits, continuing education, and amateur art clubs. But there wasn't anything real behind this passionate rhetoric. Fifteen of his clubs, dedicated to politics, music, and the performing arts, had all been developing strategic plans for the past two years. And the local branches of various societies—whose goals were to advance aviation, knowledge of chemistry, automotive transportation, equestrian sports, highway construction, as well as the prompt eradication of ethnic chauvinism—existed only in the sick imagination of the local union committee. As for the school of continuing education, of which Sardinevich was especially proud, it was constantly reorganizing itself, which, as anybody knows, means it wasn't undertaking any useful activity whatsoever. If Sardinevich were an honest man, he would probably have admitted that all these activities were essentially a mirage. But the local union committee used this mirage to concoct its reports, so at the next level up nobody doubted the existence of all those musico-political clubs. At that level, the school of continuing education was imagined as a large stone building filled with desks, where perky teachers draw graphs that show the rise of unemployment in the United States on their chalkboards, while mustachioed students develop political consciousness right in front of your eyes. Out of this entire ring of volcanic extracurricular activity that Sardinevich built around the Hercules, only two fire-breathers were active: *The Chairman's Voice* newsletter, which Sardinevich and Bomze put together during work hours each month, and a plywood board with a sign that read THOSE WHO QUIT DRINKING AND CHALLENGE OTHERS, but there wasn't a single name listed on it.

Bender was sick and tired of chasing Sardinevich around the Hercules. The grand strategist couldn't catch up with the distinguished activist no matter what. Sardinevich eluded him every time. He had just been talking on the phone in the union committee room,. The earpiece was still warm, while the shiny black receiver still had the mist of his breath on it. Elsewhere, a man with whom Sardinevich had just been talking was still sitting on the window sill. Once Ostap even saw the reflection of Sardinevich in a stairwell mirror. He leaped forward, but the mirror promptly emptied, and it only reflected the window and a distant cloud.

"Holy Mother of Divine Interception!" exclaimed Ostap, trying to catch his breath. "What a useless, disgusting bureaucracy! Of course, our Chernomorsk Branch is not without its flaws, all those little deficiencies and inefficiencies, but it's nothing like here at the Hercules . . . Right, Shura?"

The Vice President for Hoofs emitted a deep pump-like sigh. They were back in the cool second-floor hallway where they had been some fifteen times before. And so, for the fifteenth time that day, they walked past the wooden bench that stood outside Polykhaev's office.

A German engineer named Heinrich Maria Sause, brought in from Germany at considerable expense, had been sitting on the bench since the morning. He wore the usual European suit, and his embroidered Ukrainian shirt was the only sign that the engineer had already spent a few weeks in Russia—he had had enough time to visit a gift shop. He sat still, his head resting on the wooden back of the bench, his eyes closed, as if he was about to get a shave. One might even think he was snoozing. But the half-brothers, who had repeatedly raced past him in pursuit of Sardinevich, noticed that the complexion of the foreign guest was constantly changing. At the beginning of the day, when the engineer took his position outside Polykhaev's door, his face was fairly rosy. The color grew in intensity with every passing hour, and by the first break it had taken on the color of postal sealing wax. By that time, Comrade Polykhaev had probably only reached the second flight of stairs. After the break, his complexion started changing in the opposite direction. The sealing wax turned into scarlet-fever spots. Heinrich Maria started going pale, and toward the end of the day, when the director of the Hercules had probably broken through to the second floor, the face of the foreign specialist became snow-white.

"What's with him?" Ostap whispered to Balaganov. "Such a huge spectrum of emotions!"

The moment Ostap uttered these words, Heinrich Maria Sause jumped up from his bench and looked at Polykhaev's door furiously. Behind it, the phone was ringing off the hook. "*Obstrukzionizm!*" shrieked the engineer in a high-pitched voice, grabbing the grand strategist by the shoulders and shaking him as hard as he could.

"*Genosse Polihaeff!*" he shouted, jumping in front of Ostap. "*Genosse Polihaeff!*"

He took out his pocket watch, thrust it in Balaganov's face, and then went after Bender again.

"*Was machen Sie?*" asked the dumbfounded Ostap, demonstrating a certain level of familiarity with the German language. "*Was wollen Sie* from a poor visitor?"

But Heinrich Maria Sause wouldn't let go. Keeping his left hand on Bender's shoulder, he dragged Balaganov closer with his right hand and gave them both a long, passionate speech. While he was at it, Ostap looked around impatiently, in the hope of getting hold of Sardinevich, while the Vice President for Hoofs hiccuped quietly, covering his mouth respectfully and staring mindlessly at the foreigner's shoes.

The engineer Heinrich Maria Sause had signed a year-long contract to work in the Soviet Union, or, as he put it with his usual precision, at the Hercules Corporation. "Watch out, Mr. Sause," warned his friend Bernhard Gerngross, a Doctor of Mathematics, "the Bolsheviks will make you work hard for their money." But Sause explained that he wasn't afraid of work and that he had long been looking for a good chance to apply his expertise in the field of mechanized forestry.

When Sardinevich informed Polykhaev that the foreign engineer had arrived, the director of the Hercules got all excited under his palm trees.

"We need him badly! Where is he?"

"Right now, at the hotel. Resting after his trip."

"Resting? You must be kidding!" exclaimed Polykhaev. "All that money we're paying him, all that hard currency! He's to report here tomorrow, at 10 A.M. sharp."

At five to ten, Heinrich Maria Sause entered Polykhaev's office, sporting coffee-colored pants and smiling at the thought of putting his expertise to good use. The boss wasn't in yet. He wasn't in an hour later either, or two hours later. Sause started losing patience. His only distraction came from Sardinevich, who would turn up every now and then and ask with an innocent smile:

"So, *Genosse* Polykhaev isn't in yet? That's odd."

Two hours later Sardinevich approached Bomze, who was eating breakfast in the hallway, and started whispering:

"I don't know what to do. Polykhaev told the German to be here at 10, but then he left for Moscow to see about the building. He'll be gone for at least a week. Do me a favor, Adolf Nikolaevich! I've got so many things to do. Continuing education, for instance—we're having so much trouble reorganizing. Would you stay with the German and keep him busy somehow? He costs big money, you know, hard currency."

Bomze sniffed his daily meat patty for the last time, swallowed it, brushed off the crumbs, and went to meet the foreign guest.

During the next week Sause, under the guidance of the affable Adolf Nikolaevich, visited three museums, attended a performance of *Sleeping Beauty*, and sat for some ten hours at a welcoming meeting that was held in his honor. The meeting was followed by a private celebration, during which select Herculeans had plenty of fun, raised their goblets and other glasses again and again, and challenged Sause with their usual "Drink it up!"

"Dearest Tillie," the engineer wrote to his fiancée in Aachen. "I've been in Chernomorsk for ten days now, but I haven't started working at the Hercules Corporation yet. I'm afraid I won't get paid for this time."

But the paymaster handed Sause his half-month's salary promptly on the fifteenth.

"Don't you think I'm getting paid for nothing?" he said to his new friend, Bomze. "I'm not doing any work."

"Don't give it another thought, my friend!" protested Adolf Nikolaevich. "But if you wish, we can set up a desk for you in my office."

So Sause wrote the next letter to his fiancée at his own desk:

"Darling, My life here is strange and very unusual. I do absolutely nothing, yet they pay me punctually, as stipulated in the contract. I am surprised. Tell this to our friend, Dr. Bernhard Gerngross. He'd find it interesting."

When Polykhaev returned from Moscow, he was happy to hear that Sause already had a desk.

"Perfect!" he said. "Sardinevich should bring him up to speed."

But Sardinevich, who at the time was devoting all his energies to the organization of a major accordion club, dumped the German back on Bomze. Adolf Nikolaevich wasn't happy. The German interfered with his meals and generally refused to keep quiet, so Bomze dumped him on the Industrial Department. At the time, however, that department was reorganizing, which boiled down to endlessly moving their desks around, so they got rid of Heinrich Maria by sending him to Finance and Accounting. Here Arnikov, Dreyfus, Sakharkov, Koreiko, and Borisokhlebsky, who didn't speak any German, decided that Sause was a tourist from Argentina, and spent entire days explaining the Hercules's accounting system to him using sign language.

After a month, a distressed Sause caught up with Sardinevich in the dining room and started shouting:

"I don't want to get paid for nothing! Give me some work to do! If it continues like this, I'll complain to your boss!"

Sardinevich didn't like this last part of the foreign specialist's speech. He called Bomze to his office.

"What's with the German?" he asked. "Why is he blowing his top?"

"You know," said Bomze, "I think he's just a troublemaker. I'm telling you. The man sits at his desk, does absolutely nothing, makes tons of money—and still complains!"

"He really is a troublemaker," agreed Sardinevich, "a German, what can you expect? We have to resort to punitive action. I'll tell Polykhaev when I get the chance. He'll stuff him into a bottle in no time."

Heinrich Maria, however, himself decided to try to get to Polykhaev. But because the Hercules director was one of those people who "were here just a moment ago" or who have "just left," this attempt only led to the wait on the wooden bench and the explosion that the innocent sons of Lieutenant Schmidt fell victim to.

"*Byurokratizmus!*" shouted the German, switching to the difficult Russian language in agitation.

Ostap quietly took the European guest by the arm, brought him over to the complaints box that was hanging on the wall, and said, as if he was talking to a deaf person:

"Here! Understand? In the box. *Schreiben, schrieb, geschrieben.* Write. You understand? I write, you write, he, she, it writes. Understand? We, you, they write complaints and put them in this box. Put! The verb 'to put.' We, you, they put the complaints in . . . And nobody takes them out. To take out! I don't take out, you don't take out . . ."

But then the grand strategist spotted Sardinevich's broad hips at the end of the hallway and, forgetting about the grammar lesson, rushed after the elusive activist.

"Hang in there, Germany!" shouted Balaganov to the German with encouragement, hurrying after his captain.

But to Bender's utter frustration, Sardinevich had dematerialized once again.

"Now that's sorcery," said Bender, turning his head back and forth. "The man was here just a moment ago—and now he's gone."

In desperation, the half-brothers started trying all the doors one by one. But after entering the third door, Balaganov jumped back out in a panic. His face was contorted.

"Uh, uh," uttered the Vice President for Hoofs, leaning against the wall, "uh, uh, uh . . ."

"What's the matter, sonny?" asked Bender. "Was somebody mean to you?"

"In there," mumbled Balaganov, pointing his shaking hand.

Ostap opened the door and saw a black coffin.

The coffin rested in the middle of the room on a desk with drawers.

Ostap took off his captain's cap and tiptoed over to the coffin. Balaganov watched him apprehensively. A minute later Ostap beckoned Balaganov and showed him a large white sign that was painted on the side of the coffin.

"See what it says here, Shura?" he asked. "*'Death to red tape!'* Are you all right now?"

It was a magnificent propaganda coffin. On major holidays, the Herculeans carried it outside and paraded it around town, singing songs. The pall bearers were usually Sardinevich, Bomze, Berlaga, and Polykhaev himself. He was a man of democratic principles, and he had no qualms about joining his subordinates at various political marches and festivals. Sardinevich held the coffin in high regard and considered it very important. From time to time, Yegor would put on an apron and repaint the coffin with his own hands, sprucing up the anti-bureaucratic slogan. Meanwhile, the phones in his office were ringing off the hook, and head after head popped in through the cracked door and glanced around hopelessly.

Bender never got a hold of him. The doorman in the cap with a zigzag informed Ostap that Comrade Sardinevich had been there just a moment before—but he had just left for a swim at the beach, which, as he often said, helped him recharge.

The Antelopeans woke up Kozlevich, who was dozing off behind the wheel, and headed out of town, bringing Berlaga along just in case.

Was it any surprise that Ostap, who was worked up from everything that had happened that day, went straight into the water in pursuit of Sardinevich, and that he was completely unconcerned by the fact that an important conversation about dirty business dealings had to be conducted in the Black Sea?

Balaganov followed the captain's instructions to the T. He undressed the compliant Berlaga, led him to the edge of the water, and waited patiently, holding him by the waist with both hands. A difficult exchange was apparently taking place at sea. Ostap bawled like a sea lion. Nobody could make out the words. They could only see that Sardinevich attempted to head back to shore, but Ostap intercepted him and chased him further out into the open sea. Then the voices became louder, and certain words could be heard: "The Intensivnik!"—"And who profited? The Pope?"—"What do I have to do with it?"

Berlaga has long been stomping his bare feet, leaving an Indian's tracks in the wet sand. Finally, a call came from the sea:

"Send him in!"

Balaganov launched the accountant into the sea. Berlaga paddled off quickly, slapping the water with his arms and legs. Seeing him, Yegor Sardinevich dove in terror.

The Vice President for Hoofs, in the meantime, stretched out on the sand and lit a cigarette. He waited for about twenty minutes. Berlaga was the first to return. He squatted, took a handkerchief from his pocket, and said, wiping his face:

"Our Sardinevich confessed. Confronting a witness did him in."

"The creep has squealed?" asked Shura good-naturedly. He took the cigarette butt out of his mouth with his thumb and index finger and tut-tutted. Spit shot out of his mouth, swift and long, like a torpedo.

Hopping on one foot and aiming the second into his pant leg, Berlaga offered a cryptic explanation:

"I did it not in the interest of veracity but in the interest of truth."

Next to arrive was the grand strategist. He dropped on his stomach and, with his cheek on the hot sand and a meaningful look on his face, watched the blue Sardinevich get out of the water. Then he took the folder from Balaganov's hands and, wetting the pencil with his tongue, started recording the new information that he worked so hard to obtain.

The transformation of Yegor Sardinevich was amazing. Just thirty minutes earlier, the sea had embraced a most exemplary activist, a man of whom even Comrade Netherlandov, chairman of the local union, always said: "Of all people, Sardinevich would never fail us." But Sardinevich had failed them this time. And how! Instead of a lovely female body with the head of a shaving Englishman, the gentle summertime waves carried to shore a shapeless sack filled with mustard and horseradish.

While the grand strategist plundered the waves, Heinrich Maria Sause finally ambushed Polykhaev and had a very serious talk with him. He left the Hercules totally bewildered. With a strange smile on his face, he went to the post office and, standing at a tall desk with a glass top, wrote a letter to his fiancée in Aachen:

"My dear girl, I have some exciting news. My boss Polykhaev is finally sending me to a factory. But what I find incredible, dear Tillie, is that here at the Hercules Corporation this is called 'to stuff one into a bottle' (*sagnat w butilku*)! My new friend Bomze told me that I'm being sent to the factory as a punishment. Can you imagine? And our good friend Dr. Bernhard Gerngross—will he ever be able to understand it?"

CHAPTER 19
THE UNIVERSAL STAMP

By noon the following day, the Hercules started filling with rumors that the director had locked himself up in his palm-filled gallery with a visitor, and that for the last three hours he hadn't been responding to Impala Mikhailovna's knocking or to internal telephone calls. The Herculeans didn't know what to make of it. They were used to Polykhaev being promenaded up and down the hallways, or seated on window sills, or lured into nooks under the stairs; those were the places where all the decisions were made. Somebody even suggested that the boss had quit the ranks of those who "had just left" and joined the influential category of "the hermits." People like this usually sneak into their offices early in the morning, lock the door, unplug the phone, and, with the rest of the world effectively blocked off, start putting together all kinds of reports.

Meanwhile, work had to go on: documents urgently needed signatures, responses, and resolutions. An edgy Impala Mikhailovna repeatedly approached Polykhaev's door and listened carefully. Small round pearls swayed in her large ears.

"This is without precedent," the secretary said gravely.

"But who, who is in there with him?" asked Bomze, giving off a strong odor of both cologne and meat patties. "An inspector, maybe?"

"No, I'm telling you, it's just an ordinary visitor."

"And Polykhaev has already spent three hours with him?"

"This is without precedent," repeated Impala Mikhailovna.

"So how are we going to overcome this outcome?" Bomze became agitated. "I urgently need Polykhaev's signature. Here's the full report on the reasons why the premises of the former Tin and Bacon Co. do not meet our needs. I have to have a signature."

The staff besieged Impala Mikhailovna. They all held documents of varying degrees of importance in their hands. After another hour during which the rumble of voices continued behind the door, Impala Mikhailovna sat down at her desk and said softly:

"All right, comrades. Let's see your papers."

She reached into a cabinet and took out a long wooden stand. Thirty-six rubber stamps with thick polished handles were hanging on it. Expertly picking the proper stamps from their nests, she started applying them to the papers that just couldn't wait any longer.

The director of the Hercules hadn't signed papers in his own hand in a long while. Whenever the need arose, he took a stamp out of his vest pocket, breathed on it affectionately, and imprinted a purple facsimile of his signature next to his title. He really enjoyed this process, and it occurred to him that it wouldn't be a bad idea to commit some of the most common resolutions to rubber as well.

That was how the first of the rubber dictums came into being:

NO OBJECTIONS. POLYKHAEV

AGREED. POLYKHAEV

GOOD THINKING. POLYKHAEV

MAKE IT HAPPEN. POLYKHAEV

After testing the new tool, the boss of the Hercules concluded that it simplified his job significantly and thus deserved to be promoted and advanced still further. Another batch of rubber was soon put to work. This time, the resolutions were more elaborate:

ISSUE A FORMAL REPRIMAND. POLYKHAEV

ISSUE A WARNING. POLYKHAEV

ASSIGN TO A REMOTE LOCATION. POLYKHAEV

DISMISS WITHOUT SEVERANCE PAY. POLYKHAEV

The war that the director of the Hercules was waging against the Municipal Affairs Department over the building inspired a few more general-purpose statements:

I DON'T REPORT TO MUNICIPAL AFFAIRS. POLYKHAEV
ARE THEY COMPLETELY CRAZY? POLYKHAEV
LEAVE ME ALONE. POLYKHAEV
I'M NOT YOUR NIGHT WATCHMAN. POLYKHAEV
THE HOTEL IS OURS, AND THAT'S THAT. POLYKHAEV
I'M NOT A FOOL. POLYKHAEV
NO BEDS, NO SINKS FOR YOU. POLYKHAEV

This particular set was ordered in three copies. The war was expected to be protracted, and the insightful director had good reason to believe that a single set might not suffice.

The next set was ordered to meet the internal needs of the Hercules.

ASK IMPALA MIKHAILOVNA. POLYKHAEV
GIVE ME A BREAK. POLYKHAEV
EASY DOES IT. POLYKHAEV
GO TO HELL! POLYKHAEV

Naturally, the director's creative thinking went beyond strictly administrative matters. As a man of broad vision, he simply couldn't ignore the political issues of the day. And so he ordered an extraordinary universal stamp that took him several days to develop. It was a magnificent rubber creation, which Polykhaev could apply in every eventuality. Not only did it enable him to react to events expeditiously, it also relieved him of the need to think long and hard each time. The handy stamp was designed so that he only needed to fill out the blank space in order to produce a timely and appropriate resolution:

IN RESPONSE TO _____,
WE THE HERCULEANS, TO A PERSON, WILL RESPOND BY:
A) IMPROVING THE QUALITY OF OUR BUSINESS CORRESPONDENCE;
B) INCREASING OUR PRODUCTIVITY;
C) INTENSIFYING THE FIGHT AGAINST RED TAPE, OBSTRUCTIONISM,
   NEPOTISM, AND SYCOPHANCY;
D) DOING AWAY WITH ABSENTEEISM AND BIRTHDAY PARTIES;
E) REDUCING EXPENDITURES ON CALENDARS AND PORTRAITS;
F) STEPPING UP UNION ACTIVITIES;
G) CEASING TO CELEBRATE CHRISTMAS, EASTER, WHIT MONDAY,
   ANNUNCIATION, EPIPHANY, KURBAN-BAIRAM, YOM KIPPUR,

RAMADAN, PURIM, AND OTHER RELIGIOUS HOLIDAYS;

H) RELENTLESSLY FIGHTING AGAINST MISMANAGEMENT,
HOOLIGANISM, ALCOHOLISM, AVOIDANCE OF RESPONSIBILITY,
SPINELESSNESS, AND ANTI-MARXIST DISTORTIONS;

I) JOINING, TO A MAN, THE SOCIETY AGAINST CONVENTION ON
THE OPERA STAGE;

J) SWITCHING ENTIRELY TO SOYBEANS;

K) TRANSFERRING ALL PAPERWORK TO THE ROMAN ALPHABET;

AS WELL AS ANYTHING THAT MAY BE NECESSARY HENCEFORTH.

The blank space was filled out by Polykhaev himself, as needed, depending on the situation at hand.

Little by little, Polykhaev grew very fond of his universal resolution and applied it with ever-increasing frequency. In the end, he started using it to respond to the various abuses, machinations, intrigues, and outrages committed by his own employees.

For example:

IN RESPONSE TO *the brazen outrage by the bookkeeper Kukushkind, who demanded overtime pay,* WE THE HERCULEANS . . .

Or:

IN RESPONSE TO *the ghastly machinations and disgraceful intrigues by the staff member Borisokhlebsky, who requested an unscheduled vacation,* WE THE HERCULEANS . . ."—and so on and so forth.

Each situation had to be immediately responded to by improving, increasing, intensifying, doing away with, reducing, stepping up, ceasing, relentlessly fighting, joining, switching, transferring, as well as anything that may be necessary henceforth.

And only after castigating Kukushkind or Borisokhlebsky in this manner would the director apply a shorter stamp: ISSUE A WARNING. POLYKHAEV or ASSIGN TO A REMOTE LOCATION. POLYKHAEV.

Upon their first encounter with the rubber resolution, some of the Herculeans became concerned. The long list of action items made them nervous. They were particularly troubled by the Roman alphabet and the need to join the Society Against Convention on the Opera Stage. But everything worked out just fine. Of course, Sardinevich went out of his way and organized a club named "Down With the Queen of Spades!" in addition to a branch of the above-mentioned society, but that was the end of it.

As the fan-like hum of voices continued behind Polykhaev's door, Impala Mikhailovna got down to work. The stamps on the stand were arranged by size—from the smallest one, AGREED. POLYKHAEV, to the grandest, universal one—and the stand itself resembled an elaborate musical instrument in the circus, the one on which the white clown with the sun painted on his lower back plays Braga's *Serenade* with sticks. The secretary would select a stamp with a more or less appropriate response and apply it to the document at hand. She made particularly good use of the cautious stamp, EASY DOES IT, remembering that this was the director's favorite.

The work went smoothly. The stamp was a perfect substitute for the man. Polykhaev in rubber was just as good as Polykhaev in person.

The Hercules had already emptied out, and only the barefoot cleaning ladies with their dirty buckets were walking around the hallways; the last typist, who had stayed on for an hour after work in order to copy Sergey Yesenin's lines for herself —AS I LAY DOWN THE GILDED RUGS OF POEMS, I WISH TO TELL YOU WORDS OF TENDER LOVE—had already left; and Impala Mikhailovna, who had grown tired of waiting, had already gotten up and started massaging her eyelids with her cold fingers—when the door to Polykhaev's office shuddered, then opened, and Ostap Bender slowly came out. He looked past Impala Mikhailovna and walked away, waving a yellow folder with shoelace straps. Polykhaev was next to emerge from the cool shadows of the palms and ficus. Impala looked at her powerful friend and sunk silently onto the square pad that covered the hard seat of her chair. Thank God the other employees were already gone and couldn't see their boss at that moment. A diamond tear sat in his mustache, like a little bird in a tree. Polykhaev blinked incredibly quickly and rubbed his hands vigorously, as if he was trying to make fire by friction, like a native of Oceania. He ran after Ostap, smiling pitifully and stooping forward.

"So what's going to happen now?" he mumbled, rushing ahead of Ostap from one side, then from the other. "I'm not going down, am I? I'm begging you, please, please tell me, I'm not going down? I don't have to worry, do I?"

He was about to add that he had a wife and kids, and Impala and kids by her, and kids by yet another woman in Rostov-on-the-Don, but something squeaked in his throat, and he didn't say anything.

With tearful howls, he followed Ostap all the way to the entrance. The building was deserted, and they came across only two other people on the way. Yegor Sardinevich stood at the end of the hallway. Seeing the grand strategist, he clapped his hand over his mouth and stepped back into a niche. Down below, in the stairwell, Berlaga was peeking out from behind the marble woman with the electric torch. He bowed to Ostap slavishly and even uttered "How do you do?", but Ostap ignored the Viceroy's greetings.

When they reached the door, Polykhaev grabbed Ostap's sleeve and murmured:

"I told you everything. Honest! I don't have to worry, right? Do I?"

"Only an insurance policy will make your life completely worry-free," replied Ostap without slowing down. "Any life insurance agent will tell you that. Personally, I have no need for you any more. The authorities, on the other hand, may develop an interest in you fairly soon."

CHAPTER 20
THE CAPTAIN DANCES A TANGO

Balaganov and Panikovsky sat at a white table in a small refreshment bar whose sign was adorned with crudely painted blue siphons. The Vice President for Hoofs was munching on a long cream-filled pastry, making sure that the cream didn't escape from the other end. He was chasing down this heavenly chow with seltzer water flavored with a green syrup called Fresh Hay. The messenger was drinking healthful kefir. Six little bottles already stood empty in front of him, and he was busily shaking the thick liquid into his glass from the seventh. In the morning, the new secretary had distributed the pay according to the list signed by Bender, and the pals were enjoying the cool breezes that were emanating from the Italian stone slabs of the bar, from the heavy metal icebox that was filled with moist feta cheese, from the darkened cylinders of fizzy water, and from the marble counter. A chunk of ice slid out of the ice box and sat on the floor, bleeding water. It was a pleasant sight compared to the exhausted appearance of the street, with its short shadows, people beaten down by the heat, and dogs dazed from thirst.

"Chernomorsk is such a nice city!" said Panikovsky, licking his lips. "Kefir is good for the heart."

For some reason, Balaganov found this piece of information quite amusing. Laughing, the Vice President accidentally squashed his pastry, squeezing out a thick sausage-like link of cream that he barely managed to catch in midair.

"You know, Shura," continued Panikovsky, "somehow, I no longer trust Bender. I don't think he's doing the right thing."

"Watch it!" said Balaganov menacingly. "Who cares what you think?"

"No, seriously. I have a lot of respect for Ostap Ibragimovich: what a man! Even Funt—and you know how much I respect Funt—even he said that Bender is a brain. But I have to tell you, Shura: Funt is an ass! He's such a fool, I'm telling you! A wretched, miserable person, that's all! Bender, I have nothing against him. But there's something that just doesn't feel right. I'll tell you everything, Shura, like you were my brother."

Nobody had spoken to Shura like a brother since his last chat with a police detective. That's why he was pleased to hear the messenger's words and carelessly allowed him to continue.

"You know, Shura," said Panikovsky in a whisper, "I have a lot of respect for Bender, but I have to tell you: Bender is an ass! A wretched, miserable person, I swear!"

"Hey, watch it!" Balaganov warned him.

"Why are you saying that? Just think of what he's wasting our money on. Think about it! What do we need this stupid office for? It costs a fortune! Funt alone gets 120. Then there's the secretary! Then those two guys showed up and they got paid today, too. I saw it myself. They came from the employment agency! What's the point of all this? He says: For legality. I don't give a damn about legality if it costs us so much. How about those antlers? Sixty-five rubles! And that inkwell set! And all those hole binders!"

Panikovsky unbuttoned his shirt, and the fifty-kopeck dickey that was attached to his neck rolled up instantly, like a parchment scroll. But the violator of the pact was so worked up he didn't even notice.

"Yes, Shura. You and I earn our miserly wages while he enjoys all the luxuries. Tell me, did he really have to go to the Caucasus? He says it was a business trip. Yeah, right! Panikovsky doesn't have to believe everything they tell him! I was the one who went to buy the ticket for him. A first-class ticket, mind you! This fancy show-off can't even take second class! That's where our ten thousand is going! He makes long-distance phone calls, he sends urgent cables all over the world. Do you know how much an urgent cable costs? Forty kopecks per word. And I can't even afford the kefir that I need for my health. I am a sick old man. I'll tell you honestly: Bender is no brain."

"Take it easy," said Balaganov hesitantly. "Bender made a man out of you. Remember how you were running with that goose in Arbatov? And now you're working, you're getting paid, you're a member of society."

"I don't want to be a member of society!" screamed Panikovsky. Then he added in a lower voice: "Your Bender is an idiot. He started this whole stupid investigation, while we can take the money right now, with our bare hands."

At this point, the Vice President for Hoofs forgot about his beloved chief and moved his chair closer to Panikovsky. The latter, constantly pulling down his wayward dickey, apprised Balaganov of the important investigation which he himself had conducted at his own risk.

On the same day that the grand strategist and Balaganov were busy chasing Sardinevich, Panikovsky, without permission, left Funt alone in the office, snuck into Koreiko's room in his absence, and searched it thoroughly. Naturally, he found no money, but he had discovered something even better—kettlebell weights. Huge black weights, probably fifty pounds each.

"To you, Shura, I'll tell you like you were my brother. I solved the mystery of those weights."

Panikovsky finally caught the wayward tail of his dickey, attached it to the button on his pants, and looked at Balaganov triumphantly.

"What mystery?" asked the disappointed Vice President for Hoofs. "They're just regular weights for exercise, that's all."

"You know how much I respect you, Shura," said Panikovsky, growing agitated, "but you're an ass. These weights are made of gold! Don't you get it? Pure gold! They're fifty pounds each. One hundred pounds of pure gold. I figured it out right away, it's like I was hit by lightning. I stood there in front of those weights and laughed like mad. That bastard Koreiko! He had those golden weights cast and painted black, and he thinks no one will ever find out!

"To you, Shura, I'll tell you like you were my brother—you think I would have told you if I could carry them myself? But I'm a sick old man, and the weights are heavy. So I'm sharing this with you like you were my brother. I'm not like Bender. I'm honest!"

"But what if they're not made of gold?" asked the Lieutenant's favorite son, who badly wanted Panikovsky to dispel his doubts, the sooner the better.

"And what do you think they are made of?" asked the violator of the pact sarcastically.

"Yeah," said Balaganov, blinking with his red eyelashes, "now I see. What do you know—an old man figured it all out! You're right about

Bender. He's doing something wrong: writes all those papers, travels . . . We'll give him his share, though, right? That'll only be fair."

"Why should we?" protested Panikovsky. "We get everything! Now we'll live the good life, Shura. I'll get gold teeth, and I'll get married, you'll see! I swear I'll get married!"

It was decided that the precious weights should be expropriated without any further delay.

"Pay for the kefir, Shura," said Panikovsky, "we'll settle it later."

The conspirators left the bar and went wandering around the city, blinded by the sun. They couldn't wait. They spent a long time standing on bridges, their stomachs to the railings, and stared indifferently down on the roofs and streets that descended to the port. Trucks were climbing down those streets cautiously, like horses. Fat sparrows from the port pecked the pavement under the watchful eyes of filthy cats hiding in the alleys. Beyond the rusted roofs, attic windows, and radio antennas, one could see the blue water, a small tugboat racing at full speed, and a steamer's yellow funnel with a large red letter on it.

From time to time, Panikovsky would raise his head and start counting. He was converting pounds into ounces, ounces into ancient grains, and each time he'd come up with a figure so attractive it made the violator of the pact squeal ever so slightly.

Some time after 10 P.M. that night, the half-brothers were trudging towards the Bureau for the Collection of Horns and Hoofs, stooping under the weight of two large kettlebells. Panikovsky carried his share in both arms, sticking his stomach out and puffing happily. He stopped frequently, put his weight down on the sidewalk, and mumbled: "I'll get married! I swear, I'll get married!" The mighty Balaganov carried his weight on his shoulder. Sometimes Panikovsky would fail to turn the corner properly due to the weight's momentum. Then Balaganov would grab Panikovsky's collar with his free hand and send his body in the right direction.

They stopped at the entrance to their office.

"Now we'll each saw off a little piece," said Panikovsky anxiously, "and tomorrow we'll sell them. There's a watchmaker I know, Mr. Bieberham. He'll give us a good price. Unlike that government place, where you'll never get a good price."

But then the conspirators noticed a light coming from under the green office curtains.

"Who could it be, at this time of night?" asked Balaganov in surprise, bending down to peek through the keyhole.

Ostap Bender was sitting behind his desk in the lateral beam of a bright electric lamp, writing furiously.

"Writer!" said Balaganov, laughing heartily and letting Panikovsky peek into the keyhole.

"Of course," uttered Panikovsky after taking a long, hard look, "he's at it again. I'm telling you, this miserable man makes me laugh. But where are we going to saw now?"

The half-brothers lifted their weights and went on into the darkness, continuing their lively discussion about selling two pieces of gold to the watchmaker the first thing in the morning, for starters.

Meanwhile, the grand strategist was finishing his account of the life of Alexander Ivanovich Koreiko. The five little log cabins that comprised the Face the Country set all had their bronze lids off. Ostap dipped his pen indiscriminately, wherever his hand went, fidgeted in his chair, and shuffled his feet under the desk.

He had the bleary face of a gambler who's been losing all night and only at the break of dawn finally hits a winning streak. All night the banks were ahead and the cards weren't coming out right. The gambler kept changing tables, trying to outwit fate and find a lucky spot. But the cards just wouldn't behave. He already started to sweat the cards, that is, look at the first card and then squeeze out the second one as slowly as possible. He was already pushing cards over the edge of the table and peeking at them from underneath, or placing two cards face to face and opening them like a book. In other words, he went through all the motions of a loser. But nothing worked. He'd been getting mostly face cards: jacks with ropey mustaches, queens smelling paper flowers, and kings with doormen's beards. Black and red tens were showing up frequently, too. In other words, the hands were lousy—the kind that are officially known as baccarat, and unofficially as rags. And only when the chandeliers dim and go off, when losers in worn collars snore and choke on chairs under the NO SLEEPING signs, a miracle occurs. The banks suddenly start losing, the disgusting pictures and tens disappear, the eights and nines come out one by one. The gambler no longer darts around the room, no longer sweats the cards or peeks under them. He senses he's on a winning streak. The regulars crowd behind the lucky man, pull on his shoulders, and whisper fawningly: "Uncle Yura, can I have three rubles?" While he, proud and pale, turns the cards over daringly and takes the last shirts off his partners' backs amid the calls "Table nine now has spots available!" and "Fifty kopecks from each of you, amateurs!" And the green table with white lines and curves drawn on it becomes a happy and joyful sight for him, like a soccer field.

Ostap no longer had any doubts. The game was turning his way.

All that had been unclear became clear. The numerous people with ropey mustaches and kingly beards that Ostap had encountered, and who had left their traces in the yellow folder with shoelace straps, had suddenly dropped off, and the white-eyed ham-face, with wheat-blonde eyebrows and drill-sergeant jowls, came to the fore, sweeping everyone and everything else aside.

Ostap put a full stop, blotted his work with a press whose silver handle was shaped like a bear cub, and started filing the papers. He liked to keep his files in order. He admired the smoothed-out testimonials, telegrams, and assorted official papers for the last time. There were even photographs and account statements in the folder. It contained the complete story of Alexander Ivanovich Koreiko, along with palms, girls, the azure ocean, a white ship, the Blue Express, a gleaming automobile, and Rio de Janeiro, a magical city on the bay inhabited by friendly mulattos, where the vast majority of citizens wear white pants. The grand strategist had finally found the kind of individual he'd been dreaming about all his life.

"And no one can even appreciate this heroic effort of mine," sighed Ostap, getting up and tying the laces on the thick folder. "Balaganov is very nice, but dumb. Panikovsky is just a cranky old man. Kozlevich is an angel without wings. He's still convinced that we do collect horns for the manufacturers of cigarette-holders. Where are my friends, my wives, my children? I only hope that the esteemed Alexander Ivanovich appreciates my great effort and rewards it with some five hundred thousand, in consideration of my poverty. Wait a minute! After all this, I won't take less than a million, or else the friendly mulattos will have no respect for me."

Ostap got up from his desk, picked up his remarkable folder and started pacing around the empty office, thinking. He skirted the typewriter with the German accent and the ticket punch, and nearly brushed his head against the deer antlers. The white scar on Ostap's throat turned pink. His motions gradually grew slower, and his feet, clad in the red shoes he bought from a Greek sailor, started sliding silently across the floor. Without realizing it, he began to sidestep. His right arm held the folder to his chest in a tender embrace, like a woman, while his left arm stretched forward. The squeaky Wheel of Fortune was clearly heard above the city. It produced a gentle musical tone that suddenly turned into a gentle string harmony. The poignant, long-forgotten tune gave voices to all the objects found at the Chernomorsk Branch of the Arbatov Bureau for the Collection of Horns and Hoofs.

The samovar was the first to begin. A flaming ember suddenly fell out of it onto the tray. The samovar broke into a song:

> Under the sun of Argentina,
> Where the skies are blue and steamy . . .

The grand strategist was dancing a tango. His coin-like face appeared in profile. He would get down on his knee, then get up quickly, turn, and slide forward again, stepping lightly. His invisible coattails flew apart during the sudden turns.

Meanwhile, the typewriter with the German accent picked up the tune:

> . . . Where the zkiez are blue and zteamy,
> With picture-perfect ladiez gleaming . . .

The lumbering cast-iron ticket punch, who had been around, sighed quietly about times gone by:

> . . . With picture-perfect ladies gleaming,
> The tango's danced by all.

Ostap was dancing a classical provincial tango; it had been a feature of variety shows twenty years earlier, when Berlaga wore his first bowler hat, when Sardinevich worked in the Mayor's Office, when Polykhaev was taking his first test for the Imperial Civil Service, and the dummy chairman Funt was a sprightly seventy-year-old who sat in the Florida Café with other Piqué Vests and discussed the shocking news that the Dardanelles were closed due to the Italo-Turkish War. The Piqué Vests, who still had red cheeks and smooth skin back then, were going over the current political figures of the time. "Enver Pasha is a brain. Yuan Shikai is a brain. Purishkevich is also a brain, after all!" they said. And even that far back, they claimed that Briand was a brain, for he was already serving in the government.

Ostap was dancing. Palms crackled above his head; colorful birds fluttered over him. Ocean liners brushed against the piers of Rio de Janeiro. Savvy Brazilian dealers undercut coffee prices in broad daylight, while local youths enjoyed alcoholic beverages in open-air restaurants.

"I am commanding the parade!" exclaimed the grand strategist.

He turned off the lights, went out, and took the shortest possible route to Lesser Tangential Street. Searchlights crisscrossed the sky, then descended, slicing across buildings and suddenly revealing a balcony or a glass-covered porch where a startled couple would freeze up. Two small tanks with round mushroom caps swayed from around the corner toward Ostap, their tracks clattering. A cavalryman bent down from his saddle and asked a pedestrian how to get to the Old Market. In one place, Ostap's path was blocked by moving cannons. He rushed through between two artillery batteries. At another spot, policemen were hastily nailing a black GAS SHELTER sign to the door.

Ostap was in a hurry. The Argentine tango was egging him on. Paying no attention to what was going on around him, he entered Koreiko's building and knocked on the familiar door.

"Who's there?" came the voice of the underground millionaire.

"Telegram!" answered the grand strategist, winking into the darkness.

The door opened, and he entered, bumping his folder against the door frame.

At sunrise, the Vice President and the messenger were sitting in a gully far beyond the city limits.

They were sawing through the weights. Their noses were smudged with iron shavings. Panikovsky's dickey lay beside him on the grass. He had taken it off—it interfered with his sawing. The prudent violator of the pact had put newspapers under the weights, so as not to waste a single speck of the precious metal.

At times the half-brothers exchanged significant glances and went back to work with renewed energy. The only sounds heard in the serenity of the morning were the whistles of gophers and the scraping of overheated hacksaws.

"What the hell?" said Balaganov finally and stopped working. "I've been sawing for three hours now, and still no gold."

Panikovsky didn't say anything. He already knew the answer, and for the last thirty minutes, he had been moving the hacksaw back and forth just for show.

"Well, let's saw some more!" said the red-headed Shura cheerfully.

"Yes, let's," agreed Panikovsky, trying to put off the terrible moment of reckoning.

He covered his face with his hand and watched the rhythmic motions of Balaganov's broad back through his spread fingers.

"I don't get it!" said Shura after sawing through the entire kettlebell and pulling the two apple halves apart. "This isn't gold!"

"Keep sawing, keep sawing," whimpered Panikovsky.

But Balaganov was already approaching the violator of the pact, holding a cast-iron hemisphere in each hand.

"Don't come near me with that iron!" shrieked Panikovsky, running a few steps away. "I despise you!"

Then Shura drew his arm back and, groaning from the effort, hurled half of the kettlebell at the schemer. Hearing the projectile whiz over his head, the schemer dropped to the ground.

The battle between the Vice President and the messenger did not last very long. First, the enraged Balaganov gleefully stomped on the dickey, and then moved on to its owner. While pummeling him, Shura kept repeating:

"Whose idea was that? Who embezzled from the office? Who bad-mouthed Bender?"

On top of that, the Lieutenant's firstborn remembered the violation of the Sukharev pact, and that cost Panikovsky a few extra punches.

"You'll be sorry you trashed my dickey!" Panikovsky shouted angrily, protecting himself with his elbows. "I'll never forgive you for the dickey, keep that in mind! You can't buy a dickey like this any more!"

In conclusion, Balaganov took away his opponent's ratty little wallet, which contained thirty-eight rubles.

"That's for your kefir, you creep!" he explained.

The walk back to the city was joyless.

An angry Shura was walking in front of Panikovsky, who limped along behind him, sobbing loudly.

"I'm a poor old man!" he wailed. "You'll be sorry you trashed my dickey. Give me back my money."

"Just wait, you'll get yours!" said Shura without looking back. "I'll tell Bender all about it. Hothead!"

CHAPTER 21
THE END OF THE ROOKERY

Barbara Ptiburdukov was happy. She was sitting at a round table, survey-ing her household. The Ptiburdukovs' room was filled with furniture, so there was hardly any open space left. But even that small space was good enough for happiness. The lamp cast its light through the window, where a small green branch quivered like a lady's brooch. Cookies, candies, and a small can of pickled walleye sat on the table. The electric kettle cap-tured the whole of the Ptiburdukovs' cozy nest on its rounded surface. It reflected the bed, the white curtains, and the night stand. It also reflected Ptiburdukov himself, who was sitting in front of his wife, wearing dark-blue pajamas with braids. He, too, was happy. Blowing cigarette smoke though his mustache, he was using a fretsaw to make a plywood model of a country outhouse. It was a painstaking job. First, he had to carve out the walls, then put on a sloping roof, add the inside equipment, insert glass in the tiny window, and finally attach a microscopic hook to the door. Ptiburdukov toiled with passion; he thought woodcarving was the best way to relax.

Having finished the project, the satisfied engineer laughed, patted his wife on her soft warm back, and pulled the can of fish closer. At that very moment, however, somebody started banging on the door, the lamp flickered, and the kettle slid off its wire stand.

"Who could it be so late?" wondered Ptiburdukov, opening the door.

The End of the Rookery

Standing in the stairwell was Basilius Lokhankin. He was wrapped up to his beard in a white Marseilles blanket, his hairy legs showing. He held *Man and Woman*, which was thick and gilded, like an icon, to his chest. His eyes were wandering.

"Please come in," said the astonished engineer, taking a step back. "Barbara, what's this all about?"

"I came today to live with you forever," replied Lokhankin in a grave pentameter, "it's shelter that I'm seeking now from you."

"What do you mean—shelter?" said Ptiburdukov, turning red in the face. "What do you want, Basilius Andreevich?"

Barbara ran out into the stairwell.

"Sasha! Look, he's naked!" she screamed. "Basilius, what happened? Come in, for God's sake, come in."

Barefoot Lokhankin stepped over the threshold and started racing around the room, muttering: "Disaster, disaster!" The edge of his blanket promptly knocked Ptiburdukov's delicate woodwork to the floor. The engineer stepped back into a corner, with a hunch that nothing good was going to come of all this.

"What disaster?" asked Barbara. "Why are you only wearing a blanket?"

"I came today to live with you forever," lowed Lokhankin.

His yellow heel beat an anxious drumroll on the clean waxed floor.

"What are you talking about?" Barbara scolded her ex-husband. "Go home and sleep it off. Get out of here! Go, go home!"

"My home is gone," said Basilius, continuing to shiver. "My home has burned to ashes. A fire, that's what's bringing me to you. I only saved the blanket that I wear, and saved a book, my favorite at that. But since you're being so unkind and cruel, I'll go away, and damn you both for that."

Swaying in despair, Basilius headed for the door. But Barbara and her husband held him back. They apologized; they said that at first they hadn't grasped what had happened, and started fussing around Lokhankin. They brought out Ptiburdukov's new suit, underwear, and shoes.

While Lokhankin was dressing, the couple had a discussion in the hallway.

"Where are we going to put him?" whispered Barbara. "He can't stay here, we only have one room."

"You surprise me," said the kind-hearted engineer, "the man has just suffered a terrible misfortune, and all you can think of is your own comfort."

195

When they returned to the room, the victim was sitting at the table, eating pickled fish straight from the can. On top of that, two volumes of *Strength of Materials* had been knocked off the shelf—the gilded *Man and Woman* was in it's place.

"The whole building burned down?" asked Ptiburdukov with sympathy. "How terrible!"

"Well, I think maybe that's how it should be," remarked Basilius, finishing off his hosts' supper, "I may emerge from the flames a new man, don't you think?"

But a new man he was not.

After the conversation died down, the Ptiburdukovs started getting ready for the night. They set up a small mattress for Basilius on the last remaining free spot, which only an hour earlier had been good enough for happiness. The window was closed, the lights were turned off, and night entered the room. Everyone was quiet for about twenty minutes, just tossing and sighing deeply from time to time. And then Lokhankin's whiny whisper came from the floor:

"Barbara! Barbara! Hey, Barbara!"

"What now?" asked the ex-wife angrily.

"Why did you leave me, Barbara?"

Receiving no answer to this fundamental question, Basilius started whining:

"You're a floozy, Barbara! You're a she-wolf! You she-wolf you, I truly do despise you . . ."

The engineer lay in bed quietly, livid with rage and clenching his fists.

The Rookery caught fire at midnight, at exactly the same time when Ostap Bender was dancing a tango in the empty office, and while the half-brothers Balaganov and Panikovsky were walking out of town, stooped under the weight of the golden kettlebells.

Nobody's grandma was the first link in the long chain of events that ultimately led to the fire in apartment No. 3. She, as we know, had been burning kerosene in her loft because she didn't believe in electricity. For a long time after Basilius Andreevich was flogged, nothing exciting happened in the apartment, and the restless mind of Chamberlain Mitrich suffered from the idleness. So he thought long and hard about the grandma's ways and became alarmed.

"The old bat will burn the whole place down!" he grumbled. "What does she care? And my grand piano alone is probably worth two thousand."

With that in mind, Mitrich had all his belongings insured against fire. That way, he didn't have to worry about it anymore, and so he watched calmly as the grandma dragged a large murky bottle of kerosene up to her loft, holding it like a baby. The first to find out about Mitrich's prudent move was Citizen Hygienishvili, who immediately interpreted it in his own peculiar way. He came up to Mitrich in the hallway, grabbed him by the chest, and said threateningly:

"You want to burn the whole place down? You want to get the insurance money? You think Hygienishvili is a fool? Hygienishvili understands everything."

And so the hot-blooded tenant took out a large insurance policy for himself on the very same day. The Rookery was terrified. Lucia Franzevna Pferd came running into the kitchen with her eyes bulging.

"These bastards will burn us all down. Whatever you say, people, I'm off to buy my own insurance right now. We'll have a fire anyway, but at least I'll get some money. I have no desire to go penniless because of them."

The next day, everybody bought insurance, with the exception of Lokhankin and nobody's grandma. Lokhankin was busy reading *Motherland* magazine and wasn't paying attention, while the grandma didn't believe in insurance any more than she did in electricity. Nikita Pryakhin brought home his purple-edged insurance policy and studied its watermarks against the light at length.

"So the government gives us a helping hand?" he said glumly. "Offers aid to the tenants? Well, thank you kindly! So now we'll do as we wish."

He stuck the policy under his shirt and went into his room. His words made people so fearful that no one at the Rookery went to bed that night. Dunya was packing, while the other bed renters went off to stay with their friends. During the day, everyone watched everyone else, and the building was being slowly emptied of belongings, piece by piece.

There was no longer any doubt. The house was doomed. It simply had to burn down. And indeed, it went up in flames at midnight, set ablaze on six sides simultaneously.

The last to escape from the building, which was already filled with samovar smoke and streaks of fire, was Lokhankin. He tried to protect himself with a white blanket. He screamed "Fire! Fire!" at the top of his lungs, even though it was no longer news to anybody. All the Rookery tenants were already there. Inebriated Pryakhin was sitting on his trunk with metal corners. He stared mindlessly at the flickering windows, mumbling: "We'll do as we wish." Hygienishvili was squeamishly sniffing his hands, which smelled of kerosene, and he wiped them on his pants after each sniff. A flaming spiral flew out of a window and sprung open under the wooden overhang, sending sparks downward. The first window pane shattered and fell out, making a loud noise. Nobody's grandma burst into a terrifying howl.

"The house stood here for forty years," explained Mitrich with authority, walking around in the crowd. "It stood through all the regimes; it was a good one. But under the Soviets, it burned down. A sad, sad fact, citizens."

The female population of the Rookery banded together and couldn't take their eyes off the flames. Cannon-like fire was shooting from all the windows. The flames would disappear momentarily and the darkened house would seem to recoil, like an artillery piece that's just been fired. Then the red-and-yellow cloud would reappear, giving Lemon Lane a bright and festive look. It was hot. One could no longer stand near the house, so the gathering moved to the opposite sidewalk.

Only Nikita Pryakhin didn't move; he was snoozing on his trunk in the middle of the street. Then he suddenly jumped up, barefoot and wild-looking.

"Christians!" he yelled out, tearing his shirt apart. "Citizens!"

He ran away from the fire sideways, barged into the crowd, and, shouting something unintelligible, started pointing at the burning building. The crowd was rattled.

"They forgot a baby," said a woman in a small straw hat confidently.

People surrounded Nikita. He tried to push them away and get to the house.

"On my bed!" he yelled like a madman. "Let me go, let me go!"

Violent tears streamed down his cheeks. He hit Hygienishvili on the head in order to clear the way and ran into the courtyard. A minute later, he ran back out with a ladder.

"Stop him!" shouted the woman in a straw hat. "He'll burn alive!"

"Get lost!" yelled Pryakhin, setting the ladder against the wall and pushing away the young men who were trying to grab his legs. "I can't leave it. My soul's on fire!"

He kicked with his legs and climbed up the ladder, toward the smoke billowing from the second-floor window.

"Get back!" people shouted from the crowd. "What are you doing? You'll burn!"

"On my bed!" Nikita continued to bellow. "A full bottle of vodka, a big one! Three quarts! How can I leave it behind, Christians?"

With unexpected agility, Pryakhin grabbed onto the flashing and instantly disappeared, sucked in by the air stream. His last words were: "We'll do as we wish." Silence fell over the street, only to be interrupted by the bell and the trumpets of the fire brigade. Firemen in stiff canvas suits with broad dark-blue belts came running into the courtyard.

A minute after Nikita Pryakhin committed the only heroic act of his life, a large burning timber fell from the building and crashed onto the ground. The roof cracked open with a tearing sound and collapsed into the house. A shining pillar rose to the sky, as if the house had fired a cannonball toward the moon.

Such was the end of apartment No. 3, which was known as the Rookery.

The clatter of hoofs was suddenly heard in the lane. The fire lit up a racing horse cab carrying the engineer Talmudovsky. A suitcase covered with luggage labels sat on his knees. Bouncing in his seat, the engineer was leaning toward the coachman, shouting:

"I'm not staying here for another minute! Not at this salary! Go, go!"

And then his fat back, lit by the flames and the firemen's torches, disappeared around the corner.

CHAPTER 22
I AM COMMANDING THE PARADE

"I'm dying of boredom," said Ostap, "we've only been chatting here for two hours, and I'm already sick of you, like I've known you all my life. Maybe an American millionaire can afford to be pig-headed, but a Soviet millionaire must be more amenable."

"You're crazy!" replied Alexander Ivanovich.

"Don't insult me," said Bender peacefully. "I'm the son of a Turkish subject and hence a descendant of janissaries. I will not spare you if you're not nice to me. Janissaries have no mercy for women, children, or underground Soviet millionaires."

"Please go away!" said Koreiko, sounding like a bureaucrat from the Hercules. "It's past two o'clock. I want to sleep, and I have to go to work early in the morning."

"Oh, yes, I forgot about that!" exclaimed Ostap. "You can't afford to be late to work. You might get fired without severance pay. Two-week's wages are nothing to sneeze at: twenty-three rubles! It may very well last you for six months, considering how thrifty you are."

"It's none of your business. Leave me alone. Do you hear me? Get out!"

"But that same thriftiness will be your undoing. Of course, revealing your millions would be dangerous. But you're trying too hard. Have you thought of what might happen when you're finally able to spend your money? Abstinence is a dangerous thing! Somebody I knew, a teacher of French named Ernestina Iosifovna Poincaré, never once touched alcohol in her life. So guess what? Somebody gave her a shot of brandy at a dinner party. She liked it so much that she drank the whole bottle and lost her mind right there, at the dinner table. The number of teachers of French on this planet was reduced by one. This could happen to you, too."

"So what the hell do you want from me?"

"The same thing my childhood friend, Nick Osten-Backen, wanted from another childhood friend of mine, Inga Zajonc, a Polish beauty. He wanted her love. And I want yours. Citizen Koreiko, I want you to fall in love with me and hand me a million rubles as a token of your affection."

"Out!" said Koreiko quietly.

"Well now, you're forgetting again that I'm a descendant of janissaries."

With that, Ostap got up. The two of them stood facing each other. A storm came over Koreiko's face, with whitecaps flashing in his eyes. The grand strategist was smiling warmly, showing white teeth that looked like kernels of corn. The adversaries moved closer to the desk lamp, and their giant shadows stretched across the wall.

"I already told you a thousand times that I never had any millions— and I still don't," said Koreiko, trying not to blow up. "Do you get it? Do you? Now get lost! I'm going to report you."

"You're not going to report me to anybody," said Ostap knowingly. "Of course I can leave, but the moment I step out onto this Lesser Tangential Street of yours, you'll run after me, crying, licking my janissary's heels, and begging me to come back."

"And what makes you think that I'll beg?"

"You will. And that's how it should be, as a friend of mine, Basilius Lokhankin, often said. That's exactly what the Great Homespun Truth is all about. Here it is!"

The grand strategist put the folder on the table, started to undo its shoelaces slowly, and continued:

"But first let's make a deal. No dramatic moves! You are not to strangle me, not to throw yourself out the window, and, most importantly, not to die of a stroke. If you decide to experience an untimely death, you'll make me look foolish. The fruits of my lengthy and honest labors would be lost. So let's have a little chat. It is now clear that you don't love me. I'll never get from you what Nick Osten-Backen got from Inga Zajonc, my childhood friend. So I'm not going to sigh in vain or grab you by the waist. Consider the serenade over. The sounds of balalaikas, psalteries, and gilded harps have all died out. I come to you as one legal entity to another. Here's a file weighing six to eight pounds. It's for sale, and it costs a million rubles, that same million you refuse to give me as a gift because you're so stingy. So buy it!"

Koreiko leaned over the table and read:

"'The Case of Alexander Ivanovich Koreiko. Opened June 25, 1930. Closed August 10, 1930.'"

"Hogwash!" he said, shrugging. "I'm sick of this. First you bring me this money, now you come up with some kind of case. It's ridiculous."

"So are you buying or not?" the grand strategist persisted. "The price is very reasonable. For a pound of riveting information on the subject of underground commerce, I only charge 150,000."

"What information?" asked Koreiko rudely, reaching for the folder.

"The most fascinating kind," replied Ostap, politely pushing Koreiko's hand away. "The information about your second, real life, which is strikingly different from your first life, the one at the Hercules, the forty-six ruble one. Everybody knows about your first life. From ten to four, you support the Soviet regime. As for your second life, from four to ten—I alone know about it. Do you get the picture?"

Koreiko didn't answer. Shadows lay in his drill-sergeant jowls.

"No," said the grand strategist emphatically, "unlike everyone else, you came from a cow, not an ape. You think very slowly, like a hoofed mammal. I'm telling you this as an expert on horns and hoofs. So once again: I think you have roughly seven or eight million. The file costs a million. If you don't buy it, I'll take it elsewhere immediately. They won't give me anything for it, nothing. But you will be finished. I'm telling you this as one legal entity to another. I will remain the same poor poet and polygamist I was before, but, to my dying days, I will cherish the thought that I saved society from one greedy bastard."

"Show me the file," said Koreiko pensively.

"Take it easy," said Ostap, opening the folder, "I am commanding the parade. You've already received a telegram to that effect. Well, the parade has started, and I am commanding it, as you may have noticed."

Alexander Ivanovich glanced at the first page, saw a picture of himself, smiled unpleasantly, and said:

"I still don't understand what it is that you want from me. Well, why don't I take a look, out of sheer curiosity."

"I, too, was driven by curiosity," declared the grand strategist. "All right, let's get started, strictly out of curiosity—an innocent motive, after all. Gentlemen of the jury, Alexander Ivanovich Koreiko was born . . . Well, we can skip the happy childhood. In those innocent times, little Sasha wasn't yet involved in commercial plunder. Then comes rose-colored adolescence. Let's skip another page here. Now comes youth, the beginning of life. Here, it may be worth pausing for a moment. Out of sheer curiosity, of course. On page six . . ."

Ostap turned page six over and read out loud from pages seven, eight, and on through page twelve.

"And so, gentlemen of the jury, you have just learned of my client's first major operations, among them: selling government-owned medications during the famine and the typhoid epidemic, as well as working in the field of food supplies, which led to the disappearance of a food train that was headed for the famine-stricken Volga region. Gentlemen of the jury, all these facts are of interest to us strictly out of curiosity."

Ostap spoke in the awful manner of a pre-revolutionary attorney who would catch on to a certain word and then never let it go, using and abusing it throughout a long ten-day trial.

"The arrival of my client in Moscow in 1922 may also arouse curiosity . . ."

The face of Alexander Ivanovich remained neutral, but his hands felt around the table aimlessly, as if he was blind.

"Gentlemen of the jury, allow me to ask you a question. Out of sheer curiosity, of course. How much profit can two ordinary barrels of tap water possibly bring? Twenty rubles? Three rubles? Eight kopecks? No, gentlemen! They brought Alexander Ivanovich exactly four hundred thousand golden rubles. Of course, the two barrels carried the colorful name of Revenge, the Industrial Chemicals Cooperative. But let us continue. Pages 42 to 53. The location: a small gullible republic. Blue skies, camels, oases, and dandies in gilded skullcaps. My client helps build a power plant. I repeat: helps. Look at his face, gentlemen of the jury!"

Getting carried away, Ostap turned toward Alexander Ivanovich and pointed a finger at him. But he wasn't able to trace a dramatic curve with his hand, the way pre-revolutionary attorneys used to. The defendant suddenly grabbed his arm in midair and started to twist it silently. At the same time, the defendant made an attempt to grab his attorney by the throat. For about thirty seconds, the opponents wrestled each other, shaking under the strain. Ostap's shirt came unbuttoned, and his tattoo showed through the opening. Napoleon was still holding a beer mug, but he was very red, as if he had already had a few too many.

"Stop putting pressure on my psyche!" said Ostap, shoving Koreiko away and catching his breath. "I can't work like this."

"Bastard! Bastard!" whispered Alexander Ivanovich. "What a bastard!"

He sat down on the floor, wincing from the pain inflicted upon him by the janissaries' descendant.

"Our deliberations continue!" said Ostap, as if nothing had happened. "Gentlemen of the jury, you can now see that the ice has broken. The defendant tried to kill me. Out of childish curiosity, of course. He just wanted to know what's inside me. I'm happy to satisfy his curiosity. Inside, there's a noble and very healthy heart, excellent lungs, and a liver without any signs of stones. Please enter all this in the record. And now—let our games continue, as the editor of a certain humor magazine would say, opening a new meeting and looking sternly at his staff."

Alexander Ivanovich hated the games. The business trip from which Ostap returned with wine and lamb on his breath left substantial traces in the file. There was a copy of the sentence, which was delivered in absentia, blueprints of the charitable printing plant, excerpts from the profits and losses account, as well as pictures of the electric gorge and of the kings of the silver screen.

"And finally, gentlemen of the jury, the third phase in the activities of my belligerent client: a humble desk job at the Hercules for the sake of society, and intensified efforts in underground commerce for his own sake. Let us note, strictly out of curiosity, some illegal dealings in hard currency, furs, stones, and other compact staples. Let us also point out a series of self-exploding stock companies with flowery, cooperative-sounding names like the Intensivnik, the Toiling Cedar, the Sawing Aid, and the Southern Lumberjack. It wasn't Mr. Funt, the prisoner of private capital, who was in charge of all this, it was my friend the defendant."

With that, the grand strategist once again pointed at Koreiko, tracing at last the long-planned dramatic curve with his hand.

Then Ostap pompously requested the imaginary court's permission to ask the defendant a few questions, waited for a minute in order to stay in character, and inquired:

"Did the defendant have any out-of-office dealings with a certain Berlaga from the Hercules? He didn't. Right! A certain Sardinevich, also from the Hercules? He didn't either. Perfect! A certain Polykhaev?"

The millionaire clerk kept silent.

"I have no further questions. Whew! I'm tired and I'm hungry. Tell me, Alexander Ivanovich, you wouldn't happen to have a cold meat patty in your breast pocket? No? Unimaginable poverty, especially in view of the amount you wheedled out of the kindly Hercules, with Polykhaev's assistance. Here's Polykhaev's testimony in his own hand. He was the only Herculean who knew what was hiding behind that forty-six-ruble-a-month clerk. Yet even he didn't fully understand what you are. But I do. Yes, gentlemen of the jury, my client has sinned. This has been proven. But I am nevertheless asking for leniency, albeit on the condition that the defendant purchases this folder from me. I am finished."

Alexander Ivanovich came to his senses toward the end of the grand strategist's speech. He put his hands in the pockets of his summer pants and went over to the window. The young day, adorned with streetcar bells, was already filling the city with sounds.

Volunteers from the Society for Defense and Aviation were marching past the front yard, holding their rifles every which way, as if they were carrying rakes. Pigeons strolled on the zinc-plated roof ledge, tapping with their red-twig feet and flapping their wings constantly. Alexander Ivanovich, who had trained himself to be frugal, turned off the desk lamp and asked:

"So it was you who sent me all those stupid telegrams?"

"Yes," said Ostap. "'Load oranges barrels brothers Karamazov.' Pretty good, isn't it?"

"A bit silly."

"And how about that crazy bum?" asked Ostap, sensing that the parade was going well. "Wasn't he good?"

"A childish prank! Ditto for the book about millionaires. When you showed up as a cop from Kiev, I knew right away you were a small-time crook. Unfortunately, I was wrong. Otherwise, there's no way in hell you would've found me."

"Yes, you were wrong. No one is wise all the time, which is what Inga Zajonc, the Polish beauty, said a month after she married Nick Osten-Backen, my childhood friend."

"Well, I can understand the mugging, but the weights! Why did you steal my weights?"

"What weights? I didn't take any weights."

"You're just too ashamed to admit it. All in all, you did a lot of stupid things."

"Perhaps," allowed Ostap. "I'm no angel. I have my shortcomings. Well, I enjoyed chatting with you. My mulattos are waiting. Are you ready with the money?"

"Oh yes, the money!" said Koreiko. "There's a bit of a problem with the money. It's a nice folder, no question about it, wouldn't be a bad purchase. But as you were calculating my profits, you completely disregarded my expenses and direct losses. A million is a preposterous amount."

"Goodbye," said Ostap coldly, "please make sure you stay home for the next thirty minutes. A lovely carriage with bars on its windows will come pick you up."

"That's no way to do business," said Koreiko with a haggler's smile.

"Perhaps," sighed Ostap, "but I'm not a financier, you know. I'm a freelance artist and a wandering philosopher."

"So what makes you think you should get the money? I worked for it, and you . . ."

"I didn't just labor for it. I even incurred some losses. After talking to Berlaga, Sardinevich, and Polykhaev, I lost my faith in humanity. Isn't faith in humanity worth a million rubles?"

"Yes, it certainly is," assured Alexander Ivanovich.

"So, shall we go to the vaults?" asked Ostap. "Where do you keep your cash, incidentally? Not in a savings bank, I imagine?"

"Let's go!" said Koreiko. "You'll see."

"Is it far?" fussed Ostap. "I can get a car."

But the millionaire refused the car and stated that it wasn't far at all, and that they should avoid any unnecessary pomp. He graciously let Bender go first and went out after him, picking up a small newspaper-wrapped package from the table. Going down the stairs, Ostap hummed: "Under the sun of Argentina . . ."

CHAPTER 23
THE DRIVER'S HEART

Outside, Ostap took Alexander Ivanovich by the arm, and the two strategists started walking briskly toward the train station.

"You're better than I expected," Bender said amicably. "Good for you. One should part with money easily, without complaining."

"What's a million if it goes to a good man?" replied the clerk, listening for something.

When they turned onto Mehring Street, the howl of the siren spread over the city. The sound was long, undulating, and mournful. On a foggy night, a sound like this makes seamen uneasy, makes them want to ask for hazard pay, for some reason. The siren continued to wail. It was joined by a variety of horns and other sirens, more distant and even more mournful. Pedestrians suddenly sped up, as if they were being chased by a driving rain. At the same time, they were all chuckling and glancing at the sky. The fat old women who sold sunflower seeds ran with their stomachs stuck out, glass cups bouncing in rush baskets that were full of their ever-shifting wares. Adolf Nikolaevich Bomze raced across the street, cutting the corner. He managed to slip safely into the revolving door of the Hercules. A squad of mounted police reserves on mismatched horses galloped past. An automobile emblazoned with red crosses whizzed by. The street was suddenly empty. Ostap caught sight of a small herd of Piqué Vests far ahead as they detached themselves from the former Florida Café. Waving their newspapers, boater hats, and panamas, the old men went trotting down the street. But before they reached the corner, there was the deafening, cracking sound of an artillery blast. The Piqué Vests lowered their heads, froze, then turned around, and trotted back. The flaps of their woven silk jackets blew in the wind.

The maneuvers of the Piqué Vests made Ostap laugh. While he was admiring their amusing gestures and leaps, Alexander Ivanovich went ahead and opened the package he brought from home.

"Wild geezers! Vaudeville comics!" said Ostap, turning toward Koreiko.

But there was no Koreiko. Instead, the grand strategist saw a grotesque mug with the glass eyes of a diving suit and a rubber trunk, at the end of which dangled a khaki metal cylinder. Ostap was so startled that he even jumped.

"That's not funny!" he said, reaching for the gas mask. "Citizen defendant, please come to order!"

But the next moment, a whole group of people in similar masks surrounded them, and he could no longer recognize Koreiko among the dozen or so identical rubber mugs. Holding his folder close, Ostap immediately started looking at the monsters' legs, but the moment he thought he recognized Koreiko's widower pants, he was grabbed by the arms, and a spirited voice announced:

"Comrade! You've been poisoned!"

"Who's been poisoned?" protested Ostap, trying to free himself. "Let me go!"

"Comrade, you've been poisoned by gas!" repeated the orderly cheerfully. "You're in the affected zone. See, there's the gas bomb."

And indeed, a small wooden box was sitting in the middle of the street, with thick smoke busily pouring out of it. The suspicious pants had moved far away. They flashed for the last time between two plumes of smoke and disappeared altogether. Ostap fought hard and silently to free himself. Six gas masks were already restraining him.

"Plus you've been hit by shrapnel in the arm, Comrade. Don't get upset, Comrade! Please understand. You know there's a military exercise going on. We'll bandage your wounds and carry you to the gas shelter."

The grand strategist just couldn't grasp that there was no use resisting. The gambler, who had hit a winning streak at sunrise and kept surprising everybody at the table, lost everything within ten minutes to a young man who had dropped in casually, just out of curiosity. He no longer looks pale and triumphant, and the regulars no longer crowd around him, begging him for a few lucky coins. He'll be returning home on foot. A Young Communist League girl with a red cross on her apron ran up to Ostap. She pulled bandages and gauze out of her canvas bag and wrapped them around the grand strategist's arm, on top of his sleeve. She kept frowning, so as not to burst out laughing. After her act of mercy was complete, she giggled and ran to the next casualty, who obediently offered her a leg. Others tried to carry Ostap to the stretcher. Another skirmish ensued, with trunks swaying around, while the first orderly, who was in charge, continued to appeal to Ostap's conscience and other civic virtues in the loud voice of a lecturer.

"Guys!" muttered the grand strategist as he was being belted to the stretcher. "Please tell my late father, a Turkish subject, that his beloved son, who once specialized in horns and hoofs, fell like a hero on the battlefield."

In the end, the battlefield casualty recalled a few songs:

"Sleep, oh ye warrior eagles! Nightingale, nightingale, teensy bird . . ."

The stretcher started moving. Ostap fell silent and gazed into the sky, which was getting quite busy. Light-colored puffs of smoke, as dense as hearts, rolled across it. Transparent celluloid planes moved at high altitude in an irregular V formation. They emitted a resonant quiver, as if they were all connected with tin threads. The howling sirens could still be heard between the frequent artillery blasts.

Ostap was to suffer yet another humiliation. They carried him right past the Hercules. The Herculeans peeked out of the windows on all four floors of the lumber/timber enterprise. The entire Finance and Accounting stood on window sills. Lapidus Jr. teased Kukushkind, pretending that he was about to push him over the edge. Berlaga made big eyes and bowed to the stretcher. Polykhaev and Sardinevich, their arms around each other's shoulders, stood in a second-floor window, with palm trees in the background. When they spotted the bound Ostap, they started whispering and quickly shut the window.

The stretcher stopped in front of a sign that said Gas Shelter No. 34. They helped Ostap up, and since he once again tried to break free, the orderly in charge had to once again appeal for his understanding.

The gas shelter was set up in the neighborhood community center. It was a long, bright semi-basement with a ribbed ceiling, with models of military and postal aircraft suspended from it by metal wires. There was a small stage in the back of the room. Two dark-blue windows with the moon and the stars, along with a brown door, were painted on the wall behind it. The Piqué Vests, whose entire herd had been apprehended, were languishing near the wall under a sign that read: WE DON'T WANT A WAR, BUT WE'RE READY TO FIGHT. A lecturer in a green military tunic was pacing on the stage. Glancing fretfully at the door that continued to noisily admit new groups of victims, the lecturer was enunciating with military clarity:

"In terms of their effect, the poisonous chemicals used in warfare include asphyxiating agents, tear-inducing agents, lethal poisons, blistering agents, general irritants, etc. Of the tear-inducing agents, we might mention chloropicrin, benzyl bromide, bromoacetone, chloracetophenone . . ."

Ostap shifted his gloomy gaze from the lecturer to the audience. Young men were listening intently, or took notes, or were occupied with the display of rifle parts. A sporty looking young woman sat alone in the second row, gazing pensively at the painted moon.

"A nice girl," decided Ostap, "too bad there's no time for that. What is she thinking about? I bet it's not benzyl bromide. What a shame! Just this morning, I could have dashed off with a girl like this to Oceania, or Fiji, or some High Society Islands—or to Rio de Janeiro."

The thought that Rio had been lost sent Ostap pacing frantically around the shelter.

The Piqué Vests, numbering forty, had already recovered from the shock, straightened their starched collars, and launched into a heated debate about the pan-Europe proposal, the Tripartite Maritime Conference, and Gandhism.

"Did you hear?" one Vest asked another. "Gandhi arrived in Dandi."

"Gandhi is a real brain!" the other sighed. "Dandi is a brain, too."

An argument ensued. Some Vests maintained that Dandi was a place and thus couldn't possibly be a brain. Others vehemently argued the opposite. In the end, everybody agreed that Chernomorsk was about to be declared a free city any day.

The lecturer cringed again because the door opened, and two new arrivals noisily entered the room: Balaganov and Panikovsky. They were caught in the gas attack on the way back from their nighttime jaunt. After working on the weights, they were as filthy as naughty tomcats. Seeing the captain, they both looked down.

"Have you been to a dinner party or something?" asked Ostap gloomily.

He was afraid they might ask him about the Koreiko case, so he frowned angrily and went on the attack.

"Well, boys and girls, what have you been up to?"

"I swear," said Balaganov, putting his hand on his heart, "it was all Panikovsky's idea."

"Panikovsky!" the captain called out sternly.

"I give you my word!" exclaimed the violator of the pact. "I'm sure you know, Bender, how much I respect you! It was all Balaganov's doing."

"Shura!" called out Ostap even more sternly.

"How could you believe him?" said the Vice President for Hoofs reproachfully. "Do you really think I would have taken those weights without your permission?"

"So it was you who took the weights!" exclaimed Ostap. "But why?"

"Panikovsky said they were made of gold."

Ostap looked at Panikovsky. Only then did he notice that Panikovsky no longer had the fifty-kopeck dickey under his jacket, and that his bare chest was exposed for the whole world to see. Without saying a word, the grand strategist collapsed onto his chair. He started shaking and grasped the air with his hands. Volcanic thunder erupted from his throat, tears filled his eyes, and laughter that expressed all the exhaustion of the night, all the disappointment over the struggle with Koreiko that the half-brothers caricatured so pathetically—a terrible laughter rolled through the gas shelter. The Piqué Vests flinched, while the lecturer started talking even more clearly and loudly about the poisonous chemicals used in warfare.

Laughter was still prickling Ostap with a thousand tingling needles, but he already felt refreshed and rejuvenated, like a man who had gone through the entire routine at the barbershop: a close relationship with the razor, an encounter with the scissors, a sprinkle of hair tonic, and even the combing of the eyebrows with a special brush. The shiny ocean wave already lapped into Bender's heart, so when Balaganov asked him how things were going, he said everything was great, except that the millionaire had unexpectedly fled in an unknown direction.

Ostap's words didn't register properly with the half-brothers because they were thrilled that they had gotten away with the whole weights business so easily.

"Look, Bender," said the Vice President for Hoofs, "see that young lady over there? That's the one Koreiko always went out with."

"Oh, so this is Zosya Sinitsky?" said Ostap with emphasis. "Just like the poem: 'By chance, in a thunderous ballroom . . .'"

Ostap made his way to the stage, interrupted the speaker politely, and learned from him that their captivity would last for another couple of hours. He thanked him and sat down right there, near the stage, next to Zosya. Shortly thereafter, she was no longer looking at the crudely painted window. Laughing far too loudly, she was trying to tear her comb out of Ostap's hands. As for the grand strategist, he must have been talking incessantly, judging by the way his lips were moving.

The engineer Talmudovsky was next to be brought into the gas shelter. He was fighting back with his two suitcases. His ruddy forehead was damp with sweat and shiny like a crêpe.

"There's nothing I can do, Comrade!" said the man in charge. "It's an exercise! You were inside the affected zone."

"But I was in a cab!" the engineer insisted. "IN A CAB! I have to get to the station fast, it's for my work. I missed the train last night. Are you saying I have to miss another one?"

"Comrade, please understand!"

"Why should I understand when I was in a cab!" raged Talmudovsky.

He kept pushing this fact, as if riding in a cab made the passenger immune somehow and stripped chloropicrin, bromoacetone, and benzyl bromide of their deadly properties. God knows how long Talmudovsky would have continued to bicker with the volunteers had it not been for a new arrival at the shelter. He must have been not only gassed but also wounded, judging by the gauze wrapped around his head. Seeing him, Talmudovsky shut up and quickly tried to melt away into the crowd of Piqué Vests. But the man in gauze spotted the engineer's imposing figure right away and headed straight toward him.

"I finally caught up with you, Engineer Talmudovsky!" he said in a sinister tone. "On what grounds did you abandon the plant?"

Talmudovsky's small wild-boar eyes darted in all directions. Seeing that there was no place to hide, he sat down on his suitcases and lit a cigarette.

"I come to see him at the hotel," continued the man in gauze loudly, "and they tell me he checked out. I say: What do you mean he checked out, when he arrived just yesterday and must work here for a year? That's what the contract says. No, they say, he checked out, took his luggage, and went to Kazan. I thought: That's it, we'll have to start the search for an engineer all over again. But now I caught him here, sitting pretty and having a smoke. How about that? You're a job-hopper, Talmudovsky! You're destroying the industry!"

The engineer jumped off his luggage, shouting: "You're the one who's destroying the industry!" And he took his accuser by the waist, led him into a corner, and started buzzing at him like a large fly. Soon, one could hear phrases like: "With this salary . . . ," "Go find . . . ," "And the per diem?" The man in gauze stared at the engineer in exasperation.

The lecturer had already finished his oration, concluding with a demonstration of how to use a gas mask; the doors of the gas shelter had already opened; the Piqué Vests, holding onto each other, had already trotted back to the Florida; and Talmudovsky had already fought off his pursuer and escaped, calling out for a cab at the top of his lungs; but the grand strategist was still chatting with Zosya.

"What a *femina*!" said Panikovsky jealously, as he and Balaganov were leaving the shelter. "Ah, if only the weights were made of gold! I would have married her, I swear I would have!"

Hearing about the ill-fated weights again, Balaganov gave Panikovsky a painful jab with his elbow. It came just in time. Ostap appeared in the doorway of the shelter with the *femina* on his arm. He lingered over his goodbyes to Zosya, staring directly at her with yearning eyes. Zosya smiled for the last time and left.

"What were you talking about?" asked Panikovsky suspiciously.

"Oh, nothing much, this and that," replied Ostap. "Well, golden boys, back to work! We have to find the defendant."

Panikovsky was sent to the Hercules, Balaganov to Koreiko's place. Ostap himself rushed to the train stations. But the millionaire clerk had vanished. At the Hercules, his time card was still on the board. He never went home, and eight long-distance trains had left the stations during the gas attack. But Ostap didn't expect anything different.

"Well, it's not the end of the world," he said cheerlessly. "In China, for example, it would be hard to find a person: they have a population of 400,000,000. Here, it's a piece of cake: we only have 160,000,000. Three times as easy as in China. All you need is money. And we have it."

But he came out of the bank with only thirty-four rubles in his hand.

"This is what's left of the ten thousand," he said with unspeakable sadness. "And I thought we still had six or seven thousand in our account . . . How did that happen? We were having fun, we collected horns and hoofs, life was exhilarating, the Earth rotated just for us—and suddenly . . . Oh, I get it! The overhead! The organization consumed all the money."

And he looked at the half-brothers with reproach. Panikovsky shrugged his shoulders, as if to say: "You know, Bender, how much I respect you!

I've always said you were an ass!" The stunned Balaganov stroked his locks and asked:

"So what are we going to do?"

"What do you mean?" exclaimed Ostap. "What about the Bureau for the Collection of Horns and Hoofs? The office equipment? Any organization would be happy to shell out a hundred rubles just for the Face the Country set alone! And the typewriter! The hole punch, the deer antlers, the desks, the barrier, the samovar! All this can be sold off. On top of that, we have Panikovsky's gold tooth in reserve. Of course, it's not as substantial as the weights, but nevertheless, it's a molecule of gold, a noble metal."

The companions stopped outside the office. Through the open door, they could hear the youthful leonine voices of the agriculture students, who had returned from their trip, the drowsy mumblings of Funt, and some unfamiliar basses and baritones that clearly came from cattle-raising stock.

"This is an actionable offense!" roared the interns. "We were wondering from the start. In all this time, they've only collected twenty-five pounds of substandard horns!"

"You will be prosecuted!" thundered the basses and the baritones. "Where's the Branch President? Where's the Vice President for Hoofs?"

Balaganov started shaking in his boots.

"The Bureau is dead," whispered Ostap, "and we're no longer needed here. We're going to follow the shining path, while Funt will be taken to a red-brick building whose windows, due to the architect's capricious fantasy, feature heavy iron bars."

The ex-President of the Branch was correct. The fallen angels had barely put three city blocks between themselves and the Bureau when they heard the creaking of a horse cab behind them. It was Funt. He would have passed for a loving grandfather who, after lengthy preparations, was finally off to see his married grandson, had it not been for the policeman who was standing on the running board, holding Funt's bony shoulder.

"Funt has always done time," the Antelopeans heard the old man's low, muted voice as the cab was passing by. "Funt did time under Alexander II the Liberator, under Alexander III the Peacemaker, under Nicholas II the Bloody, under Alexander Kerensky . . ."

To keep track of the tsars and attorneys-at-law, Funt was counting them on his fingers.

"And now what are we going to do?" asked Balaganov.

"Please don't forget that you are a contemporary of Ostap Bender," said the grand strategist sadly. "Please remember that he owns the remarkable bag which has everything necessary for obtaining pocket change. Let's go home to Lokhankin."

A new blow awaited them on Lemon Lane.

"Where's the house?" exclaimed Ostap. "There was a house here just last night, wasn't there?"

But there was no house, and there was no Rookery. There was only a claims adjuster, who was treading on the pile of charred beams. He found an empty kerosene can in the back yard, sniffed it, and shook his head doubtfully.

"And now what?" asked Balaganov, smiling nervously.

The grand strategist didn't answer. He was floored by the loss of his bag. Gone was the magic sack that contained the Indian turban, the High Priest poster, the doctor's coat, the stethoscope . . . It had everything!

"There," Ostap finally said. "Fate plays with a man, and the man plays a trumpet."

They wandered away, pale, disappointed, and numb with grief. When people bumped into them, they didn't even snarl back. Panikovsky, who raised his shoulders during the fiasco at the bank, never lowered them again. Balaganov fiddled with his red locks and sighed dejectedly. Bender walked behind the rest, looking down and humming absentmindedly: "The days of merriment are gone, my little soldier, aim your gun." In this same condition, they finally reached the hostel. The yellow Antelope was visible in the back, under a canopy. Kozlevich was sitting on the tavern's porch. He was sucking in hot tea from a saucer, blowing the air out blissfully. His face was terracotta red. He was in seventh heaven.

"Adam!" said the grand strategist, stopping in front of the driver. "We lost everything. We're destitute, Adam! Take us in! We're sinking."

Kozlevich got up. The captain, humiliated and miserable, stood in front of him, bare-headed. Tears glistened in Adam's pale Polish eyes. He went down the steps and hugged each of the Antelopeans one by one.

"The taxi is free!" he said, swallowing his tears of pity. "Please get in."

"But we may have to go far, really far," said Ostap, "maybe to the edge of the earth, maybe even farther. Think about it!"

"Anywhere you want!" said the faithful Kozlevich. "The taxi is free!"

Panikovsky wept, covering his face with his small fists and whispering: "What a heart! I give you my word! What a heart!"

CHAPTER 24
THE WEATHER WAS RIGHT FOR LOVE

Everything the grand strategist did in the days following the move to the hostel elicited a highly negative response from Panikovsky.

"Bender has lost his mind!" he told Balaganov. "He'll drive us all into the ground."

And indeed, instead of trying to stretch the last thirty-four rubles for as long as possible by applying it strictly to the purchase of provisions, Ostap went to a flower shop and spent thirty-five rubles on a stirring bouquet of roses that was as big as a flower bed. He took the missing ruble from Balaganov. He put a note in the flowers that said: "Can you hear my big heart beating?" Balaganov was instructed to take the flowers to Zosya Sinitsky.

"What are you doing?" asked Balaganov, gesturing with the bouquet. "Why does it have to be so fancy?"

"It has to, Shura, it just has to," replied Ostap. "What can you do! I have a big heart. As big as a calf's. Plus, this isn't real money anyway. We need an idea."

With that, Ostap got into the Antelope and asked Kozlevich to take him out of town.

"I have to ponder over everything that's happened in solitude," he explained, "as well as make some necessary projections for the future."

All day long the faithful Adam drove the grand strategist along white coastal roads, past vacation homes and health resorts, where vacationers shuffled in their open-backed shoes, hit croquet balls with mallets, and jumped in front of volleyball nets. Telegraph wires hummed like cellos overhead. Summer renters dragged purple eggplants and melons in cloth bags. Young men with handkerchiefs on their hair, wet from a swim, boldly looked women in the eyes and offered their compliments, the full set of which was known to any male in Chernomorsk under the age of twenty-five. If two vacationing women walked together, the young locals would loudly say behind their backs: "The one on the side is so pretty!" And they would laugh their heads off. They thought it was funny that the women couldn't figure out which one of them was being complimented. If a woman was walking alone, the jokers would stop, as if struck by lightning, and make kissing sounds with their lips, mimicking lovelorn yearning. The young woman would blush and run to the other side of the street, dropping purple eggplants, which caused the Romeos to laugh hysterically.

Ostap, deep in thought, was leaning back on the Antelope's hard cushions. He couldn't get money from Polykhaev or Sardinevich—they were away on vacation. The insane Berlaga didn't count—one couldn't expect to get much from him. Meanwhile, Ostap's plans, and his big heart, demanded that he stay on in Chernomorsk. At this point, he would have been hard-pressed to say for exactly how long.

Hearing a familiar, otherwordly voice, Ostap glanced at the sidewalk. A middle-aged couple was strolling arm-in-arm behind a row of poplars. The spouses were apparently headed for the beach. Lokhankin trudged behind them. He was carrying a ladies' parasol and a basket with a thermos and a beach blanket sticking out of it.

"Barbara," he nagged, "listen, Barbara!"

"What do you want, you pest?" asked Mrs. Ptiburdukov without even turning her head.

"I want to have you, Barbara, to hold you!"

"How about that bastard!" remarked Ptiburdukov, without turning his head either.

And the odd family disappeared in the dust of the Antelope.

When the dust settled, Bender saw a large glass pavilion set against the background of the sea and a formal flower garden.

Plaster lions with dirty faces sat at the base of a wide stairwell. The pavilion exuded the unnerving scent of pear essence. Ostap sniffed the air and asked Kozlevich to stop the car. He got out and continued to inhale the invigorating smell through his nostrils.

"Why didn't I think of this right away!" he muttered, pacing in front of the entrance.

He trained his eyes on the sign that said CHERNOMORSK FILM STUDIO NO. I; stroked the stairwell lion on its warm mane; muttered, "Golconda"; and hurried back to the hostel.

He spent the whole night sitting at the window sill and writing by the light of a kerosene lamp. The breeze that came through the window shuffled through the finished pages. The view wasn't particularly attractive. The tactful moon lit a set that was far from palatial. The hostel was breathing, shifting, and wheezing in its sleep. Horses, invisible in the dark corners, communicated with one another by tapping. Small-time hustlers slept in horse carts, on top of their paltry wares. A horse that had gotten loose wandered around the courtyard, carefully stepping over shafts, dragging its halter behind it, and sticking its head into the carts in search of barley. It came up to Ostap's window as well, put its head on the window sill, and looked at the writer forlornly.

"Off you go, horse," said the grand strategist, "this is really none of your concern."

Just before dawn, when the hostel started waking up, and a young boy with a bucket of water was already walking among the carts, calling out in a high-pitched voice, "Water for your horses!," Ostap finished his opus, took a blank sheet out of Koreiko's file, and wrote down the title:

THE NECK
A full-length film
Screenplay by O. Bender

The Chernomorsk Film Studio No. 1 was in that rare state of chaos that only exists at horse markets, and only when the whole market is trying to catch a thief.

There was a guard sitting inside the doorway. He demanded passes from everyone who walked in, but if somebody didn't have a pass, he waved them through anyway. People wearing dark-blue berets bumped into people wearing workman's overalls, flew up the numerous stairs, and then immediately rushed down the very same stairs. They traced a circle in the hallway, stopped for a second, looked ahead, dumbfounded, and then raced back up as fast as if somebody was lashing them from behind with a wet rope. Whizzing by were assistants, consultants, experts, administrators, directors with their lieutenants, lighting people, film editors, middle-aged screenwriters, managers of commas, and keepers of the great cast-iron seal.

At first, Ostap moved about the studio at his usual pace, but he soon realized that he was failing to become part of the world that whirled around him. Nobody would answer his queries; nobody would even stop for him.

"One must adapt to the ways of the adversary," said Ostap.

He started running slowly and immediately discovered that it worked. He even exchanged a few words with somebody's lieutenant. Then the grand strategist began running as fast as he could and soon noticed that he had managed to join the crowd at last. He was running neck in neck with the chief script advisor.

"A script!" shouted Ostap.

"What kind?" asked the script advisor, maintaining his racing trot.

"A good one!" replied Ostap, overtaking him by a half-length.

"I'm asking you, what kind? Silent or sound?"

"Silent."

Gracefully raising his legs, which were clad in long thick socks, the script advisor overtook Ostap on the curve and shouted:

"Not interested!"

"What do you mean—not interested?" asked the grand strategist, losing the beat and starting to gallop.

"We're not! Silent pictures are over. Talk to the sound people."

They stopped for a brief moment, gave each other a startled look, and ran in opposite directions. Five minutes later, Bender was again racing in the right company, waving his manuscript, this time between two trotting consultants.

"A script!" offered Ostap, breathing heavily.

The consultants, trotting in unison, turned to Ostap:

"What kind of script?"

"With sound."

"Not interested," replied the consultants, speeding up.

The grand strategist lost his pace again and broke into an unseemly gallop.

"What do you mean—not interested?"

"We're not, and that's that. Talking pictures haven't arrived yet."

After thirty minutes of diligent trotting, Bender grasped the delicate state of affairs at Chernomorsk Film Studio No. 1: silent pictures were no longer being made, due to the advent of the era of talking pictures, while talking pictures were not yet being made either, due to unresolved administrative issues related to ending the era of silent pictures.

At the peak of the workday, when the assistants, consultants, experts, administrators, directors, their lieutenants, lighting people, scriptwriters, and keepers of the great cast-iron seal were all running at speeds worthy of the once-famous racehorse named Brawny, a rumor started spreading that somewhere, in some unspecified room, there was a man who was urgently developing talkies. Ostap barged into a large office at full speed and stopped, struck by the silence. A short man with a Bedouin beard and a gold pince-nez on a string sat sideways at his desk. Bending down, he was hard at work—pulling a shoe off his foot.

"How do you do, Comrade!" said the grand strategist loudly.

The man didn't answer. He took the shoe off and started shaking sand out of it.

"How do you do!" repeated Ostap. "I brought you a script!"

The man with a Bedouin beard slowly put the shoe back on and started tying the laces silently. Having done that, he turned to his papers, closed one eye, and began scribbling in miniscule letters.

"Why aren't you talking to me?" yelled Bender so loudly that the phone which sat on the movie boss's desk tinkled.

Only then did the movie boss raise his head, glance at Ostap, and say: "Please speak louder. I can't hear you."

"Write notes to him," suggested a consultant in a colorful vest who happened to race by. "He's deaf."

Ostap sat down at the same desk and wrote on a piece of paper: "Are you in talking pictures?"

"Yes," answered the deaf man.

"I brought a script for a sound film. It's called *The Neck*, a folk tragedy in six parts," wrote Ostap hastily.

The deaf man looked at the note through his gold-rimmed pince-nez and said:

"Excellent! We'll put you to work immediately. We're looking for fresh new people."

"Glad to help. How about an advance?" wrote Bender.

"*The Neck* is exactly what we need!" said the deaf man. "Wait here, I'll be right back. Don't go anywhere, it'll take just one minute."

The deaf man grabbed the script and slipped out of the room.

"We'll put you in the sound group!" he shouted, disappearing behind the door. "I'll be back in a minute."

Ostap sat in the office for an hour and a half, but the deaf man never came back. Only when Ostap stepped out into the hallway, and rejoined the race, did he learn that the deaf man had left in a car a long time ago and wasn't coming back that day. Actually, he wasn't ever coming back, because he was unexpectedly transferred to the town of Uman to raise the cultural awareness of horse cart drivers. The worst part was that the deaf man took the script of *The Neck* with him. The grand strategist extricated himself from the ever-accelerating whirl of the crowd and crashed onto a bench, stupefied, leaning on the shoulder of the doorman, who was already sitting there.

"Take me, for example!" the doorman said suddenly, apparently referring to a thought that had long been bothering him. "Terentyev, the assistant director, told me to grow a beard. Said I'd play Nebuchadnezzar, or Balthazar, in some film or other, can't remember the name. So I went ahead and grew this beard. Look at it! A prophet's beard! And now what am I supposed to do with it? The assistant director says there'll be no more silent pictures, and as for the talking pictures, he says, I won't do, my voice is unpleasant. So here I sit with this goddamn beard, like some kind of a goat! I feel funny in it, but how can I shave it off? So I just live with it."

"Is anybody filming here?" asked Bender, slowly coming back to his senses.

"What filming, are you kidding?" replied the bearded doorman weightily. "Last year, they shot a silent picture about ancient Rome. They're still in court over it, on account of criminal wrongdoing."

"Then why are they all running like that?" inquired the grand strategist, pointing at the stairs.

"Not all of them are running," said the doorman. "Comrade Suprugov, for example: he's not running. He's very businesslike. I keep thinking I should go ask him about the beard: is it going to be extra pay or a separate invoice . . ."

Hearing the word "invoice," Ostap went to see Suprugov. The doorman was telling the truth. Suprugov wasn't jumping up and down the stairs, he wasn't wearing an Alpine beret, nor foreign-made golf breeches that looked like they belonged to a tsarist police lieutenant. Suprugov offered a pleasant respite to one's eyes.

He was very abrupt with the grand strategist.

"I'm busy," he said, sounding like a peacock, "I can give you no more than two minutes of my time."

"That will do," began Ostap. "My script, *The Neck* . . ."

"Get to the point," said Suprugov.

"My script, *The Neck* . . ."

"Can't you just tell me what you want?"

"*The Neck* . . ."

"More to the point! How much is due to you?"

"Some deaf man . . ."

"Comrade! If you don't tell me right now how much is due to you, I'm going to ask you to leave. I'm very busy."

"Nine hundred rubles," mumbled the grand strategist.

"Three hundred!" said Suprugov firmly. "Take your money and leave. Keep in mind that you stole an extra ninety seconds from me."

Suprugov wrote out a note to Accounting in a bold hand, handed it to Ostap, and reached for the phone.

Stepping out of the Accounting office, Ostap stuffed the money into his pocket and said:

"Nebuchadnezzar was right. There's only one businesslike person here—and that's Suprugov, God help us."

Meanwhile, the running on the stairs, the whirling, the screaming, and the racket at Chernomorsk Film Studio No. 1 reached its peak. The lieutenants were snarling. Assistant directors were leading a black goat, marveling at how photogenic it was. Consultants, experts, and keepers of the cast-iron seal all bumped into one another and guffawed hoarsely. A woman messenger with a broom whisked by. The grand strategist even thought for a moment that he saw an assistant in light-blue pants soar above the crowd, skirt the chandelier, and settle on a ledge.

At that moment, the clock in the hallway struck.

"Bonnng!" went the clock.

Shrieks and screams shook the glass pavilion. Assistants, consultants, experts, and film editors were all streaming down the stairs. There was a wild scramble at the exit.

"Bonnng! Bonnng!" continued the clock.

Silence began emerging from the corners. The keepers of the cast-iron seal, the managers of commas, the administrators, and the lieutenants were all gone. The messenger's broom flashed for the last time.

"Bonnng!" the clock struck for the fourth time.

The pavilion was already empty. And only the assistant in light-blue pants, whose jacket pocket had gotten snagged on the bronze handle, fluttered in the doorway, squealed pitifully, and stamped the marble floor with his little hoofs.

The workday was over.

The crowing of a rooster came from the fishing village by the sea.

After the Antelopeans' coffers were replenished with cinematic cash, the captain's standing, which had been somewhat shaky ever since Koreiko had escaped, was restored. Panikovsky received a small allowance to buy kefir and a promise of golden dentures. For Balaganov, Ostap bought a jacket and a leather wallet, which was squeaky like a new saddle. Even though the wallet was empty, Shura kept taking it out and looking inside. Kozlevich received fifty rubles for fuel.

The Antelopeans were leading a clean, moral, almost pastoral, life. They helped the hostel manager keep order and became well-versed in the prices of barley and sour cream. At times, Panikovsky would go out to the courtyard, busily open the mouth of the nearest horse, glance at its teeth, and mutter, "That's a fine stallion," even though he was looking at a fine mare.

Only the captain was gone all day long, and when he finally showed up at the hostel, he was cheerful and distracted. He would sit down with his friends, who were drinking tea on a dirty glass porch, cross his strong legs, that were clad in red shoes, and say amicably:

"Panikovsky, is life really wonderful, or is it just me?"

"Where are you having such a swell time?" the violator of the pact would ask jealously.

"Come on, old man! This girl is not in your league," Ostap would say.

Balaganov laughed loudly and sympathetically, examining his new wallet, while Kozlevich chortled into his train conductor's mustache. He had already driven the captain and Zosya along the Coastal Highway on more than one occasion.

The weather was right for love. The Piqué Vests claimed that there hadn't been an August like this since the days of the *porto franco*. Night presented a clear sky, perfect for astronomic observations, while day rolled refreshing sea waves toward the city. Doormen were selling white-striped watermelons by their doorways, and the citizens strained themselves, squeezing the watermelons at both poles and lowering their ear in order to hear the desired crunch. In the evening, players returned from the soccer fields, sweaty and happy. Boys ran after them, kicking up dust. They pointed out the famous goal keeper, and sometimes even raised him onto their shoulders and carried him respectfully.

One evening, the captain advised the crew of the Antelope that they would be going on a big outing in the country the next day. Gifts would be distributed.

"Since a certain young lady will be joining our morning festivities," said Ostap significantly, "I would urge the esteemed cadets to wash their faces, clean up, and most importantly, not to use rude language during the trip."

Panikovsky became very excited, wheedled three rubles out of the captain, ran to the bathhouse, and then cleaned and scrubbed himself all night, like a soldier before a parade. He was the first to get up, and he kept hurrying Kozlevich. The Antelopeans looked at Panikovsky with amazement. He was clean-shaven and covered in so much powder that he looked like a retired MC. He kept pulling his jacket down and could barely turn his neck in his Oscar-Wilde collar.

During the outing, Panikovsky conducted himself quite ceremoniously. As he was being introduced to Zosya, he bowed graciously, but blushed so hard that even the powder on his cheeks turned red. Sitting in the car, he tucked his left foot under the seat, trying to hide the hole in his shoe where his big toe was showing. Zosya was wearing a white dress hemmed in red stitches. She really liked the Antelopeans. She was amused by the rough-edged Balaganov, who kept grooming his hair with a Sobinoff comb. At times, he cleaned his nose with his finger, after which he always took out his handkerchief and fanned himself pretentiously. Adam was teaching Zosya to drive the Antelope, which earned him her favor, too. She was a little anxious about Panikovsky, though. She thought he wasn't talking to her out of pride. But most often, her eyes rested on the captain's minted profile.

At sunset, Ostap distributed the promised gifts. Kozlevich received a keychain with a compass, which matched his thick silver pocket watch perfectly. Balaganov was presented with a leatherette-bound basic reader, while Panikovsky got a pink tie with dark-blue flowers.

"And now, my friends," Bender announced when the Antelope had returned to the city, "Zosya Victorovna and I will take a little walk. You should go back to the hostel. Nighty night."

The hostel was already asleep, Balaganov and Kozlevich were already playing arpeggios with their noses, but Panikovsky, in his new tie, wandered amid the horse carts and wrung his arms in quiet despair.

"What a *femina*!" he whispered. "I love her like a daughter."

Ostap and Zosya sat on the steps of the Archaeological Museum.

Laughing and flirting, young people strolled on the square that was paved with lava rock. Behind a row of plane trees, light sparkled in the windows of the international seamen's club. Foreign sailors in soft hats walked in groups of two or three, exchanging brief, incomprehensible remarks.

"Why did you fall in love with me?" asked Zosya, touching Ostap's hand.

"You're lovely and amazing," replied the captain. "You're the best in the world."

They sat quietly in the black shadows of the museum's columns for a long time, thinking about their little happiness. It was dark and warm, like between the palms of two hands.

"Remember I was telling you about Koreiko?" Zosya asked suddenly. "The one who proposed to me."

"Yes," replied Ostap absentmindedly.

"He's a very funny man," continued Zosya. "Remember I told you how he left town unexpectedly?"

"Yes," said Ostap, starting to pay attention, "he's very funny."

"Would you believe it, I got a letter from him today, a very funny letter . . ."

"What?" exclaimed her beau, rising to his feet.

"Are you jealous?" Zosya asked playfully.

"Well, a little. So what does this clown have to say?"

"He's not a clown. He's just a very poor, unhappy man. Sit down, Ostap. Why did you get up? No, seriously, I don't love him at all. He's asking me to come join him."

"Where, join him where?" shouted Ostap. "Where is he?"

"I'm not telling you. You're too jealous. You'd go and kill him, God forbid."

"Oh, come on, Zosya!" said the captain carefully. "I'm just curious where people find work these days."

"Oh, he's very, very far from here. He writes that he found a well-paying job. He wasn't making much here. He's helping build the Eastern Line."

"Where exactly?"

"Honestly, you're way too nosy. You shouldn't be such an Othello!"

"For God's sake, Zosya, you make me laugh. Do I look like a silly old Moor? I'm just curious where on the Eastern Line people find work."

"Fine, I'll tell you, if you insist. He works as a timekeeper at the Northern track-laying site," said the girl simply. "But it's just called a site—it's actually a train. It's very interesting, the way Alexander Ivanovich describes it. This train lays down the track. You see? And then it moves over that same track. And another train like this is moving toward it from the south. They will soon meet. Then there will be a joining ceremony. And it's in the desert, he writes, with camels . . . Isn't that interesting?"

"Fascinating," said the grand strategist, pacing under the columns. "You know, Zosya, it's time to go. It's late. And it's cold. Let's just go!"

He helped Zosya up from the steps, walked her to the square, and then hesitated.

"Aren't you going to walk me home?" asked the girl with alarm.

"Pardon?" said Ostap. "Oh, home . . . You see, I . . ."

"Fine," Zosya said drily, "goodbye. And don't come see me anymore. Do you hear?"

But the grand strategist no longer heard anything. After running for a block, he stopped.

"Lovely and amazing!" he muttered.

Ostap turned back, to follow his girl. He ran under the dark trees for a couple of minutes. Then he stopped again, took his seaman's cap off, and lingered for a few moments.

"No, this isn't Rio de Janeiro!" he said finally.

He took two more tentative steps, stopped again, stuck the cap on his head, and, without any further hesitation, rushed to the hostel.

That same night, the Antelope drove out of the hostel gates, its pale headlights on. Drowsy Kozlevich had to strain to turn the steering wheel. Balaganov promptly fell asleep in the car while the others were hastily packing. Panikovsky shifted his small eyes sadly, shivering in the cool of the night. He still had some powder on his face, left over from the festive outing.

"The carnival is over!" cried out the captain, as the Antelope rumbled under a railway bridge. "Now the hard work begins."

And in the old puzzle-maker's room, next to a bouquet of dried-up roses, the lovely and amazing one was weeping.

CHAPTER 25
THREE ROADS

The Antelope wasn't feeling well. She would stall on even the slightest incline and roll back listlessly. Strange noises and wheezing were coming from the engine, as if someone was being strangled under the yellow hood. The vehicle was overloaded. In addition to the crew, it carried large supplies of fuel. Gasoline gurgled in cans and bottles that filled every available space. Kozlevich kept shaking his head, stepping on the accelerator, and glancing at Ostap anxiously.

"Adam," the captain would say, "you're our father, we're your children. Head east! You have a great navigational tool—your keychain compass. Don't lose the way!"

The Antelopeans were on the move for the third day in a row, but no one except Ostap knew the final destination of the new journey. Panikovsky looked glumly at the shaggy corn fields and lisped timidly:

"Why are we driving again? What's the point of all this? It was so nice in Chernomorsk."

He sighed desperately, thinking of the lovely *femina*. On top of that, he was hungry, but there was nothing to eat—they were out of money.

"Forward!" proclaimed Ostap. "Stop whining, old man. Golden dentures, a nice plump widow, and an entire swimming pool of kefir await you. For Balaganov, I'll buy a sailor's suit and sign him up for elementary school. He'll learn to read and write, which at his age is a must. And

227

Kozlevich, our faithful Adam, will get a new car. What would you like, Adam Kazimirovich? A Studebaker? A Lincoln? A Rolls? A Hispano-Suiza?"

"An Isotta-Fraschini," said Kozlevich, blushing.

"Fine. You'll get it. We'll call it the Antelope II, or Antelope Junior, whatever you prefer. And now, cheer up. I'll make sure you've got the basics. Of course, my bag went up in flames, but my ideas are fire-proof. If things get really bad, we'll stop at some lucky little town and set up a bullfight, Seville-style. Panikovsky will be the picador. That alone will spur the public's unhealthy curiosity and make it a huge box-office hit."

The car crept along a wide roadway that was marked by tractor teeth. Suddenly, the driver hit the brakes.

"Which way?" he asked. "We have three roads here."

The passengers climbed out of the car and walked on a bit, stretching their stiff legs. The crossroads was marked by a tall leaning stone, with a fat crow perched on top of it. The flattened sun was setting behind unkempt corn silk. Balaganov's thin shadow stretched toward the horizon. The ground was touched by dark hues, and an early star dutifully signaled the advent of the night.

Three roads lay in front of the Antelopeans: one asphalt, one gravel, and one dirt. The asphalt was still yellow from the sun, blue vapor hovered over the gravel road, but the dirt road was barely discernible and melted into the fields just beyond the stone. Ostap yelled at the crow, which was very frightened yet didn't fly away. He paced back and forth at the crossroads in contemplation and then announced:

"I declare the conference of the roving Russian knights open! In attendance are: Ilya Muromets—Ostap Bender, Dobrynya Nikitich—Balaganov, and Alyosha Popovich—our esteemed Mikhail Panikovsky."

Kozlevich, who took advantage of the stop and climbed under the Antelope with a wrench, was not included in the ranks of the knights.

"Dear Dobrynya," Ostap instructed, "please stand on the right! *Monsieur* Popovich, take you place on the left! Shade your eyes with your hands and look forward intently."

"Are you kidding me?" said Alyosha Popovich testily. "I'm hungry. Let's go somewhere, now!"

"Shame on you, Alyosha boy," said Ostap, "stand properly, as befits an ancient knight. And think hard. Look at Dobrynya: you could put him straight into an epic. So, my fellow knights, which road shall we take? Which one has money lying around on it, the money we need for our daily expenses? I know that Kozlevich would prefer the asphalt: drivers like good roads. But Adam is an honest man, he doesn't know much about life. Knights have no use for asphalt. It probably leads to some giant state farm. We'll get lost amidst the roar of the engines down there. We might even get run over by a Caterpillar or some combine harvester. To die under a harvester—that's too boring. No, my fellow knights, the paved road is not for us. Now the gravel one. Kozlevich, of course, would like it, too. But trust your Ilya Muromets: it's no good for us either. Let them accuse us of backwardness, but we will not take that road. My intuition tells me of encounters with tactless collective farmers and other model citizens. Besides, they have no time for us. Their collectivized land is now overrun by numerous literary and musical teams that collect material for their agri-poetry and vegetable-garden cantatas. That, citizen knights, leaves us the dirt road! Here it is—an ancient fairy-tale route that our Antelope will embark on. There's Russian soul! There's Russian spirit! There, the smoldering firebird still flies, and people in our line of work can come across a golden feather here and there. Kashchey the wealthy farmer still sits on his treasure chests. He thought he was immortal, but now he realizes, to his horror, that the end is near. But we, my fellow knights, we shall still be able to get a little something from him, especially if we introduce ourselves as itinerant monks. For vehicles, this enchanted road is awful. But for us, it's the only way. Adam! Let's go!"

With a heavy heart, Kozlevich drove onto the dirt road, where the car promptly went figure-skating, listing sideways and jolting the passengers into the air. The Antelopeans were clutching on to each other, cursing under their breath, and banging their knees against the hard metal cans.

"I'm hungry!" moaned Panikovsky. "I want a goose! Why did we have to leave Chernomorsk?"

The car screeched, trying to pull itself out of a deep rut and then sunk back into it.

"Keep going, Adam!" shouted Bender. "Keep going no matter what! If only the Antelope takes us all the way to the Eastern Line, we'll bestow on it golden tires with swords and bows!"

Kozlevich wasn't listening. The wild jolting was tearing his hands off the steering wheel. Panikovsky was still restless.

"Bender," he wheezed suddenly, "you know how much I respect you, but you're clueless! You don't know what a goose is! Oh, how I love that bird! It's a heavenly, juicy bird. I swear. Goose! Bender! Wing! Neck! Drumstick! Bender, do you know how I catch a goose? I kill it like a toreador, with a single blow. When I go up against a goose, it's an opera! It's *Carmen!*"

"I know," said the captain, "we saw it in Arbatov. Better not try it again."

Panikovsky fell silent, but a minute later, when yet another jolt threw him against Bender, he started whispering feverishly again:

"Bender! It walks on the road. The goose! That heavenly bird takes a walk, and I stand there and pretend it's none of my business. Now it comes closer. It's about to start hissing at me. These birds think they are stronger than anybody, and that's their weak point. Bender! That's their weak point!"

The violator of the pact was all but chanting:

"So now it confronts me, hissing like a phonograph. But I'm not from a timid bunch, Bender. Somebody else would have fled, but me, I stand there and wait. Now it comes near and stretches out its neck, a white goose-neck with a yellow beak. It wants to bite me. Note, Bender, that I'm on the moral high ground here. I don't attack the goose, it attacks me. So, in self-defense, I grab . . ."

But Panikovsky never finished his speech. There came a horrible, nauseating crack, and the next moment, the Antelopeans found themselves lying on the road in the most peculiar positions. Balaganov's legs we sticking out of a ditch. The grand strategist had a can of gasoline lying on his stomach. Panikovsky was moaning under the weight of a suspension spring. Kozlevich rose to his feet and took a few unsteady steps.

The Antelope was no more. An ugly pile of rubble was lying on the road: pistons, cushions, springs. The copper intestines glistened in the moonlight. The car's body fell apart and slid into the ditch next to Balaganov, who had just come back to his senses. The chain crawled down into a rut like a viper. The sudden stillness was broken by a high-pitched ringing noise, as a wheel rolled in from some nearby mound, where it must have been thrown by the blast. The wheel traced a curve and landed gently at Adam's feet.

And only then did the driver realize that it was all over. The Antelope was dead. Adam sat down on the ground and put his arms around his head. A few minutes later, the captain touched his shoulder and said gently:

"Adam, we must go now."

Kozlevich got up and then quickly sat down again.

"We must go now," repeated Ostap. "The Antelope was a good, faithful car, but there are plenty of other cars out there. You will soon be able to choose any one you want. Let's go, we need to hurry up. We have to spend the night somewhere, we have to eat, we have to find money for train tickets somehow. It'll be a long trip. Come on, Kozlevich, let's go! Life is beautiful, despite certain shortcomings. Where's Panikovsky? Where's that goose thief? Shura! Help Adam out!"

They dragged Kozlevich forward, holding him by the arms. He felt like a cavalryman whose horse has been killed due to his own negligence. He imagined that pedestrians would start making fun of him.

After the Antelope's demise, life immediately became more complicated. They had to spend the night in the fields.

Ostap angrily fell asleep right away. Balaganov and Kozlevich also fell asleep, but Panikovsky spent the whole night shivering by the fire.

The Antelopeans got up at sunrise but didn't reach the nearest village until 4 P.M. Panikovsky traipsed behind the others the whole way. He limped a bit. Hunger gave his eyes a cat-like gleam, and he complained incessantly about his fate and his captain.

Upon entering the village, Ostap instructed the crew to stay put and wait for him at Third Street, while he himself went to the village council on First Street. He came back fairly quickly.

"Everything is taken care of," he said cheerfully. "They'll give us a place to stay and dinner. After dinner, we'll luxuriate in the hay. Milk and hay, remember? In the evening, we're putting on a show. I already sold it for fifteen rubles. I have the money. Shura! You're going to have to recite something from your reader, I'll be showing anti-clerical card tricks, and Panikovsky . . . Where's Panikovsky? Where on earth did he go?"

"He was here just a moment ago," said Kozlevich. But then the Antelopeans, who were standing near a wattle fence, heard a goose honking and a woman shrieking behind it. White feathers flew, and Panikovsky ran out onto the street. Apparently, this time his toreador's hand had betrayed him, and, in defending himself, he had hit the bird the wrong way. He was being chased by a woman who was wielding a piece of firewood.

"A wretched, miserable woman!" screeched Panikovsky, racing out of the village at full speed.

"What a blabbermouth!" exclaimed Ostap, not hiding his frustration. "The bastard just killed our show. Let's get out of here before they take the fifteen rubles back."

Meanwhile, the furious owner of the goose caught up with Panikovsky and managed to smack him right on the spine with the log. The violator of the pact fell to the ground, but then immediately jumped up and took off incredibly fast. Having completed this act of retribution, the woman turned around and headed back, satisfied. Running past the Antelopeans, she brandished the log at them.

"Our artistic career is over," said Ostap, hurrying out of the village. "The dinner, the night's rest—everything's ruined."

They only caught up with Panikovsky a couple of miles later. He was lying in a ditch, complaining loudly. He was pale from exhaustion, fear, and pain, and his numerous old-man's splotches were gone. He was so pitiful that the captain decided against the punishment he had been planning for him.

"So they whacked Alyosha on his mighty back!" said Ostap, walking past him.

Everyone looked at Panikovsky with disgust. And again he traipsed behind the others, moaning and babbling:

"Wait for me, not so fast . . . I'm old, I'm sick, I don't feel well! Goose! Drumstick! Neck! *Femina!* Wretched, miserable people!"

But the Antelopeans were so used to the old man's laments that they paid no attention. Hunger forced them to press on. Never before had they been in such a tough and uncomfortable spot. The road went on and on, endlessly, and Panikovsky was falling farther and farther behind. The friends had already descended into a narrow golden valley, but the violator of the pact was still silhouetted against the greenish twilight on the hill crest.

"The old man has become impossible," said the hungry Bender. "I'll have to sack him. Shura, go and drag that malingerer here!"

Balaganov reluctantly went off to do the chore. As he was climbing up the hill, Panikovsky's silhouette disappeared from view.

"Something's happened," said Kozlevich a bit later, looking at the crest where Balaganov was signaling with his arms.

The driver and the captain climbed back to the top of the hill.

The violator of the pact was lying on the road, motionless, like a doll. The pink ribbon of his tie lay across his chest. One arm was tucked under his back. His eyes looked into the sky daringly. Panikovsky was dead.

"A heart attack," said Ostap, just to say something, anything. "I can tell even without a stethoscope. Poor old man!"

He turned away. Balaganov couldn't keep his eyes off the dead body.

Suddenly, his face became contorted, and he barely managed to utter: "And I beat him up over the weights. And before that I used to fight with him."

Kozlevich thought about the Antelope's demise, looked at Panikovsky in horror, and started singing a prayer in Latin.

"Oh, come on, Adam!" said the grand strategist. "I know what you're going to do. After the psalm, you'll say: 'God giveth, God taketh away,' then: 'We're all in God's hands,' and then something totally meaningless, like: 'At least he's now in a better place than we are.' There's no need for any of it, Adam Kazimirovich. We're faced with a very simple task: the body has to be laid to rest."

It was already dark when they located the final resting place for the violator of the pact. A natural grave had been washed out by the rains at the foot of a tall stone marker. It must have been standing by the road since time immemorial. Maybe it once sported a sign like THIS LAND BELONGS TO MAJOR G. A. BEAR-WOLFSKY (RET.), or maybe it was just a survey marker from the times of Prince Potemkin—who cared anyway? They placed Panikovsky into the pit, used some sticks to dig up some dirt, and threw it on top of him. Then the Antelopeans put their shoulders to the stone, which was already loose from the passage of time, and felled it onto the ground. The grave was complete. In the flickering light of matches, the grand strategist scribbled an epitaph on the stone with a chunk of brick:

Here lies
MIKHAIL SAMUELEVICH PANIKOVSKY
A man without papers

Ostap took off his captain's cap and said:

"I've often been unfair to the deceased. But was the deceased a moral person? No, he was not a moral person. He was a former blind man, an impostor, and a goose thief. He put all his efforts into trying to live at society's expense. But society didn't want him to live at its expense. Mikhail Samuelevich couldn't bear this difference of opinion because he had a quick temper. And so he died. That's it!"

Kozlevich and Balaganov were not happy with Ostap's farewell tribute. They would have found it more appropriate had the grand strategist waxed poetic about the great services the deceased had rendered to society, about his charity to the poor, his sensitive nature, his love for children, and everything else that's usually ascribed to any dead person.

Balaganov even stepped forward to the grave, intending to express all this himself, but the captain had already put his cap back on and was walking away briskly.

When the remnants of the Antelopeans' army had crossed the valley and negotiated yet another hill, they saw a small train station on the other side.

"Here's civilization," said Ostap, "maybe a snack bar, some food. We'll sleep on the benches. And in the morning, we'll head East. What do you think?"

The driver and the rally mechanic didn't respond.

"So why are you so quiet? Have you lost the gift of speech?"

"You know, Bender," Balaganov said finally, "I'm not going. Please don't be mad, but I don't have faith anymore. I don't know where we're going. We'll get into big trouble over there. I'm staying."

"I wanted to tell you the same thing," echoed Kozlevich.

"As you wish," replied Ostap, suddenly sounding cold.

There was no snack bar at the station. A bright kerosene lamp was lit. Two peasant women slumbered on top of their sacks in the waiting area. The entire staff of the station paced on the wooden platform, staring intently into the pre-dawn darkness beyond the semaphore post.

"Which train is it?" asked Ostap.

"Unnumbered," answered the station chief nervously, straightening a red cap that was decorated with silver stripes. "A special. Delayed for two minutes. Doesn't have a green light yet."

Then there was a rumble, wires shook, a pair of small, wolfish eyes appeared, and a short, glistening train came to a screeching halt at the station. The large glass windows of the first-class passenger cars gleamed, and flowers and wine bottles in the dining car rolled right by the noses of the Antelopeans. Attendants jumped off the train with their lanterns while the train was still moving, and the platform immediately filled with cheery banter in Russian and other languages. The cars were decorated with fir garlands and slogans that read: GREETINGS TO THE HEROIC BUILD-ERS OF THE EASTERN LINE!

The special train was taking guests to the opening of the rail line.

The grand strategist disappeared. He returned thirty seconds later and whispered:

"I'm going! I don't know how—but I'm going! Want to come with me? I'm asking you one last time."

"No," said Balaganov.

"I'm not going," said Kozlevich, "I can't take it anymore."

"But what are you going to do?"

"What can I possibly do?" replied Shura. "I'll be the son of Lieutenant Schmidt again, that's all."

"I'm hoping to put the Antelope back together," said Kozlevich plaintively, "I'll go give her a good look, fix her up."

Ostap wanted to say something, but a long whistle silenced him. He pulled Balaganov closer, patted him on the back, kissed Kozlevich goodbye, waved, and ran toward the train, whose cars were already bumping together from the locomotive's first pull. But before he reached the train, he turned back, stuck the fifteen rubles he had received for the show into Adam's hand, and jumped onto the step of the car, which was already moving.

Glancing back, he saw two small figures climbing up the slope through the purple haze. Balaganov was returning to the troublesome brood of Lieutenant Schmidt. Kozlevich was trundling back to the remains of the Antelope.

PART 3
A PRIVATE CITIZEN

CHAPTER 26
A PASSENGER ON THE SPECIAL TRAIN

A short unnumbered train stood in the asphalt berth of the Ryazan Station in Moscow. It had only six cars: a baggage car, which actually housed food supplies on ice instead of the baggage; a dining car with a white-clad cook leaning out the window; the government's private car; and three sleeping cars, whose bunks, draped with austere striped covers, were to accommodate a delegation of exemplary factory workers, as well as Soviet and foreign journalists.

The train was heading for the joining of the Eastern Line.

A lengthy journey lay ahead. The workers were pushing their travel baskets, whose little black locks hung from iron rods, through the cars' doors. The Soviet press was rushing up and down the platform, brandishing their shiny plywood travel cases.

The foreigners were watching over the porters who carried their thick leather suitcases, garment bags, and cardboard boxes, which were plastered with colorful labels from travel companies and steamship lines.

The passengers had already stocked up on a book, *The Eastern Line*, whose cover featured a picture of a camel sniffing the rails. The book was being sold on the platform, from a baggage cart. Its author, a journalist named Palamidov, had already walked past the cart several times, glancing at the buyers anxiously. He was considered an expert on the Eastern Line: this would be his third trip there.

Departure was fast approaching, but the farewell scene was nothing like an ordinary passenger train's departure. There were no old women on the platform, nobody was holding a baby through an open window for a last look at its grandfather. Obviously, there was no grandfather either, a grandfather whose dim eyes reflect a fear of drafty trains, and, obviously, there was no kissing. The workers' delegation had been brought to the station by union officials, who hadn't had the chance to work out the issue of farewell kisses yet. The journalists from Moscow were accompanied by their co-workers, who were used to getting away with a handshake in situations like this. On the other hand, the foreign journalists—there were thirty of them—were headed to the joining at full strength, with their wives and their phonographs, so there was no one to see them off.

True to the occasion, the travelers talked louder than usual, pulled out their notepads for no reason, and scolded the well-wishers for not joining them on such an exciting journey. A journalist named Lavoisian was being particularly loud. He was young at heart, even though a bald pate shone through his locks like a moon in the jungle.

"You disgust me!" he shouted to those staying behind. "You can't even fathom what the Eastern Line really means!"

The hot-headed Lavoisian was so passionate, and so dedicated to print news, that he could have easily beaten up a friend or two, except that his hands were busy with a large typewriter in a heavy oilcloth cover. He was already itching to send an urgent cable to his office, but there was absolutely nothing to report.

Ukhudshansky, from a union newspaper, had been the first to arrive at the station and was strolling next to the train at a leisurely pace. He was carrying *The Turkestan Region: A Complete Geographical Description of Our Land, A Reference and Travel Book for the Russian People*, by Semenov-Tian-Shansky, which had been published in 1903. He would stop by a group of travelers or well-wishers and say, somewhat sarcastically:

"Going? Well, well . . ."

Or:

"Staying? Well, well . . ."

In this manner, he reached the front of the train. Holding his head back, he carefully studied the locomotive, and finally said to the engineer:

"Working? Well, well . . ."

After that, Ukhudshansky returned to his compartment, opened the latest issue of his union paper, and became immersed in an article, "Retail

Boards Need Improvement: Boards' Overhaul Insufficient," that he had written himself. The article reported on some meeting or other, and the author's take on the subject could be described in one sentence: "Meeting? Well, well . . ." Ukhudshansky read until the train departed.

One of the well-wishers, a man with a pink plush nose and small velvety sideburns, made a prophecy that scared everyone to death.

"I know about trips like this," he announced, "I've done them myself. I know what your future holds. There's about a hundred of you. Altogether, you'll be on the road for a whole month. Two of you will be left behind at a small station in the middle of nowhere, with no money and no papers, and, hungry and bedraggled, will catch up with the train a week later. Somebody's suitcase is bound to be stolen. Perhaps, Palamidov's, or Lavoisian's, or Navrotsky's. The victim will whine for the rest of the trip and beg his comrades for a shaving brush. He'll return the brush dirty and will lose the bowl. One of you will certainly die, and the friends of the deceased, instead of going to the joining, will be obliged to escort the remains of the dearly beloved back to Moscow. A very boring and unpleasant chore. On top of that, there will be a nasty squabble during the trip. Trust me! Someone, say, that same Palamidov, or Ukhudshansky, will commit an anti-social act. All of you will denounce him endlessly and tediously, while the culprit will moan and groan in protest. I've seen it all. You're wearing hats and caps now, but you'll come back in Oriental skull caps. The stupidest of you will purchase the full uniform of a Bukhara Jew: a velvet hat trimmed with jackal fur and a thick quilted blanket sewn into a cloak. And, of course, all of you will be singing the Stenka Razin song on the train in the evening, bellowing like idiots: 'And he throws her overboard, to the wave that happens by.' Not only that, even the foreigners will sing: 'Down the river Volga, *sur notre mère Volga*, down our Mother Volga . . .'"

Indignant, Lavoisian brandished his typewriter at the prophet.

"You're just envious!" he said. "We won't sing."

"Oh yes, you will. There's no way around it. Trust me, I know . . ."

"No, we won't."

"Yes, you will. And if you have any honor, you will immediately send me a postcard to that effect."

At this moment, they heard a stifled cry. A photojournalist named Menshov had fallen off the roof of the baggage car. He had climbed up there in order to photograph their departure. Menshov lay on the platform for a few seconds, holding his camera above his head. Then he got up, checked the shutter carefully, and headed back to the roof.

"Falling?" asked Ukhudshansky, sticking his head out the window, newspaper in hand.

"That wasn't much of a fall," said the photojournalist disdainfully. "You should have seen me fall off the spiral slide in the amusement park!"

"Well, well . . ." remarked the representative of the union paper, disappearing through the window.

On the roof, Menshov kneeled down and got back to work. A Norwegian writer, who had already put his luggage in his compartment and gone outside for a stroll, watched him with a look of whole-hearted approval. The writer had light boyish hair and a large Varangian nose. The Norwegian was so impressed by Menshov's photoheroism that he felt an urgent need to share his excitement with someone else. He marched up to an elderly worker from the Trekhgorka Factory, pointed a finger at the man's chest, and belted out in Russian:

"You!!"

Then he pointed at his own chest and exclaimed with equal force:

"Me!!"

Having thus used every single word of his Russian, the writer smiled amicably and rushed back to his car as the station bell rang out for the second time. The worker hurried to his own car. Menshov descended to the ground. Heads began to nod, the final smiles flashed, a satirist in a coat with a black velvet collar rushed by. As the train's tail was bouncing over the exit switch, two journalist brothers—Leo Shirtikov and Ian Benchikov—bolted out of the station's diner. Benchikov was clutching a Wiener schnitzel in his teeth. Leaping like young dogs, the two brothers raced down the platform, jumped off onto the oily ground, and only then, amid the ties, did they realize that they had actually missed the train.

The train, in the meantime, was rolling out of construction-filled Moscow and had already struck up its deafening tune. It pounded with its wheels and laughed diabolically under the overpasses, only quieting down a bit when it had attained full speed in the woods outside the city. It was going to trace a sizable arc on the globe, run through several climate zones —from the coolness of central Russia to the hot desert, travel past many cities and towns, and advance four hours ahead of Moscow time.

Toward the end of the first day, two envoys from the capitalist world appeared in the Soviet journalists' car. They were Mr. Heinrich, who represented a liberal Austrian newspaper, and Hiram Berman, an American. They came to introduce themselves. Mr. Heinrich was rather short.

Mr. Berman wore a hat with its brim turned up. Both of them were quite fluent in Russian. At first, everybody just stood in the corridor silently, eyeing each other with curiosity. To break the ice, they brought up the Moscow Art Theater. Heinrich praised the theater, while Mr. Berman evasively remarked that, as a Zionist, what most interested him in the Soviet Union was the Jewish question.

"We no longer have this question," said Palamidov.

"How is that possible—no Jewish question?" asked Hiram, surprised.

"No. None whatsoever."

Mr. Berman became agitated. All his life, he'd been writing about the Jewish question for his paper, and it would have been hard for him to let it go.

"But there are Jews in Russia, aren't there?" he asked cautiously.

"Correct," replied Palamidov.

"Then there's the Jewish question, right?"

"Wrong. Jews—yes, question—no."

The appearance of Ukhudshansky eased the tension in the corridor somewhat. He was headed for the washroom with a towel around his neck.

"Talking?" he said, swaying on his feet—the train was moving fast. "Well, well . . ."

As he was coming back, clean and refreshed, with drops of water on his temples, the entire corridor was already engaged in an argument. The Soviet journalists came out of their compartments, a few factory workers showed up from the next car, and two more foreigners arrived—an Italian journalist with a Fascist Party badge that depicted a lictor bundle with an axe, and a German professor of Oriental studies, who was invited to the festivities by the Soviet Society for Cultural Ties With Foreign Countries. The subject of the argument ranged very broadly—from building socialism in the Soviet Union to men's berets, which were then coming into style in the West. And no matter what the issue was, opinions clashed.

"Arguing? Well, well . . ." said Ukhudshansky, retreating into his compartment.

One could only make out individual cries above the general commotion.

"In that case," Mr. Heinrich was saying, grabbing Suvorov, a worker from the Putilov Plant, by his tunic, "what have you been yammering about for the last thirteen years? Why aren't you making the world revolution you talk about so much? Because you can't? So stop yammering!"

"We're not going to make revolution in your countries! You'll do it yourselves."

"Me? I'm not going to make any revolution."

"So they'll make it without you, and they won't even ask for your opinion."

Mr. Hiram Berman was leaning against a stamped-leather partition and watched the argument without much interest. The Jewish question had fallen through some crack in the discussion shortly after it began, and any other subject left him cold. A satirist, whose byline was Gargantua, left a group where the German professor was praising the advantages of civil marriage. He approached the pensive Hiram and started explaining something to him with gusto. Hiram tried to listen, but he soon realized that he couldn't make out anything at all. Meanwhile Gargantua, who kept on adjusting Hiram's clothing—straightening his necktie, removing a speck of something, doing up a button and then undoing it again— talked quite loudly and, on the face of it, even clearly. But he had some undefinable speech impediment that turned all his words into gibberish. The problem was aggravated by the fact that Gargantua was quite a talker, and that he demanded confirmation after every sentence.

"Isn't that right?" he would say, moving his head as if he was about to peck some bird feed with his large, well-shaped nose. "Isn't it true?"

These were the only words one could make out from Gargantua's speech. The rest fused into a wonderfully persuasive rumble. At first, Mr. Berman agreed out of courtesy, but he soon fled. People always agreed with Gargantua, so he considered himself capable of proving anything to anybody.

"See," he told Palamidov, "you just don't know how to talk to people. And I convinced him. I just proved to him that we no longer have the Jewish question at all, and he agreed with me. Isn't that right?"

Palamidov hadn't understood a word, so he nodded in agreement and turned his attention to the exchange between the German Orientalist and the car's attendant. The attendant had long been trying to insert himself into the conversation, but only now did he finally find somebody who was in his league and available. First he inquired about his counterpart's position and full name, then he put his broom aside and slowly began:

"You may not know it, Citizen Professor, but there is this animal in Central Asia, it's called a camel. It has two humps on its back. And I knew this railroad man, Comrade Bossyuk, a baggage handler, you've probably heard about him. So he climbs onto this camel, gets between its humps, and hits the camel with a whip. But the camel was mean, so it started squeezing him with its humps—almost squeezed him to death. Bossyuk managed to jump off, though. He was a tough guy, as you've probably heard. So now the camel spits all over his uniform, and it had just come back from the laundry . . ."

The evening's conversation was dying down. The clash of the two worlds ended peacefully. Somehow it hadn't ended in a fight. The two systems—capitalist and socialist—would have to coexist, willy-nilly, on the special train for about a month. Mr. Heinrich, an enemy of world revolution, told an ancient travel joke, and then everybody headed for the dining car. People walked from car to car over shuddering metal plates and squinted against the piercing wind. In the dining car, however, the passengers split into separate groups. During supper, the two sides sized each other up quietly. The outside world, as represented by the correspondents of the major newspapers and news agencies from around the globe, paid vodka its proper due and glanced with awful politeness at the factory workers in tall rough boots and at the Soviet journalists who showed up dressed casually in slippers and without their neckties.

All kinds of people sat in the dining car: Mr. Berman, a provincial from New York; a young Canadian woman, who had arrived from across the ocean just an hour before the train had departed, which was why she was still looking around in bewilderment as she hesitated over a cutlet on a long metal plate; a Japanese diplomat and another, younger Japanese man; Mr. Heinrich, whose yellow eyes were smirking for some reason; a young British diplomat with the slim waist of a tennis player; the German Orientalist who had listened so patiently to the car attendant's story about an odd animal with two humps on its back; an American economist; a Czechoslovakian; a Pole; four American correspondents, including a pastor who wrote for the YMCA paper; a blue-blooded American woman from a distinguished family with a Dutch surname, who was famous because a year earlier she had missed a train in the resort town of Mineralnye Vody and, for publicity, had hidden in the station's diner for a while, which caused an uproar in the American press. For three days, the headlines screamed "Girl from Old Family in Clutches of Wild Mountain Men" and "Ransom or Death." There were many others as well. Some were simply hostile to anything Soviet, others were hoping to solve the mystery of the Asian soul overnight, and still others were honestly trying to understand what was going on in the land of the Soviets after all.

The Soviet side dined rowdily at its own tables. The workers brought food in paper bags and went all out for glasses of tea with lemon in stainless-steel holders. The journalists, who were better off, ordered schnitzels, while Lavoisian, in a sudden bout of Slavonic pride, decided not to lose face in front of the foreigners and demanded sautéed kidneys. He didn't touch the kidneys, he had hated them since childhood, but he bristled with pride all the same and glanced defiantly at the foreign visitors. There were all kinds of people on the Soviet side as well. There was a worker from Sormovo, who had been selected for the trip at a general staff meeting; a construction worker from the Stalingrad Tractor Factory, who ten years earlier lay in the trenches opposite Baron Wrangel's troops—in the same field where his factory was later built; and a textile worker from Serpukhov, who was interested in the Eastern Line because it was going to speed up the deliveries of cotton to the textile-producing regions.

There were metal workers from Leningrad, miners from the Donets Coal Basin, a mechanic from Ukraine, and the head of the delegation in a white Russian-style shirt with a large Bukhara Star that he had received for fighting against the Emir. The diplomat with the waistline of a tennis player would have been incredulous to learn that Gargantua, the short, mild-mannered versifier, had been taken prisoner by various armed Ukrainian bands on as many as eight separate occasions, and once was even executed by Makhno's anarchists. He really didn't like to talk about it—his memories of climbing out of the mass grave with a bullet hole in his shoulder were most unpleasant.

The YMCA man would probably have gasped in horror were he to discover that the lighthearted Palamidov had chaired a Red Army tribunal; or that Lavoisian, while on assignment from his newspaper, had dressed as a woman and infiltrated a gathering of women Baptists, then wrote a lengthy anti-religious dispatch about it; or that none of the Soviets present had baptized their kids; or that as many as four of these fiends were writers.

All kinds of people sat in the dining car.

On the second day of the journey, one prediction the plush-nosed prophet had made came true. As the train was rumbling and whooping on the bridge across the Volga at Syzran, the passengers struck up the song about Razin the Volga legend in their annoying city voices. While they were at it, they tried not to look each other in the eye. The foreigners in the next car, who were unclear on the appropriate repertoire for the occasion, gave a rousing rendition of the *Korobochka,* with an equally peculiar chorus of *"Ekh yukhnem!"* No one sent a postcard to the plush-nosed man—they were too ashamed. Only Ukhudshansky held himself in check. He didn't sing with the rest of them. While the train was overwhelmed by an orgy of singing, he alone kept quiet, clenched his teeth, and pretended to read *A Complete Geographical Description of Our Land*. His punishment was severe. He succumbed to a musical paroxysm late at night, way past Samara. Around midnight, when everyone else was already asleep, a shaky voice came from Ukhudshansky's compartment: "There's a cliff on the Volga, all covered with moss . . ." The journey had gotten the better of him in the end.

At an even later hour, when even Ukhudshansky was finally asleep, the door at the end of the car opened, momentarily admitting the unfettered thunder of the wheels, and Ostap Bender appeared in the empty, glittering corridor. He hesitated for a second, then sleepily waved off his doubts and opened the door to the first compartment he saw. Gargantua, Ukhudshansky, and the photojournalist Menshov were all asleep under the blue nightlight. The fourth bunk, an upper, was empty. The grand strategist didn't hesitate. His legs weak from an arduous odyssey, irreparable losses, and two hours of standing on the car's outside steps, Bender climbed onto the bunk. Then, he had a miraculous vision: a milky-white boiled chicken, its legs pointing up like the shafts of a horse cart, sat on the small table by the window.

"I'm following in the dubious footsteps of Panikovsky," whispered Ostap.

With that, he lifted the chicken to his bunk and ate it whole, without bread or salt. He stuck the bones under the firm linen bolster and, inhaling the inimitable smell of railroad paint, fell happily asleep to the sound of creaking partitions.

CHAPTER 27
"MAY A CAPITALIST LACKEY COME IN?"

In a dream that night, Ostap saw Zosya's sad shadowy face, and then Panikovsky appeared. The violator of the pact wore a coachman's hat with a feather in it, wrung his hands, and called out, "Bender! Bender! You don't know what a chicken is! It's a heavenly, juicy bird, the chicken!" Ostap was confused and irritated. "What chicken? I thought your specialty was goose!" But Panikovsky kept insisting, "Chicken, chicken, chicken!"

Then he woke up. Bender saw the ceiling, which curved like the top of an antique chest right above his head. The luggage net swayed in front of the grand strategist's nose. Bright sunlight filled the car. The hot air of the Orenburg plains blew in through the half-open window.

"Chicken!" a voice called out. "What happened to my chicken? There's nobody in here except us! Right? Now wait a minute, whose feet are these?"

Ostap covered his eyes with his hand and he immediately had the unpleasant thought that this was exactly what Panikovsky used to do when he sensed trouble. He lowered his hand and saw two heads next to his bunk.

"Sleeping? Well, well . . . ," said the first head.

"Tell me, my friend," said the second head good-naturedly, "you ate my chicken, right?"

Menshov the photojournalist was sitting on a lower bunk; both of his arms were up to their elbows in a black changing bag. He was reloading film.

"Yes," replied Ostap cautiously, "I ate it."

"Thank you so much!" exclaimed Gargantua, to Ostap's surprise. "I had no idea what to do with it. It's so hot in here, it could have gone bad, right? Would've been a shame to throw it away, right?"

"Of course," said Ostap warily, "I'm glad I could do this small favor for you."

"Which newspaper are you with?" asked the photojournalist, who, with a faint smile on his face, was still feeling around in the bag. "You didn't get on in Moscow, did you?"

"I see you're a photographer," replied Ostap evasively. "I once knew a small-town photographer who'd only open cans of food under the red light. He was afraid they'd spoil otherwise."

Menshov laughed. He appreciated the new passenger's joke. And so for the rest of the morning, nobody asked the grand strategist any more tricky questions. Bender jumped off the bunk, stroked his stubble-covered cheeks—which made him look like an outlaw—and gave the kindly Gargantua an inquiring glance. The satirist opened his suitcase, took out a shaving kit and, handing it over to Ostap, started to explain something, all the while pecking at invisible bird feed and constantly demanding confirmation for what he was saying.

While Ostap shaved and washed, Menshov, decked out with camera straps, was spreading the word about a new small-town journalist in his compartment who caught up with the train by air the night before and polished off Gargantua's chicken. The chicken story caused quite a stir. Almost all of them had brought food from home: shortbread cookies, meat patties, loaves of bread, and hard-boiled eggs. Nobody ate any of it. They preferred to go to the dining car.

And so the moment Bender finished his morning ritual, a portly writer in a soft casual jacket appeared in Bender's compartment. He put twelve eggs on the table in front of Ostap and said:

"Eat up. These are eggs. As long as eggs exist, somebody has to eat them."

Then the writer looked out the window, observed the warty-looking plain, and remarked sadly:

"The desert is so uninspiring! But it does exist, and one has to take that into account."

He was a philosopher. After Ostap thanked him, he shook his head and went back to his own compartment to finish writing a story. A disciplined man, he had resolved to write one story every day, no matter what. He stuck to his resolution with the diligence of a valedictorian. He likely drew inspiration from the thought that as long as paper exists, somebody has to write on it.

Other passengers followed the philosopher's lead. Navrotsky brought a jar of stuffed peppers. Lavoisian brought meat patties with shreds of newspaper clinging to them. Sapegin brought pickled herring and shortbread, and Dnestrov offered some apple jam. Others showed up, too, but Ostap was no longer granting favors.

"I can't, my friends, I can't," he kept saying, "you do one person a favor, and the rest come begging."

Ostap liked the journalists very much. He would have felt touched by their generosity, but he was so full that he was completely unable to experience any emotion whatsoever. He struggled back to his bunk and then slept for most of the day.

It was the third day of the journey. The passengers were desperate for something to happen. The Eastern Line was still far away, and nothing noteworthy was going on. The journalists from Moscow, exhausted from forced idleness, eyed each other suspiciously.

"Has anybody wired anything interesting to their office?"

Finally, Lavoisian couldn't take it anymore and sent the following telegram:

"Passed orenburg stop smoke billows locomotive stack stop mood cheerful comma delegate cars talk eastern line only stop wire instructions aral sea lavoisian"

Word of the telegram got around, and a line formed at the telegraph counter in the next station. Everybody sent brief reports regarding the cheerful mood on board and the smoke billowing from the locomotive's stack.

A window of opportunity opened for the foreigners right after Orenburg, when they spotted their first camel, their first yurt, and their first Kazakh in a pointy fur hat with a whip in his hand. At the small station where the train was delayed briefly, at least twenty cameras were aimed straight at a camel's snout. This was the beginning of things exotic: ships of the desert, freedom-loving sons of the plains, and other romantic characters.

The blue-blooded American woman emerged from the train wearing dark, round sunglasses and holding a green parasol to protect herself from the sun. A gray-haired American pointed his Eyemo movie camera at her and filmed her in this outfit for a long time. First she stood next to the camel, then in front of it, and finally squeezed herself in between its humps, which had been so warmly described by the attendant. Short and nasty Heinrich weaved through the crowd saying:

"Keep a close eye on her, or she'll accidentally get stuck here, and then there will be another sensation in the American press: 'Fearless woman journalist in the clutches of deranged camel.'"

The Japanese diplomat stood right in front of a Kazakh. They eyed each other silently. They had absolutely identical, slightly flattened faces, bristly mustaches, smooth yellow skin, and eyes that were narrow and a bit puffy. They would have passed for twins, if the Kazakh hadn't been wearing a rough sheepskin coat with a cloth sash, while the Japanese wore a gray London-tailored suit; and if the Kazakh hadn't learned to read just the year before, while the Japanese had graduated from universities in Tokyo and Paris twenty years earlier. The diplomat took a step back, looked through his camera's viewfinder, and pressed the button. The Kazakh laughed, climbed onto his small ungroomed horse, and rode off into the plains.

But at the very next stop the romantic story took an unexpected twist. Behind the station one could see bright red oil drums and a new yellow building made of wood. A long row of heavy machinery—their tracks pressed deep into the ground—stood in front of it. A young woman wearing black mechanic's pants and felt boots was standing on a stack of railroad ties. The Soviet journalists took their turn. They slowly advanced toward the woman, holding their cameras at eye level. Menshov crept forward at the head of the pack. He held an aluminum film cartridge in his teeth and made a series of rushes, like a infantryman in an attacking line. But while the camel posed in front of the cameras as if he had a solid claim to celebrity, the girl was a lot more modest. She suffered quietly through a handful of shots, then blushed and left. The photographers then turned their attention to the machinery. As luck would have it, a small caravan of camels was passing near the horizon—directly behind the machines. Together they formed a perfect shot, which could be captioned "The old and the new" or "Who wins?"

Ostap woke up just before sundown. The train continued across the desert. Lavoisian wandered up and down the corridor, trying to talk his colleagues into putting out an onboard newsletter. He even came up with the name: *Full Steam Ahead.*

"What kind of a name is that?" said Ostap. "I once saw a fire brigade newsletter called *Between Two Fires*. Now that really nailed it."

"You're a real wordsmith!" gushed Lavoisian. "Why don't you just admit that you're too lazy to write for the voice of the onboard community?"

The grand strategist didn't deny that he was a real wordsmith. If pressed, he was fully prepared to say exactly which publication he represented on this train, namely, the *Chernomorsk Gazette*. But nobody pressed him, since it was a special train and therefore didn't have any stern conductors with their nickel-plated ticket punches. Lavoisian and his typewriter were already installed in the workers' car, where his idea caused considerable excitement. The old man from the Trekhgorka Factory was already working on a piece that called for a meeting to discuss industrial practices and for a literary reading on board. Others were searching for a cartoonist, and Navrotsky was charged with distributing a questionnaire that sought to determine which of the factories represented on the train was the most successful at meeting its quotas.

In the evening, a large group of newspapermen gathered in the compartment shared by Gargantua, Menshov, Ukhudshansky and Bender. They were packed in, six men to a bunk. Feet and heads dangled from above. The cool night air refreshed the journalists who had suffered from the heat all day, and the rhythmic sound of the wheels on the tracks, which had gone on for three days, created a convivial atmosphere. They talked of the Eastern Line, of their editors and office managers, of funny typos, and together teased Ukhudshansky about his lack of journalistic drive. Ukhudshansky would raise his head and reply condescendingly:

"Gabbing? Well, well . . ."

At the height of the fun, Mr. Heinrich appeared.

"May a capitalist lackey come in?" he asked cheerfully.

Heinrich settled down in the lap of the portly writer who grunted and thought to himself stoically: "If I have a lap, somebody has to sit in it. And so he does."

"So how goes the building of socialism?" asked the representative of the liberal newspaper cheekily.

It just so happened that all the foreigners on board were addressed courteously as Mister, Herr, or Signor So-and-so, and only the correspondent of the liberal newspaper was simply called Heinrich. Nobody took him seriously; they all thought he was a blowhard. So Palamidov replied to his question:

"Heinrich! You're wasting your time! Now you're going to start trashing the Soviet system again, which is boring and uninformative. We can hear all that from any nasty old woman waiting in line."

"That's not it at all," said Heinrich, "I'd like to tell you the biblical story of Adam and Eve. May I?"

"Listen, Heinrich, how come you speak Russian so well?" asked Sapegin.

"I learned it in Odessa in 1918, when I was occupying that delightful city with the army of General von Beltz. I was a lieutenant back then. You probably heard of von Beltz?"

"Didn't just hear," replied Palamidov, "I saw your von Beltz laying in his gilded office at the palace of the commander of the Odessa Military District —with a bullet through his head. He shot himself when he heard there was a revolution in your country, Heinrich."

At the word "revolution," Mr. Heinrich smiled politely and said:

"The General was true to his oath."

"And why didn't you shoot yourself, Heinrich?" asked someone from the top bunk. "What happened to your oath?"

"Well, do you want to hear the biblical story or not?" asked the representative of the liberal newspaper testily.

They kept bugging him with questions about the oath for a while, and only when he got really upset and started to leave did they agree to listen to his story.

THE STORY OF ADAM AND EVE

AS TOLD BY MR. HEINRICH

"Well, gentlemen, there was this young man in Moscow, a member of the Young Communist League. His name was Adam. And there was this young woman, Eve, also in Moscow and also a member of the League. One day these two young people went for a walk in that Moscow paradise, the Park of Culture and Rest. I don't know what they were talking about. Our young people normally talk about love. But your Adam and Eve were Marxists, so maybe they talked about world revolution. Be that as it may, it just so happened that, after a stroll, they sat down on the grass under a tree in the former Neskuchny Gardens. I don't know what kind of a tree it was. Maybe it was the Tree of Knowledge of Good and

Evil. But Marxists, as you know, don't care for mysticism. So they most likely thought it was an ordinary mountain ash. While they were talking, Eve broke a small branch off the tree and presented it to Adam. And then a man appeared. Lacking imagination, the young Marxists took him for a groundskeeper. Most likely, however, it was an angel with a flaming sword. Griping and grumbling, the angel escorted Adam and Eve to the park office, in order to file a report on the damage they had inflicted on garden property. This insignificant and mundane incident distracted the young people from their discussion of high politics. Adam suddenly noticed the lovely woman in front of him, and Eve saw the strong man in front of her. And so they fell in love with each other. Three years later, they already had two sons."

At this point, Mr. Heinrich suddenly stopped and began tucking his soft striped cuffs into his sleeves.

"So what's the point?" asked Lavoisian.

"The point is," answered Heinrich emphatically, "that one son was named Cain, the other Abel, and that in due course Cain would kill Abel, Abraham would beget Isaac, Isaac would beget Jacob, and the whole story would start anew, and neither Marxism nor anything else will ever be able to change that. Everything will repeat itself. There will be a flood, there will be Noah with his three sons, and Ham will insult Noah. There will be the Tower of Babel, gentlemen, which will never be completed. And on and on and on. There won't be anything new in the world. So don't get too excited about your new life."

Heinrich leaned back with satisfaction, squashing the kind, portly writer with his narrow, spiny body.

"All this would have been great," remarked Palamidov, "had it been supported by evidence. But you can't prove anything. You just wish it were true. There's no point in trying to stop you from believing in miracles. Go on believing and praying."

"Can you prove that it will be different?" exclaimed the representative of the liberal newspaper.

"Yes," replied Palamidov, "we can. You will see proof of it the day after tomorrow at the joining of the Eastern Line."

"Here you go again," grumbled Heinrich. "Construction! Factories! The Five-Year Plan! Don't wave your steel in my face. It's the spirit that counts! Everything will repeat itself! There will be the Thirty Years War, and the Hundred Years War, and those with the audacity to claim that the Earth is round will be burned at the stake again. They'll fool poor Jacob again, make him work seven years for nothing and then slip him the ugly, near-sighted Leah for a wife instead of the full-breasted Rachel. Everything, everything will repeat itself! And the Wandering Jew will continue to wander the earth . . ."

"The Wandering Jew will never wander again!" said the grand strategist suddenly, looking at the others with a playful smile.

"Are you saying you can prove this in two days as well?" protested Heinrich.

"I can do it right now," said Ostap graciously. "If present company permits me, I will tell you what happened to the so-called Wandering Jew."

The company gladly granted their permission. Everyone settled in to listen to the new passenger's story, and even Ukhudshansky muttered, "Telling stories? Well, well . . ."

And so the grand strategist began.

THE STORY OF THE WANDERING JEW
AS TOLD BY OSTAP BENDER

"I'm not going to recount the long and boring story of the Wandering Hebrew. Suffice it to say that this vulgar old man walked the earth for nearly two thousand years. He didn't register at the hotels, and he annoyed citizens with complaints about the exorbitant train fares that forced him to travel on foot. He was spotted on numerous occasions. He was present at the historic meeting at which Columbus ultimately failed to account for the funds that had been advanced to him to discover America. As a very young man, he witnessed the burning of Rome. For about a century and a half he lived in India, astounding the Yogis with his longevity and disagreeable character. In other words, the old man would have had a lot of interesting stories to tell, if he had written his memoirs at the end of each century. Alas, the Wandering Jew was illiterate, and on top of that, he had a memory like a sieve.

Not so long ago, the old man was residing in the wonderful city of Rio de Janeiro, sipping refreshments, watching ocean liners, and strolling under the palm trees in white pants. He had purchased the pants second-hand from a knight crusader in Palestine some eight hundred years earlier, but they still looked almost new. Suddenly the old man grew restless. He developed an urge to go to the Dnieper River in Russia. He had seen them all: the Rhine, the Ganges, the Mississippi, the Yangtze, the Niger, the Volga, but not the Dnieper. He decided he just had to take a peek at that mighty river as well.

And so right smack in the middle of 1919, the Wandering Jew crossed the Romanian border illegally in his crusader pants. Needless to say, he had eight pairs of silk stockings and a bottle of Parisian perfume on his stomach—a lady in Kishinev had asked him to take the stuff to her relatives in Kiev. In those tumultuous times, smuggling contraband on your stomach was known as "wearing bandages." The old man mastered this trick in Kishinev in no time. After making the delivery, the Wandering Jew was standing on the bank of the Dnieper, his unkempt greenish beard hanging down. He was approached by a man with yellow and blue stripes on his pants and the epaulets of Petlyura's Ukrainian army on his shoulders.

"Jew?" asked the man sternly.

"Jew," replied the old man.

"Let's go," said the man with the stripes. And he took him to his battalion commander.

"Got a Jew," he reported, pushing the old man forward with his knee.

"Jew?" asked the battalion commander with mock surprise.

"Jew," replied the wanderer.

"Then take him to the firing squad," said the commander with a pleasant smile.

"But I am supposed to be eternal!" cried the old man.
He had yearned for death for two thousand years, but at that moment he desperately wanted to live.

"Shut up, you dirty kike!" yelled the forelocked commander cheerfully. "Finish him off, boys!"

And the eternal wanderer was no more.

"So that's the story," concluded Ostap.

"I suppose, Mr. Heinrich, as a former lieutenant in the Austrian army, you are aware of the ways of your friends from Petlyura's forces," remarked Palamidov.

Heinrich got up and left without a word. At first everyone thought he was offended, but the next day they found out that the correspondent of the liberal newspaper had gone straight from the Soviets' car to Mr. Hiram Berman and sold him the story of the Wandering Jew for forty dollars. Hiram had wired Bender's story to his editor at the next station.

CHAPTER 28
A SWELTERING WAVE OF INSPIRATION

On the morning of the fourth day, the train turned east. Passing along the snowy frontal ranges of the Himalayas, rumbling over man-made structures—bridges, culverts for the spring runoff, and the like—as well as casting its quivering shadow over mountain streams, the special train whizzed by a small town that was hidden under poplars and went on twisting and turning alongside a tall, snow-covered mountain. Unable to make it straight to the pass, the special rolled up to the mountain on the right, then on the left, turned back, huffed and puffed, returned again, rubbed its dusty-green sides against the mountain, wiggled this way and that—and finally broke free. Having worked its wheels hard, the train came to a spectacular halt at the last station before the beginning of the Eastern Line.

Wreathed by fantastic sunlight, a steam engine the color of new grass stood against the background of aluminum-colored mountains. It was a gift from the station's personnel to the new rail line.

The situation with regard to gifts for anniversaries and special occasions has been problematic in this country for a fairly long time. A common gift was either a miniature steam engine, no bigger than a cat, or just the opposite—a chisel that was larger than a telegraph pole. This torturous transformation, of small objects into large ones and vice versa, cost a lot of time and money. The useless tiny steam engines would gather dust on top of office cabinets, while the giant chisel, delivered by two horse carts, would rust pointlessly and stupidly in the courtyard of the honored organization.

But the OV-class locomotive, whose complete overhaul was finished well ahead of schedule, was of perfectly normal dimensions, and the chisel that had been undoubtedly used in its overhaul was apparently also of a regular size. The handsome gift was immediately harnessed to the train, and the small *ovechka*—the little sheep—which is how the OV-class locomotives are commonly referred to inside the right-of-way, went rolling toward Mountain Station, the southern terminus of the new line, bearing a banner that read, ONWARD TO THE JOINING!

Exactly two years earlier, the first blueish-black rail, manufactured by a plant in the Urals, had been laid here. Glowing ribbons of rail had been continuously flying off the plant's rolling mill ever since. The Line needed more and more of them. The track-laying trains that were heading toward each other had entered into a competition, on top of everything else, and were moving at such a pace that their suppliers found themselves in a bind.

The evening at Mountain Station, lit by pink and green fireworks, was so wonderful that the old-timers, had there been any, would definitely have observed that they couldn't remember another evening like this. Luckily, Mountain Station had no old-timers. As recently as 1928, not only were there no old-timers, but there were no houses, no station buildings, no railroad tracks, and no wooden triumphal arch with banners and flags flapping over it, near which the special train had stopped.

While a rally was going on under the kerosene pressure lamps, and the entire population gathered around the podium, the photojournalist Menshov was circling the arch with two cameras, a tripod, and a magnesium flash lamp. The photographer thought the arch was perfect and would make a great shot. But the train, which stood some twenty paces away from the arch, would come out too small. If, however, he were to take the shot from the train's side, then the arch would be too small. In cases like this, Mohammed would normally go to the mountain, fully aware that the mountain wouldn't come to him. But Menshov did what seemed easiest to him. He asked the engineer to pull the train under the arch, in the same matter-of-fact manner a streetcar passenger might use to ask someone to move over a bit. In addition, he requested that some thick white smoke should billow from the locomotive's stack. He also demanded that the engineer look fearlessly into the distance, shielding his eyes with his hand. The crew was unsure of what to make of these demands, but they assumed that they were perfectly normal and granted his wishes. The train screeched up to the arch, the requested smoke billowed from the stack, and the engineer stuck his head out the window and made a wild grimace. Then Menshov set off a flash of magnesium so powerful that the ground trembled and dogs for miles and miles around started barking. Finished with the shot, the photographer curtly thanked the train crew and promptly retired to his compartment.

Late that night, the special train was already traveling along the Eastern Line. As the passengers were getting into bed, the photojournalist Menshov stepped out into the corridor and said plaintively to no one in particular:

"What do you know! Turns out I was shooting this goddamn arch on an empty cassette! Nothing came out."

"Not to worry," replied Lavoisian sympathetically, "it's easy to fix. Ask the engineer, and he'll reverse the train in no time. In just three hours, we'll be back at Mountain Station and you can get another shot. As for the joining, it can be postponed for a day."

"There's no way in hell I can shoot now!" said the photojournalist dejectedly. "I used up all my magnesium, or else we'd certainly have to go back."

The journey on the Eastern Line brought the grand strategist a lot of joy. With every hour, he came closer to the Northern site, where Koreiko was stationed. Besides, Ostap liked the special passengers. They were young, cheerful people, without the crazy bureaucratic streak so typical of his friends from the Hercules. For his happiness to be complete, he only needed money. He had finished off the donated provisions, and the dining car, unfortunately, required cash. At first, Ostap claimed he wasn't hungry when his new friends tried to drag him to dinner, but he soon realized that he couldn't go on like this for long. For a while, he'd been watching Ukhudshansky, who would spend the whole day by the window in the corridor, looking at telegraph poles and watching the birds fly off the wires. All along, a mildly ironic smile played on his face. He would tip his head back and whisper to the birds: "Fluttering? Well, well . . ." Curious Ostap even went as far as to familiarize himself with Ukhudshansky's article, "Retail Boards Need Improvement." After that, Bender looked the strange journalist over from head to toe once again, smiled ominously, and locked himself in the compartment, feeling the familiar excitement of the hunt.

He came back out a full three hours later, holding a large sheet of paper that was ruled like a chart.

"Writing?" asked Ukhudshansky, mostly out of habit.

"Just for you," replied the grand strategist. "I notice that you're constantly afflicted by the torments of creativity. Writing is difficult, of course. As an old editorialist and a fellow scribe, I can attest to that. But I came up with something that will relieve you of the need to wait until you're drenched by a sweltering wave of inspiration. Here. Kindly take a look."

With that, Ostap handed Ukhudshansky the sheet, which read:

THE CELEBRATORY KIT

*An Indispensable Manual for Composing
Anniversary Articles and Satirical Pieces for Special Occasions,
as well as Official Poems, Odes, and Hymns*

SECTION I. VOCABULARY

NOUNS

1. Hails
2. Workers
3. Dawn
4. Life
5. Beacon
6. Flaws
7. Banner (flag)
8. Ba'al
9. Moloch
10. Lackey
11. Hour
12. Enemy
13. Stride
14. Wave
15. Sands
16. Gait
17. Horse
18. Heart
19. Past

ADJECTIVES

1. Imperialist
2. Capitalist
3. Historic
4. Last
5. Industrial
6. Steely
7. Iron

VERBS

1. Gleam	6. Propel
2. Raise	7. Sing
3. Reveal	8. Slander
4. Glow	9. Screech
5. Soar	10. Threaten

EXPRESSIVE EPITHETS

1. Vicious	2. Savage

OTHER PARTS OF SPEECH

1. Ninth	4. So be it!
2. Eleventh	5. Onward!
3. Let!	

(Also interjections, prepositions, conjunctions, commas, ellipses, exclamation points, quotes, etc.).

Note: Commas are placed before "which," "not," and "but"; ellipses, excl. points, and quotes should be used wherever possible.

SECTION II. CREATIVE EXAMPLES
(COMPOSED EXCLUSIVELY OF THE WORDS FROM SECTION I)

EXAMPLE I. AN EDITORIAL

The Ninth Wave

The Eastern Line is an iron horse, which, raising the sands of the past with its steely gait, propels history forward, while revealing yet more vicious screeches by the slanderous enemy, upon which the ninth wave is already rising, threatening the eleventh hour, the last hour for the lackeys of imperialist Moloch, that capitalist Ba'al; yet, despite the flaws, may the banners glow and also soar by the beacon of industrialization, the beacon that gleams to the workers' hails, which, to the sound of singing hearts, reveal the dawn of new life: onward!

EXAMPLE II. A FEATURE ARTICLE

So be it!

—Onward!

It gleams to the workers' hails.

It reveals the dawn of the new life . . .

—The beacon!

—Of industrialization!

Yes, there are certain flaws. So be it. But, oh, how they glow . . . how they fly . . . those flags! Those banners!

Yes, there's Ba'al of capitalism. There's Moloch of imperialism. So be it!

But, bearing down upon their lackeys are:

—The ninth wave!

—The eleventh hour!

—The twelfth night!

Let them slander! Let them screech! Let the savage, vicious enemy reveal itself!

History is on the move. The sands of the past are raised by the striding steel.

It's the "iron horse!"

It's:

—The Eastern!

—Line!

"The hearts sing . . ."

EXAMPLE III. A POEM

A) The Twelfth Fight

The hearts all sing with steely strain,
The beacon gleams at dawn.
The vicious enemy in vain
Upon us heaps its scorn.
The iron horse, it sallies forth
To smash historic laws,

To help the workers of the Earth
Reveal their certain flaws.
Eleventh hour soars on high,
The ninth wave is aglow.
Ba'al and Moloch! Our stride
Bespeaks your final throes!

B) *The Oriental Version*
The *uryuk* blooms with fragrant strain,
A *kishlak* gleams at dawn.
And past *aryks* and alleyways
An *ishak* wanders on.

THE ASIAN FLAVOR

1. Uryuk (apricots)
2. Aryk (canal)
3. Ishak (donkey)
4. Pilaf (food)
5. Bai (a bad man)
6. Basmatch (a bad man)
7. Jackal (an animal)
8. Kishlak (village)
9. Piala (tea cup)
10. Madrasah (religious school)
11. Ichigs (shoes)
12. Shaytan (devil)
13. Arba (cart)
14. Shaytan-Arba (the Central Asian Railroad)
15. Me not understand (expression)
16. You like? (expression)

APPENDIX
Using the materials in Section I and the methodology out-
lined in Section II, one can also produce: novels, novellas,
poems in prose, short stories, sketches of daily life, fiction-
alized reports, chronicles, epics, plays, political columns,
political board games, radio oratorios, etc.

When Ukhudshansky had finally absorbed the contents of the document, his hitherto dull eyes livened up. He, who up until that moment had limited himself to covering official meetings, suddenly saw the lofty peaks of style open up before him.

"And for all that—twenty-five tugriks, twenty-five Mongolian rubles," said the grand strategist impatiently, suffering from hunger.

"I don't have any Mongolian," said the correspondent of the union paper, not letting the Celebratory Kit out of his hands.

Ostap agreed to accept ordinary rubles, and invited Gargantua, who he was already addressing as "my dear friend and benefactor," to come to the dining car. They brought him a carafe of vodka that sparkled with ice and mercury, a salad, and a cutlet that was as big and as heavy as a horseshoe. After the vodka, which made him slightly dizzy, the grand strategist informed his dear friend and benefactor, in confidence, that he was hoping to locate a certain man at the Northern Site who owed him some money. Then he would treat all the journalists to a feast. Gargantua responded with a long, compelling, and completely unintelligible speech, as usual. Ostap called the barman over, inquired whether champagne was available, and how many bottles, and what other delicacies he had, and in what amounts, and said that he needed all this information because, in a couple of days, he was planning to give a banquet for his fellow scribes. The barman assured him that everything possible would certainly be done.

"In compliance with the laws of hospitality," he added for some reason.

As the site of the joining got closer, more and more nomads appeared. They descended from the hills to meet the train, wearing hats that looked like Chinese pagodas. Rumbling along, the special train dove into rocky granite cuts, passed over the new triple span bridge, whose last girder had been installed only a day earlier, and went on to storm the famous Crystal Pass. It became famous thanks to the builders of the Eastern Line, who had completed all the blasting and track-laying in three months, instead of the eight allocated by the plan.

Life on the train was gradually becoming more relaxed. The foreigners, who had left Moscow in collars that were as hard as pharmaceutical ceramics and in heavy silk ties and woolen suits, began to loosen up. The heat was overwhelming. The first to change his uniform was one of the Americans. Giggling sheepishly, he emerged from his car in a bizarre outfit. He wore thick yellow shoes, knee-length socks with golf breeches, horn-rimmed glasses, and a cross-stitched Russian-style shirt—the kind a state-farm official would wear. And the hotter it got, the fewer foreigners remained faithful to the concept of European dress. Russian shirts and tunics of all imaginable styles, Odessa sandals, and casual slippers completely transformed the newsmen of the capitalist world. They developed a striking resemblance to veteran Soviet office workers, and one was just dying to subject them to a purge, to drag out of them what they did before 1917, to question whether they were bureaucrats or, by any chance, bad managers, and whether all of their relatives were clean.

Late at night, the diligent *ovechka* locomotive, decked with flags and garlands, pulled the special train into Roaring Springs—the site of the joining. Cameramen were burning Roman candles, and the director of the Line stood in the harsh white light, looking at the train with deep emotion. The cars were dark. Everyone was asleep. Only the large square windows of the government car were lit up. Its door opened promptly, and a member of the government jumped off onto the ground below.

The director of the Eastern Line took a step forward, saluted, and delivered the report which the whole country was waiting for. The Eastern Line, which linked Siberia directly to Central Asia, had been completed a year ahead of schedule.

After the formalities were over, the report delivered and accepted, the two men, neither of them young or sentimental, kissed.

All the correspondents, both Soviet and foreign, including Lavoisian who, in his impatience, had sent the telegram about smoke billowing from the train's stack and the Canadian woman who had rushed across the ocean—all were asleep. Only Palamidov was dashing around the freshly built embankment in search of the telegraph. He calculated that if he sent an urgent cable immediately, it would make it into the morning edition. Finally, he located the makeshift telegraph shack in the dark desert.

"Stars twinkling," he wrote, irritated with his pencil, "line completion reported stop witnessed historic kiss of line director by government member palamidov."

The editor printed the first part of the telegram but dropped the kiss. He said it was inappropriate for a member of the government to smooch.

CHAPTER 29
ROARING SPRINGS

The sun rose over the hilly desert at exactly 5:02:46 A.M. Ostap got up a minute later. Menshov the photojournalist was already decking himself out with bags and belts. He put his cap on backwards, so that the visor wouldn't interfere with the viewfinder. The photographer had a big day ahead of him. Ostap was also hoping for a big day, so he leaped out of the car without even washing. He took the yellow folder with him.

The trains that had brought the guests from Moscow, Siberia, and Central Asia formed a series of streets and lanes between them. They surrounded the reviewing stand on all sides. Steam engines hissed, and the white vapor clung to a large canvas banner that read THE EASTERN LINE IS THE FIRST PROGENY OF THE FIVE-YEAR PLAN.

Everybody was still asleep, and the cool breeze was rapping the flags on the empty stand when Ostap noticed that the clear horizon of the rugged terrain suddenly erupted with bursts of dust. Pointy hats appeared from behind the hills on all sides. Thousands of horsemen, sitting in wooden saddles and urging their long-haired horses on, hurried toward the wooden arrow that was placed at the very spot which had been chosen two years earlier as the future site for the joining of the rails.

Entire clans of nomads were approaching. Heads of household were riding, and so were their wives, straddling their horses like the men. Kids rode three to a horse, and even the mean mothers-in-law spurred their faithful mounts forward, kicking them under the belly with their heels. Groups of horsemen rustled in the dust, galloped around the field with red banners, stood up in their stirrups, turned sideways, and looked curiously at the unfamiliar wonders. The wonders were many: trains, rails, the dashing figures of the cameramen, the latticed dining hall that had suddenly risen up out of nowhere on what used to be an empty space, and the bullhorns that carried a powerful voice saying "one, two, three, four, five, six," testing the loud-speakers. Two track-laying trains—actually, two construction sites on wheels, complete with warehouses, diners, offices, bathhouses, and workers' quarters—stood facing each other in front of the reviewing stand, separated by a mere sixty feet of ties, which had not yet been stitched together by rails. That's where the last rail would be laid, and the last spike would be driven. A banner at the head of the Southern Site said TO THE NORTH!; the one on the Northern Site said TO THE SOUTH!

Workers from both sites mixed together into a single group. They were meeting in person for the first time, even though they knew and thought about each other ever since the construction had begun, when they were separated by a thousand miles of desert, rocks, lakes, and rivers. The competition between them brought the rendezvous a year ahead of schedule. During the last month, the rails were really flying. Both the North and the South were striving to get ahead and be the first to enter Roaring Springs. The North had won. The directors of the two sites, one in a graphite-gray tunic, the other in a white Russian-style shirt, chatted peacefully near the arrow, and against his will, a snake-like smile occasionally appeared on the Northern director's face. He hurried to extinguish it, and praised the South, but the smile would soon raise his sun-washed mustache again.

Ostap rushed to the Northern cars, but the site was empty. All the occupants had left for the reviewing stand; the musicians were already sitting in front of it. Burning their lips on the hot metal mouthpieces, they played an overture.

The Soviet journalists occupied the left wing of the stand. Lavoisian leaned down and begged Menshov to take a picture of him performing his professional duties. But Menshov was too busy. He was shooting the best workers of the Line in groups and individually, making the spike drivers raise their mallets and the diggers lean on their shovels. The foreigners sat on the right. Soldiers were checking passes at the entrance to the bleachers. Ostap didn't have one. The train administrator distributed them from a list, and O. Bender from the *Chernomorsk Gazette* was not on it. Gargantua beckoned the grand strategist upstairs in vain, shouting "Isn't that right? Isn't it true?" Ostap just shook his head in refusal, his eyes searching through the bleachers that were tightly packed with heroes and guests.

Alexander Koreiko, the timekeeper from the Northern Site, sat quietly in the first row. His head was protected from the sun by a tricorne made out of a newspaper. He pushed his ear forward a bit so that he could better hear the first speaker, who was already making his way to the microphone.

"Alexander Ivanovich!" shouted Ostap, folding his hands into a megaphone.

Koreiko looked down and rose from his seat. The orchestra struck up *The Internationale*, but the wealthy timekeeper wasn't paying proper attention to the national anthem. The unnerving sight of the grand strategist, running around the space that had been cleared to lay the last rails, instantly destroyed his inner peace. He glanced over the heads of the crowd, trying to figure out a possible escape route. But all around him was desert.

Fifteen thousand horsemen kept moving back and forth, fording a cold stream dozens of times, until finally they settled behind the bleachers in cavalry formation. But some of them, too proud and shy, continued to hang around on the tops of the hills throughout the day, never venturing closer to the howling and roaring rally.

The builders of the Eastern Line celebrated their victory with gusto, shouting, playing music, and tossing their favorites and heroes into the air. The rails flew onto the track with a ringing sound. They were put into place in a minute, and the workmen, who had driven millions of spikes, ceded the honor of delivering the final blows to their superiors.

"In compliance with the laws of hospitality," said the barman, who was sitting on the roof of the dining car with the cooks.

An engineer with the Order of the Red Banner on his chest pushed his large felt hat to the back of his head, grabbed a mallet with a long handle, grimaced, and hit the ground. The spike drivers, some of whom were so strong they could drive a spike with a single blow, greeted his efforts with friendly laughter. Soon, however, soft strikes on the ground began to alternate with clanging noises, indicating that, on occasion, the mallet was actually making contact with the spike. Next to take up the mallet was the regional Party Secretary, followed by members of the government, the directors of the North and the South, and several guests. It took a mere thirty minutes for the director of the Line to drive the final spike.

Then the speeches began. Each was delivered twice—in Kazakh and in Russian.

"Comrades," said a distinguished spike driver slowly, trying not to look at the Order of the Red Banner that had just been pinned to his shirt, "what's done is done, and there's no need to talk about it. But our entire track-laying team has a request for the government: please send us to a new project immediately. We work together very well now, and we've been laying down three miles of track each day in recent months. We pledge to maintain this rate and even exceed it! And long live our world revolution! I also wanted to say, comrades, that too many ties were defective, we had to reject them. This needs to be fixed."

The journalists could no longer complain about the lack of things to report. They jotted down the speeches. They grabbed the engineers by their waists and demanded information and precise figures. It became hot, dusty, and businesslike. The rally in the desert started smoking like a huge bonfire. After scribbling a dozen lines, Lavoisian would rush to the telegraph, send an urgent cable, and start scribbling again. Ukhudshansky wasn't taking any notes or sending any cables. He had the Celebratory Kit in his pocket, which would make it possible to compose an excellent Asian-flavored dispatch in five minutes. Ukhudshansky's future was secure. That's why he had more sarcasm than usual in his voice as he said to his colleagues:

"Working hard? Well, well . . ."

Suddenly Leo Shirtikov and Ian Benchikov, the ones who had missed the train in Moscow, appeared among the Soviet journalists. They flew in on a plane that had landed early in the morning, six miles from Roaring Springs, on a natural airfield located behind a distant hill. The two journalist brothers made it from there on foot. Having barely said hello, Leo Shirtikov and Ian Benchikov pulled notebooks out of their pockets and started making up for lost time.

The foreigners' cameras clicked incessantly. Throats went dry from the speeches and the sun. People glanced more and more frequently at the cold stream and the dining hall, where the striped shadows of the canopy lay on endless banquet tables that were crowded with green bottles of mineral water. Next to it were kiosks, where the revelers ran from time to time to have a drink. Koreiko was dying of thirst, but he continued to suffer under his childish tricorne. The grand strategist teased him from afar, raising a bottle of lemonade and the yellow folder with shoelace straps into the air.

They placed a little Young Pioneer girl on the table next to a water jug and a microphone.

"Well, little girl," said the director of the Line cheerfully, "why don't you tell us what you think about the Eastern Line?"

It wouldn't have been surprising if the girl suddenly stamped her foot and began: "Comrades! Allow me to summarize the achievements which . . . ," and so forth, because we have exemplary children who can make two-hour speeches with forlorn diligence. But the Young Pioneer from Roaring Springs took the bull by the horns with her little hands and belted out, in a funny, high-pitched voice:

"Long live the Five-Year Plan!"

Palamidov approached a foreign professor of economics and asked him for an interview.

"I am very impressed," said the professor. "All the construction that I have seen in the Soviet Union is on a grand scale. I have no doubt that the Five-Year Plan will be successfully completed. I'll be writing about it."

And, indeed, six months later he published a book in which he argued for two hundred pages that the Five-Year Plan would be completed as scheduled, and that the USSR would become one of the world's foremost industrial powers. On page 201, however, the professor explained that this was exactly why the Soviet Union should be crushed as soon as possible, before it brought about the death of capitalist society. The professor proved far more businesslike than the gassy Heinrich.

A white plane took off from behind a hill. The Kazakhs scattered in every direction. The plane's large shadow leaped over the reviewing stand and, folding up and down, rushed off into the desert. Shouting and raising their whips, the Kazakhs gave chase. The cameramen perked up and began winding their contraptions. The scene became even more dusty and hectic. The rally was over.

"Listen, comrades," said Palamidov, walking briskly to the diner with his fellow scribes, "let us agree that nobody will write anything banal."

"Banality is awful!" echoed Lavoisian. "It's disgusting."

And so, on their way to the dining hall, the journalists unanimously agreed not to write about Uzun Kulak, which means "the Long Ear," which in turn means "the desert telegraph." Anybody who traveled to the East had already written about it, to the point that no one could bear reading about it anymore. No stories entitled "The Legend of Lake Issyk Kul." Enough Oriental-flavored banality!

Koreiko was the only one left sitting in the empty bleachers, surrounded by cigarette butts, torn-up notes, and sand that had blown in from the desert. He couldn't bring himself to come down.

"Come here, Alexander Ivanovich!" beckoned Ostap. "Have mercy on yourself! A sip of cold mineral water! What? You don't want one? Fine, then at least have mercy on me! I'm hungry! I'm not going anywhere, you know that! Maybe you want me to sing Schubert's *Serenade* to you? Come to me, my dear friend? I'll do it!"

But Koreiko didn't take him up on the offer. Even without the serenade, he knew that he'd have to part with the money this time. Slouching forward and lingering on each step, he started coming down.

"A tricorne sits low on your forehead?" Ostap continued playfully. "And where's the gray travel coat? You won't believe how much I missed you. Well, hello, hello! How about a kiss? Or shall we go straight to the vaults, to the Leichtweiss' Cave where you keep your tugriks?"

"Dinner first," said Koreiko, whose tongue was desiccated from thirst and scratched like a file.

"Fine, let's have dinner. But none of your funny business this time. Actually, you haven't got a chance. My boys are positioned behind the hills," Ostap lied, just in case.

The thought of the boys dampened his spirits a bit.

Dinner for the builders and the guests was served in the Eurasian style. The Kazakhs settled on the rugs, sitting cross-legged, the way everyone does in the East but only tailors do in the West. The Kazakhs ate pilaf from small white bowls and washed it down with lemonade. The Europeans sat down at the tables.

The builders of the Eastern Line had endured many hardships, troubles, and worries during the two years of construction. But putting together a formal dinner in the middle of the desert was no small feat either. The Asian and European menus were discussed at length. And the issue of alcoholic beverages had also been contentious. For a few days, the construction headquarters resembled the United States just before a presidential election. The dries and the wets locked their horns in battle. Finally, the party committee spoke out against alcohol. Then another issue came to the fore: foreigners, diplomats, people from Moscow! How do you feed them in style? After all, they're used to various culinary excesses in their Londons and New Yorks. So they brought an old expert named Ivan Osipovich from Tashkent. Long ago, he was a maître d' at the famous Martyanych's in Moscow, and was living out his days as director of a state-owned diner near the Chicken Bazaar.

"So please, Ivan Osipovich," they told him at the headquarters, "we're counting on you. There will be foreigners, you know. It has to be special somehow—chic, if you will."

"Trust me," mumbled the old man with tears in his eyes, "the people I have fed! The Prince of Württemberg himself! You don't even have to pay me anything. How can I not feed people properly one last time? I'll feed them—and then I'll die!"

Ivan Osipovich grew extremely anxious. When he was told that alcohol was ultimately rejected, he almost fell ill, but he didn't have the heart to leave Europe without a dinner. The budget he submitted was substantially reduced, so the old man mumbled "I'll feed them and I'll die" to himself and added sixty rubles from his own savings. On the day of the dinner, Ivan Osipovich showed up wearing a tailcoat that smelled of mothballs. While the rally was going on, he was very nervous and kept glancing at the sun and scolding the nomads, who, out of simple curiosity, were trying to ride into the dining hall. The old man brandished a napkin at them and rattled:

"Go away, Genghis, can't you see what's going on? Oh my God! The *sauce piquante* will curdle! And the consommé with poached eggs isn't ready yet!"

The hors d'oeuvres were already on the table; everything was arranged beautifully and with great skill. Starched napkins stood up vertically, butter, shaped into rosebuds, rested in ice on small plates, pickled herrings held hoops of onions and olives in their teeth. There were flowers, and even the rye bread looked quite presentable.

The guests finally arrived at the table. They were covered with dust, red from the heat, and ravenous. None of them resembled the Prince of Württemberg. Ivan Osipovich suddenly became uneasy.

"I'm hoping the guests will forgive me" he pleaded, "just five more minutes, and then we can start! Please do me a personal favor—don't touch anything on the table before dinner, so we can do it properly."

He ducked into the kitchen for a moment, prancing ceremoniously, but when he returned with some extra-special fish on a platter, he witnessed a horrifying scene of plunder. It was so unlike the elaborate dining ceremony Ivan Osipovich had envisioned that it made him stop in his tracks. The Englishman with the waist of a tennis player was blithely eating bread and butter, while Heinrich was bending over the table, pulling an olive out of a herring's mouth with his fingers. Everything at the table was upside down. The guests were taking the edge off their hunger, chatting merrily.

"What's all this?" asked the old man, stricken.

"Pops, where's the soup?" shouted Heinrich with his mouth full.

Ivan Osipovich didn't say anything. He just waved them off with his napkin and walked away. He left all further chores to his subordinates.

When the two strategists finally elbowed their way to the table, a fat man with a pendulous banana-shaped nose was making the first toast. To Ostap's great surprise, it was the engineer Talmudovsky.

"Yes! We are heroes!" exclaimed Talmudovsky, holding up a glass of mineral water. "Hail to us, the builders of the Eastern Line! But think of our working conditions, citizens! Take the salaries, for example. Yes, they're better than in other places, no argument there, but the cultural amenities! No theater! It's a desert! No indoor facilities! No, I can't work like this!"

"Who is he?" the builders were asking each other. "Do you know him?"

Meanwhile, Talmudovsky had already pulled his suitcases out from under the table.

"I don't give a damn about the contract!" he yelled, heading for the exit. "What? Return the moving allowance? Sue me! Yes, sue me!"

And even as he was bumping his suitcases into the diners, he shouted "Sue me!" furiously, instead of "I'm sorry."

Late that night, he was already cruising in a motorized section car, having joined the linemen who had some business at the southern end of the Line. Talmudovsky sat on his luggage, explaining to the workers the reasons why an honest professional couldn't possibly work in this hellhole. Ivan Osipovich, the maître d', rode home with them. In his grief, he hadn't even taken off his tailcoat. He was very drunk.

"Barbarians!" he yelled, sticking his head out into the harsh wind and waving his fist in the direction of Roaring Springs. "The whole arrangement went to the bloody dogs! I fed Anton Pavlovich himself, the Prince of Württemberg! Now I'll go home and die! Then they'll miss Ivan Osipovich. Go, they'll say, set up a banquet table for eighty-four people, to the bloody dogs. But nobody will know how! Ivan Osipovich Trikartov is gone! Passed away! Departed for a better place, where there is neither pain, nor sorrow, nor sighing, but life everlasting . . . Ete-e-rnal mem-m-ory!"

And as the old man officiated at his own funeral, the tails of his coat fluttered in the wind like pennants.

Ostap didn't even let Koreiko finish his dessert before dragging him away from the table to settle their account. The two strategists climbed the small stepladder into the freight car that served as the office of the Northern Site and contained the timekeeper's folding canvas cot. They locked the door behind them.

After dinner, when the special passengers were resting and gathering their strength for the evening's program, Gargantua the satirist caught the two journalist brothers, who were engaging in unauthorized activities. Leo Shirtikov and Ian Benchikov were carrying two sheets of paper to the telegraph. One sheet contained a short dispatch:

"Urgent moscow desert telegraph dash uzun kulak quote long ear comma carried camps news of joining shirtikov."

The second sheet was covered with writing. Here's what it said:

THE LEGEND OF LAKE ISSYK KUL

An old Karakalpak named Ukhum Bukheev told me this legend, steeped in ancient lore. Two hundred thousand four hundred and eighty-five moons ago, the young Sumburun, a khan's wife, light-footed as a *jeiran* (mountain sheep), fell deeply in love with a young guardsman named Ai-Bulak. The elderly khan was devastated when he learned that his beloved wife had been unfaithful. The old man prayed for twelve moons; then, with tears in his eyes, he had his beautiful wife sealed up in a wooden cask, attached to it a bullion of pure gold weighing seven *jasasyn* (39 lbs), and threw the precious cargo into a mountain lake. That's how the lake received its name—Issyk Kul, which means "Beautiful women aren't very faithful . . ."

—Ian Benchikov-Sarmatsky (The Piston)

"Isn't that right?" Gargantua was asking, holding up the papers he had wrestled from the brothers. "Isn't it true?"

"It's an outrage!" said Palamidov. "How dare you write a legend after everything we talked about? So you think Issyk Kul translates as 'Beautiful women aren't very faithful?' Really? Are you sure your phony Karakalpak wasn't pulling your leg? Are you sure it doesn't mean 'Don't throw young beauties into the lake, instead throw the gullible journalists who can't resist the noxious spell of exoticism?'"

The writer in the casual jacket blushed. His notebook already contained *Uzun Kulak*, along with two flowery legends that were rich with Oriental flavor.

"I don't see any crime in it," he said. "As long as *Uzun Kulak* exists, shouldn't someone be writing about it?"

"But it's been done a thousand times!" said Lavoisian.

"But *Uzun Kulak* exists," sighed the writer, "and one has to take that into account."

CHAPTER 30
ALEXANDER BIN IVANOVICH

The hot and dark freight car was filled with thick, stagnant air that smelled of leather and feet, like an old shoe. Koreiko turned on a conductor's lantern and crawled under the bed. Ostap sat on an empty macaroni crate and watched him pensively. Both strategists were exhausted by their struggle and approached the event that Koreiko had greatly feared and that Bender had been waiting for his whole life with the indifference of government officials. It almost felt like it was taking place in a cooperative store: the customer asks for a hat, the salesperson lazily throws a fuzzy mud-colored cap on the counter. He couldn't care less if the customer buys the cap or not. Actually, the customer himself doesn't seem to be particularly engaged, and asks "Do you have anything else?" only because he's expected to. And usually this elicits the response: "Take this one, or else it'll be gone, too." And both of them look at each other with complete lack of interest. Koreiko rummaged under the bed for a long time, apparently opening the suitcase and going through it blindly.

"Hey, there, on the schooner!" Ostap called out, tired. "Good thing you don't smoke. It would be torture to ask a cheapskate like you for a cigarette. You'd never offer the whole box, fearing that they might take more than one. You'd fiddle in your pocket forever, you'd struggle to open the box, and then you'd drag out a lousy, bent cigarette. You're a bad man. Why is it so hard to pull out the whole suitcase?"

"Not a chance!" growled Koreiko, suffocating under the bed.

He didn't like being compared to a stingy smoker. At that very moment, he was fishing thick stacks of money out of his suitcase. The nickel-plated lock was scraping his arms, which were bare up to the elbows. To make things easier, he lay on his back and worked like a miner at a coal face. Husks and other plant debris, along with some kind of powder and grain bristles, were spilling out of the straw mattress right into the millionaire's eyes.

"This is really bad," thought Alexander Ivanovich, "really bad and scary! What if he strangles me now and takes all my money? Just like that. Cuts me up and dispatches the pieces to different cities on a slow train. And pickles my head in a barrel of sauerkraut."

Koreiko suddenly felt a crypt-like chill. He peeked out from under the bed fearfully. Bender was dozing on his crate, leaning against the conductor's lantern.

"But maybe I should dispatch him . . . on a slow train?" thought Alexander Ivanovich, continuing to extract the stacks and feeling horrified. "To different cities? In strict confidence. How about that?"

He peeked out once again. The grand strategist stretched and yawned with abandon, like a Great Dane. Then he picked up the conductor's lantern and started swinging it:

"Boonieville Station! Get off the train, citizen! We've arrived! Oh yes, I completely forgot: are you by any chance thinking of doing away with me? I want you to know that I'm against it. Besides, someone already tried to kill me once. There was this wild old man, from a good family, a former Marshal of the Nobility, who doubled as a civil registrar, named Kisa Vorobyaninov. He and I were business partners, searching for happiness to the tune of 150,000 rubles. And just when we were about to divvy up the loot, the silly marshal slit my throat with a razor. It was in such poor taste, Koreiko. And it hurt, too! The surgeons were barely able to save my young life, and for that I am deeply grateful."

Finally Koreiko climbed out from under the bed and pushed the stacks of money toward Ostap's feet. Each stack was neatly wrapped in white paper, glued, and tied up with string.

"Ninety-nine stacks," said Koreiko dolefully, "Ten thousand each. In 250-ruble bills. You don't need to count, I'm as good as a bank."

"And where's stack number one hundred?" asked Ostap enthusiastically.

"I deducted ten thousand. To cover the mugging at the beach."

"Now that's really low. The money was spent on you, after all. Don't be such a stickler."

Sighing, Koreiko made up the difference and received his life story, in the yellow folder with shoelace straps, in exchange. He immediately burned it in an iron stove whose chimney vented through the car's roof. Meanwhile, Ostap picked up one of the stacks to check it, tore off the wrapping, and, seeing that Koreiko wasn't cheating, stuck it in his pocket.

"But where's the foreign currency?" asked the grand strategist fussily. "Where are the Mexican dollars, Turkish liras, where are the pounds, rupees, pesetas, centavos, Rumanian leis, where are the Latvian lats and the Polish zlotys? Give me at least some hard currency!"

"That's all I've got," replied Koreiko, sitting in front of the stove and watching the papers writhe in the fire, "take this, or else it'll soon be gone, too. I don't carry foreign currency."

"So now I'm a millionaire!" exclaimed Ostap with cheerful disbelief. "A fool's dream comes true!"

Ostap suddenly felt sad. He was struck by how ordinary it all felt. He thought it odd that the earth didn't move at that very moment, and that nothing, absolutely nothing, changed around him. And even though he realized that one can't expect mysterious caves, barrels of gold, or Aladdin's light fixtures in our austere times, he still felt like something was missing. He felt a bit bored, like Roald Amundsen did, when, whizzing over the North Pole in the airship *Norge* after a life-long quest, he said flatly to his companions: "Well, we made it." Below them lay broken ice, crevasses, coldness, and emptiness. The mystery is solved, the goal reached, there's nothing left to do, time to look for a different occupation. But sadness is fleeting, because ahead, fame and glory await: choirs sing, high-school girls in white pinafores stand in formation, the elderly mothers of the polar explorers who had been eaten by their teammates weep, national anthems play, fireworks boom, and the old king presses his prickly stars and medals against the explorer's chest.

The moment of weakness had passed. Ostap tossed the stacks of money into a small bag, kindly provided by Alexander Ivanovich, stuck it under his arm, and rolled open the heavy door of the freight car.

The festivities were coming to an end. The rockets were cast into the sky like golden fishing rods, pulling red and green fish back out; sparklers burst in people's eyes, pyrotechnical comet suns swirled. A show for the nomads was taking place on a wooden stage behind the telegraph shack. Some of them sat on benches, while others watched the performance from the vantage point of their saddles. The horses neighed frequently. The special train was lit up from head to tail.

"Oh yes!" exclaimed Ostap. "A banquet in the dining car! I completely forgot! Oh, what fun! Let's go, Koreiko, my treat, I'm treating everyone! In compliance with the laws of hospitality! Brandy with a touch of lemon, game dumplings, fricandeau with mushrooms, old Tokay, new Tokay, sparkling champagne!"

"Fricandeau my foot," said Koreiko angrily, "that's how we get busted. I don't want to advertise myself!"

"I promise you a heavenly dinner on a white tablecloth," Ostap persisted. "Come on, let's go! Stop being such a hermit, make sure you consume your share of alcoholic beverages, eat your twenty thousand steaks. Or else total strangers will swarm up and polish off what should be yours. I'll help you get on the special train, they know me very well—and no later than tomorrow we'll be in a reasonably civilized place. And then, with our millions . . . Alexander Ivanovich!"

The grand strategist wanted to make everyone happy immediately, wanted everyone to be cheerful. Koreiko's gloomy face bothered him. So Ostap began working on him. He agreed that there wasn't any reason to advertise themselves, but why should they starve? Ostap himself wasn't quite sure why he needed the cheerless timekeeper, but once he got started, he couldn't stop. In the end, he even tried to browbeat him:

"You keep sitting on your suitcase, and one day the Grim Reaper will show up and slit your throat with his scythe. Then what? Won't that be something? Hurry up, Alexander Ivanovich, your meat is still on the table. Don't be such a bonehead."

After losing a million, Koreiko had become more easy-going and amenable.

"Well, maybe it's not such a bad idea to take a break?" he said uncertainly. "Go to a big city? But, of course, nothing flashy, nothing ostentatious."

"Of course not! Just two public health physicians traveling to Moscow to attend the Art Theater and take a peek at the mummy in the Museum of Fine Arts. Get your suitcase."

The millionaires headed toward the train. Ostap waved his bag carelessly, as if it were a censer. Alexander Ivanovich smiled like a complete idiot. The special passengers were strolling around, trying to stay close to the cars because the locomotive was already being attached. The journalists' white pants twinkled in the dark.

A stranger lay under the sheets on Ostap's upper bunk, reading a newspaper.

"Time to get off," said Ostap amicably, "the rightful owner is here."

"This is my place, Comrade," replied the stranger. "I'm Leo Shirtikov."

"Listen, Leo Shirtikov, don't awaken the beast in me, just go away." Koreiko's puzzled look compelled the grand strategist to get into a fight.

"Absolutely not," said the journalist feistily. "Who are you?"

"None of your damn business! I'm telling you to get off, so get off!"

"Any drunk can come in here," shrieked Shirtikov, "and violate . . ."

Ostap quietly grabbed the journalist's bare leg. Shirtikov's screams brought the entire car. Koreiko retreated to the vestibule, just in case.

"Fighting?" asked Ukhudshansky. "Well, well . . ."

Ostap, who had already managed to whack Shirtikov on the head with his bag, was being restrained by Gargantua and the portly writer in the casual jacket.

"Let him show his ticket!" yelled the grand strategist. "Let him show his boarding pass!"

The stark-naked Shirtikov leaped from bunk to bunk and demanded to see the train administrator. Ostap, who had completely detached from reality, also insisted on appealing to the authorities. The altercation ended in a major embarrassment. Shirtikov produced both the ticket and the boarding pass, and then, in a theatrical voice, demanded that Bender do the same.

"I won't do it on principle!" announced the grand strategist, hastily retreating from the site of the incident. "I have my principles!"

"Fare dodger!" screamed Leo Shirtikov, darting into the corridor naked. "Take note, Comrade administrator, there was a fare dodger in here!"

"Where's the fare dodger?" thundered the administrator, the thrill of the hunt sparkling in his hound dog eyes.

Alexander Ivanovich, who was nervously hiding behind the podium, peered into the darkness, but he couldn't make anything out. Silhouettes scuffled near the train, cigarette tips danced, and one could hear voices: "Show it to me!," "I'm telling you—on principle!," "Hooliganism!," "Isn't that right? Isn't it true?," "Shouldn't someone ride without a ticket?" Buffer plates banged, the hissing air from the brakes blew low over the ground, and the cars' bright windows started to move. Ostap was still blustering, but the striped bunks, luggage nets, attendants with lanterns, the flowers and the ceiling fans of the dining car were already coasting past him. The banquet with champagne, with Tokay old and new, was leaving. The game dumplings escaped from his hands and disappeared into the night. The fricandeau, the tender fricandeau that Ostap had described with such passion, left Roaring Springs. Alexander Ivanovich came closer.

"They're not getting away with this," grumbled Ostap. "Abandoning a Soviet journalist in the desert! I'll call on the people to protest. Koreiko! We're off with the next express! We'll buy up the entire first-class car!"

"What are you talking about," said Koreiko. "What express? There aren't any more trains. According to the plan, the line won't become operational for another two months."

Ostap raised his head. He saw the wild stars of the black Abyssinian sky and finally grasped the situation. But Koreiko's sheepish reminder of the banquet gave him new strength.

"There's a plane sitting behind the hill," said Bender, "the one that flew in for the ceremony. It's not leaving until sunrise. We've got enough time."

In order to make it, the millionaires moved at a fast dromedary's gait. Their feet slipped in the sand, the nomads' fires were burning, and dragging the suitcase and the bag, while not exactly difficult, was extremely unpleasant. As they climbed the hill from the direction of Roaring Springs, sunrise advanced from the other side with the buzz of propellers. Bender and Koreiko started running down the hill, afraid that the plane would leave without them.

Tiny mechanics in leather coats were walking under the plane's corrugated wings, which were high above them, like a roof. The three propellers rotated slowly, ventilating the desert. Curtains with plush pompoms dangled over the square windows of the passenger cabin. The pilot leaned against the aluminum step, eating a pasty and washing it down with mineral water from a bottle.

"We're passengers," shouted Ostap, gasping for air. "Two first-class tickets!"

Nobody reacted. The pilot tossed the bottle away and began to put on his wide-cuffed gloves.

"Are there any seats?" repeated Ostap, grabbing the pilot by the arm.

"We don't take passengers," said the pilot, putting his hand on the railing. "It's a special flight."

"I'm buying the plane!" said the grand strategist hastily. "Wrap it up."

"Out of the way!" shouted a mechanic, climbing in after the pilot. The propellers disappeared in a whirl. Shaking and swaying, the plane started turning against the wind. Vortexes of air pushed the millionaires back toward the hill. The captain's cap flew off Ostap's head and rolled toward India so fast that it could be expected to arrive in Calcutta in no more than three hours. It would have rolled all the way to the main street of Calcutta, where its mysterious appearance would have attracted the attention of circles close to the Intelligence Service, but the plane took off and the storm died down. The plane flashed its ribs in the air and disappeared into the sunlight. Ostap ran to retrieve his cap, which was stuck in a saxaul bush, and then said:

"Transportation has gotten completely out of hand. Our relationship with the railroad has soured. The air routes are closed to us. Walking? It's 250 miles. Not particularly inspiring. There's only one option left— convert to Islam and travel on camels."

Koreiko ignored the part about Islam, but the idea of camels appealed to him. The enticing sights of the dining car and the plane had confirmed his desire to embark on an entertaining trip as a public health physician. Nothing ostentatious, of course, but not without a certain flair.

The clans that had come for the joining hadn't taken off yet, so they were able to purchase camels not far from Roaring Springs. The ships of the desert cost them 180 rubles apiece.

"It's so cheap!" whispered Ostap. "Let's buy fifty camels. Or a hundred!"

"That's ostentatious," said Alexander Ivanovich gloomily. "What are we going to do with them? Two are enough."

Shouting, the Kazakhs helped the travelers climb between the humps and attach the suitcase, the bag, and some food supplies—a wineskin of *kumis* and two sheep. The camels first rose onto their hind legs, forcing the millionaires to bow deeply, then onto their front legs, and started walking along the Eastern Line. The sheep, attached with thin cords, trotted behind them, dropping little balls from time to time and emitting heart-wrenching bleats.

"Hey, Sheikh Koreiko!" called out Ostap. "Alexander bin Ivanovich! Isn't life wonderful?"

The Sheikh didn't answer. He had gotten stuck with a lazy camel and was furiously whacking its bald rear with a saxaul stick.

CHAPTER 31
BAGHDAD

For seven days, the camels hauled the newly minted sheikhs across the desert. At first, Ostap had a great time. He was amused by everything: Alexander bin Ivanovich floundering between the camel's humps, the lazy ship of the desert trying to shirk its duties, the bag with the million, which the grand strategist occasionally used to prod the recalcitrant sheep. For himself, Ostap took the name of Colonel Lawrence.

"I am Emir Dynamite!" he shouted, swaying on top of the tall camelback. "If within two days we don't get any decent food, I'll incite the tribes to revolt! I swear! I will appoint myself the Prophet's representative and declare holy war, jihad. On Denmark, for example. Why did the Danes torment their Prince Hamlet? Considering the current political situation, a *casus belli* like this would satisfy even the League of Nations. No, seriously, I'll buy a million worth of rifles from the British—they love to sell firearms to the tribes—and onward to Denmark. Germany will let us through—in lieu of war reparations. Imagine the tribes invading Copenhagen! I'll lead the charge on a white camel. Ah! Too bad Panikovsky isn't around anymore! He would have loved a Danish goose!"

But in a few days, when all that was left of the sheep were the cords and the *kumis* was finished, even Emir Dynamite lost his verve, and could only mutter dispiritedly:

"Lost deep in the barren Arabian land, three palm trees for some reason stood in the sand."

Both sheikhs had lost a lot of weight, become disheveled, and grown stubby beards—they were starting to look like dervishes from a parish of rather modest means.

"Just a little more patience, bin Koreiko—and we'll reach a town that rivals Baghdad. Flat roofs, native bands, little restaurants with an Oriental flavor, sweet wines, legendary girls, and forty thousand skewers of shish kebab: à la Kars, Turkish-style, Tartar, Mesopotamian, and Odessan. And finally, the railroad."

On the eighth day of the journey, the travelers approached an ancient cemetery. Rows of semi-spherical tombs stretched all the way to the horizon, like petrified waves. People didn't bury their dead here. They placed the bodies on the ground and built stone domes around them. The frightful sun glared over the ashen city of the dead. The ancient East lay in its sweltering graves.

The two strategists prodded their camels and soon entered the oasis. Poplars reflected in the waterlogged checkerboard of rice fields and lit the town all around them like green torches. Elm trees stood alone, shaped exactly like giant globes on wooden stands. Little donkeys carrying fat men in cloaks and bundles of clover started appearing on the road.

Koreiko and Bender rode past small stores that sold powdered green tobacco and stinking cone-shaped soaps that looked like artillery shells. Craftsmen with white gauzy beards labored over sheets of copper, rolling them into tubs and narrow-mouthed jugs. Shoemakers dried small ink-painted skins in the sun. The indigo, yellow, and blue glazed tiles of the mosques sparkled like liquid glass.

For the rest of the day and the following night, the millionaires slept a deep and heavy sleep at the hotel. In the morning, they washed in white bathtubs, shaved, and went into town. The sheikhs' radiant mood was dampened by their need to drag along the suitcase and the bag.

"I consider it my sacred duty," said Bender boastfully, "to introduce you to an enchanting little club. It's called Under the Moonlight. I was here some five years ago, lecturing against abortion. What a place! Semi-dark, cool, an owner from Tiflis, a local band, chilled vodka, girls dancing with cymbals and tambourines. We can spend a whole day there. Can't public health physicians have their own tiny little weaknesses? My treat. The golden calf will take care of everything."

And the grand strategist shook his bag.

However, the club Under the Moonlight was gone. To Ostap's surprise, even the street where those cymbals and tambourines once played was gone, too. Instead, there was a straight, European-style avenue, with new construction running along its entire length. Fences lined the street, alabaster dust hung in the scorched air. Trucks baked it even further. Ostap glanced briefly at the gray-brick facades with long horizontal windows, gave Koreiko an elbow, and, saying "There's another place, a guy from Baku owns it," took him to the opposite side of town. But the sheikhs didn't find the sign with the poem, that the proprietor from Baku had composed himself:

> RESPECT YOURSELF,
>
> RESPECT US,
>
> RESPECT THE CAUCASUS,
>
> VISIT US.

Instead, there was a cardboard poster in Arabic and Russian:

> MUNICIPAL MUSEUM OF FINE ARTS

"Let's go in," said Ostap forlornly, "at least it's cool in there. Besides, the public health physicians' itinerary includes a visit to a museum."

They entered a large room with whitewashed walls, put their millions on the floor, and took their time wiping their hot foreheads with their sleeves. The museum had only eight objects on display: a mammoth's tooth, which had been presented to the brand new museum by the city of Tashkent; an oil painting, entitled *A Skirmish With the Basmachs*; two emir's cloaks; a goldfish in an aquarium; a glass case filled with dried-up locusts; a porcelain statuette from the Kuznetsov Factory; and a model of the obelisk that the city was planning to erect on the main square. Right next to the model lay a large tin wreath with ribbons. A special delegation from a neighboring republic had recently delivered it, but since the obelisk did not exist yet—the funds had been diverted to the construction of a bathhouse, a far more pressing need—the delegation had made the appropriate speeches and placed the wreath at the foot of the model.

A young man, wearing a thick Bukhara skull cap on his shaved head, approached the visitors promptly and asked them, like a nervous author:

"Your impressions, comrades?"

"Passable," said Ostap.

Without missing a beat, the young man—who was the museum's director—launched into a litany of problems that his baby had to overcome.

Funding was insufficient. Tashkent had gotten off the hook with a single tooth, and there wasn't anybody to collect the local treasures, artistic or historic. And they still hadn't sent him a trained expert.

"If only I had three hundred rubles!" exclaimed the director. "I would have made it into a Louvre!"

"Tell me, do you know the town well?" asked Ostap, winking at Alexander Ivanovich. "Would you mind showing us a few places of interest? I used to know this town well, but now it seems different somehow."

The director was thrilled. Shouting that he would show them everything, he locked up the museum and lead the millionaires to the very street where they had been looking for Under the Moonlight just thirty minutes earlier.

"The Avenue of Socialism!" he announced, eagerly inhaling the alabaster dust. "Oh! What lovely air! You won't believe what it'll look like a year from now! Asphalt! Buses! The Irrigation Research Institute! The Tropical Institute! And if Tashkent won't provide research personnel even then . . . You know, they have all kinds of mammoth bones, yet they sent me just one tooth—despite the strong interest in the natural sciences in our republic."

"Really?" remarked Koreiko, looking at Ostap with reproach.

"And you know," the enthusiast whispered, "I suspect it's not even a mammoth tooth. They slipped me an elephant tooth!"

"And what about those places . . . in the Asian style, you know, with timbrels and flutes?" asked the grand strategist impatiently.

"We got rid of them," replied the young man dismissively, "should have eradicated that blight a long time ago. A hotbed for epidemics. Just this past spring, we stamped out the last of those dens. It was called Under the Moonlight."

"Stamped out?" gasped Koreiko.

"You bet! Instead, we opened a mass-dining establishment. European cuisine. The plates are washed and dried with electricity. The number of cases of gastrointestinal disease have plummeted."

"What do you know!" exclaimed the grand strategist, covering his face with his hands.

"You haven't seen anything yet," said the museum director, smiling shyly. "Let's go eat at the new dining facility."

They climbed into a cart, under a canvas canopy that was festooned in dark blue, and took off. On the way, the affable guide kept making the millionaires stick their heads out from under the canopy while he pointed out the buildings that had already been constructed, the buildings that were in the process of being constructed, and the sites where they were going to be constructed. Koreiko kept glancing angrily at Ostap. Bender turned away and said:

"What a lovely native bazaar! Just like Baghdad!"

"The demolition starts on the seventeenth," said the young man. "There will be a hospital here, and a co-op center."

"And no regrets about losing this exotic place? It's Baghdad!"

"It is beautiful!" sighed Koreiko.

The young man grew angry:

"It may look beautiful to you, you're just visiting, but we have to live here."

In the spacious hall of the new dining facility, surrounded by tiled walls, under sticky ribbons of flypaper hanging from the ceiling, the travelers dined on barley soup and small brown meatballs. Ostap inquired about wine but the young man responded enthusiastically that a natural spring had recently been discovered nearby. In terms of taste, its mineral water was superior to the famed variety from the Caucasus. As proof, he ordered a bottle of the new water, and they drank it in grave silence.

"And how are the numbers on prostitution?" asked Alexander bin Ivanovich hopefully.

"Way down," replied the implacable young man.

"Well, what do you know!" said Ostap, laughing insincerely.

But he really didn't know what was going on. When they got up from the table, it turned out that the young man had already paid for all three of them. He flatly refused to take any money from the millionaires, assuring them that he was getting paid in two days anyway, and that, until then, he'd make it somehow.

"And what about entertainment? What do you do for entertainment here?" asked Ostap without much enthusiasm. "Timbrels, cymbals?"

"Don't you know?" asked the director, surprised. "Our new concert hall opened just last week. The Bebel and Paganini Grand Symphony Quartet. Let's go right now. How could I have forgotten!"

Since he had paid for the dinner, it would have been impossible, for ethical reasons, to decline an invitation to the concert hall. After it was over, Alexander bin Ivanovich said mockingly:

"The concert hole!"

The grand strategist blushed.

On the way to the hotel, the young man suddenly told the coachman to stop. He made the millionaires get out, took their hands, and, overcome with excitement, rose to his tiptoes and led them to a small stone with a fence around it.

"The obelisk will be erected here!" he announced solemnly. "The Column of Marxism!"

As they said their goodbyes, the young man asked them to come visit more often. The good-natured Ostap promised that he'd definitely come back, because he'd never had such a blissful day in his life.

"I'm off to the station," said Koreiko when he and Bender were finally alone.

"Shall we go have a good time in some other town?" asked Ostap. "One can easily spend a few fun-filled days in Tashkent."

"I've had enough," replied Alexander Ivanovich, "I'm going to the station to put my suitcase into storage, then I'll find myself an office job here. I'll wait for capitalism. That's when I'll have a good time."

"Wait all you want," said Ostap rather rudely, "but I'm going. Today was just an unfortunate misunderstanding, overzealous locals. The little golden calf still wields some power in this country!"

On the square in front of the station, they saw a crowd of journalists from the special train, who were touring Central Asia after the joining. They all gathered around Ukhudshansky. The proprietor of the Celebratory Kit turned back and forth smugly, demonstrating his new purchases. He was decked out in a velvet hat trimmed with a jackal's tail and a cloak that had been fashioned from a quilted blanket.

The plush-nosed prophet's predictions continued to come true.

CHAPTER 32
THE DOOR TO BOUNDLESS OPPORTUNITIES

On that autumn day, filled with sadness and light, when gardeners cut flowers in Moscow parks and pass them out to children, Shura Balaganov, the preeminent son of Lieutenant Schmidt, was sleeping on a wooden bench in the waiting area of the Ryazan train station. He was resting his head on the arm of the bench, and a crumpled cap covered his face. It was clear that the Antelope's rally mechanic and Vice President for Hoofs was dejected and destitute. Crushed eggshell clung to his unshaven cheek. His canvas shoes had lost their shape and color, and they looked more like Moldovan peasant footwear. Swallows flew under the high ceiling of the airy hall.

Through its large, unwashed windows, one could see block signals, semaphores, and the other necessary objects of the railroad. Porters raced by, and moments later the arriving passengers entered the hall. A neatly dressed man was the last passenger to come in from the platform. Under his light, unbuttoned raincoat one could see a suit with a tiny kaleidoscopic checked pattern. Trousers descended to his patent-leather shoes like a waterfall. The passenger's foreign look was amplified by a fedora, which was tipped forward ever so slightly. He didn't make use of the porter and carried his suitcase himself. The passenger strolled through the empty hall and he would certainly have reached the vestibule, had he not suddenly spotted the sorry figure of Balaganov. He squinted, came closer, and observed the sleeping man for a while. Then he carefully lifted the cap from the rally mechanic's face with two gloved fingers and smiled.

"Arise, Count, you're being called from down below!" he said, shaking Balaganov awake.

Shura sat up, rubbed his face, and only then realized who the passenger was.

"Captain!" he exclaimed.

"No, no," said Bender, holding his hand out, "don't hug me. I'm a proud man now."

Balaganov started prancing around the captain. He could hardly recognize him. It wasn't only his dress that had changed; Ostap had lost some weight, a certain absentmindedness showed in his eyes, and his face was bronzed with a colonial tan.

"You're a big deal now!" gushed Balaganov excitedly. "You really are!"

"Yes, I am a big deal," allowed Bender, sounding dignified. "Look at my trousers. Europe First Class! And look at this! The fourth finger of my left hand is adorned with a diamond ring. Four carats. And what have you been up to? Still a son?"

"Oh, nothing much," said Shura uncertainly, "just little things here and there."

At the restaurant, Ostap ordered white wine with pastries for himself and sandwiches with beer for the rally mechanic.

"Tell me honestly, Shura, how much money do you need to be happy?" asked Ostap. "Count everything."

"A hundred rubles," answered Balaganov, reluctantly taking a break from the bread and sausage.

"No, no, you didn't understand me. I don't mean today, I mean in general. To be happy. See what I mean? So that you could have a good life."

Balaganov thought for a long time, smiling tentatively, and finally announced that, to be completely happy, he needed 6,400 rubles, and that this amount would make his life very good indeed.

"Fine," said Ostap, "here's fifty thousand for you."

He unlocked a square travel case on his knees and handed Balaganov five white stacks that had been tied up with string. The rally mechanic suddenly lost his appetite. He stopped eating, stuck the money deep into his pockets, and couldn't bring himself to take his hands back out.

"The platter, right?" he asked excitedly.

"That's right, the platter," replied Ostap impassively. "With a blue rim. The defendant brought it in his teeth. He kept wagging his tail until I finally agreed to take it. Now I'm commanding the parade! I feel great."

He uttered these last words without much conviction.

Truth be told, the parade wasn't going smoothly, and the grand strategist was lying when he claimed that he felt great. It would have been more honest to say that he felt somewhat awkward, which, however, he wasn't willing to admit even to himself.

A month had passed since he had parted ways with Alexander Ivanovich outside the luggage room where the underground millionaire had stored his plain-looking suitcase.

Ostap entered the next city feeling like a conqueror, but he couldn't get a room at the hotel.

"I'll pay anything!" said the grand strategist smugly.

"You're out of luck, citizen," replied the receptionist, "the entire congress of soil scientists have come down for a tour of our experimental station. Everything's reserved for the scholars."

The receptionist's polite face expressed reverence for the congress. Ostap wanted to cry out that he was the big shot, that he was to be respected and revered, that he had a million in his bag, but then he thought better of it and left in a state of utter frustration.

He spent the whole day riding around town in a horse cab. In the city's best restaurant, he had to bide his time for an hour and a half until the soil scientists, whose entire congress came to dinner, were finished with their meal. In the evening, the theater was putting on a special performance for the soil scientists, so no tickets were available to the public. Ostap wouldn't have been allowed into the theater with a bag in his hands anyway, and he had nowhere to put it. To avoid spending the night in the streets, in the name of science, the millionaire left that same evening and slept in a first-class car.

In the morning, Bender got off the train in a large city on the Volga. Transparent yellow leaves flew off the trees, spinning like propellers. The river was breathing the wind. There wasn't a single hotel with a vacancy.

"Maybe in a month or so," the hotel managers—some wore goatees and some didn't, some wore mustaches, and some were simply clean-shaven—offered vaguely. "Until they finish the third plant at the power station, you haven't got a prayer. Everything's reserved for the technical personnel. Plus, there's the regional Young Communist League conference. There's nothing we can do."

And while the grand strategist hung around the tall reception counters, the hotels' stairwells teemed with engineers, technicians, foreign experts, and Young Communist Leaguers who were attending their conference. Once again, Ostap spent the whole day in a horse cab, looking forward to the nighttime express where he could wash, rest, and sit back with a newspaper.

The grand strategist spent a total of fifteen nights on a variety of trains, traveling from city to city, because there weren't any vacancies anywhere. One town was building a blast furnace, another a refrigeration plant, the third a zinc smelter. The cities were overflowing with people who had come there for work. In the fourth town, Ostap was undercut by a gathering of Young Pioneers, and the hotel room where a millionaire could have spent a pleasant evening with a lady friend was filled with the racket of children. While on the road, he acquired various creature comforts and obtained a suitcase for his million, along with other travel gear. Ostap was already contemplating a long and comfortable journey to Vladivostok, which he figured would take three weeks, when suddenly he sensed that he'd die of some mysterious railroad malady if he didn't settle down immediately. So he did something he had always done when he was the happy owner of empty pockets. He started pretending he was someone else, cabling ahead to announce the arrival of an engineer, or a public health physician, or a tenor, or an author. To his surprise, there were always vacancies for people who were traveling on official business, and Ostap was able to recover a bit from the rocking of the trains. Once, he even had to pretend he was the son of Lieutenant Schmidt in order to obtain a hotel room. This episode plunged the grand strategist into unhappy thoughts.

"And this is the life of a millionaire?" he reflected in frustration. "Where's the respect? Where's the reverence? The fame? The power?"

Even the Europe First Class that Ostap bragged about to Balaganov —the suit, the dress shoes, the fedora—came from a consignment store, and despite their superb quality, they had one defect: they weren't his own, his original garb, they were second-hand. Someone else had already worn them; maybe for just an hour, or even a minute, but still it was someone else's. He was also hurt that the government was ignoring the dire straits of the nation's millionaires and distributed social benefits in accordance with a plan. Nothing was going right. The station chief didn't salute him, like he would have any merchant worth a lousy fifty thousand in the old days; the city fathers didn't come to his hotel to introduce themselves; the local paper didn't rush to interview him; and instead of photos of the millionaire, it printed portraits of some God-forsaken exemplary workers who earned 120 rubles a month.

Ostap counted his million every day, and it was still pretty much a million. He tried very hard, eating several dinners a day, drinking the best wines, and giving exorbitant tips. He bought a diamond ring, a Japanese vase, and a coat that was lined with fitch fur. But he ended up giving the coat and the vase to a room attendant—he didn't want to deal with all that bulk on the road. Besides, if need be, he could buy himself many more coats and vases. Nevertheless, he only managed to spend six thousand in a whole month.

No, the parade decidedly wasn't going well, even though everything was in place. The forward guards were dispatched on time, the troops arrived when they were supposed to, the band was playing. But the regiments didn't look at him, they didn't shout "Hooray" to him, and the bandmaster didn't wave his baton for him. Nevertheless, Ostap wasn't about to give up. He had high hopes for Moscow.

"So what about Rio de Janeiro?" asked Balaganov excitedly. "Are we going?"

"To hell with it!" said Ostap, suddenly angry. "It's all a fantasy: there is no Rio de Janeiro, no America, no Europe, nothing. Actually, there isn't anything past Shepetovka, where the waves of the Atlantic break against the shore."

"No kidding!" sighed Balaganov.

"A doctor I met explained everything to me," continued Ostap, "other countries—that's just a myth of the afterlife. Those who make it there never return."

"What do you know!" exclaimed Shura, who didn't understand a thing. "Ooh, just watch me have a good life now! Poor Panikovsky! He broke the pact, of course, but what the heck! The old man would have been thrilled!"

"I propose a moment of silence to honor the memory of the deceased," said Bender.

The half-brothers got up and stood silently for a minute, looking down at the crushed pastries and the unfinished sandwich.

Balaganov finally broke the onerous silence.

"Did you hear about Kozlevich?" he said. "What do you know! He put the Antelope back together, and now he's working in Chernomorsk. I got a letter from him. Here . . ."

The rally mechanic pulled a letter out of his cap.

"Hello, Shura," wrote the driver of the Antelope, "how are you doing? Are you still the son of L. Sch.? I'm fine, I just don't have any money, and the car's been acting up since the overhaul. It only runs for an hour a day. I keep working on it, I'm so sick of it. The passengers aren't happy. Dear Shura, maybe you can send me an oil hose, even a used one. I can't find one at the market here no matter what. Look at the Smolensk Market, the section where they sell old locks and keys. And if you're not doing well, come down here, we'll make it somehow. I'm parked at the corner of Mehring Street, at the taxi stand. Where is O.B. these days? Yours respectfully, Adam Kozlevich. I forgot to tell you, the priests Kusza-kowski and Moroszek came to see me at the stand. It was an ugly scene. A.K."

"I gotta go look for an oil hose now," said Balaganov anxiously.

"Don't," said Ostap, "I'll buy him a new car. Let's go to the Grand Hotel, I cabled ahead and reserved a room for a symphony conductor. You need a wash, a new outfit—a complete overhaul. The door to boundless opportunities is now open for you, Shura."

They stepped out onto Kalanchevka Square. There were no taxis. Ostap refused to take a horse cab.

"It's an antiquated conveyance," he said squeamishly, "it won't get you too far. Plus, small mice live inside the seats."

They had to settle for a streetcar. It was packed with people. It was one of those quarrel-ridden streetcars that often circulate around the capital. Some vindictive old lady starts a spat during the morning rush hour. Little by little, every passenger gets drawn into the squabble, even those who had gotten on thirty minutes after the whole thing began. The mean old lady is long gone, and the cause of the argument is long forgotten, but the screaming and the mutual insults continue to fly, while new arrivals keep joining the squabble. On a streetcar like this, the argument can drag on well into the night.

The agitated passengers quickly pulled Balaganov away from Ostap, and soon the half-brothers were bobbing at opposite ends of the car, squeezed by rib cages and baskets. Ostap hung on to a hand loop, barely managing to yank back his suitcase before it floated away on the current.

Suddenly, a woman's screams, coming from the direction where Bala-ganov was bobbing, drowned out the usual streetcar bickering:

"Thief! Get him! Look, he's right there!"

Everyone turned for a look. Enthusiasts for things like that, breathless with curiosity, started elbowing their way toward the scene of the crime. Ostap saw Balaganov's stunned face. The rally mechanic himself hadn't yet grasped what exactly had happened, but others were already firmly holding his hand, which was clutching a dime-store purse with a thin bronze chain.

"Bandit!" screamed the woman. "I just looked the other way, and he . . ."

The man who had fifty thousand rubles had tried to steal a purse that contained a tortoise-shell compact, a union card, and one ruble seventy kopecks in cash. The car stopped. The enthusiasts started dragging Balaganov toward the exit. As he was passing Ostap, Shura whispered in despair:

"I can't believe it! It was just a reflex."

"I'll teach you a reflex or two!" said an enthusiast with a pince-nez and a briefcase, gleefully hitting the rally mechanic from behind.

Through the window, Ostap saw a policeman swiftly approach the group and escort the felon down the street.

The grand strategist looked away.

CHAPTER 33
THE INDIAN GUEST

The enclosed rectangular courtyard of the Grand Hotel was filled with pounding noises from the kitchen, the hissing of steam, and shouts—"Tea for two to number sixteen!"—but the white hallways were bright and quiet, like the control room of a power station. The soil scientists, who were back from their field trip, took up 150 rooms; another thirty rooms were reserved for foreign businessmen who were trying to resolve the pressing question of whether trade with the Soviet Union could be profitable after all; the best four-room suite was occupied by a famous Indian poet and philosopher; and in a small room that had been reserved by a symphony conductor, Ostap Bender was fast asleep.

He lay on top of a plush bed cover, fully dressed, clutching the suitcase with the million to his chest. During the night, the grand strategist had inhaled all the oxygen in the room, and the remaining chemical elements could be called nitrogen only out of courtesy. The room smelled of sour wine, meatballs from hell, and something else—it was revolting beyond belief. Ostap groaned and turned around. The suitcase fell on the floor. Bender opened his eyes quickly.

"What was that?" he muttered, grimacing. "Acting like a drunken sailor in the restaurant! Or worse! Ugh! I behaved like a barroom brawler! Oh my God, did I insult those people? Some idiot there was yelling: 'Soil scientists, stand up!'—and then wept and swore that, in his heart of hearts, he was a soil scientist himself. It was me, of course! But why, why?"

And then he remembered that yesterday, deciding that he needed to start living properly, he had resolved to build himself a mansion in the Oriental style. He spent the whole morning dreaming big dreams. He pictured a house with minarets, a doorman with the face of a statue, a second living room, a pool room, and for some reason, a conference room. At the Land Use Department of the City Council, the grand strategist was told that he could indeed obtain a plot. At the construction office, however, everything fell apart. The doorman tumbled, his stone face banging loudly, the gilded conference room shook, and the minarets collapsed.

"Are you a private citizen?" they asked the millionaire at the office.

"Yes," replied Ostap, "a highly distinct individual."

"Unfortunately, we only build for groups and organizations."

"Cooperative, governmental, and non-governmental?" asked Bender bitterly.

"Precisely."

"And me?"

"And you can do it yourself."

"But where am I going to get the stones, the bolts? The molding, for that matter?"

"You're going to have to find it somewhere. It'll be hard, though: the supplies have already been allocated to various industries and cooperatives."

That must have been the reason for the outrageous scene the night before.

Still lying down, Ostap pulled out his little notebook and began to count his expenses since the time he had acquired his million. The memorable entry on the first page read:

Camel .... 180.00 r.
Sheep .... 30.00 r.
Kumis .... 1.75 r.
_____
Total .... 211.75 r.

What followed wasn't much better. The fur coat, a dinner, a train ticket, another dinner, another ticket, three turbans (purchased for a rainy day), horse cabs, the vase, and all kinds of junk. Apart from the fifty thousand for Balaganov, which didn't bring him any happiness, the million was still intact.

"They won't let me invest my capital!" fulminated Ostap. "They just won't! Maybe I should live the intellectual life, like my friend Lokhankin? After all, I've already accumulated some material riches, now it's time to start adding a few spiritual treasures. I need to learn the meaning of life, immediately."

He remembered that the hotel lobby filled up every day with young women who were seeking to discuss matters of the soul with the visiting philosopher from India.

"I'll go see the Indian," he decided. "That way, I'll finally learn what it's all about. Granted, it's a bit over the top, but there's no other way."

Without parting with his suitcase or changing out of his crumpled suit, Bender descended to the mezzanine and knocked on the great man's door. An interpreter answered.

"Is the philosopher available?" inquired Ostap.

"It depends," answered the interpreter politely. "Are you a private citizen?"

"No, no," said the grand strategist hastily, "I'm from a cooperative organization."

"Are you with a group? How many people? You know, it's hard for the Teacher to see individuals, he prefers to talk to . . ."

"Collectives?" Ostap picked up the key. "I was actually sent by my collective to clarify an important, fundamental issue regarding the meaning of life."

The interpreter left and returned five minutes later. He pulled the drapery aside and announced theatrically:

"The cooperative organization who wishes to learn the meaning of life may now enter."

The great poet and philosopher, wearing a brown velvet cassock and a matching pointy cap, sat in an armchair with a high and uncomfortable back made of carved wood. He had a dark, delicate face, with the black eyes of a second lieutenant. His beard, white and broad like a formal dickey, covered his chest. A woman stenographer sat at his feet. Two interpreters, an Indian and an Englishman, were on either side of him.

Seeing Ostap with his suitcase, the philosopher started fidgeting in his armchair and whispered something to the interpreter with alarm. The stenographer began to write hastily, while the interpreter announced to the grand strategist:

"The Teacher wishes to know whether there are songs and sagas in the stranger's suitcase, and whether the stranger intends to read them aloud, because the Teacher has already had many songs and sagas read to him, and he can't listen to any more of them."

"Tell the Teacher there are no sagas," Ostap replied reverentially.

The black-eyed elder grew even more agitated and, speaking anxiously, pointed his finger at the suitcase.

"The Teacher asks," said the interpreter, "whether the stranger intends to move into his suite, since no one has ever come to an appointment with a suitcase before."

And only after Ostap reassured the interpreter and the interpreter reassured the philosopher did the tension ease and the discussion begin.

"Before answering your question about the meaning of life," said the interpreter, "the Teacher wishes to say a few words about public education in India."

"Tell the Teacher," reported Ostap, "that I've had a keen interest in the issue of public education ever since I was a child."

The philosopher closed his eyes and started talking at a leisurely pace. For an hour he spoke in English, then for another hour in Bengali. At times, he'd start singing in a quiet, pleasant voice, and once he even stood up, lifted his cassock, and made a few dance moves, which apparently represented the games of schoolchildren in Punjab. Then he sat down and closed his eyes again, while Ostap listened to the translation for a while. At first, he nodded his head politely, then he looked out the window sleepily, and finally he began to amuse himself: he fiddled with the change in his pocket, admired his ring, and even winked quite openly at the pretty stenographer, after which she started scribbling even faster.

"So what about the meaning of life?" the millionaire interjected when he saw an opening.

"First," explained the interpreter, "the Teacher wishes to tell the stranger about the wealth of materials that he collected while learning about the system of public education in the USSR."

"Tell his Lordship," said Ostap, "that the stranger has no objections."

The gears began moving again. The Teacher spoke, sang Young Pioneer songs, demonstrated the handmade poster presented to him by the children from Workers' School No. 146, and at one point even grew misty-eyed. The two interpreters droned on in unison, the stenographer scribbled, and Ostap cleaned his fingernails absentmindedly.

Finally Ostap coughed loudly.

"You know," he said, "there's no need to translate anymore. Somehow

I've learned to understand Bengali. When he gets to the meaning of life, then translate."

When Ostap's wishes were conveyed to the philosopher, the black-eyed elder became anxious.

"The Teacher says," announced the interpreter, "that he himself came to your great country to learn the meaning of life. Only in places where the system of public education is as advanced as it is here, life becomes meaningful. The collective . . ."

"Goodbye," said the grand strategist quickly, "tell the Teacher that the stranger asks to be excused immediately."

But the philosopher's delicate voice was already singing *The Red Cavalry March*, which he had learned from Soviet children, so Ostap departed without permission.

"Krishna!" thundered the grand strategist, pacing around his hotel room. "Vishnu! What's the world come to? Where's the homespun truth? And maybe I am a fool, and I don't get it, and my life has passed without any reason or system? A real-life Indian, mind you, knows everything about our vast country, and I, like the Indian guest from the opera, keep harping about countless treasures and boundless pleasures. Sickening!"

That evening, Ostap had dinner without vodka, and for the first time ever, he left the suitcase in his room. Then he sat peacefully on the window sill and carefully studied the ordinary pedestrians who were jumping onto a bus like squirrels.

In the middle of the night, the grand strategist suddenly awakened and sat up on his bed. It was quiet, and only a melancholy Boston waltz from the restaurant was sneaking into the room through the keyhole.

"How could I have forgotten!" he said fretfully.

Then he laughed, turned the lights on, and quickly wrote out a telegram:

"Chernomorsk. Zosya Sinitsky. Account grave error prepared to fly Chernomorsk wings of love respond urgently Moscow Grand Hotel Bender."

He rang for an attendant and demanded that the telegram be sent immediately and urgently.

Zosya didn't respond. Nor did she respond to his other telegrams, which he had composed in the same desperate and romantic vein.

CHAPTER 34
FRIENDSHIP WITH YOUTH

The train was headed to Chernomorsk.

The first passenger removed his suit jacket, hung it on the curled brass tip of the luggage rack, then pulled off his shoes, raising his pudgy feet one by one almost all the way up to his face, and put on his slippers.

"So have you heard about the land surveyor from Voronezh who turned out to be related to the Japanese Mikado?" he asked, smiling in anticipation.

The second and the third passengers moved closer. The fourth passenger was already lying on an upper bunk under a scratchy maroon blanket, staring gloomily into an illustrated magazine.

"You really haven't heard? There was a lot of talk about it at some point. He was just an ordinary land surveyor: a wife, one room, 120 rubles a month. His name was Bigusov. An ordinary, completely unremarkable man, even, frankly, between you and me, quite an asshole. So one day he comes home from work, and there's a Japanese man waiting for him in his room and he's wearing, frankly, an excellent suit, eyeglasses, and, between you and me, snakeskin shoes, the latest rage. 'Is your name Bigusov?' asks the Japanese. 'Yes,' says Bigusov. 'And your given name?' 'So-and-so,' he says. 'That's the one,' says the Japanese. 'In that case, would you mind removing your shirt, I need to examine your naked torso.' 'No problem,' Bigusov says. But frankly, between you and me, the Japanese doesn't even look at his torso and goes straight for his birthmark. Bigusov actually had one on his side. The Japanese looks at it through a magnifying glass, turns pale, and says: 'Congratulations, Citizen Bigusov, allow me to present you with this parcel and letter.' Well, his wife opens the parcel, of course. And in that parcel, frankly, is a two-sided Japanese sword, sitting in wood shavings. 'So why do I get a sword?' asks the surveyor. 'Read the letter', he says, 'it's all in there. You're a samurai.' Now it's Bigusov who turns pale. Voronezh, frankly, is not exactly a metropolis. Between you and me, how can they possibly feel about the samurai down there? Very negatively. But what can you do? So Bigusov takes the letter, breaks the fourteen wax seals, and reads. And what do you know? It turns out that exactly thirty-six years earlier, a Japanese almost-prince was traveling incognito through Voronezh Province. Well, of course, between you and me, His Highness got mixed up with a Voronezh girl and had a baby with her, all incognito. He even wanted to marry her, but the Mikado nixed it with an encrypted cable. The almost-prince had to leave, and the baby remained illegitimate. That was Bigusov. And so after all these years, the almost-prince is about to die, but what do you know: he has no legitimate offspring, no one to pass the inheritance to, and on top of that, a prominent lineage is coming to an end, which for the Japanese is the worst thing. So he thought of Bigusov. Can you believe the man's luck? They say he's already in Japan. The old man died. And Bigusov is a prince, a member of the Mikado's family, and on top of that, between you and me, he got a million yen in cash. A million! To that moron!"

"If only somebody gave me a million rubles!" said the second passenger, twitching his legs. "I'd show them what to do with a million!"

The fourth passenger's head appeared in the gap between the two upper bunks. He took a good look at the man who knew precisely what to do with a million, and without saying a word, he hid behind his magazine again.

"Yes," said the third passenger, opening a small package that contained two complimentary crackers, "all sorts of things happen in the field of money circulation. This girl from Moscow had an uncle in Warsaw, who died and left her a million, and she had no idea. But somebody abroad had gotten wind of it, and within a month, a rather presentable foreigner showed up in Moscow. The wise guy had decided to marry the girl before she found out about the inheritance. But she had a fiancé in Moscow, a rather good-looking young man himself, from the Chamber of Weights and Measures. She was in love with him and naturally had no interest in marrying anyone else. So the foreigner goes crazy, keeps sending her flowers, chocolates, and silk stockings. Well, turns out this wise guy wasn't acting on his own initiative, he was sent by a partnership that had been formed with the express purpose of exploiting the uncle's fortune. They even had start-up capital of eighteen thousand zlotys. This agent of theirs had to marry the girl, no matter what, and take her out of the country. A very romantic story! Can you imagine how this agent felt? Such a huge responsibility! He received an advance, after all, and he had nothing to show for it, thanks to this Soviet fiancé! And in Warsaw, all hell breaks loose! The shareholders keep waiting and worrying, the shares plummet. In the end, the whole thing fell through. The girl married her guy, the Soviet. She never even found out."

"Stupid woman!" said the second passenger. "If only they gave that million to me!"

In his excitement, he even grabbed a cracker from his neighbor's hand and ate it nervously.

The occupant of the upper bunk started coughing demonstratively. Apparently, he couldn't sleep because of all the talking.

They lowered their voices, huddled together, head to head, and whispered breathlessly:

"The International Red Cross put a note in the papers recently that they were searching for the heirs of Harry Kowalchuk, an American soldier who was killed in action in 1918. The inheritance: a million! Actually, it used to be less than a million, but the interest had added up . . . And so in this God-forsaken village in the Volhynia . . ."

On the upper bunk, the maroon blanket jerked frantically. Bender felt terrible. He was sick of trains, of upper and lower bunks, of the entire ever-shaking world of travel. He would easily have given half a million just to be able to go to sleep, but the whispering continued:

"See, this old woman comes to a rental office and says: 'I found this pot in my basement, you know, I have no idea what's in it, so kindly go ahead and take a look at it yourselves.' So the management looks into the pot and finds Indian gold rupees, a million rupees . . ."

"Stupid woman! Why did she have to tell them? If only they gave that million to me, I would . . ."

"Frankly, between you and me, money is everything."

"And in this cave near Mozhaysk . . ."

The loud, powerful groan of an individual in grave distress came from the upper bunk.

The storytellers paused for a moment, but the spell of unexpected riches pouring from the pockets of Japanese princes, Warsaw relatives, and American soldiers was so irresistible that they soon resumed grabbing each other's knees and muttering:

". . . And so when they opened the holy relics, they found, between you and me, a million worth of . . ."

In the morning, while still in sleep's embrace, Ostap heard the sound of the blind being opened and a voice:

"A million! Can you believe it, an entire million . . ."

This was too much. The grand strategist glanced down furiously, but the passengers from the previous night were gone. They had gotten off in Kharkov at the crack of dawn, leaving behind them crumpled sheets, a greasy piece of graph paper, and bread and meat crumbs, as well as a piece of string. A new passenger, who was standing by the window, glanced at Ostap impassively and continued talking to his two companions:

"A million tons of pig iron. By the end of the year. The commission concluded that it was doable. But the funniest thing is that Kharkov actually approved it!"

Ostap didn't find this funny in the least, but the new passengers burst out laughing and their rubber coats squeaked noisily.

"But what about Bubeshko?" asked the youngest of them excitedly. "He probably has his heels dug in?"

"Not any more. He ended up making a fool of himself. But it was really something! First he started a fight . . . you know Bubeshko, he's one tough cookie . . . Eight hundred and twenty-five thousand tons and not a ton more. Then things got sticky. Deliberately underestimating the capacity . . . Check! Artificially lowering the bar—check! He should have admitted his mistakes right away, without reservation. But no! He's got his pride! Like he's a blue-blood or something! Just confess—and that's the end of it. But he had to do it piece by piece. Wanted to protect his reputation. So he did this Dostoyevskian song and dance: 'On the one hand, I admit, but on the other, I have to point out . . .' But what is there to point out, that's just spineless wiggling! So our Bubeshko had to write another memo."

The passengers laughed again.

"But even then he didn't say a word about his opportunism. So it went on and on. Every day, a new memo. Now they want to set up a special section for him—Corrections and Disavowals. He knows he's dug himself into a hole, and he wants to get out, but he made such a mess that there's nothing he can do now. He really lost it in his latest memo: 'Yes, I admit my mistake . . . but I consider this memo insufficient.'"

Ostap had long ago left for the washroom but the new passengers still hadn't finished laughing. When he returned, the compartment was swept clean, the bunks lowered, and the attendant was on his way out, holding down a pile of sheets and blankets with his chin. The young men, who were not afraid of drafts, opened the window, and the autumn breeze thrashed and rolled around the compartment like an ocean wave locked inside a box.

Ostap threw the suitcase with the million onto the luggage net and made himself comfortable on the lower bunk, glancing amicably at his new neighbors. They were settling into the first-class car with unusual gusto. They kept looking into the mirror on the door, jumping up and down on the couch to test the strength of its springs and cushions, admiring the quality of the smooth red upholstery, and pressing all the buttons. From time to time, one of them would disappear for a few minutes, then return and confer with his companions in a whisper. Finally, a girl dressed in a men's woolen overcoat and tennis shoes with strings laced around her ankles, in the ancient Greek style, appeared in the doorway.

"Comrades!" she said firmly. "That's not very nice. We want to ride in luxury, too. We ought to switch at the next station."

Bender's companions started hooting in protest.

"Oh, come on. Everybody has the same rights as you do," continued the girl. "We already drew lots. It fell to Tarasov, Parovitsky, and myself. Off you go to third class."

From the ensuing ruckus, Ostap deduced that they were members of a large group of engineering students who were returning to Chernomorsk after their summer internships. There weren't enough seats in third class for everybody, so they had to purchase three first-class tickets and split the difference among the whole group.

Consequently, the girl stayed put, while the three firstborns cleared the premises with belated dignity. Their places were promptly taken by Tarasov and Parovitsky. Without delay, they started jumping on the couches and pressing all the buttons. The girl jumped enthusiastically along with them. After less than thirty minutes, the original trio barged into the compartment, drawn back by their nostalgia for lost splendors. They were followed by two more, with sheepish smiles, and then by another one, with a mustache. He was scheduled to ride in luxury the following day, but he just couldn't wait that long. His arrival was greeted by particularly excited hoots, which drew the attention of the car attendant.

"That's not good, citizens," he said officiously. "The whole gang is here. Those from third class, please leave. Or I'm going to the boss."

The gang grew quiet.

"But they are our guests," said the girl, disconcerted. "They were just going to sit here with us for a while."

"It's against the rules," insisted the attendant, "please leave."

The mustachioed one started backing toward the exit, but at this point, the grand strategist inserted himself into the dispute.

"Come on, pops," he said to the attendant, "you shouldn't be lynching your passengers unless you absolutely have to. Is it really necessary to stick to the letter of the law like this? You should be hospitable. You know, like in the East. Let's step out, I'll tell you all about it."

After a chat with Ostap in the corridor, the attendant embraced the spirit of the East so ardently that he vanquished all thoughts of ousting the gang and instead brought them nine glasses of tea in sturdy holders, along with his entire supply of crackers. And he didn't even charge them.

"As dictated by the customs of the East," explained Ostap to his company, "in compliance with the laws of hospitality, as a certain employee of the culinary sector used to say."

The favor was granted with such grace and ease that it was impossible not to accept it. The cracker packages rustled as they were being ripped open. Ostap passed around the tea like a host and soon became friends with all eight of the male students and the female one.

"I have long been interested in issues of universal, equal, and direct education," he babbled happily, "I even discussed it recently with an amateur Indian philosopher. An exceptionally erudite man. No matter what he says, they immediately put his words on a phonograph record, and as the old man is quite a talker—yes, he does have this weakness—his records ended up filling eight hundred railcars, and now they make them into buttons."

Having started with this free improvisation, the grand strategist picked up a cracker.

"This cracker," he said, "is just one step away from being a grindstone. And that step has already been taken."

Warmed up by witticisms of this sort, their friendship blossomed quickly, and soon the whole gang was singing a ditty under Ostap's direction:

Peter, Tsar of great renown,
Has no kinfolk of his own.
Just the serpent and the steed—
That's his family indeed.

By the end of the day, Ostap knew everybody and was even on a first-name basis with a few of them. But a lot of what the youngsters were talking about was beyond his grasp. Suddenly, he felt incredibly old. In front him was youth—a bit rough, straight as an arrow, and frustratingly uncomplicated. He was different when he was twenty; he had to admit that he was far more sophisticated—and rotten—at that age. He didn't laugh back then, he smirked. But these kids were laughing their hearts out.

"What are these pudgy-cheeked kids so happy about?" he thought with sudden irritation. "I'm starting to envy them, I really am."

Although Ostap was undoubtedly the center of attention for the whole compartment and talked incessantly, and although they treated him very nicely, they showed him neither Balaganov's adoration, nor Panikovsky's craven submission, nor Kozlevich's loving devotion. In these students, he sensed the superiority that the audience feels toward an entertainer. The audience listens to the man in the tailcoat, laughs at times, applauds him half-heartedly, but in the end it goes home and no longer gives him another thought. The entertainer, on the other hand, goes to the artists' club after the show, hovers gloomily over his plate, and complains to a fellow member of the Art Workers' Union—a vaudeville comedian—that the public doesn't understand him and the government doesn't value him. The comedian drinks vodka and also complains that nobody understands him. But what's not to understand? His jokes are old, his techniques are old, and it's too late to learn new tricks. It couldn't be clearer.

The story of Bubeshko, who had set the bar too low, was told once again, this time specifically for Ostap's sake. He went to third class with his new friends to try to convince the student Lida Pisarevsky to come visit them. He was so effusive and eloquent that the shy Lida did come over and join in the general pandemonium. The sudden closeness went so far that in the evening, while strolling along a platform at one of the longer stops with the girl in a man's overcoat, the grand strategist took her almost as far as the exit semaphore, where, to his own surprise, he confided in her using rather sappy language.

"You see," he expounded, "the moon, that queen of the landscape, was shining. We sat on the steps of the Archaeological Museum, and I felt that I loved her. But I had to leave that same night, so the whole thing fell through. I think she's mad at me. Actually, I'm pretty sure she is."

"You had to go on a business trip?" asked the girl.

"Sort of . . . You could say it was a business trip. Well, not exactly a business trip, but an urgent matter. Now I'm suffering. In a grand and foolish fashion."

"This can be remedied," said the girl, "simply redirect your excess energies to some kind of physical activity. Saw firewood, for example. It's a new trend these days."

Ostap promised to redirect, and although he couldn't imagine how he'd be able to replace Zosya with sawing firewood, he felt a whole lot better. They returned to their car looking conspiratorial, and later kept stepping out into the corridor and whispering about unrequited love and the new trends in that field.

Back in the compartment, Ostap continued to do his utmost to get the gang to like him. Thanks to his efforts, the students came to see him as one of their own. The rube Parovitsky even slapped him on the shoulder with all this might and exclaimed:

"Ostap, why don't you come study with us? I'm serious! You'll get a stipend, seventy-five rubles a month. You'll live like a king. We've got a cafeteria; they serve meat every single day. And later, we'll do an internship in the Urals."

"I already have a degree in the humanities," said the grand strategist hastily.

"So what do you do now?" asked Parovitsky.

"Oh, nothing special . . . finance."

"You work in a bank?"

Ostap looked at the student ironically and suddenly blurted out:

"No, I don't work. I'm a millionaire."

Of course, this kind of pronouncement didn't mean much and could have easily been turned into a joke, but Parovitsky laughed so hard that the grand strategist felt hurt. He was overwhelmed by the urge to dazzle his companions and gain even greater admiration from them.

"So how many millions do you have?" asked the girl in tennis shoes, hoping for a funny response.

"One," said Ostap, pale with pride.

"That's not much," countered the guy with a mustache.

"Not much! Not much!" cried the rest.

"Enough for me," said Bender solemnly.

With that, he picked up his suitcase, clicked its nickel-plated latches, and poured the entire contents onto the couch. The paper bricks formed a small, spreading mound. Ostap flexed one of them; the wrapping split open with the sound of a deck of cards.

"Ten thousand in each stack. That's not enough for you? A million minus some small change. Everything's here: the signatures, the security thread, the watermarks."

In the silence that followed, Ostap raked the money back into the suitcase and threw it onto the luggage net with a gesture that seemed regal to him. He sat down on the couch again, leaned back, spread his feet wide, and surveyed the gang.

"Now you know that the humanities can be profitable, too," said the millionaire, inviting the students to have fun together.

The students were silently inspecting various buttons and hooks on the ornamented walls of the compartment.

"I live like a king," continued Ostap, "or like a prince, which, come to think of it, is pretty much the same thing."

The grand strategist waited a bit, then fidgeted nervously, and exclaimed in a friendly way:

"What is bothering you devils?"

"Well, I'm off," said the one with the mustache after a brief period of contemplation, "back to my place, to see what's going on."

And he darted out of the compartment.

"Isn't it amazing, isn't it wonderful," gushed Ostap, "just this morning, we didn't even know each other, and now it feels as if we've been friends for years. Is that some kind of chemistry or what?"

"How much do we owe for the tea?" asked Parovitsky. "How many glasses did we have, comrades? Nine or ten? We should ask the attendant. I'll be right back."

Then four more people took off, driven by the wish to help Parovitsky deal with the attendant.

"Shall we sing something?" suggested Ostap. "Something tough. For example, 'Serge the priest, Serge the priest!' Shall we? I have a lovely Volga bass."

Without waiting for an answer, the grand strategist hastily started singing: "Down the river, the Kazanka river, a blue-gray drake is making its way . . ." When the time came to join in the chorus, Ostap waved his arms like a bandmaster and stamped his foot on the floor, but the powerful choral burst never materialized. Only the shy Lida Pisarevsky peeped, "Serge the priest, Serge the priest!," but then she cut herself short and ran out.

The friendship was dying before his eyes. Soon the only one left in the compartment was the kind and compassionate girl in tennis shoes.

"Where is everybody?" asked Bender.

"Right," whispered the girl, "I'd better go take a look."

She leaped for the door, but the heartbroken millionaire grabbed her by the arm.

"I was kidding," he muttered, "I do have a job . . . I'm a symphony conductor! I'm the son of Lieutenant Schmidt! My father was a Turkish subject . . . Honest!"

"Let me go!" whispered the girl.

The grand strategist remained alone.

The compartment was shaking and creaking. The teaspoons spun inside the empty glasses, and the entire herd was slowly creeping toward the edge of the table. The attendant appeared at the door, holding down a stack of fresh sheets and blankets with his chin.

CHAPTER 35
HOUSEWIVES, HOUSEKEEPERS, WIDOWS, AND EVEN A DENTAL TECHNICIAN— THEY ALL LOVED HIM

Roofs were clattering in Chernomorsk, and the wind romped through the streets. An unexpected northeaster assailed the city and chased the fragile Indian summer into the garbage cans, drains, and corners, where it was expiring amidst charred maple leaves and torn streetcar tickets. Cold chrysanthemums were drowning in the flower ladies' tubs. The green shutters of locked-up refreshment stands banged in the wind. Pigeons were saying, "You throoh, you throoh." Sparrows kept warm by pecking at steaming horse manure. People struggled against the wind, lowering their heads like bulls. It was especially hard on the Piqué Vests. The gusts blew the boater hats and panamas off their heads and rolled them across the wood block pavement down toward the boulevard. The old men ran after their hats, expressing their outrage and gasping for air. Sidewalk gales carried the pursuers so fast that at times, they would overtake their own headgear before finally regaining their composure at the wet feet of a dignitary from the time of Catherine the Great, whose bronze statue stood in the middle of the square.

At the taxi stand, the Antelope creaked like a ship. Kozlevich's vehicle used to look oddly amusing, but it had become a pitiful sight: the rear left fender was held on by a rope, a piece of plywood had replaced a large portion of the windshield, and instead of the rubber bulb that played the maxixe, which was lost in the wreck, a nickel-plated chairman's bell was hanging from a string. Even the steering wheel upon which Adam Kozlevich rested his honest hands was a bit askew. On the sidewalk, next to the Antelope, stood the grand strategist. Leaning against the car, he was saying:

"I lied to you, Adam. I can't give you an Isotta-Fraschini, or a Lincoln, or a Buick, or even a Ford. I can't buy a new car. The state doesn't consider me a legitimate customer. I'm a private citizen. Anything I could find for you in the classifieds would be the same kind of junk as our Antelope."

"Don't say that," protested Kozlevich, "my Lorraine-Dietrich is a fine vehicle. If only I could find a used oil hose—then who'd need a Buick?"

"That I have," said Ostap. "Here. But that's all I can do for you, dear Adam, when it comes to mechanized means of transportation."

Thrilled with the hose, Kozlevich inspected it thoroughly and started fitting it in right away. Ostap pushed the bell, which produced an officious ring, and said emotionally:

"Have you heard the news, Adam? Turns out, each individual is under the pressure of a column of air that weighs 472 pounds!"

"No, I haven't," said Kozlevich. "Why?"

"What do you mean, why? It's a medical fact. And lately, it's been very hard on me. Just think of it! Four-hundred-and-seventy-two pounds! It weighs down on you day in and day out, especially at night. I can't sleep. What?"

"No, no, I'm listening," replied Kozlevich softly.

"I don't feel well at all, Adam. My heart is too big."

The driver of the Antelope chuckled. Ostap went on babbling:

"Yesterday, an old woman approached me on the street and offered me a permanent needle valve for a Primus stove. You know, Adam, I didn't buy it. I don't need a permanent valve, I don't want to live forever. I want to die. I've got all the tawdry symptoms of being in love: loss of appetite, insomnia, and a maniacal desire to write poetry. Just listen to what I scribbled down last night, in the flickering light of an electric bulb: 'I recollect that wondrous meeting, that instant I encountered you, when like an apparition fleeting, like beauty's spirit, past you flew.' It's good, isn't it? Brilliant? And only at sunrise, just as I finished the last lines, did I realize that this poem had already been written by Pushkin. Such a blow from a literary giant! Excuse me?"

"No, no, please continue," said Kozlevich warmly.

"So that's my life," continued Ostap, his voice shaking. "My body is registered at the Cairo Hotel, but my soul is taking a break, it doesn't even want to go to Rio de Janeiro any more. And now this atmospheric column—it's choking me."

"Have you seen her?" asked the forthright Kozlevich. "I mean Zosya Victorovna?"

"I'm not going," said Ostap, "on account of my bashful pride. She awoke the janissary in me. I sent this heartless woman 350 rubles worth of telegrams from Moscow and didn't even get a fifty-kopeck response. And that's considering I've had any number of housewives, housekeepers, widows, and even a dental technician—they all loved me! No, Adam, I'm not going! See you!"

The grand strategist returned to the hotel and pulled the suitcase with the million from under the bed, where it sat next to a pair of worn-out shoes. For a while, he stared mindlessly at it, then grabbed it by the handle and went outside. The wind gripped Ostap's shoulders and dragged him toward Seaside Boulevard. It was deserted. The white benches—covered with romantic messages that had been carved in summers past—were empty. A low-sitting cargo ship with thick upright masts was skirting the lighthouse on its way to the outer roadstead.

"Enough," said Ostap, "the golden calf is not for me. Whoever wants it can have it. Let him be a free-range millionaire!"

He looked back and, seeing that there wasn't anybody around, threw the suitcase onto the gravel.

"It's all yours," he said to the black maples and bowed graciously.

He started walking down the tree-lined alley without looking back. First he moved slowly, at a leisurely pace, then put his hands into his pockets—they were suddenly getting in his way—and speeded up, in order to allay his doubts. He forced himself to turn the corner and even started singing, but a minute later he turned around and ran back. The suitcase was still there. However, a rather unremarkable-looking middle-aged man was already approaching it from the other side, bending down and reaching for it.

"What the hell are you doing?" yelled Ostap from afar. "I'll show you how to grab other people's suitcases! You can't leave anything even for a moment! Outrageous!"

The man shrugged sullenly and retreated. And Bender went trudging on with the golden calf in his hands.

"Now what?" he wondered. "What do I do with this goddamn booty? It's brought me nothing but anguish! Should I burn it?"

The grand strategist found this thought intriguing.

"Actually, there's a fireplace in my room. Burn it in the fireplace! That's regal! An act worthy of Cleopatra! Into the fire! Stack after stack! Why should I waste my time on it? No, wait, that's stupid. Burning money is in poor taste! It's ostentatious! But what can I do with it, other than party like a swine? What a ridiculous situation! The museum director thinks he can slap together a Louvre with just three hundred rubles. Any organized group of waterworks employees or something—or a playwrights' cooperative—can use a million to build a near-skyscraper, complete with a flat roof for holding open-air lectures. But Ostap Bender, a descendant of the janissaries, can't do a damn thing! The ruling working class is smothering a lone millionaire!"

Wondering what to do with the million, the grand strategist paced through the park, sat on the parapet, and stared morosely at the steamer that was rocking outside the breakwater.

"No, fire is not the answer. Burning money is cowardly and inelegant. I need to come up with a strong statement. What if I endow the Balaganov Scholarship at the radio technicians' correspondence school? Or buy fifty thousand silver teaspoons, recast them into an equestrian statue of Panikovsky, and install it on his grave? Have the Antelope encrusted with mother of pearl? And maybe . . ."

The grand strategist jumped off the parapet, fired up by a new thought. Without even a moment's pause, he left the boulevard and, firmly resisting the onslaughts of both head and side winds, set out for the main post office.

There, at his request, the suitcase was sewn into a piece of burlap and tied with a string. It looked like an ordinary parcel, one of the thousands that the post office accepts every day, the kind people use to send salt pork, fruit preserves, or fresh apples to their relatives.

Ostap picked up an indelible pencil, waved it excitedly in the air, and wrote:

Valuable
To: THE PEOPLE'S COMMISSAR OF FINANCE
Moscow

Thrown by the hand of a mighty postal worker, the parcel tumbled onto a pile of oval-shaped sacks, bags, and boxes. Stuffing the receipt into his pocket, Ostap noticed that a slow-moving geezer with white lightning bolts on his collar was already taking the cart with his million into the next room.

"Our deliberations continue," said the grand strategist, "this time without O. Bender representing the Deranged Agrarians."

He lingered under the post office archway for a long time, alternately congratulating himself and having second thoughts. The wind snuck under Ostap's raincoat. He shivered, and began to regret that he never bothered to buy another fur coat.

A young woman stopped for a moment right in front of him. She threw back her head, looked at the shiny face of the post office clock, and moved on. She wore a rough lightweight coat that was shorter than her dress and a dark-blue beret with a childish pompom. She held down the flap of her coat, which was being blown by the wind, with her right hand. The captain's heart fluttered even before he recognized Zosya, and then he started following her over the wet slabs of the sidewalk, subconsciously maintaining a distance. Occasionally, other people stepped between them; then Ostap would walk out onto the street, peering at Zosya from the side and preparing his talking points for the upcoming face-to-face.

On the corner, Zosya stopped in front of a stand that was selling accessories and studied some brown men's socks that were dangling from a string. Ostap patrolled nearby.

Two men with briefcases were having a heated conversation on the curb. Both wore fall overcoats, their white summer pants showing underneath.

"You didn't leave the Hercules a moment too soon, Ivan Pavlovich," said one, clutching his briefcase to his chest, "they're having a vicious purge right now. It's brutal."

"The whole city is talking about it," sighed the other.

"Yesterday, it was Sardinevich," said the first man lustily, "standing room only. At first, everything was hunky-dory. When Sardinevich told his life story, everybody applauded. 'I was born, he said, between the hammer and the anvil.' By that he meant that his parents were blacksmiths. But then somebody from the audience asked: 'Excuse me, do you happen to remember a trading company called Sardinevich & Son Hardware? You're not that Sardinevich, by any chance?' And this idiot blurts out: 'No, I'm not that Sardinevich, I'm the son.' Can you imagine what they'll do to him now? Category One is all but assured."

"Yes, Comrade Brinetrust, it's tough. And who are they purging today?"

"Today's a big day! Today it's Berlaga, the one who tried to sit it out in the nuthouse. Then it's Polykhaev himself, along with Impala Mikhailovna, that snake, his illegitimate wife. She wouldn't let anyone at the Hercules breathe easily. I'm going there two hours early, or else I'll never get in. Also, Bomze's coming up . . ."

Zosya started walking again, and Ostap never found out what happened to Adolf Nikolaevich Bomze. He couldn't care less, though. He had already come up with an opening line. The captain quickly caught up with the girl.

"Zosya," he said, "I'm here, and this fact is impossible to ignore."

He uttered these words with unbelievable impudence. The girl flinched, and the grand strategist realized that his opening had sounded phony. He changed key, spoke rapidly and incessantly, blamed circumstances, said that his youth hadn't passed the way he had pictured it as a child, that life turned out to be harsh and low, like a bass key.

"You know, Zosya," he said in the end, "every single person, even a party member, is under the pressure of an atmospheric column that weighs 472 pounds. Haven't you noticed?"

Zosya didn't say anything.

They walked past the Capital Hill movie theater. Ostap quickly glanced across the street, at the building that just a few months earlier had housed the bureau he had founded, and gasped quietly. A large sign stretched across the entire length of the building:

> HORNS AND HOOFS STATE ENTERPRISE

In every window, one could see typewriters and portraits of political leaders. A sprightly messenger, who looked nothing like Panikovsky, stood at the door with a satisfied smile. Three-ton trucks, loaded down with horns and hoofs that met the industry's standards were driving in through an open gate that bore the sign MAIN WAREHOUSE. Ostap's baby had clearly taken the right path.

"The ruling class is smothering me," said Ostap wistfully, "it even took my offhand idea and used it to it's own advantage. And I got pushed aside, Zosya. You hear? I got pushed aside. I'm miserable."

"A heartsick lover," said Zosya, turning to Ostap for the first time.

"Yes," agreed Ostap, "I'm your typical Eugene Onegin, also known as a knight who's been disinherited by the Soviet regime."

"A knight? Come on!"

"Zosya, don't be mad! Think of the atmospheric column. I even have a feeling that it puts a lot more pressure on me than on other people. On account of my love for you. Besides, I'm not a union member. That's another reason."

"And also because you tell more lies than other people."

"This is not a lie. It's a law of physics. But maybe there really isn't any column, and it's just a fantasy?"

Zosya stopped and started taking off a glove that was the color of a gray stocking.

"I'm thirty-three years old," said Ostap hastily, "the age of Jesus Christ. And what have I accomplished thus far? I haven't created a teaching, I wasted my disciples, I haven't resurrected the dead Panikovsky, and only you . . ."

"Well, see you," said Zosya. "I'm off to the cafeteria."

"I'll have lunch too," announced the grand strategist, glancing at the sign that read THE CHERNOMORSK STATE ACADEMY FOR SPATIAL ARTS VOCATIONAL COLLEGE. MODEL FOOD PREPARATION FACLITY. "I'll have some model borscht du jour at this academy. Maybe it'll make me feel better."

"It's for union members only," warned Zosya.

"Then I'll just sit with you."

They went down three steps. A young man with black eyes sat deep inside the model training facility, under the green canopy of a palm tree, and studied the menu with a dignified expression.

"Pericles!" called out Zosya before she had even reached the table. "I bought you socks with double-knit heels. Here, please meet Femidi."

"Femidi," said the young man, giving Ostap a friendly handshake.

"Bender-Transylvansky," replied the grand strategist snidely, instantly realizing that he was late to the feast of love, and that the socks with double-knit heels weren't just a product of some pseudo-invalids' co-op but a symbol of a happy marriage that had been sanctified by the office of the civil registrar.

"Wow! Are you really Transylvansky as well?" asked Zosya playfully.

"Yes, Transylvansky. And you're not just Sinitsky anymore either, are you? Judging by the socks . . ."

"I am Sinitsky-Femidi."

"For twenty-seven days now," announced the young man, rubbing his hands.

"I like your husband," said the disinherited knight.

"I do too," retorted Zosya.

While the young spouses were eating navy-style borscht, raising their spoons high, and exchanging glances, Ostap examined the educational posters that were hanging on the walls with annoyance. One of them read: AVIOD DISTRACTING CONVERSATION WHILE EATING, IT INTERFERES WITH THE PROPER SECRETION OF STOMACH JUICES. The other was in verse: FRUIT JUICES HAVE BENEFICIAL USES. There wasn't anything else for him to do. It was time to go, but a shyness that had materialized out of nowhere was getting in the way.

Ostap strained his faculties and offered: "The remains of a shipwreck float in this navy borscht."

The Femidis laughed good-naturedly.

"And what line of work do you happen to be in?" Ostap asked the young man.

"I happen to be the secretary of the painting collective of railroad artists," answered Femidi.

The grand strategist slowly began to rise from his chair.

"Oh, so you represent a collective? I'm not surprised! Well, no more distracting talk from me. It might interfere with the proper secretion of stomach juices that are so vital to your health."

He left without saying goodbye, bumping into tables while making a beeline toward the exit.

"They snatched my girl!" he muttered outside. "Straight from her stable! Femidi! Nemesidi! Femidi, representing the collective, snatched from a lone millionaire . . ."

And that was when Bender remembered with striking clarity and certainty that he no longer had the million. He kept turning this thought over while he was already running, slicing through the crowd like a swimmer who is trying to break the world record slices through the water.

"Look at this self-appointed St. Paul," he grumbled, leaping across flower beds in the city park. "Money means nothing to this s-son of a bitch! A goddamn Mennonite, a Seventh-day Adventist! If the parcel is already gone—I'll hang myself! Those Tolstoyan idealists ought to be killed on the spot!"

After slipping twice on the tiled floor of the post office, the grand strategist raced up to the window. In front of it was a small, silent, and stern line of people. In the heat of the moment, Ostap tried to stick his head into the window, but the citizen who was first in line raised his sharp elbows nervously and pushed the intruder back a little. Like clockwork, the second citizen also raised his elbows, muscling the grand strategist even farther away from the coveted window. Elbows continued to rise and stretch in total silence until the brazen trespasser ended up where he rightfully belonged—at the very end of the line.

"I just need . . ." started Ostap.

But he didn't finish. There was no use. The line, stony and gray, was as impregnable as a Greek phalanx. Everybody knew their place and was prepared to die defending their petty rights.

Forty-five minutes later, Ostap was finally able to insert his head into the postal window and boldly demanded his parcel back. The clerk coldly returned the receipt to Ostap.

"Comrade, we don't give parcels back."

"What! You already sent it?" asked the grand strategist in a shaky voice. "I brought it here just an hour ago!"

"Comrade, we don't give parcels back," repeated the postal worker.

"But it's my parcel," said Ostap gently, "it's mine, you see. I mailed it, now I want it back. You see, I forgot to put in a jar of preserves. Crabapple preserves. Please, do me a big favor. My uncle will be so mad. You see . . ."

"Comrade, we do not give parcels back."

Ostap glanced back, looking for help. Behind him was the line, silent and stern, well aware of all the rules, including the one which said that parcels cannot be given back to the sender.

"Just one jar," murmured Ostap, "crabapples . . ."

"Send the jar in a separate parcel, comrade," said the clerk, softening. "Your uncle will survive."

"You don't know my uncle!" said Ostap excitedly. "Besides, I'm a poor student, I don't have any money. Please, I'm asking you as a civic-minded citizen."

"See what you've done, comrade," said the clerk plaintively. "How am I supposed to find it? We have three tons of parcels over there."

But then the grand strategist launched into such a pitiful and nonsensical spiel that the clerk went to the other room to look for the poor student's parcel. The hitherto silent line promptly started raising hell. They scolded the grand strategist for his ignorance of the postal regulations, and one woman even pinched him angrily.

"Don't ever do this again," exhorted the clerk, tossing the suitcase back to Bender.

"Never again!" swore the captain. "Student's word of honor!"

The roofs clattered in the wind, the streetlights swayed, shadows darted over the ground, and rain crisscrossed the headlight-beams of the automobiles.

"Enough of these psychological excesses," said Bender with great relief, "enough anguish and navel-gazing. Time to start living the life of the hard-working rich. On to Rio de Janeiro! I'll buy a plantation and bring in Balaganov to serve as a monkey. He'll fetch me bananas from the trees!"

CHAPTER 36
A KNIGHT OF THE ORDER OF THE GOLDEN FLEECE

An odd-looking man was walking at night through the marshy delta of the Dniester. He was enormous and shapelessly fat. He was tightly enveloped in an oilcloth cloak with its hood raised. The odd man carefully tiptoed past stands of cattails and under gnarled fruit trees as if he were walking through a bedroom. At times, he would stop and sigh. Then a clunking sound, the kind produced by metal objects that were striking against each other, came from under the cloak. And each time after that, a particularly fine high-pitched jingle would hang in the air. Once, the odd man stumbled over a wet root and fell on his stomach. That produced a very loud bang, as if a set of body armor had collapsed onto a hardwood floor. The odd man stayed on the ground for a while, peering into the darkness.

The March night was full of sound. Large, well-shaped drops were falling from the trees and plopping onto the ground.

"That goddamn platter!" whispered the man.

He got up and walked all the way to the Dniester without further incident. Then the man lifted the hem of his cloak, skidded down the bank, and, struggling to maintain his balance on the wet ice, ran toward Romania.

The grand strategist had spent the whole winter preparing. He had purchased American dollars, that featured portraits of presidents with white curly hair, gold watches and cigarette cases, wedding rings, diamonds, and other valuable toys.

He was carrying seventeen massive cigarette cases with monograms, eagles, and engraved inscriptions like:

TO EVSEY RUDOLFOVICH CUSTOMEIR,

DIRECTOR OF THE RUSSO–CARPATHIAN BANK AND OUR BENEFACTOR,

ON THE DAY OF HIS SILVER WEDDING ANNIVERSARY,

FROM HIS GRATEFUL CO-WORKERS.

TO HIS EXCELLENCY M. I. INDIGNATYEV

UPON COMPLETION OF THE SENATORIAL AUDIT,

FROM THE STAFF OF THE CHERNOMORSK MAYORAL OFFICE.

But the heaviest of all was a case with the dedication: TO MR. CHIEF OF THE ALEXEEVSKY POLICE PRECINCT FROM THE GRATEFUL JEWISH MEMBERS OF THE MERCHANT CLASS. Below the dedication was a blazing enamel heart pierced with an arrow; it was clearly supposed to symbolize the love of the Jewish members of the merchant class for Mr. Chief.

His pockets were stuffed with rings and bracelets that had been strung into necklaces. Twenty gold pocket watches, suspended from sturdy twine, formed three layers on his back. Some of them ticked annoyingly, giving Bender the sensation that insects were crawling over his back. Some of the watches were gifts, as evidenced by the engravings on their lids: TO OUR BELOVED SON SERGE CASTRAKI IN RECOGNITION OF HIS PERFORMANCE AT SCHOOL. Above the word "performance," someone had scratched the word "sexual" with a pin. This must have been the work of young Castraki's buddies, all losers like himself. Ostap had long resisted buying this indecent watch, but he did in the end, because he had decided to invest his entire million in jewelry.

All in all, the winter was very busy. The grand strategist was able to acquire only four hundred thousand rubles worth of diamonds, and only fifty thousand in foreign currency, including some questionable notes from Poland and the Balkans. He had to spend the rest on heavy stuff. It was particularly hard to move with a golden platter on his stomach. The platter was large and oval-shaped, like the shield of an African tribal chief. It weighed twenty pounds. The captain's powerful neck was weighed down by a bishop's pectoral cross that was inscribed, IN THE NAME OF THE FATHER, THE SON, AND THE HOLY SPIRIT, which he had purchased from the former deacon of the Orthodox cathedral, Citizen Overarchangel-sky. Above the cross, a little ram cast in gold dangled on a magnificent ribbon—the Order of the Golden Fleece.

Ostap bargained hard for this Order with a peculiar old man who may even have been a Grand Duke, or else a Grand Duke's valet. The old man was asking an exorbitant price, pointing out that very few people in the world had this particular decoration, most of them royals.

"The Golden Fleece," muttered the old man, "is awarded for the utmost valor!"

"Then I qualify," replied Ostap, "and besides, I'm only buying this ram for scrap."

The captain wasn't telling the truth, however. He fancied the medal from the start and had decided to keep it for himself, as the Order of the Golden Calf.

Driven by fear and expecting the crack of a rifle shot at any moment, Bender raced to the middle of the river and then stopped. All that gold was heavy: the platter, the cross, the bracelets. His back was itching under the dangling watches. The bottom of the cloak had gotten soaked and weighed a ton. With a groan, Ostap tore off the cloak, dumped it on the ice, and continued running. This revealed his fur coat—a stupendous, almost unbelievable fur coat, easily the single most valuable object Ostap had on his person. He had built it over the course of four months, like a house, preparing blueprints and gathering materials. The coat had two layers: genuine sealskin lined with unique silver fox. The collar was made of sable. That coat was amazing! A supercoat with chinchilla pockets, which were stuffed with civilian medals for bravery, little neck crosses, and golden bridges—the latest in dental technology. The grand strategist's head was crowned with a towering cap. Not just a cap—a beaver skin tiara.

All this magnificent freight was supposed to provide the captain with an easy, care-free life by the warm ocean, in the city of his childhood dreams, among the palms and ficus on the balconies of Rio de Janeiro.

At three o'clock in the morning, the restive descendant of the janissaries stepped onto the other, foreign shore. Here, it was also quiet and dark, it was also springtime, and drops of water were falling from the trees. The grand strategist burst out laughing.

"Now, a few formalities with the kindhearted Romanian counts—and the path is clear. I think a couple of medals for bravery would brighten up their dull frontier existence."

He turned toward the Soviet side, stretched his chubby, sealskin-clad arm into the melting haze, and announced:

"Everything must be done according to the proper form. Form No. 5: saying farewell to one's country. Well, *adieu*, great land. I don't care to be a model pupil and receive grades for my attention, diligence, and behavior. I'm a private citizen, and I have no obligation to show interest in silage pits, trenches, and towers. I don't have much interest in the socialist transformation of men into angels and holders of passbooks at the state savings bank. On the contrary. My interest lies in the pressing issue of kindness to lone millionaires . . ."

At that point, saying farewell to one's country according to form No. 5 was interrupted by the appearance of several armed men, whom Bender identified as Romanian border guards. The grand strategist gave a dignified bow and clearly enunciated the phrase he had learned by heart for this very occasion:

"*Traiasca Romania mare!*"

He gave a friendly look to the border guards, whose faces he could barely make out in the murky light. He thought the guards were smiling.

"Long live great Romania!" repeated Ostap in Russian. "I'm an old professor who escaped from the Moscow Cheka! I barely made it, I swear! Allow me to greet you as representatives . . ."

One of the guards came right up to Ostap and, without saying a word, took the fur tiara off his head. Ostap made a motion to reclaim his headgear, but the guard pushed his hand back, again without a word.

"Come on," said the captain good-naturedly, "please keep your hands to yourself! Or I'll report you to the *Sfatul Ţării*, your Supreme Soviet!"

Meanwhile, another guard began unbuttoning Ostap's stupendous, almost unbelievable supercoat with the speed and ease of an experienced lover. The captain jerked. As a result, a large woman's bracelet fell from one of his pockets and rolled away.

"*Branzuletka!*" shrieked the guards' officer in a short coat with a dog-fur collar and large metal buttons on his prominent behind.

"*Branzuletka!*" cried the others, rushing Ostap.

Getting entangled in his coat, the grand strategist fell on the ground and immediately sensed that they were pulling the precious platter out of his pants. When he got up, he saw that the officer, with a devilish smile on his face, was holding up the platter, trying to determine how much it weighed. Ostap grabbed his possession and tore it out of the officer's hands, then immediately received a blinding blow to the face. The scene unfolded with military swiftness. Trapped in his coat, for a while the grand strategist stood on his knees and fought off the attackers, hurling medals for bravery at them. Then he suddenly felt an immense relief, which enabled him to deliver a few crushing blows. As it turned out, they had managed to rip the one-hundred-thousand-ruble coat off his back.

"Oh, so that's how you treat people!" shrieked Ostap, casting wild glances around.

There was a moment when he was standing with his back against a tree and bashed his foes over the head with the gleaming platter. There was a moment when they were trying to rip the Order of the Golden Fleece from his neck, and the captain swung his head around like a horse. There was another moment, when he held the bishop's cross with the words IN THE NAME OF THE FATHER, THE SON, AND THE HOLY SPIRIT high above his head and screamed hysterically:

"Oppressors of the working masses! Bloodsuckers! Capitalist stooges! Bastards!"

As he screamed, pink saliva ran from his mouth. Ostap fought like a gladiator for his million. Again and again, he threw the attackers off his back and rose up from the ground, looking ahead with bleary eyes.

He came back to his senses on the ice, his face smashed up, wearing only one boot, without the fur coat, without the engraved cigarette cases, without the watch collection, without the platter, without the foreign money, without the cross or the diamonds, without his million. The officer with the dog-fur collar stood high on the bank and looked down at Ostap.

"Bloody persecutors!" shouted Ostap, raising his bare foot. "Parasites!"

The officer slowly pulled out his pistol and cocked it. The grand strategist realized that the interview was over. Hunching over, he started limping back toward the Soviet shore.

Smoky white fog was rising from the river. Bender opened his fist and saw a flat copper button, a lock of someone's coarse black hair, and the Order of the Golden Fleece, which had miraculously survived the battle. The grand strategist gave his trophies and what was left of his riches a blank stare and continued on, slipping into ice pits and flinching from pain.

A lengthy and loud cannon-like boom made the surface of the ice tremble. The warm wind was blowing hard. Bender looked down and saw a large green crack running through the ice. The ice field under him rocked and began to tilt into the water.

"The ice has broken!" cried the grand strategist in horror. "Gentlemen of the jury, the ice has broken!"

He began leaping over the widening cracks between the ice floes, desperately trying to reach the same country he had bid farewell to so arrogantly just an hour earlier. The fog was lifting sedately and slowly, revealing ice-free marshes.

Ten minutes later, an odd-looking man with no hat and only one boot stepped onto the Soviet shore. Without addressing anyone in particular, he loudly announced:

"Hold the applause! As the Count of Monte Cristo, I'm a failure. I'll have to go into apartment management instead."

TRANSLATORS' NOTES

CHAPTER I

Lieutenant Schmidt—A Russian naval officer who was executed for his role in the revolution of 1905. Lt. Petr Schmidt had only one son.

The New Economic Policy (NEP)—The policy of the Soviet government in the early 1920s that promoted cooperative and private enterprise, which explains the abundance of small businesses in the novel. The NEP was followed by forced industrialization (the first Five-Year Plan) and the replacement of private establishments with state-owned ones, as depicted later in the novel.

CHAPTER 2

Chernomorsk (literally, a city on the Black Sea)—Unquestionably Odessa, the city in Ukraine where both Ilf (1897-1937) and Petrov (1903-1942) were born and grew up. In 1999, a small sculpture of the Antelope and its crew was installed in the courtyard of the Odessa Literary Museum.

CHAPTER 3

Gnu antelope—Another name for the African wildebeest.

Lorraine-Dietrich—An early French carmaker that was active until the 1930s; it was based in Alsace-Lorraine, hence the French-German name.

Maxixe—A Brazilian tango that was briefly popular in the early twentieth century. Mentioned in the writings of F. Scott Fitzgerald, among others.

CHAPTER 4

The purge—The novel accurately depicts the early purges, the campaigns to remove people of "non-proletarian" origin from Soviet organizations and institutions. Category Two involved dismissal and was comparatively mild, Category One essentially made the victim an unemployable pariah.

CHAPTER 8

The Proletkult—"The Proletarian Culture," an early Soviet cultural and educational institution.

CHAPTER 13

Corps of Pages—An exclusive and highly privileged military school in Imperial Russia. All students also doubled as court pages.

Gymnasium—The fifth grade of pre-revolutionary classical gymnasium was roughly equal to grade nine or ten of present-day American high school.

CHAPTER 14

The Red Putilov—A major industrial complex in St. Petersburg. At the time, it still bore the name of its pre-revolutionary owner.

CHAPTER 24

The Eastern Line—In real life the Turksib, the Turkestan-Siberia Line; one of the major projects and symbols of the first Five-Year Plan. Ilf and Petrov traveled to the Turksib joining ceremony with a group of journalists and writers.

CHAPTER 27

The Park of Culture and Rest—A multi-use park in central Moscow. Offered amusements, as well as lectures and variety shows, hence the "culture." Later known as Gorky Park.

CHAPTER 32

"On that autumn day, filled with sadness and light . . ."—September 1, traditionally the first day of the school year, when younger children are expected to bring flowers to school.

". . . There isn't anything past Shepetovka."—This landlocked Ukrainian town used to be near the Soviet-Polish border.

CHAPTER 33

The Indian guest—A character from *Sadko*, an opera by Rimsky-Korsakov.

CHAPTER 34

". . . Kharkov actually approved it."—At the time, Kharkov was the capital city of Ukraine and thus an important administrative center.

"Peter, Tsar of great renown . . ."—A reference to the famous Bronze Horseman, a massive equestrian statue of Peter the Great in St. Petersburg. The horse is trampling a large snake.

CHAPTER 35

"I recollect that wondrous meeting . . ."—Translated by Walter Arndt. In: *Pushkin, Alexander. Collected Narrative and Lyrical Poetry.* Ann Arbor: Ardis, 1984.

APPENDIX

In the first version of The Golden Calf, *which appeared in the magazine* 30 dnei *and was completed in June (or July) of 1931, Chapter 34, "Friendship with Youth," was followed by a final chapter, numbered 35 and entitled "Adam Says We Have To." It was partly identical to Chapter 35, "Housewives, Housekeepers, Widows, and Even a Dental Technician—They All Loved Him," as it appeared in the book version. However, following "He shivered, and began to regret that he never bothered to buy another fur coat," the story line took a different turn.*

•

CHAPTER 35
Adam Says We Have To

The high pitched ringing of the chairman's bell that announced the approach of the Antelope distracted Ostap from his thoughts. Spotting the captain, Adam Kazimirovich stopped the car and beckoned Ostap with his finger. The granddaughter of the old puzzle-maker sat behind the driver, looking the other way.

"The taxi is free, please get in," invited Kozlevich, "I've been looking for you all over town, I even went to the Cairo Hotel. Please."

The driver of the Antelope reached back and opened the door.

"Ah, Kozlevich!" said Ostap cheerfully, without looking at Zosya. "How's the oil hose? Is it working?"

"Get in, get in!" repeated Kozlevich sternly.

"I'd rather walk," said the captain, climbing into the car.

The chairman's bell rang loudly, and the Antelope, limping on its front wheel, slowly started moving. Zosya was carefully reading the store signs on the right side of the street. Ostap stared at Adam's back.

"Am I bothering you, by any chance?" he asked after a long silence.

"You're sitting on my dress. Please move over," said Zosya without turning her head.

"Fine," said the disinherited knight sarcastically.

The ensuing silence was interrupted by a crack and a barely audible curse uttered by Kozlevich. The Antelope stopped. The driver climbed under the car, while Zosya bent over the door and started giving him useless advice. Two men with briefcases were having a heated conversation on the curb. Both wore fall overcoats, their white summer pants showing underneath. Their conversation soon caught Ostap's attention.

"You didn't leave the Hercules a moment too soon, Comrade Counterproducteff," said one, "it's hell on earth right now. Brutal!"

"The whole city is talking about it," sighed the other.

"Yesterday, it was Sardinevich," said the first man lustily, "standing room only. At first, everything was hunky-dory. When Sardinevich told his life story, everybody applauded. But then somebody from the audience asked: 'Excuse me, do you happen to remember a trading company called Sardinevich & Son? You're not that Sardinevich, by any chance?' And this idiot blurts out: 'No, I'm not that Sardinevich, I'm the son.' Can you imagine what they'll do to him now? Category One is all but assured."

"Yes, Comrade Brinetrust, it's horrible. And who are they purging today?"

"Oh, today's a big day! Berlaga, you know, the one who tried to sit it out in the nuthouse. Then it's the maestro Polykhaev himself. Also Impala Mikhailovna, that snake, his wife. She wouldn't let anyone at the Hercules breathe easily. I'm going there two hours early or else I'll never get in. Also, Bomze's coming up . . ."

Kozlevich climbed back into the driver's seat, the car moved forward, and Ostap never found out what happened to Adolf Nikolaevich Bomze. At the moment, he couldn't care less.

"You know, Zosya," said Ostap, "every single person, even a party member, is under the pressure of an atmospheric column that weighs 472 pounds. Haven't you noticed?"

Zosya didn't say anything.

The Antelope was creaking past the Capital Hill movie theater. Ostap quickly glanced across the street, at the building that a few months earlier had housed the bureau he had founded, and gasped quietly. A large sign stretched across the entire length of the building:

> HORNS AND HOOFS STATE ENTERPRISE

In every window, one could see typewriters and portraits of political leaders. A sprightly messenger, who looked nothing like Panikovsky, stood at the door with a satisfied smile. Three-ton trucks, loaded down with horns and hoofs that met industrial standards, were driving in through an open gate that bore the sign MAIN WAREHOUSE. Ostap's baby had clearly taken the right path.

"The ruling class is smothering me," repeated Ostap, "it even took my off-hand idea and used it to it's own advantage. And I got pushed aside, Zosya. You hear? I got pushed aside. I'm miserable. Tell me something comforting."

"After everything that happened," said Zosya, turning to Ostap for the first time, "you're the one who needs comforting?"

"Yes, me."

"You have no shame."

"Zosya, don't be mad! Think of the atmospheric column. I even have a feeling that it puts a lot more pressure on me than on other people. On account of my love for you. Besides, I'm not a union member. That's another reason."

"Why are you always telling lies?"

"This is not a lie. It's a law of physics. But maybe there really isn't any column. I don't understand anything anymore."

Chatting like this, the passengers of the Antelope looked at each other with affection. They didn't notice that the car had already been stopped for several minutes, and that Kozlevich was looking at them, twisting his conductor's mustache up with both hands. After finishing with his mustache, Adam Kazimirovich climbed out with a groan, opened the door, and loudly announced:

"Please get out. We're here. It's not even four o'clock yet, you've got just enough time. They do it fast here, it's not like the church, with its Chinese ceremonies. You'll be done in no time. I'll wait for you."

The stunned Ostap looked forward and saw a small, ordinary-looking gray house with the most ordinary-looking gray sign that read THE OFFICE OF THE CIVIL REGISTRAR.

"What's that?" he asked Kozlevich. "Do we have to?"

"Absolutely," replied the driver of the Antelope.

"You hear, Zosya? Adam says we absolutely have to do it."

"Well, if Adam says so . . ." said the young woman, her voice faltering.

The captain and the old puzzle-maker's daughter went into the small gray house, while Kozlevich climbed under the car again. His plan was for the Antelope to reach its top speed on the way to the bride's home—eight miles per hour. To achieve that, he had to check a few things first.

He was still lying under the car when the newlyweds came out of the office.

"I'm thirty-three years old," said Ostap sadly, "the age of Jesus Christ. And what have I accomplished thus far? I haven't created a teaching, I wasted my disciples, I haven't resurrected anybody."

"I'm sure you will still be able to resurrect somebody!" said Zosya, laughing.

"No," said Ostap, "it won't work. I've been trying to do it all my life but never could. I'll have to go into apartment management instead."

With that, he looked at Zosya. She wore a rough lightweight coat that was shorter than her dress and a dark-blue beret with a childish pompom. She held down the flap of her coat, which was being blown by the wind, with her right hand, and on her middle finger Ostap noticed a small ink stain that she had gotten when she signed her name in the wedding register. In front of him stood his wife.

Ilya Ilf (1897–1937) and Evgeny Petrov (1903–1942) met in Moscow in the 1920s while working on the staff of a newspaper for railway workers. The foremost comic novelists of the early Soviet Union, the pair wrote two of the most revered and loved Russian novels, *The Twelve Chairs* and *The Golden Calf*, as well as various humorous pieces for *Pravda* and other publications. Their collaboration came to an end with the death of Ilya Ilf after his tuberculosis turned for the worse while the pair traveled the United States researching the book that would become *Little Golden America*.

Konstantin Gurevich is a graduate of Moscow State University and the University of Texas at Austin. Helen Anderson studied Russian language and literature at McGill University in Montréal. Married to each other, they are both librarians at the University of Rochester, and this is their first major translation together.

Open Letter—the University of Rochester's nonprofit, literary translation press—is one of only a handful of publishing houses dedicated to increasing access to world literature for English readers. Publishing ten titles in translation each year, Open Letter searches for works that are extraordinary and influential, works that we hope will become the classics of tomorrow.

Making world literature available in English is crucial to opening our cultural borders, and its availability plays a vital role in maintaining a healthy and vibrant book culture. Open Letter strives to cultivate an audience for these works by helping readers discover imaginative, stunning works of fiction and by creating a constellation of international writing that is engaging, stimulating, and enduring.

Current and forthcoming titles from Open Letter include works from Argentina, Catalonia, France, Germany, Iceland, and numerous other countries.

www.openletterbooks.org